THE RED RIDER

A Retelling of Little Red Riding Hood

Rebecca Fittery

Copyright © 2021 Rebecca Fittery

All rights reserved

The characters, places, and events portrayed in this book are fictitious. Any similarity to real persons, living or dead, is coincidental and not intended by the author.

No part of this book may be reproduced, or stored in a retrieval system, or transmitted in any form or by any means, electronic, mechanical, photocopying, recording, or otherwise, without express written permission of the publisher.

ISBN-13: 978-1-7361122-1-2

Cover design through Canva
Map design through Inkarnate

To my friend Alison Souders. I always say that the characters I write aren't based off of people I know, and that's true. But it's also true that the best of Red is the best of you: brave, fierce, adventurous and strong. Thanks for a friendship stretching decades, and for your wicked sense of humor. Life is better with you in it.

CONTENTS

Title Page
Copyright
Dedication
MAP OF ISTOIRE
MAP OF SHERWOOD
PROLOGUE   1
CHAPTER ONE   8
CHAPTER TWO   23
CHAPTER THREE   38
CHAPTER FOUR   49
CHAPTER FIVE   59
CHAPTER SIX   76
CHAPTER SEVEN   88
CHAPTER EIGHT   94
CHAPTER NINE   107
CHAPTER TEN   118
CHAPTER ELEVEN   126
CHAPTER TWELVE   135
CHAPTER THIRTEEN   148
CHAPTER FOURTEEN   158

CHAPTER FIFTEEN	169
CHAPTER SIXTEEN	185
CHAPTER SEVENTEEN	194
CHAPTER EIGHTEEN	207
CHAPTER NINETEEN	218
CHAPTER TWENTY	232
CHAPTER TWENTY-ONE	239
CHAPTER TWENTY-TWO	250
CHAPTER TWENTY-THREE	262
CHAPTER TWENTY-FOUR	272
CHAPTER TWENTY-FIVE	279
EPILOGUE	281
Afterword	283
About The Author	285

MAP OF ISTOIRE

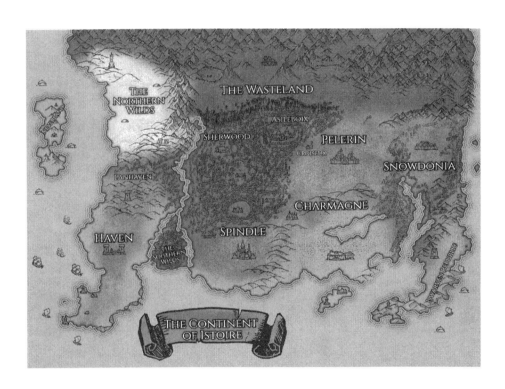

MAP OF SHERWOOD

PROLOGUE

Bare feet pounded the ground, tiny gasps of dirt protesting the abuse. Red laughed up at the sun peeking between rows of sunflowers as she ran, her favorite crimson cape flying behind. It was warm enough that she didn't need the cape, but she wore it anyway. Her mother had just added a strip of fabric to the hem so that it came down almost to her ankles again, promising to add more if she grew taller before winter.

The red cape made her feel alive and pretty. It was her mother's warm love, wrapped around her in protection. It was a cheerful splash of color against snow in colder months.

"It makes you visible to hunters too, darling," her mother's voice sounded in Red's mind. She had meant it as a reassurance. The crimson color ensuring someone wouldn't hit her by mistake during rambles in the forest, but the thought made Red shiver.

Instead of slowing as she hit the tree line, Red pumped her legs harder. Dodging pine and oak, beech and maple; the sticks and stones on the forest floor made no impression on her leathery feet.

Grandma must be close by now, she told the wolf in her mind, feeling it perk up in interest. The wolf's consciousness had started trickling through only a few months ago; a sign of her approaching womanhood, or so her mother claimed. Red didn't know what that meant, but she did know that having a wolf to talk to meant a friend always nearby. *I wish the wolf were out here too, so I could hold it.* Something in the way it behaved in her mind told her she was a puppy. She was sure to be soft and cuddly.

You'll like Grandma, Red told her happily. *Grandma gives the best hugs, and she always fixes things. After all, she used to rule two countries! Now my cousin rules one and my uncle rules the ours. Grandma helps them but has more time for visiting. She says I'm her favorite person to visit!*

Visits from Grandma had become more frequent in the last few years. After Papa died, Mama had become quieter. The sunny giggles and adventures in the forest seemed to have died with Papa. Mama's love was gentler now, more like a blanket to snuggle up with near the fire. Her face seemed lined and heavy, although her eyes smiled everytime she looked at her daughter and her hugs were tighter and more frequent.

Red didn't mind so much, especially now that she had the wolf. *But that's why I named you Elne,* Red told her wolf. *Elne means courage, and that's how you make me feel. Mama needs us to be courageous.*

But no need to worry about that now. Red reassured her wolf as she scrambled over a log, the bark scraping against her calves. *Grandma's arriving to fix whatever's worrying Mama.*

The trees began to thin as Red approached a narrow stream. She put on one last burst of speed, panting loudly. Pushing branches aside, she burst out of the undergrowth, scaring several birds who squawked loudly in protest. Driving her feet hard into the dirt, she bunched her muscles and sprung out in a mighty leap across the creek.

"Yes!" she crowed triumphantly as she reached the other side, wobbling slightly on the edge of the bank. "I did it!" Elne yipped in approval.

Red's foot slipped out from under her as she tried to maintain her balance. Mud caked between her toes as she scrabbled for purchase, only to be washed away in a shock of icy cold water as they broke the surface of the stream below. Reaching out wildly, she managed to wrap her fingers around a hefty root further up the bank and haul herself up, trying not to get her tunic dirty; or worse, her lovely red cape.

She grinned back at the creek once she regained her feet. *That's only the second time I've jumped all the way across.* Her bruised knees were testament to all the times she had tried before.

Stooping to pick up a couple of sticks, Red ambled over to the wooden bridge nearby. Plopping down on the edge, she dangled just above the surface of the water, enjoying the sensation of the air drying her still wet feet as she swung them back and forth. After watching the fish swimming below for awhile, she tossed the sticks she had gathered off the far side of the bridge, then scrabbled on her knees to the other side and waited for them to appear. The funny one with a crook in it was first, racing down a faster course of the river, while the longer, straighter one followed serenely a moment later.

A jingling clatter reached her ears, pushing her mouth into a grin. *Grandma!* It had to be her. The only other people that drove to Barnsdale Lodge were farmers with creaking wagons, an altogether different noise.

Red pushed up and ran off the bridge, skipping down the path toward home a little way before stopping off to one side. She bounced on her heels in anticipation as a large carriage appeared, several soldiers riding out in front.

Red capes, just like mine, Red thought with pride. Her smile grew wider as the front rider shouted something back to the others. The carriage began to slow as it passed over the bridge, finally halting next to Red. She reached up and pulled open the door, her Grandmother's form appearing as it started to swing open.

"Grandma! I couldn't wait for you at home, so Mama said…" she trailed off as the door swung the rest of the way open, revealing a pale girl, not much older than Red, seated beside her Grandma. Red's brow furrowed in surprise, although her smile didn't dim.

"Marian! I didn't know you were coming! Robin already started his apprenticeship so he's not here… but didn't you start your training too?" Red glanced between Marian and her Grandmother, her confusion growing as she noticed the look on their faces.

"Grandma, why are your eyes so big?" she asked. A sick feeling started to grow in the pit of her stomach. *Grandma wasn't supposed to look afraid. Grandma fixed things that made you afraid.*

A shadow shifted across from Marian and Grandma, leaning forward until it crossed into a beam of light.

"Prince John?" The sight of his dark hair and oily smile rang a note of alarm in Red's mind. He was her mother's half brother, the youngest of Grandma's children. She had noticed anytime the family got together that her mother didn't like him: feared him even. The anxiety in Red's stomach skittered up her spine. Elne growled nervously in her head.

"Red," Prince John drawled, "I shouldn't be surprised to find you out in the forest, streaked in dirt. You've always been half feral, haven't you?"

Red shied away from his words, remembering why she didn't like him. His tone sounded light and amused, but there was always an edge to it. Like when Mama was warning her to behave in public or else she'd be in trouble at home, but worse somehow. Red didn't like it.

"No matter," John continued to himself, "a feral child may suit my purposes even more."

Grandma's stiffened in her seat, her eyes narrowed at her son, while Marian seemed to shrink a little.

Something isn't right, Red thought to Elne. The wolf pup growled, and Red suddenly noticed that one of the outriders had slipped off his horse and was approaching the carriage. Instead of looking toward the occupants, his eyes were trained on Red.

Alarm thrilled through her body, and instinct took over. Stumbling backward, Red turned blindly and put on a burst of speed, sprinting away from the ruined welcome.

"Get her. Now!" John's harsh yelling spurred Red's legs to move faster. Sticks snapped under her feet as she dodged trees and rocks. Her cape caught on branches and bushes that seemed to tug at her, threatening to hold her until the soldier caught up.

Boots pounded the ground, not far behind. Her eyes flitted frantically, looking for escape. A turn in the creek came into view and without thinking, she gathered her courage and leaped, scaling it with inches to spare. Relief swept through her momentarily, followed by a renewed sense of panic as the soldier behind her cursed. A minute later, a splash sounded. *He fell in the stream!* Red crowed to Elne, flashing her eyes back to see the fast moving current pulling at him, his heavy chain mail thwarting his efforts to haul himself out.

Red pumped her arms with a renewed effort. She didn't know where she was going, but she needed to go. *Maybe we'll find a cave. There's lots around here. Robin would know if her were here.*

Hoofbeats sounded and Red looked up, all the breath leaving her lungs in a moment of terror as she caught sight of a horse barreling straight toward her. She dove out of the way just in time, rolling to a stop when her shoulders cracked against a tree trunk.

Hands grabbed her roughly as she got to her feet, and her heart plummeted.

"Come here, girly," the soldier demanded irritably. "The Prince has plans for you."

"Why? I haven't done anything wrong! What could he want with me?" Red panted, her voice wavering.

"How should I know? Depends on how your magic is manifesting, don't it?" The soldier's voice was impatient as he hauled her along by her upper arm. He grabbed the reins of his horse and walked them both back toward the carriage. Red's terror subsided a little at his words. *Maybe John's just checking to see if my magic came in, so he knows where to place my apprenticeship. I'll be old enough in a few years anyway.* Elne's restless energy crashed against Red's own, the two of them sharing anxiety and a desire to reassure one another.

The carriage door was still open as it came into view, and the soldier shoved her up through it. Red fell onto the seat next to John.

"Are you allri… John no!" Grandma cut off with a gasp as John grabbed Red's chin roughly.

He sneered as he examined her, his voice oddly smooth even as his eyes betrayed the depth of his anger. "If you ever run from me again, darling niece, I'll have you whipped."

Red's fear was drowned in a surge of rage at her uncle's threat. *He's supposed to be the Prince - the one that takes care of our land. Not the one who goes around punishing little kids!* Marian's soft whimper sounded from the other side of the carriage, drawing Red's gaze. She looked at Marian properly for the first time. Her face was cast in shadows, tear trails glimmering on her cheeks. The sight of brave, laughing Marian reduced to a trembling rabbit stoked the flames of Red's anger even more. Elne's growls echoed in her mind and drowned out all thought. *I need to fight, to push back at the bully in front of me so he knows who he's dealing with,* Red told Elne. Elne growled her agreement, tinged with anxiety. In a flash, Red ducked her chin and bit down onto John's fingers as hard as she could.

He yelped, prying his hand from between her teeth as blood welled out of her bite mark. "You *dare* bite your sovereign?!"

Red spat his blood out of her mouth, spraying it across his face. "Mama says you're not the rightful sovereign, so I don't think it counts, *dear* Uncle." She gave him a hard look, before flicking her eyes to Marian.

John followed her gaze, his shock hardening as he looked at Lady Marian. "So your mother thinks little Lady Marian would do a better job than I would?" The anger in his voice was replaced with silky speculation. He turned his attention back to Red, heedless of the blood dripping off his hand and on to his lap. "I look forward to changing her mind soon." His voice hissed slightly on the last word, and Red's righteous anger was shaken by a wave of doubt at the strange light in his slitted eyes.

The carriage started forward with a jerk, almost casting Red to the floor. Her Grandma leaned forward to steady her with a look of warning in her eyes. Red settled back, inching as far away on the seat from John as was possible. He ignored her, watching blood drip steadily from the bite in his hand, doing nothing to stem the flow. His mouth was twisted into a strange smile and his eyes gleamed.

Elne whimpered in her mind as Red shivered, pressing herself into the corner of the bench. *What is John planning?*

CHAPTER ONE

Red - Twelve Years Later

Hoofbeats pounded a steady staccato. My breaths seemed to come in time with my horse's as I leaned over her neck, eyes focused on the border ahead of us. The sun had just passed it's zenith, shining through murky cloud that crept south from the Wasteland, infecting the clear, high blue skies over Sherwood. The difference between my country and the Wasteland wasn't always so stark, but on days like today the sky proclaimed the border's location for miles; pristine blue under assault from tendrils of sickened cloud-smog. Just looking at it made your lungs seize.

The sight pulled a cough from my chest, a visceral reaction to the memory of breathing the filthy miasma on countless missions. As leader of the most elite border unit in the Sherwood, you'd think my lungs would be used to it by now. I've spent almost as much time in and around the Wasteland as I have at home.

I pushed thoughts of home aside as Barnsdale Lodge flashed through my mind. *Don't go there.* Elne growled in agreement. *Not safe,* her tone warned me. Although there was no threat to us there now, she wasn't wrong.

A shape flashed in the corner of my vision and I squinted through the murky fog. The path I was riding on branched just ahead. I had been planning on taking the lefthand one, which looped back toward Sherwood. My scouting shift would be over soon so I was due to meet up with my unit. But if there was something in the Wasteland, I needed to know.

"Whoa," I called softly, slowing to a walk. The right hand fork shifted into a steep incline for a few yards, and was pitted with rocks and roots. I didn't want to injure my horse, or alert anything out there to my presence. As we reached the top of the slope, I scanned the leaden depths beyond the border.

There.

Elne's attention pricked up in my mind, and I could imagine her ears moving forward. *That was definitely something.* My eyes caught motion again, the ghost of a shape half formed in the fog. I sucked a breath through my teeth.

"It's just possible…" I muttered to myself, my heart increasing in tempo. Elne surged in recognition of a possible hunt and I let myself be carried along in her sudden bloodlust, kicking my mount into motion again, urging her faster and faster along the track.

Ahead of us, the shape appeared again, half seen, but visible enough to make me sure. *It's that monster. The one from my mission.*

Kill. Destroy. Avenge. Elne's thoughts were never coherent but I could sense her intention and my own rage joined to hers until it consumed both of us.

We rushed closer and closer to the mist, my entire focus narrowed to my horse, my bloodlust, and the smog ahead, searching, straining, anticipating that cursed form to appear again.

"Red!"

A noise broke through the haze in my mind.

"Red! Stop!"

Why is that sound familiar? I wondered, Elne snapped at my distraction, annoyed.

"Red what are you doing?!"

Eileen. My mind snapped out of the bloodlust of the hunt and

I glanced in the direction of the words. Sure enough, there was Eileen O'Dale, racing behind me, her face set grimly.

Elne snarled, urging me forward but I snarled back at her, slowing to a trot and then walk, and finally stopping to wait for my friend and fellow warrior, Eileen O'Dale.

"Eileen. What happened? Why are you out here?"

"What do you mean? You were supposed to report back an hour ago! Why are *you* out here?"

I raised my eyebrows, glancing back at the sickly looking sun.

That's right, I was supposed to report back at noon. I had completely forgotten my self imposed time constraint on scouting ahead of the unit.

"...obviously we all know our orders, and it's not as if chaos would break out, but you *are* the Captain. It looks bad if you're lax about reporting. I've told you before - you shouldn't even ride scout anyway!"

"Eileen!" I snapped, the truth in her reminders of my duty stinging like alcohol in a wound. "I saw the monster."

"What?" Her eyes darted to the Wasteland, alert and searching.

"It was there, just beyond the border. I was tracking it."

Her eyes dimmed and flicked back to me. "Are you sure?"

"*Yes*, I'm sure. I *saw* it. Clear as anything."

"I don't know, Red, I've been chasing you, trying to get your attention. I didn't see anything."

My brow furrowed. Elne snuffled in my mind, dismissing Eileen's words. *She's the best tracker we have,* I reminded Elne. *Her hawk vision wouldn't have missed anything.*

"You probably weren't looking at the Wasteland if you were following me. Why didn't you call out to me?"

"I did call out! Several times! You must have heard me. Why didn't you stop?"

I shook my head, glancing back toward the roiling fog of the border. Elne's desire to resume the hunt surged against my mind but I pushed her back. *Can't abandon the pack,* I reminded her sternly. She subsided irritably.

"Look, Trewe would have noticed if something was there," Eileen argued, referencing her own beast companion. "He would have sharpened my vision enough to see it too. Probably just the fog twisting upon itself. It's in fine form today."

Irritation flared at her assertion, but I knew she wasn't lying. She had just as much reason as I did for revenge.

She patted her horse's neck as it shook it's head and snorted, but kept her eyes focused on me. "Anyway, we had a call come in over the moonstones. Base camp has a POW. Didn't you see the message?"

I looked down at the moonstone broach fastening my dark cloak over my black leather jerkin. It was pulsing, the light spelling out a message in code. *POW. Base camp.* I double tapped the jewel's smooth surface to turn it off.

How distracted was I? If I hadn't noticed the flashing glow of the message, inches from my face, nor heard Eileen calling out to me, what did I miss during the last couple hours of scouting? I scowled.

"It looks like I have things to see to. Must've gotten too caught up in scouting. I should leave that to you and Hreremus."

"Well, we appreciate the break of course, but we've been sitting on our hands at Asileboix since the battle, so it wasn't necessary."

I gave a hearty chuckle, hoping the sound would clear away the slight tension between us. "Let's get back. You're probably right. The border magic is particularly strong today."

Eileen looked relieved. "I told them to meet us at the Old Maid's stone. They should get there soon."

"Good. We'll camp there tonight and press on toward base camp in the morning. I'm curious to see about this POW situation."

Eileen gave a salute as I turned my horse and led us back, Elne's displeasure coloring my thoughts.

* * *

"Oi Captain, you get lost?"

Broc's amused voice reached my ears as Eileen and I rode up to our meeting place, making me grin.

"Yes Broc, that's why they made me Captain - so I'd have an entire unit to babysit me."

A rumble of laughter swept through my company and I flicked my eyes over each soldier. They looked relaxed, unconcerned about my missed check in. *Good. Don't need them doubting me.*

"Thought I saw something along the border, but it turned out to be a false alarm." I glanced up at the sun's progress. It had slipped further down the sky while Eileen and I rode toward Old Maid's stone. "We'll sleep here for the night. Should make base camp by lunch tomorrow."

I slipped from my horse, pulling it forward to one of the hitching posts near the stone. Old Maid's stone was a well known camping spot, being slightly sheltered and easily defensible, as well harboring a freshwater spring. It was used often enough that the locals had put up hitching posts and built fire circles, stocking well seasoned firewood under a neat lean-to nearby. It was almost a luxury for patrols used to sleeping rough.

"I'll be dreaming of a hot lunch tonight," Broc said cheerfully to Edith as everyone pulled bedrolls and tarps from their saddlebags. My first squadron, set up their tents around mine, as usual. The rest of the company fanned out in an orderly fashion, those assigned to the first watch forming our perimeter as the rest of us prepared for our hard earned sleep.

She just chuckled, but her older twin, Edda laughed as her stomach rumbled loud enough for everyone to hear, "You won't be the only one Broc. I've had fresh baked bread on my mind since we left Asileboix."

The other sibling pair in my first squadron, Wystan and Barden, were busy setting up their shelter next to the sisters. Rather, Wystan was setting it up. Barden was too busy bothering

Broc and Eoforde about extra provisions to be of assistance. Nothing unusual there. One of my scouts, Aeflaede, took pity on Wystan, catching a pole just before it fell to the ground and offering him a rare smile. I raised my eyebrow at the sight. *Is there something between them?* It wasn't unusual for married couples to serve in the same unit in Sherwood, but I had never had any in my company, let alone my most elite first squadron. *I probably still won't have one. Aeflaede and Wystan are so reticent they'll never reveal their true feelings without some sort of a push.* I shrugged. As long as it didn't effect their work, it wasn't my business.

My soldiers continued chattering to each other as they set up camp, happy to be off their horses after a long day, and the comfort of base camp within reach. I couldn't bring myself to join in as I usually did, the experience at the border still haunting my mind.

Eileen pitched the tent she shared with the other scouts, Aeflaede and Hreremus, close to my own. I was the only one of our company that didn't have a tent mate. I slept alone, always. I couldn't be responsible for what I did to anyone startling me out of my sleep. Instead of seeming strange, it just added to my reputation as the fearsome Red Rider. Only a few knew why I was so jumpy in my sleep. Eileen was one, and she had been treating me almost like a mother hen the last few months. My slip up in the woods would probably make it worse. She puttered around in the space between our shelters, reorganizing her pack, checking the fire incessantly, and shooting covert glances my way, her brow puckered. Every movement she made irritated me further. By the time she sat down next to me, just outside my tent, I was ready to snap.

"You ready to talk about what happened out there?" She asked in a low voice. I sat as still as I could, trying not to betray my inner turmoil. *She's just concerned, that's all. Just a good friend. And better Lieutenant.*

"Red, I've told you before that I'm worried -" I cut her off by standing up abruptly. I was in no mood to discuss her feelings.

Let alone mine.

"I'm heading to bed. If Hreremus turns up with anything unusual to report, wake me immediately. Otherwise, I'll see you in the morning." Ignoring the way she pressed her lips together, barely holding in a scolding, I turned and stalked into my tent, mind buzzing.

I had been *sure* it was that Beast, the same one from the skirmish where we lost Rapunzel's unit. Something had been off about that fight. The Beasts too organized, fighting in sync too much to be a coincidence. And that one monster, the Beast Captain, as I had taken to calling it, seemed to direct them all without speaking.

Elne's angry irritation spilled across my mind again. She wanted to break off from the group, go back to the Wasteland alone and track the monster down. I growled softly.

The pack comes first, Elne, you know that. She withdrew into herself, her irritation less abrasive, but still simmering. After a quick meal and approval of the watch schedule, I lay down on my bedroll, restless, but knowing I needed sleep. My mind turned to the message over the moonstones.

A POW? Where would base camp come across a POW? They were close to our border with the Wasteland, so I could only assume it was a Beast. But why they would keep it prisoner instead of killing it outright was beyond me.

Elne snapped at my thoughts, her focus still on the Wasteland. I pushed her aside once more and closed my eyes for sleep.

* * *

We arrived at base camp just in time for lunch. The scent of roasted beef had been drifting toward those of us with heightened smell capacities for the last mile. We were practically slobbering by the time we picketed our horses.

"I'll bring a bowl to your tent, Captain," Barden called with a smile as the others hustled toward the mess.

"Bring one for Eileen too, will you?" I asked, signaling to Eileen to follow me. Barden nodded, jogging to catch up with his older brother. Eileen trailed me into my temporary headquarters, crossing her arms as I put down my saddle packs. I pulled a string of weapons out of my pack and took off the ones I kept strapped to my body, laying them out across my wide desk. I always gave them a quick clean after time in the field.

"You're getting reckless," she said, her scowl permeating her voice.

I stilled, hand hovering over a pair of knives I usually kept strapped to my calves.

"I didn't ask you here for commentary on my behavior," I replied, keeping my tone light and tamping down Elne's ferocious response to the insubordination of a beta in our pack.

"I'm not scolding you, I'm just saying, you've become increasingly reckless since the loss of Rapunzel's unit, and- "

I interrupted, my own snarl mingling with Elne's. "I *definitely* didn't bring you here to discuss that incident. If I am being reckless, that's my own concern, not yours. You'll stick to your orders, soldier."

"Red, please-"

I cut her off again. "Lieutenant, I called you here because we have a prisoner to handle. Should I call for Wystan instead?"

She shook her head, not able to keep the frustration off her face. "No, Captain."

"Good. Once we've had a chance to eat I'll have Reynold report on the situation."

"Food, Captain," Barden's voice called from outside my tent.

"Come in," I ordered, glancing away from Eileen's irritated stare.

Barden pushed through the door flap, holding two steaming bowls of beef stew, followed quickly by Wystan, holding another two. He handed one to me, and the other to Eileen before grabbing his own bowl from Wystan. I sat down at my desk while the other three took their seats, the brothers murmuring quietly to each other while Eileen and I sulked. We had all been friends long enough that we didn't need to pretend in front of each other.

As I finished my meal, my good humor returned. *Warm food in a belly will do that.* Barden tipped back in his seat, starting up an old argument with Eileen about fletching arrows. My eyes crinkled as Eileen jumped right into a treatise on hawk feathers, a passion of hers due to her inner beast companion. I caught Wystan's attention when he looked over to roll his eyes at me.

"Go find Reynold and ask him to report in to me here. I want a brief on the prisoner."

He nodded, passing out through the entrance, only to pop his head back in a second later.

"Cap, Reynold's already headed this way, and he has a stranger with him."

I raised my eyebrows in surprise. "So not a Beast then? Stay, since you're here. This may get interesting."

Wystan ducked back out to shout to Reynold, then went to stand near Eileen and Barden, their argument forgotten. I stood up as well, clearing my half cleaned weapons to one side, and buckling my sword back on. *Wouldn't do to make a poor first impression, would it?* I asked Elne. Her disinterest drifted across my thoughts and I almost laughed. A sword wouldn't be much help in the close quarters of my tent, but I still had knives strapped to my bracers, and I preferred bare knuckle combat anyway. A grin of anticipation crept across my face as I leaned a hip against my desk. Reynold pushed through a moment later, holding the tent flap back as a man passed through after him.

He was definitely as stranger. Mostly clean-shaven, with a healthy shadow on his jaw, unlike the custom here in Sherwood. *Handsome even so,* I couldn't help but note. He wore leather and chain mail emblazoned with Pelerine military insignias, although much worse for the wear at this point.

"Captain, welcome back. This is Eduoard Marchand, the guest we messaged you about. He was brought here by the Gypsy Prince himself, half dead from a lizard Beastie." Reynold's eyes glimmered with mirth as he stared at the back of Marchand's head, and I cocked my head to the side as I studied the man standing stiffly in front of me.

So this is Eddie Marchand, Belle's onetime betrothed, I thought to myself, scrutinizing every detail. I hadn't thought to ask Belle what he looked like, but he resembled just about every Pelerine man I had met. Prim, arrogant, and slight whiff of superiority hanging around him like a cloak.

His eyes flitted over the occupants of the tent, lips pursing slightly as they traced over me and Eileen. The corner of my mouth quirked up as he addressed himself to Wystan and Barden.

"Excuse my ignorance sirs, but which one of you is Captain Hood?" he asked, with a polite bow.

The brothers shared an incredulous glance. Eileen stared blankly. I couldn't hold back a laugh, drawing Eddie's disapproving gaze toward me as I looked at the offended faces of the others. I flicked my head toward the door, and they filed out silently, Barden shaking his head as he gathered our empty bowls.

"You too, Reynold," I instructed. He raised his eyebrows at me and I gave him a look. "Wait outside with Eileen while I speak to Captain Marchand."

He shrugged and swept out. I relaxed and turned my attention back to the prisoner. Captain Marchand stared at me, color creeping up his neck as confusion warred with disgust on his face. His reaction amused me, though Elne continued to dismiss the entire situation.

"Welcome. Eddie, is it? You'll have to excuse my soldiers, they assume everyone knows of the famous Red Rider."

Eddie swallowed and cleared his throat a few times. "Please excuse me, Madame Hood. I had no idea the Captain was a woman."

"Captain Hood, thank you, or Red," I responded, my smile growing. "And it would be Mademoiselle, if I were to allow you to call me that."

His discomfort grew, the color creeping up along a pair of

neck tattoos that extended to his ears, before reddening his cheeks. *How fun this is,* I thought to myself. No one had dared be disgusted, or have any negative reaction toward me for years. *Save Eileen, I suppose. But hers is out of concern, not disdain.* As the great Red Rider, I elicited only reverence or fear. Eddie appeared to think me hardly worth his notice.

"I apologize, *Captain* Hood. I'm from Pelerin and we do things quite differently there, you must understand. In truth, I was taken here without my knowledge. I would like to return home as soon as possible. I'm sure you're aware of the great battle that was fought at the border of Pelerin and Asileboix not long ago. I need to get back and check on my family as soon as possible. I fear everyone I love may be dead."

Elne perked up at the mention of a battle, and I had to work to keep from rolling my eyes at her. She subsided as she realized there was no imminent fight.

"Well, Eddie - I can call you that, can't I?" I asked, smiling all the wider. He nodded stiffly.

"I have some good news and some bad news for you. Which do you want first?"

He frowned, apprehension creeping across his face. "The bad news, please."

"I'll start with the good, then," I responded, tamping down my rising grin. "All your loved ones are safe and well, so there's no need to worry on their account."

His frown became deeper. "What would you know of my loved ones?"

"Quite a bit, actually. My cousin is married to the Princess of Asileboix. I believe you knew her as Lady Belle Montanarte?"

The prisoner's face went slack. I continued on cheerfully.

"I left them about a week ago, both happy and healthy, praise the Lady. Your family is fine, as well as the Montanartes. And I believe a person named Monsieur LeFeu is working on regaining his ability to walk before his wedding." I couldn't help delivering a sugar coated barb, worthy of my sister-in-law, Marian. "Actually, they're all doing quite a bit better since you disappeared."

He flinched, his words finally coming back to him. "That *is* good news. I must see them as soon as possible. I'm sure they're wondering what happened to me."

"Ah yes, now we come to the bad news. They are indeed wondering about your fate. In fact, it was a topic of discussion at the Council of Asileboix. You're being considered a hostile in all our countries, which means you're now a prisoner of war."

Eddie's nostrils flared, disdain quirking one eyebrow again. "I have to wonder why you would want to provoke Pelerin with such an action. As a Captain in their army, I'm not without rights."

"It was Pelerin that denounced you loudest," I informed him, nonchalantly.

He stiffened, bowing his head and staring at the ground in horror. I fiddled with one of my rings, a thick band of iron, studded with needle sharp spikes. Twisting it around so that the spikes faced downward, I gently curled my hand into a fist, pricking the skin just below the base of my thumb. Keeping my fist curled to prevent the blood welling up and dripping down my hands, I pushed off of my desk, approaching Eddie.

"Now, it's not so bad. You won't have to bear with me too long. I'll be taking you to the Duke and Duchess in Nottingham immediately. You'll like them much more than a rough and tumble soldier like me."

His eyes flicked up to mine and I reached out gently, taking his hand between both of mine. It was warm, calloused by swordplay and hard work. His hand tightened on mine reflexively and my lips parted to feel the gentle strength of his grip, soft and sure. The disdainful anxiety that had hovered over his brow slid away as our eyes locked, and I knew he felt the same thrum of awareness.

I slammed that feeling down before I could explore it further. Pasting a cheerful grin on my face, I pressed my ring into the corresponding point on his palm, and slipped my wound up to meet his. His eyes hardened again as he tugged his hand away, but I followed the movement easily, muttering the spellwork as I did.

As I finished, the binding spell tugged on my heart, and I stumbled closer as he did the same, our heads knocking painfully. I gasped, wrenching my hands away and staring at the bloodied one in confusion. Elne finally took an interest in my affairs, growling at my discomfort.

"What did you do?!" Captain Marchand demanded angrily. He pulled out a handkerchief and pressed it to the wound, his chest heaving as if he just finished a sprint.

I gathered my wits about me again, teeth grinding as I pasted on another cheerful smile.

"Nothing to worry about, Captain Marchand. Just a binding spell to keep you close. We use it on all prisoners during transport. I set it relatively loosely. You don't have to stay by my side, but you won't be able to get more than half a mile away from me without your feet leading you back."

"Is that what this feeling is, then? The pain in my chest?"

"Yes," I lied, not wanting to examine the corresponding pull inside me, emanating from my chest and drifting toward him. *That's never happened before,* I thought to Elne. She settled down again, uninterested now that she knew the blood had to do with a spell.

"I demand you remove it, immediately. You've placed this evil on me without my consent, and it's already doing something... " he rubbed his uninjured palm over his heart, disgust written on every feature.

"Sorry, not until I release you into Robin's custody, or over my dead body," I laughed.

"I'll take whichever one is faster," he snarled angrily.

I raised my brows. "I'd like to see you try, soldier. I've been dead bored since the Battle of Asileboix anyway." I leaned closer and gave him a conspiratorial smirk. "I suggest you wait until I'm asleep. You'll have a better chance if you sneak up on me in bed."

His skin flushed around his tattoos again as he glanced to my cot, just beyond my desk. My heart stuttered into a new rhythm as I realized how my words sounded, my eyes tracing the bob of his throat as he swallowed heavily. I rushed to correct myself. "I didn't mean-"

He cut me off, speaking at the same moment. "I would never hurt..."

I huffed a breath. "Let me heal the cut at least." I suggested, pacing back toward him, my injured hand held out.

He jerked his away. "More magic? No thank you."

"Looks like you've already benefited from healing magic," I said, motioning to his gypsy tattoos. His lips pressed together and I found myself wanting to coax him out of his buttoned up disapproval. "It's not going to hurt. And it won't leave a mark. My magic doesn't work that way."

He wavered for a moment before unwrapping his hand and holding it out. I took it gingerly, trying not to notice the rasp of his skin on mine. Quickly, I spoke the healing words over both our wounds. He tipped his face down to watch as the cuts knit together seamlessly. When the spell finished, he made a gentle noise of surprise before wiping the remaining blood off of both our hands before I could clean them with magic. I let him, holding still beneath his unexpected gentleness.

A clatter sounded just outside my tent and we sprung apart, the guilty look on his face matching my own. His handkerchief fluttered to the ground near my feet and I bent to pick it up.

"Captain, urgent message for you." Eileen's voice called through the tent fabric.

"Come in." I responded, clearing my throat and offering Eddie's handkerchief back to him. He motioned for me to keep it and I rolled my eyes, tossing it behind me onto the surface of my desk.

Eileen stepped through with a messenger, followed by Reynold.

"Beast pack spotted on the border, Captain, right near the gap in the wall at the river," the messenger puffed out hurriedly. "The field scout isn't close enough to engage and requests back up."

"How many?" I barked out, ignoring the way Eddie's body

suddenly tensed next to mine.

"Just five that he saw, one of them was huge."

The Beast Captain. Elne's bloodlust surged across my mind again and I gave into it willingly.

"Leave it with me, Sergeant. I'll handle them on my own." I reached back for my water flask, sitting on my desk, leaving the half cleaned knives where they were. I had enough weapons to dispatch five Beasts easily. *And I'll be taking the big one down with my bare hands,* I promised Elne, grimly.

"Red, what are you thinking going out on your own?" Eileen challenged me as I swept out of the tent. I growled at her without thinking, jogging over to my horse and mounting in a liquid motion. *She just wants a chance for revenge on the Beast Captain too,* I told Elne, *but it's going to be all ours.*

CHAPTER TWO

Eddie

My jaw dropped open as the female Captain stormed out of the tent, growling, yes actually growling, at the other female warrior.

She seriously thinks she can take five Beasts herself? I glanced around at the other occupants of the tent. Neither Reynold nor the scout looked concerned, although the other woman muttered something incoherent.

"She'll be fine, Eileen, I don't know why you're so concerned," Reynold said in an amused tone.

My eyebrows rose again. "She'll be fine?!" I finally burst out. "One woman against *five* Beasts?"

The messenger's wheezing had lessened in volume, but his voice was still breathless as he responded. "She's the Red Rider, of course she'll be fine. They say her eyes glow red when she catches sight of a Beast, and don't stop until they're all slain. She'll never be defeated."

Reynold chuckled and shook his head. "Is that what you were told, laddie?" Eileen threw up her hands in disgust and stormed out.

An array of weapons sitting on the Captain's desk caught my eyes. I grabbed two knives and followed on Eileen's heels.

"Are you going to get help for her?" I asked, as I strapped the scabbards onto my forearms. I could see Red slowing to a stop in front of a group of horses not far away.

Eileen scoffed, turning to face me with her hands on her hips. "You heard the Captain. I've been ordered to stay here. Are you suggesting insubordination?"

"No, but sometimes a leader's choices need to be called into question. It seems like she trusts you."

"What's it to you, prisoner? I may disagree with her right now, but she's still my commanding officer." She tossed her bright red hair over her shoulder and crossed her arms, glaring at me.

I shook my head. *These Sherwoodians are insane.* "Well she didn't order me to stay. Give me your sword and I'll be her back up." I held my hand out and she looked at me skeptically. I stared back incredulously.

"So you're not afraid to let her run into a one on five Beast fight, but you think *I'm* going to somehow kill her? I assume you heard her put that binding spell on me. I'll have to follow her anyway."

She shook her head slowly, glancing down at my outstretched hand. "No, I didn't hear. The tents have privacy spells on them." She hesitated for a moment, eying the scar on my hand, a few smears of drying blood still evident. Nodding once to herself, she reached around her waist and unbuckled her sword.

"I like to think I'm a good judge of character, and I have a good feeling about you." She pulled back as I reached for her sword. "I hear you attacked Prince Andrus. If you try something like that here, with our Red Rider, not only will you fail, but every Sherwoodian will take an ounce of flesh from you in punishment. Your death will be slow and vicious. We're not as nice as our Asilean cousins." Her eyes bored into me, something sharp and aquiline about her gaze made me feel as if I were a field mouse about to be torn apart by a bird of prey.

I pressed my lips into a firm line. "I'm not about to besmirch my honor by attacking a woman. I'm going to protect her."

Eileen's face broke into a sudden smile, her shoulders shaking as she held her sword belt out to me. "How noble of you, Captain Marchand. Let's get you a horse to aid you on your quest. I'll feel better knowing someone has her back."

I strapped her sword to my waist as we jogged toward a group of horses tied to a hitching post. Even now, Red was disappearing from view beyond the edge of the camp.

"I hope you can ride bareback," Eileen said as she cupped her hands to boost me onto a dark colored mare.

"Well enough," I replied, hesitating only a moment before stepping up into her hands and heaving myself onto the horse's back. Eileen bent down to untie the picket line and I nudged the beast forward as soon as she was free. Eileen called out to the sentries as I rode to the edge of camp, and they allowed me to pass without issue.

Urging the horse faster, I found a tentative rhythm between us as I navigated a small forest tracking, hoping it was the one Red had used. I caught a glimpse of her as I rounded a curve and exhaled in relief.

What am I doing? I berated myself. I shouldn't feel relieved to keep her in sight. I should be letting her die in reckless pride, releasing me from this binding spell and enabling me to escape home. *No doubt the feeling is part of the spell. Besides, no man of honor would allow a lady to go into danger alone. I couldn't live with myself.*

Not that Red seemed like much of a "lady". She was distractingly female of course, but tall and muscular instead of dainty; scarred and tattooed instead of smooth skinned. Even now, her half braided black hair streamed out behind her as she rode ahead. She wasn't wearing a helmet. *Neither am I*, I realized with a jolt. *This can only end in disaster.*

Red must have sensed me, because she glanced back, hair blowing across her face to obscure her expression. She turned forward again, urging her own mount all the faster.

Finally, she began to slow, and I was able to gradually pull alongside her.

"What are you think-"

"Shhh," she ordered tersely, eyes darting around as we approached the wooden border palisade ahead of us. There was a gap in the rudimentary wall, allowing an oily, slow moving river to flow down from the Wasteland.

"Has there been a drought?" I asked in a whisper, indicating space between where the fence ended, and the waterline began. It seemed obvious that the palisade usually extended partially into the river, but the riverbed was dry for several feet on either side, leaving enough room for someone to easily walk around the wall.

Red shot me a glance. "No actually, but the river has become smaller and fouler in recent years, it's one of the reasons we…" she trailed off, examining me speculatively. "Never mind that. What are you doing here?"

"Giving you back up, since you ordered your soldiers to stay away. *What* are you doing now?!" I added in exasperation as she slid from her mount.

She laughed quietly, a slightly unbalanced sound that echoed oddly in the misty air. "The Beasts are probably still on the other side. The horse won't want to cross if she can help it and I fight better on the ground anyway." She offered the reins to me. "Here, why don't you lead her back to camp for me. I'll find my way on foot. I think camp is less than half a mile away, so you'll be fine."

I looked at her outstretched hand in disdain. *Why is she insane? And why do they all follow her blindly?*

"No thank you, I'll picket mine too, if only to save it from dying with us." I slid down off my horse, patting her side and leading her to a stand of trees, Red following.

"Fine. I'll go across first. You can follow if you like." She glanced at me as we finished securing our mounts. "I'll admit I'm intrigued to see if you're going to try and kill me when I'm distracted by the Beasts. I'm not sure you have it in you, *Captain* Marchand."

Anger at her deliberate smear on my honor flared inside. "I *don't* have it in me, *Captain* Hood. In Pelerin, we have more integrity than that. I'm here to prevent you from killing yourself, Lady knows why."

Red's mouth twisted into the approximation of a grin and she patted her weapons to make sure they were secure.

"We'll see. Just don't get in my way once the fighting starts. I can't be responsible for your safety since I didn't ask you to follow me."

"I'm definitely not holding you responsible for my safety," I hissed sarcastically. Red's shoulders shook in laughter as she turned away, stalking toward the entry point into the Wasteland.

The sky turned murky overhead as we passed through. I was used to the sight from battles at the Pelerine border, but it had never been this thick and cloying. Red's entire body was alert, tense as she scanned the fog. I trailed a few steps behind, my posture defensive, but relaxed. We could see clearly for about a dozen yards on either side, after that visibility faded swiftly into monotonous haze, the grayish brown grass and sparse, stunted trees blending into smothering sky.

My eyes were drawn to Red as we slowly crept forward. If I could set aside her gender, she seemed a competent enough soldier. Almost eye level with me in height, and at six feet I was not exactly short, her armor and leggings did little to conceal her muscular body. Nothing like the petite form fashionable in Pelerin.

I twitched my eyes away, willing my thoughts from the brutish woman ahead of me. Pivoting slightly, I kept her in the corner of my eye while maintaining a line of sight behind us. I felt, rather than saw her stiffen a minute later.

She broke away silently, sprinting toward an equally noiseless shadow. I watched, disoriented, until another shadow appeared to my left.

The Beasts.

Training kicked in like clockwork. Sprinting toward the hunched shape, my brain barely registered it's resemblance to a distorted terrier before I sliced my unsheathed sword in a downward attack to it's neck. The Beast stepped aside and I drew a little slice, instead of removing it's head. I turned as I stumbled past, keeping my hips toward it and my sword in front. It's snout curled savagely, beady eyes red-rimmed and angry. We came together again, charging forward at the same moment. I blocked a series of lunging bites, teeth snapping and growls tumbling from it's mouth. Adrenaline flowed along my veins, my limbs liquid and almost weightless.

There! I spotted an opening as the Beast jumped up at my neck, my arms striking just before it reached my skin. I pulled my sword from it's side in a twisting motion, blood following as it came free. The creature twitched one, twice, and then lay still, angry eyes turning glassy.

Whirling, I sought Red, finding her a few yards away, surrounded by three more bodies. *Three?!* She seemed unfazed, standing straight and tall, a hand on one hip, the other hanging at her side, loosely clutching a knife.

Three, and she hasn't even drawn her sword. Respect colored my perception of her, previously just an exasperated scorn. I turned in a circle, checking our perimeter as I drifted slowly in her direct. My neck snapped toward her as she spoke into the gloom.

"So you're the big one they mentioned, huh. What a shame. I was expecting your boss."

She stood nonchalant as a hulking shadow paced forward in a measured tread. A twisted, misshapen humanoid bear revealed itself, fangs dripping thick strings of saliva, snout pulled back in a snarl.

Red responded with her own snarl, and I was shocked to catch a glimpse of prominent canines extending down from her upper jaw, her nose elongated as if part of a wolfish snout. I shook my head and the vision was gone, her back toward me as she took off toward the remaining Beast.

"Red, wait for - " I cut off, stuttering into my own sprint. She clearly wasn't going to stop now, and I doubt she even heard me. *What, exactly, is wrong with her?!*

Wild laughter reached my ears as she made contact with the remaining Beast. My heart jumped to see that she still hadn't pulled out her sword, slicing at the it's snout with only a knife and dodging a powerful swipe from it's claws. My lungs screamed as I forced my muscles to their breaking point, desperate to reach her before she committed suicide by bear.

The Beast finally caught sight of me barreling toward them, unable to stop itself from issue a roaring challenge. Red plunged her knife deep into it's throat, tearing across savagely in a jerking motion, blood spilling down her arm and misting across her chest and face.

She stepped away as the monster collapsed with a thud and I skidded to stop beside her. I stared at the beast's unmoving carcass, one of the biggest I had ever seen.

"Well that wasn't nearly as much fun as I thought it would be," Red complained with a small laugh. I turned my shocked gaze toward her. She ignored me, crouching down over the scrubby grass and attempting to wipe some of the blood off her arm without much success.

"Fun," I repeated, tonelessly. "You came here, on your own, to fight five Beasts, for *fun?!*" My voice ended in a shout, deadened by the fog swirling around us.

She glanced up into my eyes, a smirk playing around her lips. "Yes, *Eddie.* Some of us like to have a bit of enjoyment from time to time. But I suppose you wouldn't understand. You look like you've never had any in your entire life."

I spluttered, shoving my sword point down into the ground at my side. "Of course I have fun. But you're the leader of a military unit! You can't just go charging off to fight Beasts, out manned and unprotected. You have a *duty* to your soldiers to conduct yourself properly. How will you maintain their respect if you're acting like a reckless youth?!"

"Is that why you look like you've eaten sour grapes? Because it's the only way you could get *your* soldiers to respect you?" she asked, rising back to her feet only marginally cleaner and cocking her head to the side to study me.

Anger clouded my vision as her obtuseness clashed with the lessening adrenaline in my blood. "I do *not* look like I've had sour grapes. And if I do, it's only been since I met *you,* and your sorry excuse of leadership."

I expected her anger to flare at my disrespectful comment, but she merely took a step or two closer, her lips dropping open in a little smile. My eyes traced a splatter of red blood that lay across them.

"You do," she insisted, her tone light. "Your lips are either pressed into a thin line, or, like now, pursed together like…" she reached a hand out toward my mouth, but I caught it in mine before she could make contact.

"Don't touch me."

Her eyebrows lifted and her smile grew. "Noted. But I think you're the one touching *me* right now."

My grip jumped, tightening for a moment as if to crush her strong fingers beneath mine. She seemed unconcerned, her eyes trailing along the new tattoos spilling down my neck, reminding me of their existence. I released her hand with a push.

Ripping a handkerchief out of a pocket, I offered it to her.

"Here. Use this. We can clean up a little more at the river once we're on the other side."

"Yes, sir," she said mockingly, taking the handkerchief from my hand with a flourish. I rolled my eyes and led the way back to the wall.

❋ ❋ ❋

We made it back across the border without incident and without seeing any other Beasts. The oily sheen on the sluggish water of the river gave me pause, but we washed with it anyway. Anything better than the stench of Beast blood on our armor and weapons.

A tautness thrummed in my chest as we rode back to camp. *Who is this woman?* A Captain, a warrior; reckless, bloodthirsty, confident. *And beautiful,* my traitorous mind couldn't help whispering. To be fair, she was beautiful, but in a strong, unapproachable way. Too dangerous and sharp to be inviting.

Not that I want an invitation, I instructed myself sternly. She was the opposite of how a proper woman should behave, and my sense of honor and rightness rebelled at it.

"Go back to your tent when we arrive. You can move about freely since I bound you, no need for a guard. But don't bother trying to escape," Red called back as the camp came into view. "For one thing, you can't, and for another, I'll feel your attempts."

"There's no need to remind me," I replied testily, "I've seen enough magic by now to know it's real. I wouldn't waste my time on it."

"Oh?" She twisted in her saddle, settling a crooked grin on me. "How will you spend your time, then? Screwing up your courage to do what you must, I imagine. As I said, you'll be free only when we reach Nottingham or upon my death. Shall I expect a visit tonight when I'm sleeping?"

Red's form, relaxed and sleeping, her face peaceful and void of that perpetual smirk stole through my mind. I shoved it aside before it could take root, replying stiffly, "I would never approach a lady's bed like that, no Pelerine of integrity would, regardless of your customs in Sherwood."

She pulled a face and turned back around, giving a sign to the sentries as we passed through the camp entrance, before guiding our horses back to their picket lines.

"You're right," she said conversationally as we slid off and secured our mounts, "better to wait until I'm properly exhausted. If I woke up in the middle of my own murder, it wouldn't go well for you."

I spluttered as she sauntered off, her deep chuckle drifting back. *These people have no decency. None,* I thought in disgust. Turning aside, I focused on rubbing down my horse, nodding hello when a squire appeared to take care of Red's mount. The familiar actions soothed the roiling unrest inside, and I felt a little better as I wandered toward my assigned tent, almost happy at the fact that Reynold was no longer required to trail me everywhere.

"Prisoner!" Reynold's voice boomed out, just as I reached my tent. I looked over to find him a row away, seated at a cook fire next to Eileen.

"Come and join us, I made extra," he invited with a smile. "The rest of the game we caught while on the road, with some spice and vegetables I begged off of cook. Can't let it go to waste." After a quick once over, Eileen bent over her steaming bowl, ignoring me.

I cast a longing glance at the freedom of my tent, but turned my feet toward the hot food instead. Giving Reynold a nod of thanks as he offered me a dish of piping hot stew, I settled down on a tree stump and began wolfing down the food.

"So, did she give you a chance to help, or were you just there for a show?" Reynold asked, chuckling.

I grunted around a searing hot mouthful of potato and venison, burning my throat slightly as it went down.

"I told you," Reynold directed at Eileen, nudging her. She shot him a glare as her food almost slopped over the side of the bowl.

"Good for you for being right. But there could have been more than just the five spotted. Everyone should have back up when they go into a fight."

"Not our Captain, though, surely!" The crunch of footsteps sounded behind me and I turned, just as something flew through the air to my right. I flinched, only to realize it had been a bread roll.

"Ar, it's the prisoner I've heard so much about now, isn't it? Sorry to startle you, young man. Here's to make up for it." A hulking giant of a man stood a pace away, proffering a rough bread roll to me.

I accepted it cautiously, and he broke into a gap-toothed grin, tossing another roll to Eileen before sitting down next to me. My eyes lingered on the stark white stripe running down the center part of his rough black hair.

"These were the last ones for the day, and I had to beg 'em off Cook. He said he'll have bread with dinner, that is if Edda and me don't eat it all before you lot have a chance." He winked as

Reynold chuckled, then turned his attention back to me. "I'm Broc," he said with a nod.

"Eddie. Thank you for the roll."

"Ah well, prisoner, we understand you Pelerines are used to fine dining. Don't want to shock you all at once with our rough ways, do we now, Reynold."

"He's not so bad," Reynold replied with a laugh. "Seems used to camp life at least. Haven't heard a complaint from him since he got here. Though that could be him trying to stay in our good graces for release."

"Ah, I heard about that. You went off after the Cap'n earlier, didn't you? Thought she'd need back up." Broc chuckled around a mouthful of stew. "Our Red Rider don't need help with five wee Beasties, but you weren't to know that I suppose."

My brow furrowed. "I've heard that term before. What is a Red Rider?"

"*The* Red Rider, my lad. Do you mean to tell me you haven't heard of her?!" Broc's jaw hung down in astonishment.

"Not in Pelerin," Eileen spoke up, setting her empty bowl down on her lap. "My Dad's been there in his travels. He says they have naught to do with us in Sherwood. Their rulers favored Prince John."

"Darkness take him!" Reynold spat. Eileen raised an eyebrow.

"Don't give me that look, you don't know what it was like." Reynold scolded her, then shared a glance with Broc. He grunted and focused back on his food, his cheery look turned grim.

"I fought like the rest of you, old timer, by Red's side," Eileen replied testily.

"Yes but you only came of age toward the end. That Prince was a pit of lies, his mind more Beast than man. And he tried his best to keep or kill the Captain. If she weren't..." he trailed off, shaking his head and gazing into the fire.

"Enough of that. He's worm food now, and can trouble us no more," Broc declared, turning his attention back to me. "I can't believe you don't know about our Red Rider. Have you heard none o' the tales?"

I shook my head. "Everyone here seems to hold her in high respect, I gather. But no, I don't know what she's done to deserve the name."

"Wasteland's Watch, man! Eileen, you're a bard's daughter. Tell him all about it. So long as he's here we can educate a poor ignorant Pelerine like him. When he goes back he can spread her fame across his land too."

Eileen rolled her eyes, leaning forward to scoop some ash from the edge of the fire into her bowl. "I'm a bard's *daughter*, not a bard, as I keep reminding you."

"Yes," Reynold responded, grinning between her and Broc, "but you're the closest thing we've got to a storyteller. Unless you'd rather have me do the honors?"

"Lady's Bow, no! Spare us your ramblings." Her shoulders shook with laughter as she swirled the ash around the bowl, cleaning the remains of her stew away before dumping it on the edge of the fire. The two men settled back as she stacked her bowl and spoon next to Reynold's and gathered her words.

"You know of the time we call the Interregnum here, yes?" she asked me, and I nodded. "Good. Maid Marian, as she was known then, was still a minor and so not yet able to rule in her own right after her grandfather died. Her uncles acted as regent for her, one after the other. Each met an untimely end until the only one left was John. Instead of fulfilling his office, he seized power for himself, playing off the fears and factions that have always plagued our country. He was successful for a time." Eileen looked at her hands thoughtfully, the others listening quietly although they must know the story as well as she did.

"Red was only twelve when he seized the throne. Not only was he Marian's uncle, but Red's as well. Her father was a well known keeper of the old ways, and had died in an uprising against John. To keep Red's mother from seeking aid from Asileboix, he drafted Red into the military. First as a Forester, but then when she… started showing talent despite her age, he transferred her to a border unit. Instead of dying in battle, as he no doubt expected, she thrived at every turn, fighting harder, and longer, and better than those twice as experienced."

Murmurs of agreement sounded from the men and I stared into the fire, trying not to imagine the horrors a teenage Red must have faced, knowing all too well what they were from my own experiences at the Pelerine border these last few years.

"Her fame grew across the land. She was legendary as a brutal fighter who never refused a mission and never lost. Finally John sought to use her to solidify his own power, which had been waning after Marian passed the age of inheritance. He thought he had stamped out all loyalty and honor from our Captain, his own twisted mind not capable of understanding some of us don't long only for power." Eileen shook her head as the others murmured in angry remembrance. She tossed a stick onto the fire, making the embers jump and sending a few sparks into the air before continuing.

"His mistake. He recalled her from the border, making her Captain of his own personal guard, using her fame and popularity to bolster his own. She performed her duty well until the resistance gave her an opening. Then she hunted him down like the dog he was." A chorus of growls went up around the fire, and I noticed in surprise that two women had joined our group, twins by the look of them.

I cleared my throat. "So she killed him, and set Marian on the throne."

"Heavens no," Eileen said, brow furrowed. "She captured him as he ran, dragging him back to the Nottingham Castle while Robin and Marian dealt with his supporters. They tried him for his crimes, and he was executed."

I raised my eyebrows, surprised at the adherence to rule of law by the Sherwoodian people. They were known in Pelerin for their brutality, but it seemed that their current leaders at least aimed for more. "I see. But, why The Red Rider? I don't understand where the name comes from." I darted a glance around the group as everyone shifted in their seat.

"No one knows for sure," one of the twins whispered solemnly. "I heard it's because she wept tears of blood as she fought along

Robin and Marian in the revolution. Crying for each traitorous Sherwoodian she had to cut down when they wouldn't accept their rightful rulers."

My eyes widened in shock and a shiver passed down my spine as I thought of Red, only a few years ago, meting out death in the Sherwoodian civil war. *Has she only known bloodshed and betrayal?*

A charged silence sat around the fire for a moment, broken after a moment by a cough from Reynold, followed by a chuckle from Broc that sparked an cascade of laughter from the others.

"Edda," Reynold crowed, wiping tears from his eyes, "You got me, I don't mind admitting. I thought I'd heard them all over the years but that one was a peach."

Edda grinned, a flush of pride on her cheeks.

"I don't know where you get these ideas," her twin accused, her nose wrinkled although a faint smile hovered on her lips. "That was just disgusting."

"I don't know how it came to me. Only, I could imagine our Captain doing such a thing. She loves Sherwood with every bone in her body, but that wouldn't stop her from doing her duty," Edda replied. The others nodded, their amusement fading.

"So what, then?" I asked, unable to feel too acrimonious that I had been duped. "Where did her name come from?"

"It's not her name, prisoner," Eileen's voice cut across the others. "It's her title. It's who she is."

"Aye," interrupted Broc, grinning again, "and it's why she don't need no Pelerine nursemaid following her around to fight a few Beasties. Why, I was there the day she cleared out that whole den on her own, weren't I, Reynold?"

Reynold nodded, crossing his arms across his chest. "She's always testing herself, our Captain, even from that first day she came to our unit, smaller than a whippersnapper and fiercer than a wolf cub."

"And that's exactly why she shouldn't be going out there without backup!" Eileen cut in, her tone exasperated. "She's not the Red Lady. She's not immortal. She'll get herself killed for no reason one of these days. The foreigner could see it right off." She shot an approving glance my way, surprising me.

Broc slapped me on the shoulder, almost shoving me off my seat. "He's alright, I reckon, this one. Though we'll be keepin' an eye on you, never fear," he warned with a laugh. "Now off with youse all. I'm needing my bed soon."

The twins stood up and Eileen walked around the fire to join them. The ducked their heads together, quickly engrossed in their own discussion as they wandered away. Broc took my bowl and he and Reynold nodded before heading back toward the mess tent, hands full of dirty dishes.

Once I was alone, my hand sought the pocket with my good luck charm, out of habit more than anything else. I pulled it out, rubbing the frayed silk with my hand as I had done a thousand times before. Only this time, I no longer felt the warm reassurance of my path ahead like I usually did. *Maybe it doesn't hold luck for me anymore,* I thought, staring at it uneasily. Red's story jumped to the front of my mind, and I stuffed my charm away again. It was a reminder of a charmed childhood, one that wasn't available to everyone apparently. *Well Creator, if you're out there, I could use a new good luck charm.* There was no response, so I sat staring at the fire awhile longer, wondering how I could make my own luck.

CHAPTER THREE

Red

We made good time back to Nottingham, our capitol city. The promise of good food and entertainment, the the ability to see family for those who lived in the city was cheering to each of us, our prisoner included. Eddie Marchand seemed to get along with just about everyone. He was pleasant, witty, and proved himself handy with a weapon when he sparred with Reynold and Broc in the evenings. The only time he looked at all disgruntled was when someone performed magic, or when I teased or flirted with him.

I don't know what made me do it. Some perverse need to make someone feel as out of control as I felt. It wasn't right, really, since he was my charge. I was careful not to cross any lines but I couldn't seem to help myself.

A loosening recklessness had been unleashing inside me for the last several months. *No, longer.* Maybe I've always lived with it, this feeling like a shooting star. I've been burning, incinerating all the parts of myself that aren't hard and dangerous. For a long time I burned alone, never letting anyone close enough to know how consumed with rage I was already. Victory over John granted me a safe place, and people praised me as a bright guiding star, but instead of settling down I've been burning hotter. Eileen had noticed, and a few of the others.

There was a feeling of inevitability in my mind. I was a meteor streaking brightly across the arc of my life, and since my failure at the border a few months ago, my incendiary end seemed imminent. Something about Marchand's presence seemed liable to ignite that final descent, and I couldn't resist helping it along.

My eyes slid to him now, riding off to my right before refocusing on the road ahead. He had born my teasing stoically, hiding his disgust with moderate success. He tried but couldn't completely hide the answering spark that flared in his eyes during our exchanges, which made it all the more interesting. Still, I knew my interest in him was a flash in the sky, a fleeting flare of brilliance. It had to be. I would be handing him off to Robin in a few hours, and then hopefully be sent to the Wasteland to fix my mistakes. That was the only ending for us.

I glanced back at Marchand again, catching his brown eyes on me. They were focused on my tattoos, which traced the curve of my hairline from my ear to my temple. A frown marked his brow, provoking my grin.

"You disapprove," I told him, more of a statement than a question.

His eyes flicked to mine, his flushing as he realized I had noticed his stare. He shrugged.

"I'm not exactly comfortable with tattoos, I'll admit. In Pelerin they are considered barbaric and signs of …"

"Magic?" I supplied, my grin growing wider.

"Well, yes. And of course they are. But I assume you didn't have a choice in your healing, or the wound that necessitated it. Besides, I have a few of my own by now, I can't exactly disapprove, can I?"

My eyes flicked to his tattoos, a complicated whirling line of runes tumbling down each side of his neck. They were enticing. *Where do they end?* I wondered, eying the collar of his shirt.

I fought my own flush and turned my head forward, wrenching my thoughts back to our conversation. "No, I didn't have a choice in my healing. At the time, I wished for death instead. But Elne was right, it was better to live, and the tattoos have been a reminder that everything could always be worse." I grinned, my canines bared as Elne stirred sleepily in my mind.

"Elne?"

"My companion," I explained, purposefully vague. His face cleared. No doubt he thought Elne was a lady's maid. If he knew I communed with a disembodied wolf in my mind, he's be a little more lively.

As we exited the woods, the city of Nottingham rose before us. Most prominent were the cathedral and castle, of course, but the houses and municipal buildings crowded together in a cheerful way, presenting a comfortable looking city of wood and stone. Smokefires rose up here and there, and the verdant green of animal pastures spread out between us and the central gate. A peaceful and pleasing sight.

I hated it.

Behind those walls lived many hardworking, honest people, but the city also housed political factions and the leftovers of John's supporters. Robin and Marian had built peace in the last handful of years, but vipers hid even in their own supporters. Marian had enough cunning to keep them all in check, but I hated their politics, as well as the memories that lived here.

You're nothing but an attack dog. The stones whispered to me in John's voice. I ignored them as usual. A swish of a cape caught my eye as someone passed out of the main gate, walking just as *he* used to; a steady, measured tread. My heart froze, but a moment later and the man's hood fell back, revealing fair hair and a friendly countenance. Not John. *John's dead.* Eddie's voice jolted me back to reality.

"Is this Nottingham?" Eddie asked.

"Are ye daft, man?" Reynold asked from behind us. "Of course it's Nottingham. What else would it be?"

I snorted and moved toward the front of the line. Eddie trailed in my wake, staying a horse length away.

We wound through the city toward the castle. Townspeople stopped and saluted with a fist over their heart as usual, but I kept my focus on the road, ignoring everyone else. The Red Rider let nothing distract her from her mission.

As we finished stabling our horses, Marian appeared at the entrance of the castle to welcome us. She was glowing, nearing the end of her pregnancy and dressed in flowing green that set off her auburn hair. Slinging my pack over my shoulder, I couldn't help glancing at Eddie as I tightened the strap, observing his reaction to my sister-in-law.

His whole face had softened at the sight of her. *Of course,* I thought bitterly, *she's exactly the type of woman he'd admire. Just like Belle, gracious, beautiful, and classically feminine.* Marian had won the love of all of her subjects, even those that objected to her for idiotic reasons like her gender or motherhood. They sang praises about her gentleness and mercy, her patient good humor and how she listened wholeheartedly to anyone who crossed her path. It irritated me that I even cared that Eddie would be taken in by her.

The first of my soldiers had reached Marian, and her charm was turned on full bore. I reminded myself to keep the cynical smirk off my face. Easy enough to do. *I've spent most of my life masking what I'm truly feeling. I suppose it's hypocritical of me to mock Marian for doing the same.* After all, she *was* a paragon of virtue in some regards. But the virtues she had in spades were much harsher, much more practical, and much more suited to ending a civil war than the ones she displayed with her public persona.

She softly welcomed each warrior that came toward her, shaking hands and accepting bows, answering questions about her condition, and Robin, and the other children. Finally it was only myself and Eddie. I accepted a kiss on each cheek from her.

"Welcome home, sister," she said with a gentle smile.

"Sister-in-law," I reminded her, pulling my lips into a tight smile. "The Creator didn't see fit to grant me full sister-ship with you, my Lady."

"No indeed, but I claim it anyway, dear Red."

I bowed stiffly as she turned to Eddie, her too sweet voice grating on my nerves. "And you must be Captain Marchand. We heard of your plight and are glad to see you safe. Red will show you to your quarters. My Lord Robin will call for a meeting to discuss your situation within the hour, do not worry." She turned back to me. "I've had him put in the chambers across from yours, as you are his keeper. Bess will find you when Robin is ready."

I bowed again, waiting impatiently as Eddie took Marian's proffered hand and bent over it in a courtly fashion. She always inspired such platonic dedication from men like him, the chivalrous and genteel, especially in her current condition.

"The baby is well?" I asked in an undertone as we turned toward the castle doors. She crooked an eyebrow at me and dipped her chin. "Very well, and active. She'll be as difficult as Richard, I swear." I grinned. My nephews were rays of sunshine in the shadowy halls of Nottingham. "Well, maybe it will be a boy as well, and keep his brothers in line."

Marian stuck her nose in the air, confident in her predictions as always, and motioned for me to follow Eddie into the castle. We took leave of her in the entrance hall, and I marched toward our rooms as Eddie trailed behind, casting concerned glances as Marian lumbered gracefully toward Robin's study. I rolled my eyes. Yes, Marian was nearing the end of her pregnancy, but despite the air of delicate fragility she managed to project, she was a strong as an ox. I knew for a fact that she had spent most of her last labor dictating tax collection policy for the southern part of the duchy. She had stopped only for a few minutes to have Richard, then picked up where she left off. Nothing and no one got in her way.

We arrived at our rooms and I left Eddie in his with a sense of relief. The desire to needle him had left with our entry to the castle; his reaction to Marian serving as a reminder that his disgust for a woman like me was all too real. His propensity to be duped by beauty was just as disgusting to my own ideals. *He'll be out of my hands in an hour. Then I can get back to real work.*

✽ ✽ ✽

After cleaning up and changing, I barely had time to re-braid my hair before Bess' knock sounded on the door.

"Lord Robin sent for you, Captain," she told me with a warm smile. "He's in his study."

"Thank you, Bess. I'll go there directly." She bobbed a curtsy and trundled off toward the stairs.

I walked across to Eddie's room and knocked briskly. The door swung open after a moment, revealing a much neater version of him than I had met a few weeks ago. When I had left him in his room his jaw had sported a scruffy stubble. Now, his face was smooth again, and I watched a drop of water slip from the short, dark locks behind his ear, coaxed downward by gravity. *What is it about him that's so fascinating?* I asked myself, half curious, half irritated. To cover the direction of my thoughts I adopted a warm grin.

"Well, Captain, your time under my care is about to come to an end. Let's go see my brother."

He nodded, pulling the door shut behind him as he followed me down the corridor. As we entered the Great Hall, a flash of red hair caught my eye and I saw Eileen stride out of the corridor leading to my brother's offices. I frowned as I traced her purposeful stride. *What business could she have there?* She was too far away to ask and I didn't want to draw attention by shouting across the busy hall. She disappeared out the main entrance without a glance in my direction.

Eddie pulled alongside me, my gait having slowed almost to a stop as I watched Eileen. He shot me a puzzled look.

"Do you not know where your brother might be?"

I rolled my eyes and picked up speed again, ignoring Elne as she pulled at me to check in with Eileen first, to investigate a potential wayward pack member. *Humans aren't like wolves, Elne,* I reminded her sternly. *We have our own business to attend to, not just pack business.* I could tell she disagreed but she retreated from my mind again. Passing by the grand staircase leading to upper level audience chamber, I led Eddie into a small warren of offices. Stopping before the door at the very back, I knocked twice and stepped inside, waiting for Eddie to pass through before closing it behind us.

The office was warm and full of yellow sunshine, softening the colors of the tapestries on the stone walls with hazy warmth. Bookshelves, stuffed to the gills with manuscripts and tomes lent the air a papery smell, interwoven with something green. My eyes flicked toward the fireplace. As had become Marian's wont, it was filled with a number of potted plants. There would be no need for a fire until Autumn returned, and she hated inefficient spaces. A small movement caught my eye, and I was startled to find her seated on a padded window seat, recessed along the curved outer wall of the tower. *Of course she's here. She wouldn't miss this interview for the world.* She smiled sweetly in response to Eddie's bow. Elne growled in agreement with my irritation, almost causing me to chuckle.

My brother leaned forward in his chair, setting his elbows on the desk in front of him and lacing his hands together. His brown eyes were serious as he assessed Eddie. Robin surreptitiously rubbed the calluses of is draw fingers against his knuckles, a tell that betrayed his conflicted thoughts he's had since he was a boy. The corner of my mouth quirked up to see it.

"Well, brother, it's good to see you too," I said, amusement coloring my voice.

His mouth pressed into a wry smile as he transferred his attention to me. "Yes, Red, welcome back. I've received reports that you've been indulging in your usual habit of fighting to victory, this time for Asileboix's benefit. Well done."

I pasted my smirk on all the harder as some of my mirth lessened. Robin, I knew, wouldn't intend the bite in those words, but I saw Marian's hands still for a fraction of a second behind him, and knew her eyes were on me. She never forgot anything, certainly not the stain of losing Rapunzel's unit last year.

"And this must be Captain Marchand," Robin continued, looking back at Eddie gravely. "I've heard that you are seeking passage back to Pelerin."

"Indeed, Sir. Although Captain Hood here has assured me of my family's wellbeing, I would like to see them for myself. I'm sure you understand. And of course, we all feel more comfortable in our own countries, don't we?" Eddie ended his speech with a respectful smile.

Marian made an adjustment to her embroidery hoop while my brother considered Eddie in silence. Robin shifted in his chair, glancing over at Marian replying. "Indeed, I can well understand that desire.". Impatience to move past this prisoner transition overtook me and I sniffed, drawing Robin and Eddie's eyes toward me.

"So, you'll be releasing him home. A bit of a surprise, given my report from the Council. Either way, it's not my concern." Twisting one of the brass knuckles I wore disguised as a ring, I held my hand out to Eddie. "Here, I'll release our binding." His eyes flicked from my outstretched hand up to my face, his expression unreadable.

"That won't be necessary," Robin interrupted, just as Eddie began to close the distance between us, his own hand reaching toward mine.

I whipped my gaze back to my brother, my body still turned toward Eddie. Robin stared at me implacably, eyebrow raised and lips pressed together. *Oh no. Not good.* Whenever he looked at me like that, he invariably issued an order he knew I wouldn't like. While he usually valued my insight, when he looked like this, I knew I wouldn't be able to change his mind from whatever ill advised task he was about to dump on me.

I braced myself as he stood from behind his desk, clasped his hands behind his back and transferred his attention back to Eddie.

"Captain Marchand, I will *not* be releasing you from our custody. You were captured during a military engagement, and while I do not believe you were acting against Sherwood, I've received reliable reports that you acted directly against the leader of our most stalwart ally. I will not risk insulting Prince Andrus by releasing you just yet. Besides which, our reports from the Pelerine government indicate that you are being considered an outlaw. Home, for you right now, may not be the refuge you think it."

Eddie stared at Robin as he spoke, color draining from his face, his hand still hovering between us. I kept my own outstretched arm still, impatient to release my charge.

"Robin, surely I don't need to be here while you discuss his fate. Let me release him. I'll send his new guard in when I leave."

"No, Red. Have a seat."

I drew my hand away from Eddie and turned toward Robin more fully, crossing my arms over my chest. "I'll stand, thanks brother."

He let out an exasperated snort, the sound familiar from our childhood spats. "Fine, stand then, *little* sister." I gritted my teeth but kept a lid on the flare of irritation from Elne that colored my thoughts. Robin continued in a more controlled manner, addressing Eddie.

"You are still under guard, but I do not intend to lock you up. The Princess of Asileboix has entreated me to be merciful with you, stating that your character is honorable. To that end, you will be placed under guarded house arrest until I come to an agreement with the Asilean and Pelerine governments."

A sense of foreboding rolled across my gut and Elne snapped to attention in response to my anxiety. Eddie's mouth was pressed in a thin line and I could almost feel the tension rolling off of him, but he made no comment. Robin continued, nodding to an envelope on his desk.

"Red, your orders are in there. Your unit is long overdue for a break, so I'm putting you on leave until Yuletide."

A shock went through me, every muscle in my body tensing. *No.*

"You'll return home to Barnsdale Lodge with Eddie. I'm entrusting you with his care until this matter is settled."

"No," I growled, my jaw finally unclenching. Eddie stiffened beside my and I could feel his eyes on me. *No doubt shocked at my disregard for the chain of command,* some part of my brain sneered. But when the chain of command is your idiot older brother, challenging his idiot ideas is my birthright. *Of course, he knows how I feel about Barnsdale - this doesn't sound like him.*

"This isn't you," I told Robin, turning my anger toward Marian instead. "This is your doing, isn't it!?"

Marian set aside her embroidery with graceful movements, placing her hands on her rounded belly and giving me a gentle but reproving look.

"Dear Red, I am not your commanding officer, as you well know, but I happen to agree with my husband's orders. You've been on duty too often these last years. You need rest. There is no safer place than Barnsdale Lodge for Captain Marchand to serve out his house arrest. It solves both problems neatly, I must say. Besides, your mother misses you."

I scoffed loudly, "Did she tell you that? Did she write in her last letter, 'Oh Marian, do convince Robin to let my dear daughter come home for once, I long to see her.' No, the 'neatness' of this solution smacks of you, Marian. As usual, you've arranged everything to your own desire, no matter the discomfort it causes someone else." I drew in a deep, shaky breath. Marian hadn't flinched a muscle during my tirade, although I knew her well enough to know that fixed expression meant she was concentrating on hiding her true reaction.

"That's enough, *Captain* Hood," my brother interrupted. "You have your orders. I know you don't like them, but it's your duty to carry them out. They will not be changed."

I stared at Robin, aware that resentment was pouring out of my eyes, even as I fought to keep my mouth shut. His anger at my words to Marian gave way slightly to understanding and concern. He took a few steps toward me from around his desk, seeming to think better of it after a minute and stopping before he reached me.

"Red, your reaction just confirms reports I've received of your recklessness in the last few months. I know you want to fix…" he trailed off as I shot him a warning glare. "In any event, even if you don't want a break, your unit need one. The decision has been made."

"Then add me to whichever unit is scheduled for border duty next. They wouldn't say no to having the Red Rider," I demanded, my voice tight.

"The answer is no. You're going to Barnsdale Lodge. Do I need to provide you with an escort?"

"No, *Sir.*" I bit out, whirling toward the exit. I stopped as I closed my hand around the latch. "If those are my orders, we'll be leaving tomorrow, unless you have any other tasks for me."

"No Red, none at all," he replied, tiredly. I swept from the room, Elne's snapping matching my own mood.

CHAPTER FOUR

Eddie

I flinched as the wooden door of the study bounced off the door frame, Red's athletic form visible through it, striding purposefully away. Her attitude reminded me of a wounded bobcat I had stumbled across once while hunting with my best friend, Henri LeFeu. It's back leg had been caught in a trap, and it was clearly in pain. We had tried to help it, as a healthy predator population was good for the balance in the woodland on my father's estate, but it hadn't trusted us, striking out defensively every time we made a motion toward it. In the end, we had to put it down. It had mangled the original wound so badly in it's wild attempts to free itself and fight us off. Healing would have been impossible. Something about Red's interaction with her brother reminded me of that wild inability to accept help.

"Captain Marchand," Lord Robin's voice drew my attention away from Red's retreating form. I looked back to where he examined me gravely, just a few feet away.

"Do not attempt to escape. I am sure Red has already explained the limitations of the binding spell. If you harm anyone under my care, you will suffer immediate punishment. I am trusting the word of the Asilean Princess as to your honor, but I can assure you, I care nothing for her wishes in comparison to the safety of my people."

"Our people, darling," Lady Marian said, coming quietly to stand beside her husband, tucking one hand under his arm and leaning against him slightly. She gave me an understanding smile. "Captain Marchand, we have your word that you will abide by our wishes, do we not?"

I couldn't bring myself to smile back, but my gaze softened. "You have my word that I will not harm any of your people unless in self defense. And I will go with Captain Hood to this Barnsdale Lodge while I await your negotiations. If Belle is truly alive, and advocating on my behalf, I am content to wait." I left the *for now* off of my words as I bowed to them, although it echoed in my mind. I still wasn't wholly convinced that all was as these Sherwoodians represented. I had hoped that Lord Robin and Lady Marian would release me.

Wait to see which way the wind is blowing. Surely it will be easier to escape from some country lodge than Nottingham Castle. I'll figure out what to do about that spell later.

I kept my eyes trained on the floor. Although Lady Marian seemed like the embodiment of goodness itself, there was something about her gaze that indicated she saw more about your thoughts than you might like. It wasn't necessarily a bad trait, it wasn't comfortable to be around.

"There now, we have his word. Do see our castellan about anything you may have need of before you leave in the morning. A change of clothes, or any toiletries you didn't carry with you. I'm sure she can sort something out for you."

I bowed again as she and Lord Robin dismissed me, glancing back just before I clicked the door shut. Robin stared down at his wife, a sad expression on his face, as she cupped his cheek, whispering something in his ear.

A pang went through my chest at the sight, which I quickly stuffed away. That was exactly the sort of relationship I wanted for myself, the sort I almost had with Belle. *No, don't go down that trail,* I instructed myself sternly. *That sort of relationship had never been on the table, even if you thought it was. You know better now.*

The knot in my chest grew harder as I rounded the tower staircase and walked back toward the Great Hall. *Stop being so dramatic,* I ordered myself. *You're not lovesick over Belle. She was right when she said it was more the idea of 'us' than the actual 'us' you loved.*

Still, as I continued toward my chambers, the ache in my chest got worse. I found myself turning, rubbing my aching heart as my feet led me toward the front doors of the castle. No one challenged me as I went through them. My fuzzy thoughts had devolved to focus solely on the ache in my chest and the desire, the *need* to walk. My feet took me across a gravel drive that led to the main road in the city. Again, I wasn't challenged as I left the city gates, although I noted the guard's curious looks as walked through.

Has someone put a spell on me? I wondered fuzzily. *Is this what it feels like? I wonder what I'm going to do.* My actions no longer felt under my control, although I didn't feel as if someone was commanding me. More as thought I was walking toward my fate, all other options closed to me.

A moment of clarity stole across my mind as the ache in my chest let up just a fraction. *Someone did put a spell on you - Red's binding spell.* She had said we were bound to stay within a half a mile of each other. I judged that the cleared farmland surrounding the castle was just over a half a mile wide. My steps were still leading me purposefully in the direction of the woods beyond. *She must be out there. Still in a high temper no doubt.* I fought the urge to roll my eyes. *And this is the famous Red Rider.*

By the time I reached the woodline, the pain in my chest had lessened considerably, and I could have easily stopped. But I found that I could still sense a tug on my heart if I concentrated, and, curious now, I continued on more slowly, concentrating on the sensation as my guide until it suddenly faded.

I glanced around, confused. There was no sign of Red in the forest undergrowth I had wandered into, but since I no longer felt any vestiges of the spell, she had to be nearby.

"Red?" I called, glancing around in the leafy undergrowth. "I know you're here somewhere. I got my first taste of that spell you put on us, thank you *so much* for that." Not a sound in response. I shook my head. I had seen soldiers in moods like she had been in. They either needed someone to bash some sense back into their heads, or they would cause their own death within a fortnight.

"Don't you think it's time to end this little hissy fit? If I understood correctly, we have a journey to prepare for, and I need help finding supplies."

Still no reply. I decided to press one of the buttons that I had noticed seemed to get to her during our verbal sparring in the last few weeks - her competency as a soldier. "It's none of my business how you people conduct business in Sherwood, but if I had treated my commanding officer the way you did yours, I would have been flayed alive."

A slight whisper sounded behind me, not to my ears, but as a prickle on my arms.

Whirling, I blocked her strike just in time, my forearm jarring against hers as I pushed her arm to the side, grappling to gain control of her wrist. She stumbled as she threw a punch with her other hand, pushing me back against a wide tree trunk. I deflected the force of her blow with my other hand, scrabbling to grab that wrist as well.

"That can be arranged," she hissed as she pinned me to the trunk with her hips, wrenching down to pull her wrists out of my grasp. Our strength was well matched, but I proved the winner, pulling her back as she tried to push away from me. With a quick motion, I crossed our wrists against our chests tugging her around and pressing her back against the tree instead, forcing her to look at me.

Her teeth were bared, canines showing and longer than I remembered, a wild look burning in her storm grey eyes, only an inch from my own. Something in me broke open to that wildness. I wanted to push her as far she would go, see how bright her fire could flare; and simultaneously capture her for myself and tame her, to soften her spirit to a warm glow.

What does she taste like? A memory spilled across my tongue - something I had tried in the capitol once. Dark chocolate flavored with southern peppers: bitter, strong, a velvety sweetness that made you crave more. My heart pulled toward her, wanting to drink her in.

Her eyes traced the direction of my thoughts and I saw her pupils widen slightly. She inhaled a tiny breath through open lips, so close to mine; if either of us dared to cross the distance.

Taste her, something traitorous in my mind urged, and my neck moved forward infinitesimally before revulsion flared against at my base instincts. *You just fought a **woman**, and now you're trying to seduce her,* I accused myself. Red's expression shuttered as my lips twisted in self-disgust. I released her, pushing back several paces to put distance between us.

She's your jailer, and an enemy. I reminded myself, trying to draw breath back into my lungs. Red seemed more controlled now, her temper having receded back to the noisy quiet I had come to associate with her as she tugged on the bottom of her black leather jerkin, not meeting my eyes.

"Let's go," she growled darkly. She led the way out of the woods, striding purposefully toward the castle, obviously wishing to leave the moment behind us. I was happy to do the same, but a part of me couldn't help lengthening my own stride until I was beside her, satisfied as I noted a flicker of irritation cross her face when she quickened her pace to get ahead of me. I matched it easily, even as I knew the gentlemanly thing would be to allow her to proceed me, as she so obviously wished. There was something in the air in Sherwood that seemed to bring out the worst in me.

※ ※ ※

A flash of red hair met our eyes as we re-entered the castle grounds. Eileen was sitting on a bench, staring down at her hands. I felt Red stiffen beside me before changing her course and marching directly over to her. I followed more slowly.

"I know it was you," she accused, coming to a stop and setting her hands on her hips as Eileen looked up. "I'm your friend, and your commanding officer, and yet you went behind my back to Robin! We have work to do, we can't afford to sit out of rotation."

Eileen frowned, concern etched on her face. "I've been telling you that you're too reckless, but you won't listen. I can't let you destroy yourself, either as a friend, or as an officer."

Red bristled as she looked down at Eileen, but the other woman didn't flinch, just held Red's eyes steadily. After a charged silence, Red's shoulders relaxed slightly.

"You shouldn't have done it."

"Well, it's done. And you would have done the same in my place. Everyone needs a break sometimes, Red."

I flicked my gaze between the two women. Neither of them betrayed much emotion, but they seemed to read each other's thoughts easily. The type of camaraderie that could only come from a long friendship.

Red released a charged breath and then chuckled. "I suppose it has been some time since we've had a real break. I'm not saying I agree with what you did, but as you said: it's done." Eileen cracked a smile and Red rolled her eyes. "Give your little ones a kiss from me when you get home. And say hello to your husband. You'll enjoy your time off at least."

"I will. I'm leaving at first light. Come and visit us if you can."

Red nodded and turned around, noticing me again with a surprised look.

"You're still here? Come on then, let's go eat."

I followed her a half step behind this time as we marched into the castle. Her interaction with Eileen was strange. Their relationship obviously had a long history. Neither of them had apologized, or really justified their actions. But they seemed to have settled their differences without that. The officer in me was irritated by the fact that a junior team member had gone behind a superior's back. But the soldier in me knew firsthand what could happen if a reckless officer went unchecked. Not only the officer's life, but the lives of his men could be lost. *Her men. Her soldiers,* I corrected myself. *Nothing here is normal.*

The dining hall proved to be a long room that took up almost half of one of the towers. Narrow tables trailed the length of the room, and people in what looked like servant's uniforms sat among nobles and guards. At one end there was a buffet piled high with dishes to choose from. The other end held an empty head table, used by the Duke and Duchess during feast days, no doubt.

I followed behind Red, taking a plate and filling it at the buffet before finding a seat among some soldiers I was acquainted with from her unit. She began eating with focus as soon as we sat down, ignoring her subordinates except for a nod and a grunt when they questioned her about their release. The others had already eaten their fill, and were instead swapping stories about what they would do with their extended leave.

"Our father will put us to work, no doubt. He won't have to hire extra hands for harvest if we'll be there," one of the twins said morosely.

"If I have my way, I'll help Ma in the shop instead," the other twin said with a devious smile, making her sister perk up.

"Now there's an idea. Think she'll take two of us?"

"There won't be room for both of us, and it's my idea!"

Broc rumbled a laugh from where he sat between them. "Ah the problems of youth. If you's slacked in your duties here like you's are plannin' to at home, you'd be dead by now, the pair of you!" The twins rolled their eyes at each other while Broc continued speaking. "Now I'm glad to be home myself. My missus writes that our older daughter fancies herself in love. Seems I'm needed to knock some sense into her suitor so the timing's perfect. Besides, my son and his wife are expectin' my first grandchild. I'll actually be home to meet the wee mite. I can hardly wait."

"Hmm. Very domestic, the lot of you," an older warrior named Eoforde interrupted, talking around a mouthful of food. "I'll be staying here as usual. Put some rotations in with the castle guards to give them a break. Reckon you'll do the same, eh Hreremus?"

The quiet scout nodded, coloring as Broc let out a guffaw and elbowed him. "He'll be staying here all right, but he's got domestic plans of his own, don't he?"

"Really?" Edith squealed, echoed by Edda. "Tell us!"

Hreremus blushed harder into his drink as Broc leaned in conspiratorially. I felt myself leaning in to catch his words before realizing what I was doing and straitening back up. *Why are you interested in a bit of Sherwoodian gossip?*

"He's got his eye on a scribe in the library. A quiet thing, jus' like himself. They'll never come together if you ask me. Neither one'll be able to manage the words between 'em."

"Hreremus we'll help!" Edda volunteered, eyes alight with interest. "Tell us which one and we'll talk to her for you."

Edith shushed her. "Leave him alone. He needs to figure it out on his own or not at all." She turned to Hreremus, who was edging out of his seat. "Besides, if you're too shy to talk to her, you could always write letters back and forth!"

"If you take my advice, Hreremus, you'll forget about it. Starting a family and keeping it is hard enough in this line of work. You're a good scout. Focus on that instead," Eoforde grunted.

Broc chuckled at Eoforde's surly statement and turned his attention to me. "And you'll be going with our Red Rider to the Lodge from what I hear, Eddie."

"That's right," Red chipped in as she stood from the table, empty plate and cup in hand. "He's under house arrest with me, so pray for the poor sod when you think of it." She flashed a smile as the others laughed, then added in an undertone to me, "we leave at dawn. I'll arrange with the Castellan to get your things packed, and a few supplies you'll need until we get to the Lodge. Be ready." I nodded and she strode away without a backward glance. I turned back to her companions.

"Yes, it seems I'm to await my fate at Barnsdale Lodge. Is it far from here?"

"Well, it's a fair walk to be sure. You'll be on the road several days at least, more depending on the weather. We're due for some good rain," Broc answered, with Eoforde nodding sagely across from him.

My eyebrows shot up. *Surely I misheard him.* "Did you say walk?"

"Yes, lad," Eoforde replied, brows furrowed. "We don't have enough horses to be justifying gallivanting off home. They're needed up at the border. Besides, they don't do well on the terrain you'll be traveling. Most of us walk. Don't be slowing down our Captain now. She has enough on her shoulders without a bit of baggage like you." The twins shared a stifled laugh at this speech, while Broc rolled his eyes.

Hreremus spoke in my hearing for the first time, causing a hush to fall over our little section of the table as everyone strained to hear his soft words.

"Mind Eoforde's words, Captain Marchand. If you try attempt to betray our Red Rider on your journey, you'll learn the true origin of her name."

I leaned forward, curiosity ignited. "And what is that?"

Hreremus swallowed nervously, eyes darting between me and his food. "On the night of a full moon, as we're having in two days time, her wolf appears to destroy anyone marked as her enemy, leaving a river of red behind it."

My eyes widened in horror at the picture he painted, before narrowing in suspicion. "A river of blood, huh?"

The others burst out laughing, and Eoforde almost choked on his food in mirth, washing it down with a quick swallow of beer.

"Hreremus, you've been saving that one up, haven't you!?" Edda accused between chuckles. Hreremus nodded, sending me an apologetic shrug as he dug back into his own food. I couldn't help chuckling a bit myself.

"One of these days you'll tell me the real story, but I won't believe it because of all these tall tales!" I protested, making them laugh all the harder.

Later, as we were leaving the dining hall, Broc pulled me aside while the others went their separate ways.

"Mind you don't try anything with our Captain though, Eddie. If you even think it, we'll destroy you slowly and carve up everything you've ever held dear, understand?" He stared hard at me, every trace of good humored friendliness wiped from his face as if it had never been there.

I nodded and he broke out into a warm smile again.

"Well that's settled. Pleasant journey, and farewell, in case we never see you again."

He strode off as well, whistling a merry tune slightly off key. I stared for a moment before forcing my feet toward the stairs. *Can I wait for the government to bring me home again? These bloodthirsty Sherwoodians just might kill me for fun in the meantime.*

CHAPTER FIVE

Red

My knees ground against the stone floor of the transept, barely feeling the chill as it seeped through my trousers. I rested my head against the side of my grandmother's tomb and drew in a deep breath filled with dust and incense. The monks had just finished their morning prayers, filing out as I entered the cathedral, so I knew I had only a few minutes before the nuns would be entering to complete their prayers as well. The high church diocese controlled the Nottingham Cathedral, which meant they followed strict rules around serving the faith, unlike the low church diocese more common in rural areas. The church was one area even Marian had found resistant to change from John's reign.

I sighed. I didn't really want to think about him. My uncle was long dead. "It seems he's still hunting me, Grandma," I whispered. Taking one more deep breath, I opened my eyes and leaned against the tomb as I stood, brushing off my hands and knees before folding my arms and making a face at the effigy of my grandmother on the top of her tomb. She was depicted in long robes and a crown on her head, the expression on her face solemn and wise. A far cry from the laughing, kindly woman I had known.

"You told me to trust the wolf inside all those years ago. That together she and I would conquer the evil we faced." Elne felt smug and I shrugged. "You were right of course. We did defeat John in the end, at least physically. But Grandma, I hear his whispers in my mind even now. Poisoning my thoughts. And Elne… sometimes I think we aren't good for each other. We urge each other into danger. It's addicting." Elne's smugness vanished at my words and feelings and she drifted away with a huff.

I scuffed my boot along the church floor, wishing my real grandmother was hear to talk to. *She would know just how to help me. How to banish John from my mind. How to feel comfortable with my role in life. How to let myself live at all…*

"They put me on leave!" I told her indignantly, leaning my hip against the tomb. "Well, worse than that, it's a working leave! I have to guard this Pelerine prisoner who is simply infuriating!" Eddie's face flashed into my head and I pushed it away quickly. I didn't really want to spend the few moments I had alone at my grandmother's tomb complaining about him. "That doesn't really matter. It's more going to Barnsdale and dealing with Mother. I can't stand being there for very long. And Elne's even worse. We've grown as strong together as you always thought we'd be, but she disappears from my head for days, weeks even, when I go home." I hesitated, lowering my voice even more. "And to be honest, the whole reason I'm on leave to begin with is because our decision making has become clouded lately. I find myself fixated on going back into battle as soon as I can, and Elne feels the same. We're never so alive as when we're fighting for our lives. I know that's the Sherwoodian way, but it's become something more." I sighed. "Robin and Marian think I need a break. Eileen reported on my too. I guess they can't all be wrong, but I don't see how sitting around Barnsdale is going to change Elne and me." *I guess Eddie might make my head explode before we get too far into our stay at Barnsdale and then I won't have to worry about anything anymore.*

I traced the fingers on the effigy's hands, cold and smooth and folded as if in prayer. Although Grandmother had prayed often, I never remembered her folding her hands in such a high church pose. She usually muttered her prayers as if she was having a conversation with the Creator, who seemed mostly to listen instead of answer back. A shiver crept up my arm, just as I heard the main doors creak open in the nave, no doubt letting the nuns in for their prayers. I turned back to Grandmother.

"You told me to trust the wolf inside. I've always done that. But now I'm worried that me and Elne aren't trustworthy anymore. We lost a team in the Wasteland a few months ago. We can't focus on our mission half the time. And we don't fit in anywhere…" A flash of white caught my eye as the nuns filed passed the transept I was in, their heavy gowns flowing behind them as they walked. None of them spared a glance my way, although that was probably because of the elaborate coif and veils they wore as part of their religious habits. I watched as they prepared for their prayer service, then turned back to Grandmother with a half smile.

"I have to be off to collect Eddie and start for Barnesdale. He's the Pelerine I told you about, the one I'm stuck with for months. I just need to hold on long enough to defeat that Beast Captain I told you about last time. It's a wolf Beastie, coincidentally. So maybe me and my big bad wolf companion are exactly the ones fated to defeat it." I couldn't help laughing under my breath at my silliness. "If you can put in a good word with the big man upstairs, I would appreciate it. I can't defeat that it if Robin won't let me back in the field. Surely the all powerful Creator could do something about that."

One of the initiates at the back of the group of nuns turned my way, identifiable because of the simple, heavy veil she wore instead of the ornate headdress and wimple. Whether she could see me under that veil I had no idea, but I was obviously being too loud. With one last glance at my grandmother's cold effigy, I paced out of the nave and toward the main door, passing through the church as silently as possible.

When I got outside, I headed straight toward the castle door where I was due to meet Eddie. Although it wasn't nearly as dark as it had been when I entered the cathedral the sun wasn't fully up yet. The only evidence of it's presence was a glowing ember in the east. Thin clouds stretched out across the sky in long, lazy tendrils, but there was no threat of rain. Elne drifted around the edges of our connection, unsettled as she usually felt when we visited Barnsdale Lodge. I folded my arms as Eddie came into view. He looked tired but made no protest when I informed him that we would be walking to our destination.

"A carriage would mean following the roads the entire way, which would end up taking even longer. Besides the horses are needed elsewhere," I explained, half expecting remarks upon the discourtesy of the Sherwoodian people from Eddie.

He shrugged. "Eoforde told me last night. He said the terrain wasn't good for them anyway."

"That's true," I replied, surprised at his quick acceptance. *Maybe he's not as soft as the other Pelerines I've met.* "It's a little hilly, but the bigger problem is that there aren't many good paths to follow. The forest can be quite dense."

He shrugged his pack a little higher on his shoulders, glancing up at the sky.

"It should take a week at most, unless the clouds open up," I reassured him, not completely sure why I felt the need to defend my choices to my 'guest'. Irritation flared and I turned without another word, leading the way toward the gates.

The first day was easy going. We followed the main road southwest, eventually branching off on a smaller road, and stopping at The Creaking Bough for the night, the famous Inn from the revolution. The barman was full of outrageous stories as usual, supplemented by even more unbelievable ones told by his wizened mother from her perch in the corner by the fire. She had even prim and proper Captain Marchand in deep belly laughs by the time we went to our beds.

The next day was gray. An hour after we started, we split off the country road onto a hunting track, which forced us to go single file. By noon, we had turned into deeper woodland, the light that filtered through the trees casting a gloom over everything.

"How can you be sure we're going the right way?" Eddie finally asked as we stopped for a break.

"Compass spell," I replied tersely, taking a swig from my water pouch. He looked at me strangely but I didn't care. I was tired already. Elne's constant stream of low level agitation was draining, not to mention my own anxiety. The discomfort of traveling would be nothing compared to spending the months ahead at our destination. *I could tear Robin to pieces.* Elne echoed her agreement.

"I should have guessed," Eddie said, looking at me with a furrowed brow. "And I suppose you're used to this trip by now, since it's your home."

"It's not my home," I spat, swinging my pack back on my shoulders and starting forward again. Elne snuffled at my smug triumph as Eddie scrambled to keep up. My smoldering irritation kept additional conversation at bay for the next few hours.

We camped outdoors that night, far from any civilization. Eddie broke his silence as we finished our meal, watching as I bent to scoop ash from the fire into my bowl to clean it.

"Lord Robin made it sound like Barnsdale was your home, but you say it's not." My hands continued to move in lazy circles, rubbing the ash around to clean out my bowl but not really concentrating on my task. His eyes were glued to me, taking in every detail while I fought sudden flashes of memories his question provoked.

Warm summer breezes moving through the wheat field, my father's laughter mingling with my mother's. The sting of the acorns Robin tossed at me for interrupting his game with Marian. Sitting in Mama's lap while she hummed a tune and rubbed slow circles on my back. Watching my father and brother leave the farm for Robin's apprenticeship. Father's body coming back after the rebellion. Mama broken. Robin gone. Marian caught. And John... I shivered violently, Elne whining in my head and snuffling.

I sensed Eddie's eyes still on me, missing nothing, and let Elne's defensiveness over my still vulnerable memories overtake me. My canines grew sharper and longer, and I felt my nose wrinkle and eyes burn as they tinged with red.

"Because it brings out the wolf in me," I snarled, turning to face him fully.

It was his turn to shudder, and he pulled away from across the fire, a stricken look on his face. Elne crowed at his disgust. Although I was happy he had stopped pushing, I couldn't help feeling flat. *He's right to be repulsed. The only thing that's left of me is ugly and brutal.*

He retreated under his tarp while I put out the fire, collapsing under my own shelter not long after.

Heavy rain streaked down my face and permeated my cloak, creating a chilled armor between me and the warm, humid air. Eddie had been trudging behind me most of the day, accepting a heat charm without comment after the morning passed and the storm only got worse.

I looked down to check my compass spell. We were still on course, so we should be coming across the River Tricher very soon. If I had managed things properly, we would be near the old bridge. Whether it was safe to cross right now would remain to be seen. Reaching the bottom of a rocky slope, I stilled, straining to hear. Eddie pulled up short just behind me.

"Is that the river?" He asked, ears picking up the rushing sound I had heard a moment before.

"Got to be. Sounds like it will be too full to cross though."

I felt, rather than heard him sigh behind me, his steamy warmth breaking through the chill on my back. Instinctively, I rocked back toward it, but quickly corrected into a rolling step forward. Whatever twisted attraction I felt for him needed to be buried.

He should be gone by now, I complained inwardly. Elne ignored it. She had been quiet the whole day, retreating into wherever she went when our minds weren't touching. A cold, wet slog through the woods wasn't her cup of tea. *If I could retreat somewhere I would too.* Instead I was pushing back wet branches and trying not to let my irritation with the world come out by letting them spring back and smack Eddie in the face.

"Don't tell me this is the crossing you mentioned," Eddie moaned as the small river came into view.

Putting my hands on my hips, I scanned the swollen riverbank, pointing to a spot a few yards down stream. "Right there. Let's go look."

Our approach did little to assuage our fears. Dirty brown water heaved in the deep river channel, having already begun to spill over the sides, testing the ground around it with watery tentacles.

Friar Tuck had showed me this broken down bridge soon after the Interregnum and I had used it ever since. My visits to Barnsdale Lodge had been few over the years, so I had never needed to cross during such bad weather.

"I can see why you called it a 'crossing' instead of a bridge. It barely warrants the word." Eddie didn't even attempt to hide his dissatisfaction, grabbing a tree branch and poking the one remaining log that spanned the river. Half rotted, with broken boards hanging like crooked teeth toward where the other support beam must have once lain, half of the remaining piles had been swept aways since my last trip.

I grabbed the tree branch from his hand with an angry swipe and dashed it into the river. The water tossed it about violently before sucking it downstream and out of sight.

"Very mature," Eddie commented tersely, brushing his hands together to wipe off the dirt from the branch.

"There's no sense poking it with a stick, it's rotten enough that you might send the whole bridge crashing down," I shot back acidly.

"I thought we agreed that it's not a bridge."

"It spans the river, and is big enough to walk across if you're careful, so technically it's a bridge."

"Well, color me impressed with the marvels of Sherwoodian engineering then. Shall I lead?"

I stared at him incredulously, "Across the bridge? I don't think so. We'll have to camp here tonight and try it tomorrow once the rain has subsided."

"It doesn't look like it's going to let up anytime soon. By tomorrow morning the water might be up to the bridge and then we won't be able to cross at all. You said there's an inn not far away on the other side. I'm sleeping there tonight."

My eyes shot heavenward as I clamped my hands on my head in frustration, quickly dropping them when it only served to squeeze water out of my damp hood in rivulets down the side of my face.

"I know it will be uncomfortable, but we aren't exactly under a deadline. Let's camp here tonight and figure out what to do in the morning. I'm sure you're missing your precious little Pelerine manor house, but you can stand a little discomfort, can't you?"

He pressed his lips together in response to my mocking tone. "You know what, fine. You want to believe that about me, that's great. But I'm crossing. You said the inn was less than half a mile away from the bridge earlier. You can camp out here, while I sleep in a warm bed tonight, resting my dainty Pelerine bones in something approaching comfort instead of this nightmare."

He whirled around, stepping onto the log with a few strides. The beam sunk into the muddy earth a little with his weight but held steady. I rushed over, shouldering my pack a little higher as I bent to hold the end of the log steady.

"You're out of your mind! And you called *me* reckless when we met! At least I was fighting an enemy!"

"Hey, if you want to die of hypothermia tonight, that's your choice. Then I can scamper off home with nothing in my way," he retorted, keeping most of his concentration on his next few steps.

My concern increased as he moved away, watching as his heel depressed the rotten wood a little more with each step toward the middle of the beam. "At least let me reinforce it with a little magic. I'm not a fairy engineer, but I'm sure I could do *something* - " I sucked in a breath as he reached the middle, stopping over the central pile, one of the few that remained.

He inhaled an answering breath, craning his neck back to me with a challenging smirk on his face. "No! No magic. I'm already halfway to a hot dinner and a warm bed. Want to put money on whether I make it the rest of the way?"

I glared at him reprovingly, a clump of hair slipping out of my braid and partially obscuring my view of him. "You're halfway to releasing me from guard duty by your untimely death. I don't exactly care except I'll have to explain all this to Robin and Marian, and they'll think I made you do it."

Eddie laughed, throwing his hands out to keep his balance as he wobbled slightly. He turned forward again as he regained his equilibrium, casting a measuring look toward the opposite bank.

"I think if I just take a few more steps, I could jump the rest of the way."

A ripple of tension passed through my muscles at his words. "That wood is so rotten you'll just send your foot through it and tumble into the river. And I won't be fishing you out, I can promise you."

His deep chuckle reached my ears, just audible over the rushing torrent. "No, I don't expect you would. I can't picture you fishing at all, actually. Not enough patience." He took a cautious step forward, rocking the log slightly as I strained to keep it steady from where I crouched.

"I'll have you know that I'm quite - " my words cut off as he plunged through the rotten wood and into the angry flood below.

My body sprang into motion even as my mind stayed blank. Unbuttoning my cloak, I pulled off my brooch and clipped it onto my leather jerkin before tossing the rest of the fabric away. I shrugged off my pack, and starting sprinting downstream, eyes scanning the water for Eddie.

There! His pack surfaced, bobbing against the rock. No sign of the man himself. Elne's consciousness bumped into mine as she sense my hunt. Her interest dimmed a little as she realized there was no imminent battle, but she lent me her heightened senses all the same.

Scents rushed at me, cold water, woodrot, damp leaves, broken rocks; no human smell detectable with all this rain confusing things.

A flash of white caught my eye as it thrashed out of the water; Eddie's arm, scrabbling at a rock on the other side of the swollen stream. His cloak had caught on a branch and was pulling at his throat, choking him. He pushed off of the boulder as best he could with one hand, scrabbling at the clasp as I moved down the riverbank toward him.

"Eddie!" I called, shouting to be heard above the roaring water. His eyes caught mine as he finally released the clasp, but his hold on the rock slipped and he was torn from the rock by the angry current.

"No!" I screamed, part desperation and part anger that he had let go of his anchor. *Where is he now?* I needed to get him out quickly, before he was smashed to pieces on a rock, or chilled to the point of hypothermia. I had a fair amount of magecraft but my healing skills were minimal, focused on battle wounds. I wouldn't be able to work a miracle.

His form surfaced from the frothing water again, heading toward a curve in the river. Sprinting to get ahead of him, my eyes caught a place in the water that looked deep and clear of rocks. Pulling in as deep a breath as I could manage, I dove in, just before I calculated Eddie would reach it.

A long minute of muffled panic passed before I muscled my way back to the surface, eyes straining for Eddie's shape as I fought to keep my head up. Something bumped into my back and a choking noise reached my ears over the rushing water. I kicked into a turn, spinning far enough to catch a glimpse of Eddie, just as his head slipped under the water again. I thrashed wildly until my hand made contact. Gripping his arm, I pulled him to the surface with a mighty heave, sending my own head under as I did so.

My lungs burned, then screamed, as I focused on pouring magic into my leather jerkin, reinforcing it against the blow

I knew would be coming when we crashed onto the rocky riverbank at the bend up ahead. I kicked hard, managing to steal a breath and a quick look around before the churning current and Eddie's massive weight pushed me under again. Gripping him tight, I threw up a last minute shield of pure magic around our heads, draining my energy recklessly.

A jarring smack reverberated through my bones as we hit the rocks. I sent a pulse of magic through my body, checking for injuries. My magic infused shield had worked, preventing major damage. I felt Eddie's legs slip around the side of me as the water spun us, followed by an audible crunch. His agonized scream a moment later confirmed the limits of my shield spell.

Scrabbling against the rocks with one hand, I kept Eddie anchored to me with the other. He began pulling himself up the bank as well, gasping moans escaping with each breath as the water battered this way and that, threatening to pull us around the river bend back into it's violent current.

"On three," I told Eddie, as I felt him gain a good hold. He gave a terse nod of agreement so I braced against the rocks and tightened the hold I had around his waist with my left hand. "One, two, three -," I strained upward, levering him up with a might heave until I felt his upper body go over the top of the river bank. His scream barely registered in my ears as I clawed at the rocky riverbank, ripping the skin on my fingers and knuckles and tearing several fingernails as I prevented myself from being swept under again.

I waited for a heartbeat, watching the rain flush rivulets of blood down my hands to join the muddy water as I caught my breath and steeled my muscles. Eddie's legs hung limply to my right, and I wondered if I should help push him the rest of the way up before I climbed to the top. My thoughts were becoming foggy with cold. *Get out of the water, then pull him up.*

Taking a huge gulp of air, I bunched my muscles, roaring pain stabbing through the shredded skin of my hands. A final burst of adrenaline took the edge off as I hauled myself over the riverbank. My eyes squeezed shut against a splatter of mud from my landing, their cold, viscous weight sliding down my skin as I lay for another moment drawing in ragged gasps of air.

Alive. Still alive, I commented to Elne, as she growled in approval. I was triumphant too; not at securing more time for my pitiful existence, but in winning against death's latest attempt to conquer me. Death will win eventually, of course. It's inevitable mastery was a soothing thought rather than something to rail against. But death only needed one victory, and was as liable to come quietly in someone's sleep just as much as in a glorious sacrifice. Before I let that happen, I wanted as many contests as I could manage, leaving a string of outrageous victories for the people to sing about whenever they thought of their Red Rider. Every win made me feel more alive, even as it decreased the odds in my favor.

A frenzied laugh bubbled out of my chest as I crowed in triumph, wiping the mud off my face and propping myself up on my elbows. I looked over at Eddie to share my elation and cut my laugh short. He was utterly still, his body collapsed along the ground, his face turned away from mine. I pulled my legs up from the bank and scrambled around to crouch at his side and peer into his face.

His eyes were closed. My fingers flew to his neck - no sign of a pulse. I reached out tentatively with my magic, scrabbling to get a read on his vitals just as my eyes caught the slight rise of his shoulders as he inhaled. Relief swept through me and I closed my eyes, concentrating on my limited healing knowledge.

My magic brushed his being and I could sense his erratic heartbeat. Spiky heat pulled at my senses from several directions. I followed the sharpest stabbing down to his left leg and hissed a breath through my teeth.

It was broken. Badly. My eyes flew open and I glanced down, noting the sickening angle at which it still hung off the riverbank. My magic continued to explore and I closed my eyes to concentrate.

The bones in his lower leg were mangled. *I don't even know if I should attempt a healing there.* The left femur had a tiny crack in it, which I might be able to manage if I rested for awhile. I traveled along the remaining heat spikes in his energy, finding numerous bruises and cuts. His left wrist had something wrong with it, probably a sprain, and I could sense deep bruising on his ribs, potentially a few cracks along the left side. His neck seemed fine enough, and his head was perfect.

My eyes flew open as I completed my rough exam. "Well, you may not walk again properly if I can't get help soon, but at least you'll keep you looks," I told his unconscious form. Rain slid down his forehead and over closed eyes, tracing a path until it dripped off the end of his nose. His unresponsiveness, combined with the chill and my decreasing adrenaline pushed my foggy brain forward.

"Lady's breath and Beastie's death," I cursed, as I looked him over, wondering what I should do first. "Let's get him fully out of this treacherous river, before it decides it wants us back," I told Elne, looking around for something I could use as a splint. She didn't bother replying in any meaningful way, just continued feeding me her more powerful senses and shoring up my energy supplies. My eyes caught upon a sturdy branch nearby. I pulled it over, using it to lever myself up. As I put my full weight on my right leg, a stabbing pain shot up from my ankle.

"Don't tell me. Don't bleedin' tell me," I threatened my magic, sending an exploratory tendril down to confirm. "A sprained ankle. Just great." I must have twisted it when I heaved myself out of the water. Now that that my adrenaline had all but left me, the aches and pains of our adventure in the river were pulling at my endurance, and sleep beckoned to my tired limbs.

Elne nudged my thoughts. I could feel her intention, urging me to heal my ankle and take a rest. I huffed in exasperation, testing my weight again. Pain flared. It wasn't good, but I could put some weight on it.

"It'll have to do for now. My energy is low. I'll need all my magic to get this Pelerine lump under shelter somewhere." Elne whined in my head but subsided.

Using just a touch of magical force, I broke the stick in my hands, looking around for some fabric or something to help make a splint. Neither one of us had our packs or cloaks on anymore.

Maybe I can summon them? I thought, without much hope. Summoning took an inordinate amount of power and skill, and right now I had neither. Tracing the path of the river, I squinted in the distance but saw nothing I recognized. We had come further than I thought and were on the opposite bank from where we started. I knew that this side of the river was strewn with rocky outcrops that would make walking back upstream toward the inn difficult. In any case, our gear was too far away to summon, even if I exhausted myself trying.

Looking back at the two halves of the branch in my hand, I sighed. *Nothing else for it then.* Placing one branch on either side of Eddie, I untucked my tunic and tore a wide strip off the bottom before sitting at the edge of the riverbank next to where his broken leg dangled over the side. Pulling out a small knife I kept strapped to my boot at all times, I cut off the bottom portion of his trousers, exposing his leg to the knee. *Thank the Lady.* No bones were poking through his skin, but his leg was canted at an odd angle. My eyes kept sliding away from the wrongess of it. I forced myself to ignore that and perform a quick examination. He had enough cuts from his bumpy ride down the river that infection would be a problem. Focusing back on the material I still held from his pant leg, as well as my own tunic, I held it alongside the sticks toward his leg. Summoning my magic, I sent it out in a rush, pushing the pieces of my makeshift splint into place along his lower leg, wrapping and tying the branches off securely with the pieces of shirt fabric.

"Terribly crude, but it will have to do," I told the still unconscious Eddie. Grabbing his hands, I took a deep breath to steady myself, and sent another wave of magic along his body, using every scrap of remembered magical engineering and medical training I had ever received to support his broken form while pulling it the rest of the way onto the bank.

After setting him down gently, I flopped down, propping

myself against a nearby tree trunk. My well of magic was quickly running dry. Like most Sherwoodians, I had a certain amount of innate magic, which not only allowed me to connect with Elne as a companion, but also expressed itself in a personal affinity. Mine happened to be hand fighting, which is why I preferred using my fists or knives in a fight. The priests claimed innate magic was a sign of our that our people were descended from the Shepherds, or from some of the other ancient magical beings that once walked this land unhindered. *Right now I wish I had a hundred Fae ancestors. I could use a bigger well of magic.* Unfortunately, I only had what I had, and hand fighting wasn't going to be useful right now anyway. Like any magician, I could pull magic from the environment, from the very essence of the woodland and earth itself at times, but it worked like any muscle - too much strain in too little time and you could injure yourself badly, or even die. "You'd like that wouldn't you," I muttered to my old nemesis, Death. "I'm not there yet, so don't get your hopes up." I glanced over at Eddie. "And stop sniffing around him too. It's not our day." *At least I hope it's not our day.* If I wanted to save us I would need to eat and sleep soon and replenish my energy. Before that, we needed to find shelter. Weariness ate at my bones.

If I had made a stretcher first, I could have lifted him onto it at the same time I pulled him up from the riverbank, I realized, a wave of frustration washing over me as I realized my inefficiency was costing me energy, and potentially our lives. Elne sent a disgruntled wave of emotion my way, layered with a suggestion to leave the wounded enemy where he lay and take care of my own needs. I pushed back, saying out loud, "Go away if you aren't going to help." She growled irritably and retreated from my mind again. If she had a corporal form she would have tossed her head as she left.

My hands went to where I had hastily pinned my moonstone brooch to my leather jerkin. It felt cool beneath my touch and I looked down, rolling my eyes to see that it had been broken. *Of course it has. Why not?* Summoning help wouldn't be an option, even if anyone with a linked brooch was in range. Since we were in the middle of a forest that hadn't required a Forestry patrol group since the end of the Interregnum, it was doubtful anyone would have received a signal anyway.

My hand dipped into a pocket in my jerkin, pulling out my heat charm and wrapping my fingers around it while my increasingly fuzzy thoughts drifted along the list of things I needed to do.

Find shelter. Find food. Eat, sleep. Heal myself. Heal Eddie. Find help.

Eddie would need help before his lower leg began to set on it's own. Maybe even sooner if I had missed some internal bleeding, or if there was any infection. But first of all we needed shelter. The rain was getting worse and night was beginning to descend judging by the deepening gray filling the gaps between rain drops.

My compass charm, worked into the same banded jasper stone that housed my heat charm, pulsed beneath my fingers, sending me a rough image of the way I needed to go to get to the broken bridge that had gotten us into this mess. It was several miles away, meaning the inn was even further. No way I could make it there on foot, and I had nothing to write with to send a message, if I even had enough magic left to transport it.

Eying the bands of reddish brown on my spelled stone, I thought back through all the magic I knew, and a moment later, made a clumsy adjustment to the compass charm's target. Casting it outward in a wide direction, it gave me a feeble impression of the nearest building. My eyes flicked in the direction it indicated - just beyond a thick stand of trees, maybe fifty yards away. Relief swept through me.

"You can do this," I told myself sternly, pushing to my feet and ignoring the pain in my ankle as well as the instinct to dull it with magic. I would need every scrap of power I had left to get us to this shelter and dried off. *I have no idea what we'll do for food - don't think that far ahead.*

"At least you've given me plenty of water!" I shook my fist at the sky, taunting Death, who apparently hadn't give this round up yet. Working quickly now that I had a purpose, I created a crude stretcher, using the rest of my tunic as well as Eddie's shirt. I shivered uncomfortably under my soaking leather jerkin, knowing that a descent into hypothermia was quickly becoming the biggest threat for both of us. With a combination of brute force and magic, I pushed Eddie onto the stretcher, picked up the side near his feet with my hands, and used the last of my magic to pull up the other side of the stretcher, managing to lift it several inches off the ground. Limping, I followed my compass charm until a small cabin came into view, gingerly pushing Eddie before me.

The door was latched, but not locked, and the inside proved to be cold and dusty. It looked disused, but was stocked as if the owner expected to come back someday. A pallet lay in the corner, a thick blanket rolled up and waiting at the foot of it. I lugged Eddie toward it, kicking the blanket out to cover the hard pallet, and shifting him as gently as possible off the the stretcher and onto the bed. Tossing the stretcher away, I pulled off Eddie's soaking pants, then threw another blanket from a nearby pile over him. Dust wafted through the air as I stumbled around, sending me into a coughing fit, tears streaming down my face as I tried o take stock of our surroundings.

A neat stack of firewood and kindling near the fireplace caught my eye. *Bless you, whoever owns this cabin.* Opening the flue, I sent a quick prayer up that there wasn't anything caught in the chimney and set about starting a fire. That done, my strength left me. I stripped down to my soaked undergarments, sent a quick request to the Creator that Eddie wouldn't wake up before I could get us both dressed again in the morning, and climbed under the cover next to him, our chilled flesh greeting each other with grudging shivers as I waited for heat to build between us.

CHAPTER SIX

Eddie

My entire body ached. *What is it about Sherwood that leaves me waking up like this more often than not? Another reason to find a way home soon.* My hazy mind hovered just beyond consciousness, instinctively knowing that as soon as I woke up I would have to deal with whatever was causing that fuzzy ache all over.

Something whispered across the bare skin of my right shoulder, a tiny warm breeze. *I wish that would stop.* I shrugged my shoulder slightly, rubbing against a silky mass. I froze, my eyes snapping open to the sight of Red's black hair spilling across my shoulder and chest. She was nuzzled up against my shoulder, her breath skittering across it and tickling my skin, one hand curled up around my bicep.

What is she doing?

With sudden clarity, I realized I was practically naked, and since she was pressed against my side, I could feel that she was too. Awareness swept across my entire body, and with it, the full depths of pain I had been avoiding. My left leg throbbed angrily, and I groaned through gritted teeth.

Either I was louder than I thought or Red hadn't been sleeping very soundly, because she jerked awake, half sitting up and pulling a knife out from under the pillow. She looked steadily outward for a minute, tensed to defend against an attack, but when no threat materialized, I watched her back stiffen, the muscles relaxing slowly even as her shoulders tensed higher. I flushed again, realizing that the reason I could see her muscles relaxing was because I was staring at her almost completely bare back. Slowly, she turned her head to the side, flicking a glance at me between tendrils of hair. The moment of quietness while we eyed each other was full, with what I couldn't say. Tension? Embarrassment? Curiosity?

Red opened her mouth but before she could say anything, an agonizing stab of pain from my leg ripped another groan from my mouth, and I felt her push off the bed. I lay my head back on the pillow, eyes closed and teeth gritted, until the feeling subsided again. My eyes opened to reveal Red standing next to the bed again, fully clothed in an ill fitting pair of breeches and a worn tunic.

She saw my gaze and shrugged, hands on her hips. "My clothes are still drying. I found these in a cupboard over there."

My eyes traced in the direction she pointed and I could see a few cupboards near a large fireplace. What was left of my own tattered clothing was laid out, drying by the fire. A flash of blue caught my eye. *My good luck charm. How on earth did it survive our swim?*

"I've been thinking I need to get a new good luck charm, and now I *know* I do," I said, jutting my chin toward where it sat. Red raised her eyebrows, then shrugged her shoulder. "I don't waste my time with luck. It certainly didn't save you from the river. Hard work and magic did that."

"Point taken," I replied, not having the strength to argue.

"How are you feeling?"

I drew in a shaky breath. "If I had to put it into words, like I've been swept into a raging river and battered against rocks and who knows what else until I was half drowned," I said, attempting a smile.

She raised an eyebrow. "What a vivid imagination you have," she quipped before turning serious again. "I've done an examination, and your left leg is broken in two places, one of them quite badly. You have other injuries that I can probably take care of, but you'll need a real healer to deal with your leg. I've only been trained to patch up wounds during battle enough to get someone back to a real doctor."

I nodded, sucking in a breath and wincing as one of my ribs twinged. Red's face softened and she sat gingerly on the side of the bed.

"I have a little more energy now. I can ease your pain if you'll let me."

I nodded, watching in confusion as she placed a hand over my heart. She closed her eyes and started murmuring softly before I realized her intent. A wave of relaxation swept over me, dulling the pain to a more acceptable level.

"I didn't realize you meant magic," I said, not able to keep the accusation from my voice as she opened her eyes again. She snatched her hand away from my chest, leaving behind a circle of warmth where our skin had met.

"I thought it was obvious." She stood abruptly, pacing over to the fireplace and kneeling to build up the embers.

"What sort of tattoo will I have because of that healing?" I asked, my mind flying back to the tattoos I had gained only a week before at the hands of a Gypsy Prince. I grimaced. Now I would have more for my collection, yet another mark to set me apart when I made it to Pelerin.

"If that's your concern, don't worry," she scoffed, adding logs over the embers methodically. "Only Gypsy magic will give you tattoos. It's an honor to bear them if you're lucky enough to be healed by one with the gift. I'm just a normal magician. I pull magic from the world around us, not from your fate or life force like the gypsies can do. My magic will wear off eventually, so you may be wishing you had a tattoo by the day is out." She twisted the hair hanging just past her shoulders into a quick braid and then crouched forward, blowing deep breaths under the stacked logs until the embers flared high enough to catch. Soon yellow flames danced along the wood, sending a wave of heat through the cabin.

I glanced around curiously, able to take interest in our surroundings a bit more now that pain wasn't gnawing at my thoughts. We were in a rustic, one room cabin. If I had to guess, it was used for hunting, based off of the equipment hanging on the walls, interspersed with mounted horns. The fireplace held rudimentary cooking implements. There was a sink and table with chairs in the opposite corner, a set of shelves holding household items, and a locker, probably for more weapons. I was laying on the only bed in the room, taking up most of the wall at this end of the cabin.

I looked back at Red, who was rummaging in a chest of drawers. She muttered under her breath, pressing her lips flat as she sorted through the contents. Finally, she pulled out a heavily patched hooded cape, shaking a layer dust off before putting it on.

"I need to forage for food. I'll try to set a few traps while I'm out. It's still raining, so I doubt I'll have any luck with game, but I'm sure I can find something for the pot. Just rest while I'm gone. We'll figure out what to do next once we have food in our bellies.

Once she was gone, I inched my way over to the chamber pot, grudgingly thankful that whatever spell she had put on me meant I could do so on my own. After a brief rest, I hobbled toward the same chest of drawers she ahd found the cape in and pulled out a faded tunic. It fit, and although I could see another pair of trousers, I left them alone, knowing I wouldn't be able to pull them over the splint on my leg. I lay back down in bed, completely exhausted from my exertions.

My stomach was rumbling audibly by the time she returned, arms full of greens and limping.

"What happened?" I asked, nodding at her leg as she limped over to the sink.

"Souvenir from our trip down the river," she said with a tired grimace, dumping the vegetables into the sink and stomping back outside. She came in a minute later with a pitcher full of rainwater, pouring some in a glass and downing it in one go before refilling and offering it to me. I drank greedily, the cold water sitting heavily in my empty stomach. I wachted with hungry impatience as she set about preparing the food and dumping it into a pot over the fire. She murmured a few words as she stirred it, then laid her cape out to dry before settling into a chair.

"I've spelled it to cook faster without spoiling the food. Reynold taught me the trick years ago. It won't taste great but I'm too hungry to care right now."

"Thank you," I said, propping myself up on my elbows. "For the food and for, you know, saving my life."

Our eyes met across the room and I was struck by how stark the shadows under her eyes were. They clashed with her pale skin. Something inside me rose up at that look and I wished I was uninjured, that I could take some of the burden of our situation off of her shoulders. That *I* could look after *her*. Her teeth flashed, and a look of hearty good humor settling over her face that didn't quite reach her shadowed eyes. A wall between her true feelings and me - an outsider. Her instinct to hide herself only made me want to break any barriers down more. *But you are an outsider,* I reminded myself. *You have nothing in common with her, or this place.*

Turning back toward the fire, she stretched her feet toward the flames. "Well, I haven't saved us yet, but thanks all the same."

I frowned, settling back onto the bed. There had been a moment of vulnerability between our unfiltered, exhausted selves. That smile was a mask. She was putting a wall between us again. *I suppose that's her prerogative.* After all, I was an outsider. *And a prisoner,* I reminded myself wryly. But I couldn't deny that the facade she was putting on only made me want to know the true Red even more. *How many masks does she wear? And what happened to the irritating Red from our rides?* She had spent the last week needling me almost every chance she got. Flirting outrageously when we were out of earshot of the others, seeming almost to enjoy the looks of disapproval I sent her way. She had obviously been trying to make me uncomfortable, maybe in retaliation for that moment of sparks between us when we first met. I pushed my thoughts away, stuffing my rebellious heart aside. I didn't want to examine whatever it thought it had felt for this woman. *It's probably a side effect of the binding spell.*

Her voice broke into my thoughts and I jumped, heat flooding my face as I realized I had been frowning at her for the last few minutes. Thankfully she still wasn't looking my way.

"My moonstone brooch was damaged, so I can't send a message," she said matter-of-factly. "There's no paper here to write on, to fly one the old fashioned way, and even so, that takes a lot of effort and I'm exhausted." Red looked back over at me. "I modified my compass spell while I was foraging so I was able to figure out where we are. There's a Friary that would be in range of my moonstones if I can fix them. I know the Friar that runs it. He's a skilled healer. He would answer my summons and care for us without hesitation."

"Sounds perfect. Can you fix your... brooch?" I glanced at the jeweled pin she fiddled with in her hand.

"I believe so. Luckily the spellwork wasn't damaged, I just need to repair the stone so it's usable again."

"Excellent. When can we expect help?" I asked, slightly cheered by the idea that my body might be fixed soon, even if by magic.

Red's fingers stilled as they traced the crack which marred the surface of the smooth gray stone. "That's the thing. I can fix the stone, but it will take a lot of effort. I'll need to rest overnight in order to pull enough magic to make it work. And..." she hesitated, looking back at me with that tired look again. "I won't have enough energy for anything else. No healing, no speeding up dinner, and especially no relieving your pain. Probably for most of the day."

I swallowed hard. Although I had only been conscious for a few minutes before her pain spell, it had been agonizing. *A whole day?* I grit my teeth. *Just do what's in front of you, until you can move forward,* I instructed myself sternly.

"Okay," I finally responded. "Then that's what we'll do." She nodded, then turned to check on our food. Apparently determining it was done, she poured two bowls out and brought one to me. We both shoveled down the simple meal, which tasted better to my starving stomach than any other food in recent memory. My belly full, lethargy spread across my body and I dozed while Red cleaned up, memories of campaigns meals with my friend LeFeu dancing across my mind.

Red's brisk footsteps broke into my daydreaming as she approached the bed. I opened my eyes to find her standing with her hands on her hips and her mouth pressed into a thin line. Shadows had fallen across the cabin since we had eaten and night had settled outside the dirty windows.

"This is the only place to sleep, so I'm afraid we'll have to share the again," she informed me in clipped tones. I nodded, ignoring the blood rushing in my ears as I moved over and she pulled back the covers, gingerly sliding in next to me.

"Let me check on your injuries," she whispered once she was settled. I nodded, then felt her hand skim across my chest, settling over my heart. My pulse raced at her touch and I stared at the fingers splayed across my chest. *Can she feel my heartbeat?* I wondered, my eyes tracing across lightly scarred knuckles, up her wrist, along her strong arm, until they found her face. Her eyes were closed, her brow furrowed in concentration as she worked her way through my injuries. She sucked a tiny breath through her teeth after a minute, and I felt her fingertips flex.

"What is it?"

Her eyes flashed open, staring directly into mine and blinking. "Your leg is worse," she said bluntly. "I *think* you have an infection. This isn't the sort of magic I'm trained in so I'm not sure. Best not to worry about it. If all goes well, I'll get a message to Friar Tuck tomorrow and he'll be here the next day. He *is* a healer so he'll be able to take care of it."

I nodded and swallowed dryly, my thoughts fractured between her words and the feel of her hand still on my chest. She pulled back, hesitating for a moment before giving my shoulder a light squeeze of reassurance, before turning on her side and settling in to sleep. I drew a deep breath, turning over her words and the events of the last day as I chased shadows across the ceiling.

"Why did you jump in after me?" I asked into the dark silence after awhile. I hadn't meant to give voice to the question that had rattled around my head all day, but the quiet darkness seemed to invite questions.

She turned back toward, eyebrows raised in disbelief. "Would you have rather drowned?"

"No, not at all. But it was reckless of you to come after me. You could have died too, and I'm just a prisoner. I think your brother was right to put you on leave if that's the sort of thing you're doing. I wasn't worth it."

Her face shuttered closed and she turned away again, her back tense. "I'm not afraid to help someone in need. And don't say that."

"What? The truth?" I couldn't help the note of scorn that entered my voice.

"No. That you're not worth it. You may be a fancypants Pelerine, but every life with a good heart is worth it. You want to talk about reckless? You were the one being reckless by going over that rotten bridge. You're an idiot, but you're an idiot with a good heart."

The mixture of insult and compliment in her response befuddled my tired brain. After a moment, she turned to look at me with a grin. "And I don't know why you're admonishing me for jumping in. If I had died saving you, you could be off to Pelerin without anyone the wiser by now."

I snorted. "Not with this leg. We'd just be sleeping together in a watery grave instead of a cozy bed." I stiffened at my awkward phrasing but she just laughed.

"That may be so, but don't worry yourself. I'm the Red Rider. Saving people is what I do. Now, go to sleep. My spell is going to wear off soon and you'll want to be unconscious by then. I can't renew it until I'm done with the stones."

Who saves the Red Rider? I wondered, as I watched her shift around to get comfortable. From the lines of constant tension I had observed over the short week that I had known her, I knew the answer: *no one.* My heart rebelled at that thought. She held a lonely position. It was obvious that she was strong enough to bear it, but everyone needs someone to have their back. Even someone like the Red Rider.

✻ ✻ ✻

When my eyes peeled open in the morning, I wanted to close them again immediately. They felt scratchy and sunken. My whole body was roasting and every muscle and bone complained. Red had obviously been up for some time, stirring another pot of stew at the fireplace.

When she came over with my bowl, she pressed a deliciously cool hand to my forehead. "As I thought. You have a fever. I can't use magic to heal it, but I did see some herbs yesterday that might help. I'll be back in a bit." Red limped out the door, and I concentrated on eating my food and doing my best to prepare myself for the day. By the time she came back, dripping from the continuously falling rain, I was half asleep again. I watched through slitted eyes as she moved around the room methodically, heating water, preparing the herbs and steeping them into a tea. She helped me sit up, pressing a cup to my lips and laying a cool, damp cloth on my neck, which broke through the haze in my mind for a little while. I watched her wolf down her own food, then drift over to a chair by the fire, and hunch over her broken moonstone.

The instinctual loathing of magic that had soaked into my bones from childhood seemed blocked by my dry, fever filled thinking. I watched without condemnation, only a foggy interest while Red worked on her stone, knitting it back together again little by little. Periodic flashes of light were the only visible sign of her magic from where I sat. My eyes closed and I dozed for I don't know how long, surfacing to pain filled consciousness only to drift back into fever filled sleep. The one nice thing about my fever was that it dulled my perception of the pain in my leg to a muted roar. Everything seemed muted at my body burned and my mind drifted, untethered. She didn't *seem* to be doing much each time I opened my eyes, just sitting hunched over her brooch, but the effort obviously exhausted her. Finally, she sat back, her face almost as gray as the surface of her stone, and sighed, the noise drawing me from my stupor.

"It's done," she announced, noticing my gaze. "It feels like the spellwork is safe. I sent a message out to Friar Tuck. As long as it's working, and he's in range, it will go through. He should get here by tomorrow I would think."

She stood, pinning her mended brooch near the collar of her borrowed shirt before shuffling over to the stew pot, keeping our meager food warm, and pouring a bowl for each of us. We ate quietly, neither one of us having the energy to think, let alone speak.

The shadows were lengthening, and I could see Red swaying on her feet as she washed dishes. I racked my fevered brain for ways I could keep her awake, grateful for the care she was providing both of us. A question that had bounced around my mind since we met tumbled out of my mouth.

"Why are you called the Red Rider?"

She slowed as she finished washing the last bowl, but didn't stop her chores. She didn't answer either, setting aside the dish and adding a few more vegetables from our store into the pot to cook overnight. Only when she was done at the fireplace did she turn, her face inscrutable.

"Only people I trust implicitly know the full truth behind that name."

"Fair enough," I replied with a hazy smile. "But Red can't be your name. What *is* your real name?"

She laughed tiredly. "I'll give you the same answer as before. Only those I trust know my given name. I don't go by it anyway.

I'm not that person anymore. I never can be again. I'm Red."

We examined each other quietly, our filters gone save tiredness and fever. I could feel how weak I was, laying in a bed, my skin tight and hot. Her granite strength seemed diminished as she stood before me. We were both at our weakest: vulnerable to each other, but not friends.

"Why did you attack Andrus?" She asked, breaking into my lazy thoughts. I raised my eyebrows, trying to remember that day through the fog of sickness.

Why did I attack him? Oh yes, he was attacking Belle. But was he? At the time it had seemed obvious, but now I wasn't sure. A picture of the prince crouching over Belle surfaced in my mind. His posture may have been defensive, not aggressive toward her. Maybe he *had* been trying to protect her. My ears listened the sound of her getting ready for bed as I thought about her question. It wasn't until she was settled in gingerly beside me, that I could formulate a coherent response.

"I thought he was attacking her. They were arguing about something, and I thought he was going to hurt her, especially considering what he is..." I flicked my eyes over, but Red was staring at the ceiling. "I mean, I thought that all magic users were evil. That someone like him could never have good intentions."

"And now?"

"Well, I wouldn't say that I'm ready to go preach the wonders of magic to my fellow Pelerines, but I've been saved by it twice. I can't exactly criticize, can I?"

She snorted, shooting an amused look my way. "Very diplomatic."

I grinned back at her, my amusement fading after a minute. "I guess if I'm telling the truth, I attacked the Prince out of ignorance and jealousy. I had a right to fear him I think. After all, I was raised to believe people like him are monsters. I didn't know any better then. I do now, obviously... if he truly is as good as you claim."

Red rolled her eyes and looked back up at the ceiling. I gazed blearily at her profile as my fevered brain processed my changing understanding of the world of magic. "I had loved Belle my whole life. She was the perfect woman to my mind. She was supposed tobe mine, and that Beast took her from me. Not just physically, but her heart too. He owns it in a way I never have… and from what Belle said, never could. If I'm honest, I hated that truth, and I hated him."

Red's mouth firmed into a taut line while I spoke. "She's not a possession to be had, Marchand. But I'll give you this, there probably isn't a woman more deserving of devotion than Rosebelle. She's intelligent and cunning, but also warm and caring. You don't meet a person like that very often. It's usually either one or the other. And you're the type of man who couldn't help worshiping someone like her."

My brain stumbled along her words as I felt myself sinking into unconsciousness. "Yes, worship is exactly right…" I mumbled, thinking back to Belle's accusations. *I never loved 'her', just worshiped who I thought she was. I never felt concern over her, or a desperate desire to know her fully, to let her know what's inside my heart.*

As my eyes dragged shut I felt Red sigh quietly next to me. A memory of the terror I felt when I realized she had jumped in after me in the river streaked across my brain. *Foolish, reckless woman. If she had died…* my brain supplied a thousand ways she could have suffered and been lost over the course of the night, and I slept fitfully.

CHAPTER SEVEN

Red

"Elne, don't bite my ankle." I could hear my voice talking to my companion as I slipped toward consciousness, the pain of my sprained ankle mingling with my dreams. I had been dipping in and out of sleep all night. As exhausted as I was, my sprained ankle couldn't be fully ignored, and the little energy I was able to put toward pain management I gave to Eddie. The alternating waves of chills and heat shed from his body during the night were another reason I didn't sleep well. His fever was in full force, and there was little I could do about it.

You can brew some more fever tea. My body followed my brain's suggestion, swinging my legs out of bed, and shambling toward the fireplace. I was so tired, and my ankle hurt badly enough, that I didn't even feel a prick of shame in leaning on a sturdy branch I had found when foraging the last two days. The cabin was small, but any amount of movement was becoming a test of resolve.

The fire was still burning strong, it's orange glow mingling with the gray dawn to cast enough light to see. I had periodically built it up overnight to continue cooking our food and keep the drafty cabin warm. I placed another log on before pulling our pitiful vegetable stew away.

"Mushy, and bland, but probably good for us," I told Elne. She snuffled around the edges of my mind, irritability over my injury the main emotion I felt from her. Picking up a small pot I had filled with clean water last night, I placed it on the cooking hook that had recently held our stew, and swung it over the flames to boil. While I waited, I grabbed another bowl of water which I had placed next to the sole small window in the cabin. A steady stream of air filtered through it's rickety casement, chilling everything nearby. The water was cold, so I pushed two rags into the bowl to soak, before wringing them out and limping over to Eddie. Sitting on the edge of bed, I wiped his forehead with one before laying it across his neck. Then I propped my leg up and wrapped the other around my aching ankle.

I studied Eddie's face as I waited on the water. His eyes flickered under closed lids, playing out a fever dream. If they snapped open right now, I would be staring into accusing depths, dark blue like the night sky.

"Ugh." I wrinkled my nose. *Why of all people, do I find _him_ so attractive.* I was still not quite used to his relatively clean shaven face, but I had to admit to myself that the dark brown days old stubble suited him. It gave him an air of instability that belied the careful, principled, conventional man I had observed over the last week or so.

Is that it? He's so prim and proper you just want to shake his calm self control? My eyes passed over his fair skin, dotted here and there with the old scars of a soldier, noting his tattoos with interest. *I guess I _do_ like the idea of shaking his world up, otherwise those tattoos wouldn't please me so much.* He would carry them with him always, a constant reminder that magic saved his life. The corner of my mouth curved into a smile.

I pulled the rags off of his neck and my ankle and hobbled back over to the fireplace to check on the water. It was just about to boil so I perched on a stool to wait and felt my eyes drawn back toward Eddie. Begrudgingly, I had to admit that there was something about the way he treated me that made me feel alive. His frank disapproval of my recklessness, my magic, my profession probably should have put me off, but somehow only drew me to him all the more. He had generally been respectful, but he had also been direct and unafraid in his judgment of me. Few acted that way toward me these days. Those who knew me well enough to see a person beyond just the Red Rider, like Robin and Eileen, were too afraid of hurting me to speak plainly. There was an highhandedness about Eddie that I both liked and rebelled against.

A stab of pain from my ankle cleared my thoughts for a moment, and when they returned, they were more orderly. *Get him out of your head,* I told myself sternly. *You enjoyed flirting with him, true, but it was supposed to be a game for a few days. Now you'll have to live with him, and encouraging whatever spark is between you is a bad idea.* I rubbed my chest over my heart absently. *Your feelings are probably a result of a botched binding spell anyway.*

The bubbling of the water reached my ears and I quickly pulled it out, replacing it with the stew to keep warm, before steeping the willow bark and mint directly in the hot water.

I could hardly wake Eddie fully enough to drink it, finally succeeding to rouse him just enough to swallow the whole cup with a little magic, exhausted though I was. He sunk back to sleep almost immediately, the tea seeming to have little effect.

After eating a little stew and failing to wake Eddie enough to feed him, I lay down again, listening to the renewed pounding of the rain on our cabin roof. The world seemed to have shrunk into this little room; to the next thing I needed to do to keep us alive. Friar Tuck had sent a confirmation message back through the moonstones last night. Just simple code. *Received. Understood. Tomorrow.*

"He knows this cabin, thankfully," I mumbled out loud to Elne. "He probably shouldn't be out in all this rain, but I hope he gets here quick. Although if it weren't for Eddie's injury I wouldn't mind staying here a little longer…" I trailed off as a surge of stymied anger rolled off of Elne in response to bringing up Barnsdale Lodge. "I know, girl. But we can't sacrifice Eddie just to keep away from ghosts. Besides the fact that it wouldn't be right, he's my charge, so that makes him part of the pack, sort of." Elne's disbelief butted up against my thoughts before she made herself scarce.

※ ※ ※

The door frame shook under a barrage of thumping knocks, and I caught myself instinctively crouching in front of our bed, knife in hand, before realizing who it must be. Still, I hobbled over and into a better defensive position before calling for the Friar to enter. *Better to be prepared for an enemy and find a friend than to open the door too soon.*

The door creaked open, revealing a soaked form in drab brown, an ample belly preceding the rest of him into the room. I relaxed, leaning against the wall to take the weight off my injury.

"Red, my girl, I'm sorry for the delay," he said, turning to shut out the rain lashed afternoon sky, and pulling off his dripping cloak. "Your message said you have an injured companion. And what of you?" His kind brown eyes peered at me from a wrinkled, sun tanned face, taking in my hunched posture and the way I favored my right leg. He was middle aged, and still very fit, although having softened around the middle considerably over the years of peace.

"I'm fine," I assured him, motioning toward the bed. "My charge is the one who is in danger." I followed Tuck over to the bed, trying to disguise my limp as best I could so as not to draw his attention.

"We were swept into the river trying to cross up near the Blue Boar Inn. I haven't had the time or energy to heal much. His leg's the worst."

Friar Tuck sat down on the edge of the bed, settling his bag on the floor and stretching his hand out to Eddie's forehead and then heart.

"Fever set in too," he murmured to himself as he started his examination. He settled back, looking at me grimly when he had finished. "I wish I had gotten here sooner. He must be in terrible pain. I can set it back to rights tonight, but I won't be able to heal it fully. It will take several spells, and he'll still need to rest for a few days once I'm done."

He cocked his head as I shifted gingerly on my feet. "And let's do your examination now, if you please." I pursed my lips, but nodded to him to get it over with. He made a tsking sound as he pulled his hand and magic away, frowning at my ankle. "I'll heal you first, then you can get to work making a good meal with the food I've brought. I'm sure the two of you are starved, not to mention that I'll be hungry enough for ten once I'm done my spellwork!"

"Go on, then," I replied with a slightly shaky laugh, relief that real help had arrived making me feel a little dizzy. "You know I'm not talented in cookery but I'm sure all of our appetites will be forgiving of any mistakes I make."

Tuck grinned at me, pulling out his amulet and motioning for me to sit. He made quick work of my ankle and other minor injuries, then handed over his bag. I pulled out a number of goodies, devouring a meat pastie before getting to work concocting a meal for us.

A golden glow spilled into the room as Friar Tuck started on Eddie. Now that my own injuries were gone, the only remnant a twinge now and again from my ankle, I hustled around the room, preparing food and assisting Tuck. The healing took more than an hour, and Tuck's swarthy tan had a grey tinge too it by the end.

"There. His leg is set. The rest of his injuries are healed, and the fever is already going down. He'll be waking up any minute. No doubt he'll be needing food more than both of us combined."

"Well, he'll have to make do with venison stew. I added your food to my own concoction from last night, and it's pretty tasty."

"Give us a bowl then, lass, and I'll be the judge of that," Tuck grinned cheerily at me, dimples showing on his cheeks.

Eddie stirred as I handed Tuck his bowl. Those blue eyes flashed open, pinning me as I sat down where Friar Tuck had been only minutes before.

"I feel better," he said, almost suspiciously.

"Friar Tuck is here. He healed you." I jerked my head toward the Friar and Eddie's eyes flicked to him, and expression of gratitude washing over his face.

Friar Tuck paused in the act of shoveling stew into his mouth to grin at Eddie. "Pleased to meet you, Captain Marchand. I've only set the left leg, not healed it completely. Although hopefully my pain spell hasn't worn off enough yet for you to feel it."

"I feel much improved, thank you sir," Eddie said, nodding at the Friar and attempting to sit up. I bent forward to help, slipping my hands under his shoulders to support him. The muscles in his jaw twitched at my touch and I couldn't help feeling a surge of satisfaction that my touch meant something. *Could be revulsion, could be the same spark I feel, but it's something,* I thought to Elne. Her only reaction was boredom and I fought not to roll my eyes.

CHAPTER EIGHT

Eddie

"So why doesn't your healing magic create a tattoo?" I asked the jovial man sitting at the table near my bed. Red had scarfed down her own stew faster than either of us, then promptly curled up in a chair near the fire and dozed off. Friar Tuck and I had finished at a slower rate, the Friar talking a mile a minute in between bites. His cheerful outlook permeated every word he spoke, putting me at ease quickly.

"Ah yes, I can see you've been a patient of a Romany at some point," he replied, nodding to my neck tattoos and settling his folded hands on top of his large belly. "What happened?"

I squirmed in my seat, careful not to move my newly re-set left leg as I found a more comfortable position. "A Romany Prince found me after I had been captured by a lizard Beast. He removed as much of the poison from of me as he could, then took me to another gypsy. Together they healed the rest of my injuries. I have another tattoo on my shoulder."

Friar tuck whistled. "The Romany Prince you say? And he needed help? You must have been all but dead."

"So they told me. I only remember bits and pieces of it."

"The Romany are usually strong healers due to the nature of their magic. They rarely need help from another healer like us magicians. The Prince is the strongest of all. If he needed another to complete the healing they must have narrowed your fate considerably indeed."

I couldn't keep the skepticism from showing on my face. "Narrowed my fate? I don't believe in destiny. And even if I did, what would that have to do with healing?"

The Friar's belly jiggled as he laughed. "Son, that's how the Romany heal. Their people have been gifted with a certain amount of power over fate. Not much, not like the ancient Shepherds. But it's said that they were gifted long ago by the Last Shepherd, the Black Prince, before his disappearance." I frowned, concentrating on remembering my lessons from Chapel in my youth. *Shepherds are the deities the Creator supposedly sent to guide our world from the beginning, like the Lady. But I haven't heard of them giving gifts before they disappeared.*

Friar Tuck settled himself more comfortably in his seat. He took a quick swig of the ale he had bought with him as he organized his thoughts. "Most know that Romany can read a person's palm to reveal their fate. Their healing and growing magic is all tied together with their ability to read. Instead of pulling magic out of the world around us, like I do as a common mage, or from within as a fairy or fae would do, they pull it from all your possible fates; and from the chords you've already chosen."

I shook my head, trying to hide my chuckle. "You mean to tell me that these tattoos are pieces of my fate, used in healing?"

"Precisely! At any given moment, we all have infinite choices available to us, infinite threads of fate. Most of the time, there are only a few likely courses we will take, based off of our personalities and patterns, and the choices we've made previously. A Romany healer is taught to examine those possible threads of fate, gather some of the least likely ones, and use their potential power to invoke a healing. The deeper the wound, the more potential fates will be needed. At a certain point, if the wound is too difficult, they may need assistance from another Romany to keep track of all the fates they are using up, and the ones they are leaving alone so a person still has their likely choices ahead of them. For someone close to death, you would need many Romany healers. The Prince can do the work of five, it's said. If he needed help, then you were truly marked by death."

My mind was soaked in disbelief, but I was curious despite myself. "So according to you, since I almost died, the Prince would have used up many of my potential fates? Wouldn't I feel something like that?"

"How would I know?" The Friar laughed in response. "I've never been in that position myself. I've felt the strain of making a momentous choice though," he continued, sobering at the thought. "The feeling of loss as you make a choice and don't know if it was the 'right' one, or finding out later what might have happened if you chose differently."

He paused, eyes turned inward on some memory. "Ah well," he continued, cheering himself up with another swig of ale, "whether you can feel it or not doesn't matter to the facts. You've found yourself without a lot of choices at the moment I dare say, haven't you? That should be proof enough of what I'm telling you!"

My eyebrows jumped in surprise as he subsided into a quiet chuckle. I still didn't exactly believe him, although it's not as if I had any understanding of 'normal' magic either so draining power out of potential fates seemed to make as much sense as anything else these days, but he had a point. Only half a year ago I had left the military, a thousand opportunities spread in front of me. Belle had taken a few of those plans away by her own choices. The others had seemed to be in the palm of my hand, but after the battle at the Shrine with the Beasts and Asileans, I had found myself with very little to decide day to day. I was a prisoner, bound to Red, stuck in a foreign country for a time. If I ever made it back to Pelerin, the tattoos visible on my face and neck would restrict how I could operate within society. No one would want to interact with someone marked by Gypsies.

Even now, my choices were almost nonexistant. I was bedridden in injury, my gear and even half my clothes swept away by the river, dependent on Red and the Friar in front of me to keep me alive.

I shrugged slightly. *If my fates were taken to heal me, but I wouldn't have used them anyway, then it doesn't seem to matter much. It's no different from any other day - just deal with the situation in front of you, and move on to the next.*

Friar Tuck left me to my thoughts, bustling around collecting his gear and pulling on his cape. He came to stand in front of me and offered his hand, which I shook heartily.

"I need to leave, unfortunately. The rain seems to be tapering off finally, which will help my journey home."

"In the dark? Can't you stay? We can put a blanket on the floor or something." I looked around, trying to find a place for him to sleep instead of consigning him to a journey through the woods at night.

"No I can't I'm afraid, even if you had a bed fit for a king to offer me. It's summer harvest time at the Friary. I'll be needed at the crack of dawn. Red can finish your healing over the next few days now that your bones are set. If you're careful it won't take long. My Friary is on the way to Barnsdale Lodge so you must stop in for the night when you get moving again. I'll check on my work then." He winked, bent over Red to pull her blanket up to her chin, and slipped out into the night.

✳ ✳ ✳

We settled into a slow rhythm at the cabin over the ensuing days. I moved from the bed to a chair in front of the fire in the mornings, and helped with whatever chores I could do from my seat. Red left to forage after breakfast to supplement the food Friar Tuck had brought us. In the evenings, we ate together. Sometimes there was quiet conversation, but more often than not, I ended up staring at the fire while Red busied herself with some chore or another. Then she would help me back to bed, pour another round of healing spells into my leg, and we would both fall into an exhausted sleep. Our days weren't exactly cheerful but there was a steadily growing sense of reliance on each other as we worked side by side, doing what we were able to help the other.

A few days after Friar Tuck's visit, she began helping me walk again. At first our touch was awkward, even though we had been sharing a bed for almost a week. But she kept a serious demeanor, a far cry from the teasing flirtatiousness I had come to expect when we first met. Her entire personality seemed to have changed since our plunge in the river. Instead of the sparkling, unpredictable, reckless soldier from before, Red was now a serious, quiet, careful person. She took care of both of us with restless efficiency, and without complaint. I was beginning to understand why her soldiers seemed to respect her so much. It was unnerving. *It's more unnerving to let someone else take care of me, let alone that it's her.*

"I think you're well enough to walk to the Friary tomorrow. Are you up for it?" Red's grey eyes flicked toward my leg.

I pushed off the tree I had been leaning on, during a break in my walking exercises. "How far is it again?"

"About ten miles. If we start in the morning, even taking it easy, we should make it there by nightfall. There are two hunting trails that we can follow most of the way, so it won't be slogging through undergrowth."

"Then let's do it. It will be nice to have real food, and company again." I grinned, but my smile faltered suddenly. "Not that your company hasn't been... adequate." I gaped, my mouth suddenly as dry as my thoughts. *What in the world is happening to me?* Red had thankfully turned to lead the way back to our cabin, so I couldn't see her face. "What I mean to say is that I'm grateful for everything you've done for me. Truly."

She opened the front door as I walked toward it, meeting my eyes as I passed her. "It's my job, Eddie. I've been charged with your security. At the rate we're going so far, I'd say I've been under-performing."

I chuckled as I passed through, glad she hadn't taken offense.

We spent the rest of the day packing, and after a final healing session, quickly fell asleep.

The walk to the Friary was grueling but uneventful. Red insisted on shouldering the pack that Friar Tuck left. Unencumbered, I managed a slow and steady pace and we entered the ancient Friary's grounds much earlier than anticipated. The sight that unfolded before our eyes as we left the tree line was freeing after so much time confined to the cabin and walking through dense forest.

Late afternoon sunlight shone onto long fields. Endless rows of lavender ran out before us up to the walls of an ancient church. The air outside the canopy of trees felt light and warm. Golden sunlight diffused over the crops and the sight of workers moving steadily among the rows settled a sense of peace over my chest.

"This seems like a place of goodness," I murmured, my eyes soaking in the tranquil scene.

"It wasn't always so," Red replied, her voice achingly somber. She drew a steady breath and smiled. "Under the Friar and Friaress, it has become a haven."

She moved forward with a quick step, and I followed in her wake a little more slowly, wondering what sad history the Friary must hold to have provoked such a response from Red.

A worker peeled off from the others as we neared the Abbey walls, and I recognized Friar Tuck's wide grin.

"Welcome, travelers. Most welcome, indeed. Wren is expecting you inside. Go ahead in, and I shall see you at supper." He shook hands with both of us, clapping us each on the shoulder. "You're hardly limping at all, Captain Marchand," he commented after Red thumped his shoulder back and started for the door.

"Yes, I'm feeling much better. It's still difficult for me to wrap my mind around what you mages are capable of..." I shook my head.

"It is wonderful, isn't it? Although no more wonderful than anything else of the Creator's handiwork." He beamed at the rows of lavender extending beyond us.

"You'd better run along after Red. You'll get lost in the Friary quick enough without a guide. I'll check on your leg after supper if that suits you."

"It does. Thank you."

He waved me off and I found Red waiting for me in the Cloister, just inside the Abbey doors. We continued on in silence through a maze of passages and rooms until we found the kitchens. There I was introduced to Friar Tuck's wife, Wren, and all of their children. We passed several hours in noisy busyness, helping Wren prepare supper, and at least on my part, answering the children's endless questions about Pelerin. We ate with gusto after the Friar appeared, the food simple, but abundant.

I lay awake that night, pondering my day. Tuck and Wren were kind and generous. Their children were all adopted, I discovered, orphans from the civil unrest of the past decades in Sherwood. They seemed to do everything with a current of cheerful noise, playing as they worked, and working as they played. Red had been less quiet than at the cabin, playing games with some of the children, and listening with a smile as Wren relayed the news of the area. I had never seen her so relaxed. *Is that what she's truly like? Or is she actually the challenging tease I met originally? Or the serious person from the cabin?*

The home brewed mead and ale that Tuck insisted I try after dinner buzzed around my head as I realized that I was sleeping alone for the first time in a week. With more than a little chagrin, I had to admit that I missed Red's presence.

Stop that. You just miss a warm body. When you get home you should buy a pet dog if this is how you're going to be.

My cheerful grin slid off my face. This Abbey had been the homeliest place I had been to in a long time. Even more homely than Croiseux Manor. I didn't like that feeling one bit. The world I understood was in Pelerin. Sherwood was a feral country, full of wild people and strange wonders. I didn't want to feel at home here. I didn't want to be finding anything in common with these people.

I tossed and turned most of the night, the walls of the

monastic cell I had been given seeming to crowd my thoughts.

* * *

Trilling birdsong flew in through my ears and flitted around my brain. My eyes opened to the plain, cream colored walls of the Friary. I smiled at them as peace settled over my chest and spread along my limbs. The cheery notes from the bird rang out again and I rolled off my pallet, drawn to the small window and quickly finding the maestro responsible for welcoming me into a new day.

The light was soft and muted, the sun not yet fully visible over the horizon, but already I could see workers moving along the rows in the field. The sight of prosperous occupation sparked an urge to join them, be a part of providing for the greater community. A little tan and gray songbird fluttered across my vision, winging it's way somewhere else, so I turned back toward my room, taking a few minutes to stretch before dressing for the day, marveling once again at my fully healed leg.

I hesitated outside Red's room after I stepped into the hall. I had gotten used to seeing her first thing in the morning during my convalescence in our cabin. **The** *cabin. Not ours. Someone else's cabin.* Not wanting to dig into that train of thought, I continued down the hall. *There's not reason to check in with her first. She'll know you haven't run off since the spell binds you. Besides, she might already be up and about. She seems like an early riser.*

The scent of bread and bacon reached my nose as I descended the staircase near the kitchen. My stomach rumbled happily as I stepped across the threshold and waved to Friaress Wren, busy chopping vegetables at the work table. Children seemed to be occupying every other surface of the room, eating breakfast or helping Wren. The smaller ones were chasing each other around, earning periodic reminders from their mother to keep away from the oven. Two boys breezed in through a side door, stopping to grab a few rolls and pieces of fruit before announcing their departure to the orchard.

I grabbed a plate and let Wren fill it with an assortment of food before settling at one end of the kitchen table, enjoying the warm chaos surrounding me, and the simple food in front of me.

Just as I finished the last crumb on my plate, Friar Tuck trundled into the room, balancing a load of equipment and buckets and just barely managing to hang on to them as on of the children dashed across his path on her way outside.

"Slow down!" Tuck called after the girl, laughing and shrugging the contents onto the table next to me. "Have you had your breakfast Eddie?" he asked, wobbling a little as one of his boys cannoned into him, giving his father a fierce hug and yelling something incoherent before shrieking and tearing off again as one of his brothers turned the corner of the table holding out an enormous frog.

"Put that outside right now!" Tuck yelled to the boy sternly, casting a glance toward his wife and lifting his eyebrows at me. "If Wren sees it she'll be out of sorts all morning."

"What's that my love?" Wren called from where she and her two older children worked.

"Nothing to worry about!" Tuck called back. "Just talking to my friend Eddie here. We'll headed out to the beehives in a minute."

Wren cast a smile our way before turning to adjust her daughter's grip on the paring knife she was using. "That sounds nice. Fresh honey will go perfectly with the biscuits I'm making for lunch today."

Tuck chuckled and turned back to me. "What do you think? Red will probably sleep for a few hours yet. Would you like to help me harvest some of our famous honey?"

"Of course. Actually, I have a little experience with beekeeping, although a refresher would be nice," I replied, standing and accepting his help securing the sleeves of my shirt and pants with twine, and pulling on gloves and a veiled hat. We grabbed a couple of buckets each, as well as the rest of his equipment, and marched through one of the numerous side doors. The quiet of the courtyard was startling as we stepped outside the buzzing friary kitchens.

Friar Tuck noticed my shell shocked expression and laughed heartily. "Yes, we can be a bit much, can't we? Usually Wren runs a tight ship, but she insists on giving the children complete free time on Saturday mornings. They're a bit like a thunderstorm of cheerfulness."

It was my turn to chuckle as I fell into step beside him. "I have to admit, I'm surprised Red wasn't downstairs already. But maybe that sort of chaos isn't her thing."

"Not at all! She's as ready to jump into their games as anyone else, but she usually sleeps late when she visits. The Friary calls to something different in everyone who visits, and she hears the call to rest loudest of all." Friar Tuck stopped to open a gate that crossed our path, and we came to the first of several stand of beehives not long after.

We stopped, laying out our equipment carefully as Friar Tuck ran through a list of instructions. The sun had fully risen by now, warming our skin as we started smoking out the first hive. Memories from my youth of helping Monsieur Comfry at the Dower House with his bees mingled with my concentration on the present. The buzz of the insects reminded me of a spring rainshower, at times worried and anxious, and other times steady and soothing as the smoke calmed their fears.

When we had filled our buckets with the appropriate amount of honeycomb from at least four hives, we took a few minutes to cover and secure our prizes before heading back to the house.

"Some of my favorite passages in the Book of Creation are analogies to the collection of honey," Friar Tuck mused as we secured the last covering over the precious honey.

"Is that right?" I asked politely, trying to remember if I had read any of them over the years. I had attended Chapel consistently each week with the rest of my family, but I had never loved reading the ancient religious texts the priest taught from on my own. The only passage I could remember was something about a lion and a honeycomb, but I didn't think that ended well for the man that found the honeycomb. *Or was it the lion that faced a bad ending?*

"Yes, honey is often used as a sign of the Creator's love for us, proof that he wants to give us good and sweet things, not just the essentials to keep us going. When I can pour fresh honey and butter on bread just pulled out of the oven, I know that's true!" Tuck declared, looking at me with twinkling eyes.

I quirked an eyebrow and smiled. "That sounds delicious. Although I would say that the bees provided the honey, the cows the butter, and Wren probably made the biscuits, not the Creator."

Tuck tipped his head back with laughter, shaking his head as he adjusted his grip on his full buckets. "You wouldn't be wrong Captain Marchand, I'll have to agree with you there."

"I suppose you'll tell me that the Creator created the bees and cows and even Wren, so he's responsible for it all," I said, provoking another round of laughter from Tuck.

"Well, I won't disagree with you on that either, although that makes the Creator sound like he's trying to steal credit from the others." I joined in as Tuck chuckled to himself again. He cocked his head to the side for a thoughtful minute before replying to my implied accusation.

"The way I see it, the Creator's love for us is not *just* in the literal sweetness of the honey, but in the way we all work together to produce and enjoy it. Not just us humans, but the bees of course, and other animals who keep the bees in check by eating them or tasting their honey too. Even the fact that the bees produce it by pollinating plants. Because they do that, those plants can grow and provide food for others, or even just grow into beautiful flowers for no other reason than to exist and be beautiful." I cast a surprised glance his way, adjusting my grip on my buckets. He sounded very different to the teachers we had at Chapel that I was used to. He navigated some uneven ground in our path and continued on. "The very ground benefits from the presence of those plants too as they prevent erosion from the soil, and give purpose to rain and sunshine. When we enjoy the honey we harvest, we're enjoying the work and purpose and beauty of the whole family that the Creator has intertwined here, and the way we each have a small part in the balance that creates a better whole. It's good to enjoy sweetness. But even sweetness can become flavorless if we forget our part in our family."

I kept my eyes on the gravel path in front of us, following Tuck back to the Abbey and into an underground storage area while I thought over his words. I had grown up listening to the priest at chapel speak about right and wrong, that it was the only way I had ever thought about our religion. *Right and wrong is important, of course, but maybe I'm missing something bigger about our purpose for being here.* Fragments of my feelings upon returning from the War to Croiseux Manor drifted across me. The itchiness at settling down to work in my father's business and learn how to run the manor. The thread of guilt that wove it's way through all my actions as part of me knew I didn't want to be there. The corner of disgust in my mind towards myself as I wished to be back on the battlefield.

I hadn't been feeling much of that since my capture. I had thought it was because I was so focused on understanding my position and finding a way to return home. But maybe it was because here in Sherwood, brutality and warmth seemed to coexist in a way that wasn't possible in Pelerin. There was less focus on what was right and wrong, and more focus on what was needed to make a better whole for everyone. Just like a bee stinging someone taking it's honey wasn't necessarily wrong, my pride over my skill in battle against an enemy that would destroy the wholeness and balance of a place like the Friary, or my home in Croiseux wasn't something to hide. I didn't need to do that here. People seemed to be warriors and farmers. Fighters and friars. They would defend what needed defending without apologizing for it, so long as it contributed to the wholeness of everything that was intrinsically good. Friar Tuck's voice shook me from my thoughts and I realized he had secured the other two buckets of honey we had harvested before I had finished storing my own in the cool cellar shelf.

"Come on son, Red will be up by now. Let's get back for a quick spot of lunch. I'll check on the final healing spell I placed on you last night to make sure it's complete." I gave Tuck a sheepish smile and followed him out of the cellar, the new thoughts he had given me buzzing around in the back of my brain as we walked away.

CHAPTER NINE

Red

Our time at the Abbey was like a dream. The good kind, not my usual nightmares. Tuck and Wren's magic had run deep into the earth here over the years, their goodness no doubt multiplied by the creator. They have turned this place from a whitewashed tomb into a life-giving sanctuary. As much as my soul cherished the rest, now that Eddie was fully healed we needed to press on. Besides, as much as I loved it, I didn't belong in this place full of peace and light. I had been formed for shadows and war. Time to move on.

"Are you sure we can't stay here longer?" Eddie asked as we waved our last goodbyes and followed the road away from the Abbey. "This place seems as secure as any. They could probably use our help with the harvest. You've haven't exactly been quiet about your reluctance to go to Barnsdale Lodge."

I wasn't about to explain my complex reasoning to Eddie. No doubt he would try to calmly debate with me until he succeeded in extending our stay. Elne's nerves fluttered around the back of my mind. If she could manifest physically she would be pacing and snapping. She always felt uncomfortable around too much goodness too.

"It's time to move, Pelerine. We've been delayed long enough. Besides, the Abbey is still in Sherwood. Why would you want to stay in a place so blatantly filled with magic?" I snapped.

"Back to calling me Pelerine, huh?" He scratched behind his ear and jogged a step or two to come beside me. My desire to be the leader mingled with Elne's desire to put someone in their place, but I shoved both feelings down.

Eddie continued talking, ignoring my moodiness. "You're right, the magic there is almost palpable. At least I assume that's what the warm, glowy, honey-like feeling was."

A smirk lifted the corner of my mouth at the bemused look on his face. "Yes, that was Tuck and Wren's magic. Tuck is a healer and Wren is a grower. Their magic has intertwined over the years to both heal and grow the Abbey. It's overpowering, isn't it?"

Eddie looked thoughtful. "I wouldn't say overpowering, but it makes itself known. Sort of invades your chest and gently corrects your errors, if that makes sense." He laughed and shook his head. "I can't believe I'm saying this, but the Abbey reminded me of home. Of Croiseux Manor."

My eyes snapped forward on the trail and I gave into my instinct to be in front, stepping fast enough to draw ahead of him half a pace. "So was Croiseux filled with magic, then? Seems strange for a Pelerine manor house."

"No, not magic, just love," Eddie panted slightly as he pulled abreast of me again. "Why are you walking so fast? My leg feels fine, but I don't know that I'm up for running the whole way. You said it would be another day or two until Barnsdale."

I slowed my pace, casting him a resentful look. "Of course we can slow down, if you can't handle the pace. I'm just used to people who can keep up with me."

Eddie tipped his head back and laughed. "Well, this Pelerine weakling would appreciate a more reasonable pace, if you can manage."

I slowed a little more until we were walking at a more normal pace. I had expected Eddie to lose his temper at my remarks. Most people did when you challenged their ego, but Eddie didn't seem to have much need for defending himself. His calm self assurance just made me jumpy.

"I suppose I could see why someone as restless as you might not want to stay in a place as peaceful as the Abbey," Eddie mused aloud a few minutes later. "Is Barnsdale Lodge like the Abbey? Is that why you aren't happy about staying there for the next few months? I confess, I won't mind at all if that's the sort of house arrest I have to look forward to."

I scoffed. "Barnsdale Lodge, like the Abbey? If you grew up in a large manor filled with love, you'll be disappointed. Barnsdale is nothing like the place we just left."

The crunch of our boots and whoosh of our breath stretched between us for a few minutes as my thoughts turned toward 'home'.

"Barnsdale is like the Abbey in one way. It isn't what it once was. The Abbey used to be a symbol of oppression and twisted religion. Now it's been healed. The Lodge used to be a place of warmth and family. Now it's a just a grave marker."

I could feel Eddie's eyes on me, but he didn't push me any further and I didn't feel like expanding on my words. He seemed to finally sense that I needed space. The rest of the day was spent in relative silence.

We stopped at a well known camp site as the afternoon began to wane. Eddie set up our tent while I foraged for firewood. The feeling of being alone for a few minutes was a relief, but did little to calm the simmering anxiety in my chest. Going home always made me anxious, but usually I could console myself with the thought that I could leave in a few days or a week. This time, I'd be stuck for months, living in and around the setting of my torturous launch into adulthood. More than a decade had passed since that time, but the place still taunted me with memories of my weakness. *If I could burn it down I would.* But it was my mother's home, and supported too many people's livelihoods to be destroyed in attempt to free me from my past. I had my orders. So I would just have to find a way to put one foot in front of the other for the next few months.

After heating our food over the fire, we sat staring at the

flames until nightfall. There was nothing to say to each other beyond communication over our camp or plans for the next day. My racing brain couldn't help finding meaningless tasks to complete, and I was jumping up every few minutes to attend to some small chore: fetching water, cleaning our dishes, gathering more firewood, reorganizing my pack. Eddie watched me with steady eyes, but refrained from putting his thoughts into words.

Why isn't he more unsettled? He's the prisoner here, not me. If he guessed my state of mind, he didn't ask, and I didn't ask the secret to his unflappable calmness. *Maybe that sort of tranquility was a gift. Creator, I assume you can't be too interested in the affairs of mud dwellers like me, but could you throw a little of that peace my way for once?* I waited a moment, but nothing changed, as usual. If the Creator hadn't been interested in saving me from John's torture all those years ago, I don't see why he'd be interested in sparing my feelings now.

When we settled into our tent that night, my resentment of Eddie's immovable serenity grew higher and higher. But as his breathing settled into rhythmic calm, I couldn't help being glad to have his presence by my side in the dark again. His peace couldn't reach me, but it was nice to curl up next to.

❋ ❋ ❋

Elne grew quieter with every step as we started out the next day, withdrawing apologetically as she often did during trips to Barnsdale. She was the first to protest any potential threat to my wellbeing, but there were no threats at the Lodge, only memories and ghosts. Not something a wolf was equipped to handle. I didn't begrudge her absence. If I could hide away from it I would too.

Instead I was left on my own. The lack of my wolf's reassuring presence in my mind made me jumpy. Eddie noticed, but instead of saying anything, just kept a little more space between us, allowing me to take the lead.

We crossed the small wooden bridge leading to Barnsdale Lodge just before sundown, spilling out into the hayfields as golden beams kissed the tops of tall grass. It should have been a pretty scene, pastures and crops surrounded on all sides by ancient forest, and the old Lodge in the center of it all. Perhaps it appeared so to Eddie. But instead of golden warmth, I felt a steady chill emanating from the house, streaking out lazily to touch every part of the estate.

It's like any other visit. Just get through the day. It occurred to a part of my brain that I should explain my family dynamics to Eddie before we arrived, but the rest of me was too frozen and too determined to just get through the evening to care. We marched toward the whitewashed walls of the Lodge, Eddie creeping steadily closer until he was walking next to me again. I didn't bother trying to put him in his place. Elne was gone so I didn't even have her irritation over alpha rank to contend with. Eddie was the only warm spot left to me.

The thick wooden doors of the lodge creaked open as we neared the house, and Mrs. Reed appeared from behind them, wiping her hands on her apron.

"Welcome home, Lady Hood. It is good to see you." She curtsied, and I felt Eddie's surprised gaze from beside me. I motioned for her to rise.

"Thank you Mrs. Reed. I hope you received Friar Tuck's notice about our delay."

"Oh yes ma'am, we did. And very sorry to hear of it, we were. But you look hale and hearty now, so all's well that ends well. And is this our other guest? Your usual quarters are all prepared if you want to rest from your journey before dinner."

"Yes please. This is Captain Marchand. Have you put him in the room next to mine?"

"Yes ma'am. But I beg that you would reconsider, especially since you'll be here some time. John Reed and I would happily move out of yours and Robin's old rooms. Tisn't right."

Martha always referred to her husband by his full name, and vice versa, a quaint custom in this area of the country. A leftover from when Fae walked these woods, generations ago before they left our shores. Referring to someone by their full name left less of an opportunity for an eavesdropping Fae to interfere with your intentions.

I realized Martha and Eddie were both looking at me curiously while my thoughts had wandered. *Keep yourself together. You're a warrior. A house means nothing.* I drew in a fortifying breath. "That's enough of that Mrs. Reed. You know I prefer the rooms over the kitchens. Oh and, I would like for you and Mr. Reed to join us at dinner this evening."

Nodding, she stepped aside, holding the door open. I jerked my head to Eddie, took a fortifying breath, and stalked into the stone and wood building.

Barnsdale Lodge had begun life as a Normagnian Keep during the wars of succession. The ancient tower stood even now, proud and menacing. Later generations had added a small series of additions in stone and wood, almost completely obscuring it, and the tower itself was hardly ever used these days. My father had reinforced and refurbished most of the maze of living quarters when my mother married him, but there had been no updates since he died. My mother couldn't bear change, and the Lodge wasn't decrepit enough for Robin to force the issue.

Although technically Barnsdale Lodge would be left to me upon Mother's death, Robin had taken over management at my request. Mr. and Mrs. Reed had been hired from a nearby hamlet after the revolution to care for my mother. To be within easy distance of her, Robin had all but forced the couple to take over our childhood rooms, even though they had protested at the thought of living above their station. They rooms weren't opulent by any means, but they were nicer than anything else in the county. Mrs. Reed always had a whiff of disapproval around her mouth when I came to visit, trying various ways to get me to use my old room. Instead, I opted to stay in a small, but perfectly adequate set of disused servant's quarters above the kitchen. Robin and Marian generally stayed in Marian's ancestral home, Locksley Hollow. It was only a half hour ride away. No one else ever came.

I showed Eddie to our rooms, not even sparing a glance to see how he reacted to his sparse bedroom and what would be our shared bathroom, crammed together at the end of a loft above the kitchens. Instead I retreated to re-familiarize myself with my own four walls. Whatever his reaction was, it would be nothing to the surprise of meeting my mother.

* * *

A few hours later, I leaned my back against a support post in the open loft area outside our rooms, waiting for Eddie to appear so I could lead him to dinner. The scent of our soon-to-be meal wafted up from below. My nose inhaled a promise of deliciousness, but my roiling stomach rebelled at the thought of food in addition to the awkward resettling ahead of us. Mrs. Reed bustled around downstairs, issuing last minute instructions to herself in a steady stream of low comments.

Since it was my first dinner home, I had made a slight effort to look like a Lady of the Manor. A very slight effort, consisting mainly of donning a plain dark blue dress and coiling my hair into a heavy bun at the base of my neck. Thick, wavy tendrils were already starting to escape, creating a halo of shadow around my face, but it was the best I cared to do.

Mrs. Reed had just left with the first tray of food for the dining room when Eddie appeared. I pushed off the support beam and started down the steep stairs to the first floor without a word. He followed, saying something, but I couldn't hear and didn't care to ask for a repetition. *Why are you so nervous? Dinner will be a disaster, like always. Who cares?*

"Red!" Eddie touched my elbow, startling me slightly, and I spun to face him, my gaze taut. His concern was palpable. "I asked if you're alright. Has something happened?"

I just stared at him. Part of my mind was fumbling for something to say, while another, disconnected part had continued down the passage to the dining area where my mother waited.

"Red?" Eddie's hand reached out toward my shoulder tentatively. I flinched away just before he could reach me. *How can I explain the agony waiting for us? Explain my mother? Can't he feel the weight of the old tower? Hear the echo of long ago screams from the terror still haunting it?* I shook my head slightly. *No, he probably can't. He was raised in a different world. None of that would hold weight for him.*

"The first course is already being served. We're late," I said, my tone emotionless. Eddie's hand dropped to his side and I turned to lead us down the hall.

With every step I gathered courage and momentum so that by the time I pushed through the dining room doors, I breezed right over to my mother, touching a kiss to the crown of her head and murmuring hello as I continued to my usual chair at the other end of the table.

Mr. and Mrs. Reed jumped to their feet as I entered, casting nervous glances around the room. An awkward pause reverberated on the walls while I took my seat and Eddie hovered nearby.

When no one spoke, he cleared his throat and turned toward my mother. "Excuse my intrusion, and please allow me to introduce myself, madame. I am Captain Eduoard Marchand, at your service. I am here as your daughter's charge, as you no doubt know."

My mother's vague, grey blue eyes fluttered toward Eddie, not quite looking him in the eye, but taking him in with a wan smile. "It's lovely to meet you, Captain Marchand. My step-son Robin did inform me that you would be my guest. Welcome to Barnsdale Lodge. It will be wonderful to have some company. Do have a seat."

Eddie executed a short bow, taking the seat to my mother's right with a charming smile. Mr. Reed was seated directly to my right, and I could feel him stealing glances at me. Ignoring him, I dug into my food with haste, not because of Mrs. Reed's delicious concoctions so much as I simply wanted to be doing something that would speed my exit from this room.

I ate mechanically, ignoring all as the rhythm of conversation between Mother and Eddie evolved from a stilted politeness to a slightly more natural exchange of pleasantries. *How typical that Eddie's charm would break through her vagueness.*

"My daughter? Do you mean Lady Marian?" Mother's wistful voice flowed into my ears from across the table. "She's my daughter-in-law. I had always wished for a daughter, so when Robin finally married I was filled with joy. And I've known Marian since she was born, so she's been like a daughter all these years anyway." She smiled vaguely and swallowed a spoonful of soup, as Eddie shot a glance my way. I avoided his eyes but couldn't help a detached curiosity about how this conversation would unfold. Mr. And Mrs. Reed had stiffened beside me, and I could feel Mrs. Reed's desire to step in. I doubted her sense of propriety would allow it.

"I'm sorry Madam, I had thought that you were Red's mother."

"Call me Marie, please. And thank you, it *is* wonderful to be a mother. Robin is my step-son you know, but we were as thick as thieves when he was young. Mischievous boy but his heart was always sturdy."

Eddie frowned, setting his soup spoon down and glancing between Mother and me. I concentrated on shoveling my food into my mouth.

"Shall we get the next course?" Mrs. Reed interjected, standing quickly and practically hauling Mr. Reed out of the room with her.

Eddie watched them go, then glanced at the empty place next to him. "Is your mother indisposed tonight Red? I was hoping she would be joining us."

I gave a tight smile to the table top. "Yes she is indisposed, and yes she is joining us. You're sitting right next to her."

He turned back to look at my mother. "I'm confused. I'm so sorry, are you Red's aunt? You look too much like her to not be family, but..."

My mother beamed at Eddie, eyes darting around the room as usual while she spoke, but her nervous enthusiasm was fixating on Eddie. "Yes I am an aunt, to the Prince of Asileboix if you can believe it." She leaned forward conspiratorially. "I don't usually tell people this because you never know how they will use the information, but you have a trustworthy sort of face Captain Marchand so I don't mind trusting you. *I* was actually born a Princess of Asileboix! I gave it all up to marry Robin's father. He was the love of my life. Yes, my brothers were princes all, and I a princess." Eddie listened politely, trying to follow the train of her conversation, but his confusion was palpable.

Mother sighed, turning back to the last of her soup. "But that was all a long time ago. And I *did* long for a princess of my own you know." Her voice turned plaintive and I could've sworn she said it in my general direction, if I didn't know any better. *Don't get your hopes up. She'll never acknowledge you. Just eat and get out of here.* My stomach clenched and my skin felt clammy. *I wonder if my skin is as grey as my eyes. As grey as this stone. As grey as a wolf...*

As if on cue, Mr. And Mrs. Reed appeared with the rest of our food. We were all more subdued as we finished the meal. Eddie didn't attempt to engage my mother in conversation, and I could feel him sneaking glances at me now and again. They were easy to ignore. With Elne still gone from my mind, I felt frantic in the emptiness, desperately latching on to anything that would distract me. Taste and texture of my food. Scents in the air. The feeling of the spoon in my hand and the light in my eyes. *Anything but the tower. Think of anything but there.*

Finally the meal was over. I stood from my chair abruptly, Eddie and the Reeds following suit more slowly.

"Mother, I'm glad to see you're in good health. I'll retire to my rooms tonight and check on you tomorrow." I sketched a bow as my mother concentrated on her napkin, folding the cloth fastidiously.

Eddie caught up to me just as I stepped onto the breezeway connecting the Lodge to the kitchen building. It skirted the base of the old tower a short way and I never liked to linger. Grey, weeping stone loomed up on one side, and a wooden railing hemmed me in on the other. I turned, shrugging off the hand he had put on my shoulder.

"*What* was that about?" he asked, his eyes a mixture of confusion and concern. "Who was that woman? Why wouldn't she look at you?"

I caught myself leaning away from the stone wall next to me, ever so slightly, and sternly stood up straighter. Tapping my fingers against my leg, I looked out across the grounds.

"She's my mother, Lady Marie Hood. She suffered greatly under Prince John's rule. She has no memory of me, and won't acknowledge me. No one has been able to cure her, and she gets agitated if anyone insists on speaking about me for too long. I should have told you before." I shrugged my shoulders lamely, only half focusing on our conversation. *Is the tower leaning toward me now?* I examined the stones next to me out of the corner of my eye. *Are they? Probably not. That wouldn't make sense, would it?* Eddie started speaking again and my mind drifted back toward our conversation.

"…would have appreciated a little preparation for all of that, yes. But I can understand not wanting to talk about something so painful. I'm sorry, she must have suffered something very traumatic to have that happen."

I grimaced. "Don't be sorry. The one who did it to her is dead. She's safe." Pulling a breath through my nose, I turned and started back toward our rooms, Eddie trailing behind. The leftover scent of our dinner swirled around us as we mounted the stairs to our rooms. *Just get to your room and you'll be safe too.* As I opened my door, I threw a muttered 'goodnight' over my shoulder and stepped across the threshold eagerly. *Safe.*

Later, as I settled in to the quiet dark of my room, falling deeply toward oblivion, the color behind my closed eyelids shifted from black to stone grey. The scent of dust and iron filled my nostrils just before I fell asleep, too late for me to claw my way back to consciousness.

CHAPTER TEN

Eddie

Bloodcurdling screams reached my ears, mingling with my dreams for a minute before I snapped fully awake. Shooting out of bed, I hovered, wrestling my brain out of it's sleepy fog and trying to identify the direction of the noise.

Red. It's Red! Grabbing a knife from under my mattress, I ripped open my door, charging the few steps down the tiny passage to her room and bursting through the closed door. My eyes searched frantically for her attacker, slipping across the darkened lumps of her dresser, chair, and bed. Finally, they settled on the only person in the room: Red. She was hunched in her narrow pallet, blanket and pillow half tumbled to the floor in a tangled mess. Sheathing my knife and setting it on her dresser, I stepped over them to the edge of her bed. Her screams had subsided into a pitiful whimpering. The desperate sound grated against my heartstrings as I tried to calm my own breathing.

She's fine. Wake her up so she doesn't make that noise. Crouching beside her bed, I gently shook her shoulder, my eyes glued to her face so I could catch the moment she returned to the present. I didn't want her attacking me in confusion as she surfaced.

Eyelids snapped open, her pale eyes glowing like moonlight in the darkness of her room. Wide, terrified, they locked onto mine, a question forming faintly on her brow.

"You're safe. Just a dream. All is well." I squeezed her shoulder lightly as I spoke, trying to imbue some of my calmness into her bones. Her eyes stayed on mine as her own breathing slowed. After a minute, she pushed up and swung her legs around to sit on the edge of her bed. I let my hand fall away but stayed crouched in front of her, waiting for her to speak.

"Thank you. If you hear me again just ignore it."

"Ignore it?" I repeated in surprise.

"Actually, I'll soundproof my room tomorrow, so you won't be bothered again."

"But... soundproofing won't fix anything. It will just ensure I can't hear if you *do* need help. How often do you have these nightmares?"

"Almost every night. And I don't need help."

"I've *never* heard you scream like that before. You sounded..."

"Weak?" Red supplied, anger threading through her voice. "They're not real. I can't control whether I have a nightmare or not. But they're not real. And I'm *not* weak." She stared at me fiercely, the muscles on her arms taut with nerves.

"I didn't say that," I admonished her, holding up my hands, trying to follow the direction of her thoughts. "But if you have these every night, how haven't I heard you cry out before now? I shared a bed with you for almost a week!" A flush swept across my face and I was grateful the darkness of the room would hide it.

Her posture relaxed slightly as she thought for a moment. "No, I guess I didn't have any nightmares while I slept next to you. Maybe I was too tired."

I studied her, sifting through her words. She reminded me of some of the men I knew on the front. So used to suffering quietly that they ignored the need to care for themselves during and after the fight. If they didn't find a way to break that habit they usually ended up being sent home with a few less limbs: or dead. *Maybe that's why Red is so out of control. She hasn't found a way to confront whatever horror stalks her, and she doesn't have a way to break it's hold over her.*

She obviously needed someone to help find a way to treat the root of her problems, but it was too late in the evening to figure out what they were. We needed a solution for the moment.

"Would you like to sleep with me?" I asked suddenly, acting impulsively on a fleeting idea.

"Get out," she growled, and I rocked back on my heels.

"I wasn't suggesting... what I meant was that we've slept near each other before. It's the same as the cabin."

"Get out!!"

I pushed up from the floor, edging my way out of her room and shooting one last glance at her hunched form as I closed the door. *Leave her alone for now*, I ordered myself. I was exhausted and wanted to succumb to the gravity of my bed anyway. *You have months ahead of you to find a way to help.*

* * *

Red's distinctive rapping on my door awoke me the next morning. She always ended her knocks with a double tap that made me want to snap to attention. I glanced toward my window, just a tiny rectangle located near the ceiling. Grey light filtered through, doing nothing to entice me from my broken sleep. Red's knock sounded again. I pushed out of bed, straightening my shirt before opening the door.

"Let's go spar. Then we'll get breakfast and meet with Mr. Reed."

I nodded, closing the door again and taking a few minutes to get ready. I grabbed my knife on the way out and met her in the loft area, following silently as she led the way across the small courtyard, past a walled garden, and through a gate toward what seemed to be a kitchen garden. In the corner was a small grassy space, the edges littered with pots and heaps of soil grouped around a long work bench, obviously used for transplanting and garden work. We put our weapons down on the bench, and started a series of warm ups, neither of us speaking. Red seemed full of strictly contained energy, not even sparing a glance in my direction. For my part, I kept my attention on my breathing and stretching out the kinks in my back. She would make her thoughts known when she was ready. *I just need to make sure I'm ready to hear them.*

Just as golden streamers began to invade the cloudy grey sky, Red called me to the center of the space.

"Let's begin. We'll need to meet here every day to keep our skills sharp. I don't intend to get soft during our penance here. And since I'm in charge of you, that means you won't be allowed to slack off either."

"I'm more than happy to be your partner, Red. You could have just asked."

"I'm not asking, I'm telling you how it's going to be. Understood?"

I fought a smile as I stared back into her eyes. She was trying to assert herself over me to make up for her vulnerability last night, but she didn't realize there was no need for it. I didn't intend to fight her authority, or undermine her. Unless I was released from the spell that bound us, I had no choice but to find a way to bide time here. She wanted to assert dominance over me, but I didn't have any argument to her being in charge. I only wanted a way to become her friend. My urge to smile drooped as I traced the dark circles under her eyes and pallor of her skin. *She obviously didn't sleep again last night. She needs an outlet for some struggle that she's in, someone to break her aggression on. I can provide that.*

"I understand," I answered quietly. She nodded and dropped into a loose fighting stance. I mirrored her posture, grinning as I continued my train of thought. "And just so *you* understand, I don't intend to spar with you, I intend to beat you so thoroughly you'll be *asking* me to teach you instead of ordering me around. *That's* how it's going to be. Understood?"

A flood of anger surged through every line in her body, spilling out of her eyes and filling her previously tense posture with aggression. *Well that was a little more of a reaction than I was expecting, time to put my money where my mouth is!*

She muttered something under her breath and I felt a pulse in the air, rushing through me from tip to toe.

"Wait a minute! You didn't say anything about using magic!" I exclaimed.

"I've shielded us both so we won't sustain serious injuries," she replied sardonically. "Don't be such a baby. Whoever draws first blood wins."

My jaw dropped open. "I'm not going to cut you!"

Her teeth flashed. "Then you'll lose, Pelerine."

We lunged for our weapons at the same time. She had two knives and shortsword, I had only the single knife she had given me for protection after the skirmish at the border. I lunged backward as I snagged it from the table, putting distance between us. She took her time strapping her knives on her arm bracers while I thought, keeping her body turned towards mine.

I can't cut her! How could I do that to a woman? My sense of honor recoiled at it. *She's a skilled warrior, so it's not exactly the same as cutting one of my sisters. Still, why would she think I'd be okay with hurting her like that?* I huffed out an annoyed breath, watching as she grabbed her unsheathed shortsword and gave a few practice thrusts, grinning all the while, no doubt guessing the direction of my thoughts from the expression on my face.

She knows I'll have a problem with those rules. And I definitely do. But I'm more concerned that the spell isn't strong enough and she wants me to hurt her for real. She's in that state of mind. How can I test it?

"How do I know that your spell is going to work?" I called over to her as we began to circle each other. "What if I accidentally cut too deep? I can't heal you.

"Are you saying you're too chicken to fight me properly? I'm not surprised, Pelerine."

"Stop calling me that. And you know I'm not scared to fight you, I just don't want to hurt you."

She laughed. "Don't worry, you'll never even get close enough to try. And I promise not to aim for your vitals, or that handsome face."

I cocked an eyebrow. *Flirting Red is back, is she?* This woman had more masks than a masquerade ball. Still, I wanted a way to verify the spell, even as the competitive side of me burned to show her up.

That's it. A sudden thought occurred to me and I grinned. "You promise to heal me if I get hurt, correct?"

A look of disgust passed over her face at my supposed cowardice. "Yes, Eddie, I'll heal your precious, delicate skin when I inevitably pink you, don't worry."

I lifted my knife in response and she tensed, preparing for my attack. Instead, I ran the blade down the top of my forearm, pressing lightly at first, then a little harder to test the strength of the shield. The spell allowed a small cut, worse than a papercut, but not bad enough to require stitches. I could feel a layer of resistance build as I pressed harder, not allowing me to cut any deeper. *Okay good, the spell won't allow us to truly hurt each other.*

"What are you… seriously?! Are you trying to forfeit already? I thought you were man enough to at least *try*." Red's voice wavered between disgust and derision as she sheathed her short sword and stalked toward me.

"Technically, I've just won the first round."

She scoffed as she came to a stop in front of me, reaching out for my arm. "Really? And how to do you figure that?"

I grinned as she muttered a spell, sinking a golden glow of magic into my arm. "You said whoever drew first blood. You didn't say it had to be on the other person."

Her grip tightened and her jaw ground audibly in response to my words. "What a clever Pelerine I've got for myself. Ugh! I can't stand people who do that." She examined her healing handiwork and then folded her arms across her chest.

"People who follow the rules?" I asked innocently.

She closed her eyes. "People who follow the letter of the rules, and ignore the spirit."

I grinned even wider, tightening my grip on my knife. "There's a saying in Pelerin that the spirit of the law resides in the letters.

If the spirit is missing, you must check the spelling."

"Fine." She opened her eyes, pinning me with a sarcastic gaze. "The new rules are these: first one to draw the *other person's* blood wins the round, we'll continue for at least five rounds without stopping to heal, unless one of us calls a forfeit. If you injure yourself, you lose. Are those tight enough for you?"

"Yes, ironclad." I kept my expression nonchalant as I whipped up my knife, tracing it lightly down her cheek and pressing just hard enough to draw a pink line.

She stood in shock as I danced away, and I couldn't help laughing.

"I said no face hits!" she protested angrily.

"You said you wouldn't damage *my* handsome face. I made no promises about yours." Her anger grew along with my grin until it released in the loudest frustrated growl I've ever heard. She whipped both knives out of her bracers and charged toward me with ground eating strokes.

"Lady's tears," I cursed, leaning forward on the balls of my feet as I braced for contact.

I lost every round after that in quick succession. There were a few bouts where I pinked her only a second after she got me, but most of them were short and brutal. I lay on the ground panting when she called an end to our session. She healed the few cuts I had opened on her with a muttered spell, then knelt by my side, sinking magic into my skin with mumbled incantations.

I reveled in the warmth of her magic as it swept over my aching wounds, leaving refreshment and energy in it's wake. Her brow was serious, the tension from earlier lessened, but anger still danced in the set of her mouth. When she was done, she pushed up, straightening her tunic and brushing off her pants while I stood to do the same.

"I'm impressed you can keep your focus so well, even while you're angry. Most people become sloppy when they're mad, but you were even better than the matches when we were traveling with your unit," I commented, watching her expression. Her eyes tightened, resembling the grey stone walls of the Lodge's ancient tower.

"Then keep that as a reminder. You know *nothing* of what I'm capable of. Don't cross me. And don't get in my way."

I shrugged my shoulders as she stalked away. It seemed I had lost this sparring match in more ways than one.

CHAPTER ELEVEN

Red

Eddie followed in my wake as we headed back for breakfast. We ate in the kitchen without much conversation, our clothes damp from sweat and dew, as well as a little blood. My skin itched while they dried in the warm air as Mrs. Reed managed a number of simmering pots. She had just left to take a tray to my mother when her husband poked his head through the door.

"I'm ready for you's now, Lady Red." I nodded, standing and dumping my dish into the sink before following him in the courtyard, Eddie my shadow.

Mr. Reed acted as the farm manager, and was slowly apprenticing his son, who was about my age and also named John, on his duties. There were no nearby towns, only a hamlet about half a mile away, where his son lived, and then no one until Locksley Hollow, a half a mile in the other direction.

"We're glad ta have some extra help through the rest of summer and harvest season, I can tell you Lady Red. My son has been pushing to experiment with a new schedule of crop rotations and I finally agreed this year. I bin callin' myself a fool ever since, wonderin' how we're to keep up with this new plan and the animals. With the two of you's here, and the workers from the hamlet every now and again, we'll be right as rain."

I nodded and he continued on, detailing the farm operations as we walked through the main barn, the pastures and the crop fields. I asked questions here and there, but soon fell silent as Eddie's bright interest led the two men into a steady discussion of farming techniques.

Mr. Reed's son, John Jr., joined us near the outer pasture. He doffed his cap to me, welcoming me home with full deference, but was soon pulled into the lively conversation on crop selection and rotation. I chimed in now and again, keeping my tone light and hearty, as I usually did when dealing with members of the public, but it was a battle to keep a lid on my restless irritation. Mrs. Reed had asked during breakfast if we could move a few large items out of the storage area in the old tower once we were done with the farm work for the day. I had agreed, and she thanked me apologetically, knowing I never set foot inside unless strictly necessary.

Our inevitable trip to the tower was growing in my mind as the men chattered on. I reached for Elne again but caught only a brief wave of fear and loathing before she skittered off to wherever she was hiding. *On my own then.* I glanced at Eddie. *Not exactly on my own, I guess, but he isn't exactly what I had in mind.*

The sun had passed it's zenith by the time the Reeds excused themselves to take their lunch under a stand of trees. Hunger gnawed at my belly just as strongly as the evil of the tower gnawed at my mind.

"Let's go," I snapped at Eddie as our two companions left us. He shot me a confused and slightly offended look. I turned and stomped along the perimeter of the pasture's fence, to where it turned and headed back toward the Lodge. Eddie jogged to catch up to me.

"What's this all about?" he demanded, pulling slightly ahead of me so he could see my face.

I bit back a snarl and refused to look at him. "I'm tired of the chattering. We need to get back for lunch." *Half a lie,* I admonished myself, memories of the cold tower store room like a sinkhole in my mind. I feared if I stepped back into it, I might not come out.

"This is exactly the problem!" Eddie exclaimed, putting his hand on my arm and pulling me to a stop to face him. "You wear so many masks I don't even know which one is you! You're angry and surly one minute. You're jovial and kind when you're talking to people like the Reeds. You ignore your own mother ignoring you. You're obviously capable of great things as an officer, but you're reckless in ways you'd never tolerate in one of your soldiers. And your nightmares… you're afraid of *something* or you wouldn't have sounded like you did last night. You have too many walls and fake versions of yourself layered over something. Tell me who the *real* you is!"

Waves of bitterness, and fear, and a longing swept over me. They melted together in a shield of anger as I rounded on him. "The *real* me?! Who do you think you are to ask me that? *No one* shows their real self all the time. And why would you think I would choose to be so vulnerable to someone like *you?*" I ripped my arm out of his grasp and he set his jaw, throwing his hands up in exasperation.

"No one shows their real self?! What sort of cynical, bitter world do you live in? Yes people put up boundaries sometimes, but what you see is what you get generally. *I* certainly don't go around pretending to be something I'm not. You like to keep reminding me that I'm Pelerine, to remind me that I don't belong here and can't. And you know what, that's fine. I wouldn't want to belong here if it means I have to play games every second of the day. It's childish." His chest heaved as he finished his tirade, his usual steady calm dissipated in the wake of offended pride.

His anger just served to ignite mine further. "What do you know of Sherwood to say that we're only playing games?! You grew up in a land of golden sunshine and glorious peace from all accounts. This is the first time you've had to confront something other than your fragile idea of reality, and all you can do is sneer at how the rest of us cope with the evil we've had to vanquish? Don't make me laugh, Eddie!"

He stepped closer at my threat, angry blue eyes staring

directly into my own in a challenge that even the absent Elne couldn't ignore. I felt her snarling temper sweep over my own, overwhelming my fragile control.

"Don't make you laugh?! At what? My challenge to be better? To be more authentic? To face whatever is haunting you? Everyone treats you like you're some sort of untouchable saint, but all I see is a woman hamstrung by fear and weakness."

Elne's protective anger burst out of control at his accusation of weakness, and I growled, showing my teeth as I felt my jaw start to lengthen and fur burst out along my skin. Elne urged me to attack him and I followed blindly, throwing a wicked punch at the side of his head. He managed to duck just in time, and I roared, kneeing him in the gut before he could get away. He doubled over in pain as my surge of triumph mingled with Elne's. My eyes focused on the side of his neck and the urge to rip into the unprotected area swept over me. My claws hadn't fully extended yet so I reached for a knife on my bracers, only to discover I wasn't wearing them. The unexpected lack of weaponry shot through my brain and I recovered myself for a moment, a cacophony of hormones, and rage, and vulnerability battered me, the real me, Red the broken and brittle and strong. Eddie stared up at my partially transformed face with horror as he straightened up in front of me. I stood frozen, snarling and scared at my loss of control.

"No," I gasped, as Elne urged me to put him in his place. "Run!" Eddie didn't move, so I did, turning and loping into the forest. *Get away*, I told myself. From Eddie, from my mother, and away from that cursed tower.

I ran blindly, crashing through the trees without even trying to hide my trail. Arms pumping, feet finding purchase among the rocks and leaves on the forest floor, I dodged trees and leaped over fallen branches. I ran until the pull on my chest threatened to steal my consciousness.

I stopped, hand over the squeezing tug on my ribcage, and fell to my knees. The earth was slightly damp, seeping through the knees of my work trousers. As my adrenaline started to ease, I felt my jaw moving back into the place, and the little patches of white and black fur that had rippled up from my skin along my arms and shoulders dissipate. I lost track of time as I kneeled, focusing on my calming my breathing and the rushing of blood in my ears.

We started to transform, I scolded Elne. *Are we children that we can't control ourselves?* Her shame mingled with an insistent worry that Eddie would harm us and upset the pack.

"He's *not* truly part of the pack, Elne," I scolded between breaths. I turned, sitting down heavily on a small pile of leaves and leaned against a tree trunk, tilting my head back and closing my eyes. *Even if he is pack, he wasn't completely wrong in what he said. What he and Eileen both have been saying. We're out of control. We've been running scared from that tower for the last decade. Maybe we do need to fight these ghosts.*

I breathed out a sardonic laugh, the burn in my lungs beginning to subside. "If even Robin can see it, then it must be getting bad."

"See what?"

I jumped in my seat, opening my eyes to find Eddie only a few paces away. In my distracted state of mind I hadn't noticed the sound of his approach nor the lessening pull of the binding spell in my chest.

We stared at each other for a loaded moment. Elne growled in my head at the intrusion, but I snarled back in my mind. She retreated at the strength of my anger and I felt bad for a moment. We would have to sort this mistake out later. I turned my attention to the man in front of me.

"Me." I gestured to myself. "The heaping mess you see in front of you. Robin doesn't exactly excel at reading people fully. He's like you. What you see is what you get. Isn't that how you put it? So if he can see that I'm going off the rails and banish me here, then I must really be a mess."

Eddie observed me, a sense of gravity hanging around him even as he hesitated to form a response. I heaved a sigh.

"I'm sorry about that. About transforming. I lost control.

It could have ended badly." I smacked my head at a sudden thought. "And you probably had no idea what was happening. I forgot that you're Pelerine, and I've never explained my shift."

He shifted uncomfortably on his feet, opening his mouth to respond before I cut him off.

"We don't usually talk about it to outsiders. Not even the Asileans know we can transform using our companion's traits at will. They can only transform at the full moon. If you attacked Andrus because of his transformation, I had better watch my back, huh?" I smiled at him crookedly. He didn't smile back, his eyes flicking between my upturned mouth and the tears glittering in my eyes. *Don't let them spill,* I told myself sternly, closing them. *You don't deserve your own tears.*

"I'm sorry for what I said, or at least, the way I said it," Eddie replied quietly.

My eyes flew open in surprise. "Why? You only spoke truth, at least to an extent. You don't know me fully, but that doesn't mean you can't see what's in front of you."

"You're right, I don't know you," he admitted, walking slowly to a tree trunk near mine and sliding down to sit against it. "That's what was making me so angry. I used to think I was good at reading people. But then it turned out that I never knew Belle properly… the woman I was in love with for most of my life! And I was wrong about Prince Andrus apparently too. And my superior officers, my King and country apparently trying to pin the consequences of their actions on me… everything I know to be true and good in this world is shifting, and I took that feeling of being untethered out on you, just because I've seen so many faces of you that it bewilders me."

I frowned, digging in the muddy earth beside me with my fingers as I listened, the ache in my soul soothed slightly to hear that someone else felt out of control. *That's probably a terrible thing to feel,* I scolded myself, but I couldn't really feel ashamed.

Eddie laughed and I glanced back to him. His eyes were following the lines I was tracing in the earth, but I could tell his mind was elsewhere.

"Belle compared me to a benevolent dictator once. And I'm starting to think she was right. There's this need... compulsion maybe; I feel that I have to put things in their proper place. To dig at something until I understand it completely. To have mastery over it. Not to control necessarily, but to know and understand where everything goes so that I can keep it all in it's place." I felt his eyes on my face, and heard the apology in his voice. "And that extends to people of course. I want to think I understand those around me so that I can help them be their best self. But when I don't have the measure of something, or some*one*, it gets under my skin. Combine that with the recent challenges to my understanding of how the world works and you get the theatrics you witnessed today I guess."

We sat in silence for awhile, the sounds of birds trilling above and the wind ruffling leaves in the trees. The noises combined to anchor me in the moment and soothe the unsettled bits of my heart.

"Everyone wants control," I remarked after awhile. Eddie grunted and I could feel him look over at me. I grabbed a stick and ran my thumb along the rough bark before snapping it in half and tossing the pieces away. Something compelled me to continue speaking, unburden myself to this foreigner who saw beyond the person and life I had crafted for myself in response to John's long ago violence.

"I don't want to control anyone but myself. But I'm starting to realize that my past might be controlling me instead. When I ran into battle that day you met me, it was a little reckless, yes. But I've done that sort of thing so many times before just to feel alive that it's become commonplace. I'm the Red Rider. I defeat my enemies. No one questions that anymore." I plucked another stick off the ground and tapped the tips of my boots with it. "I shouldn't have to be facing down death just to feel alive. But I don't know how to live any other way." Several heartbeats stretched between us and I forced myself to exist fully in that quiet moment, to not worry what Eddie thought, or try to justify my own admission, or berate myself with accusations. The desire to do any and all of those things itched at my soul.

"I can understand that," Eddie replied quietly. "You want to stay with what you know. What you're good at. I felt the same after the end of the Beast War..." he shuddered involuntarily, drawing my eyes. A sad smile pulled at his lips. "Sitting at the desk at home, the place I had been dreaming of for years. It was killing me. And not in a meaningful way, for the good of my country like a battlefield death would mean. It was killing who I was, and who I felt like I should be. Maybe that's why I ended up getting things so twisted..." He shook his head, balling his hands at his side.

"No. That's not true. I was just an idiot who thought he was in love with Belle and that he knew everything about this world. My hubris could have killed people and places I didn't know were good. Thankfully it seems like my mistakes haven't ruined things permanently. As my punishment I'm a prisoner in a strange land to a wolf woman." He grinned more widely. "It was a wolf, wasn't it?"

I rolled my eyes, but couldn't help answering his grin with my own. "Yes, I'm a wolf shifter. Gold star for you. My animal companion is called Elne, but she's not a big fan of yours. She thinks you don't know your place."

His grin faltered at my words, his eyes drifting back to where his hands lay folded in his lap. "Well, this... Elne, as you called her, may be more right than you know. I once had my entire life figured out. Now I'm not sure what new reality will come upon me from one day to the next."

"Well, for the next several months, your reality is going to be helping me with farm work every day, you can count on that," I teased with a smile, brushing off my hands and crossing my arms.

He laughed, and I felt a spark ignite between us, a recognition of a kindred spirit.

"Look," he said, observing me hesitantly, "I know I'm technically a prisoner, but it seems like we're both in need of a friend. We're actually the same rank, so if we had met in other circumstances, we would be on equal footing. Is there any way, while we're here at Barnsdale at least, that we could just be friends? I have no angle, I swear. I'm not trying to gain your trust to escape or something." He huffed a laugh. "I'm not even sure if I have another home to go to anymore... too much has changed. I just want to help you, if you'll let me. And if you would let me be a friend, I think you could help me too."

Pushing back against the tree trunk for leverage, I got to my feet and walked over to him. He took my outstretched hand, and I pulled him up as well. Searching his eyes, I looked for signs of guilt or deception, but found none. *Belle spoke of him as honorable to a fault. He obviously has his own issues, but he treats me like a person instead of a hero. I could use a little more of that in my life.*

His brow furrowed as I made my examination. "Are you putting a truth spell on me?" he asked, disapproval coloring his voice slightly.

I chuckled and dropped his hand. "No Eddie, I don't need magic for everything. Just considering your offer."

"Well?"

"Friends while we're at Barnsdale. It's a deal." His sudden smile set me off balance for a minute, and an urge to make him laugh nudged at me.

"Although I'm suspicious that you're only wanting to be my friend so that I don't beat you thoroughly in our sparring sessions during our stay."

He tipped his head back in a belly laugh, the sound strangely soothing to my raw soul. "I wouldn't dream of it! Although I admit I probably won't attempt to make you angry before we start tomorrow. I could use with a few more victories on our next go." We turned back toward the Lodge, falling into an easy step beside each other. *A friend,* I thought happily. *It sounds nice.*

CHAPTER TWELVE

Eddie

I peered around the side of the hay wagon, then turned away, shielding my eyes as I scanned the field for Red's distinctive form. We had just finished loading our last wagon for the day, and I wanted to head home to wash and change before dinner.

We had been here a month, and June was getting ready to turn into July. After our rocky beginning, Red and I were quickly becoming true friends. The ache in my heart for home had lessened the closer we grew, and I felt peace settle over me as we focused on farm chores and sparring. My place in Barnsdale felt more comfortable everyday, and the sense that I could build something real here lurked around the corners of my mind.

Everyone I met was fascinating. I got to know the Reeds, and the workers that came over from the hamlet, and even started visiting with Marie in the evenings, discussing everything from the farm work we finished that day to what life was like in Pelerin. I still itched to be home and see my family frequently, but my worries lessened as I focused on the tasks we needed to get through the day.

Nights were more interesting. The evening after we decided to be friends, Red had come to my roo, as I was getting in to bed. She had stood in the doorway, shifting from one foot to the other.

"I didn't have time to put a soundproofing spell up today, and I'm too tired now. It's not something I'm skilled at."

I stared at her, comprehension slowly dawning on me. She looked as if she wanted to say something more, but nothing else escaped her lips. The tired wheels of my brain churned to life, seeking a way to solve her problem without forcing her to sacrifice her pride after our tentative truce. I glanced back at my relatively comfortable bed, wondering if I was making a mistake.

"Well, you didn't have the nightmares while we were... you know. Sleeping together. *Next* to each other, I mean." I cleared my throat awkwardly. "I saw some bed pallets out in the loft area. We could sleep there tonight. That way I could wake you up if you start having trouble."

Relief filled her eyes and she nodded once, then turned back toward her room. I gathered up my pillow and all the blankets I could find, trudging out to the darkened loft area with them. The bed in my room was a straw and wool filled mattress. A bed fit for a king in comparison to the wooden sleeping pallets lining one wall of the loft. *I wonder if that's what the kitchen servants sleep on at Croiseux?* I knew some of the lower orders of servants shared large sleeping areas like this loft, but I had never thought to look into their arrangements. *Well, you'll get firsthand experience now.*

Red was already there, laying thick wool blankets over the two pallets closest to the outer wall. After a few quiet communications on who would sleep where, we settled in for the night. The thick blankets Red had found made for a more comfortable bed than I had anticipated, and we both fell asleep quickly.

She didn't have any nightmares that night.

Nor did she on any night afterward, as we continued sleeping out in the loft. Each morning, we woke to the sound of Mrs. Reed starting breakfast below. Donning our work clothes, we started the day with a sparring match, sometimes going at it with aggressive abandon, other days methodically teaching each other the fundamentals of our own country's styles of combat.

Afterward, we would devour an enormous breakfast before starting our portion of the farm work. Red took little interest in the running of the estate, but given my background with Croiseux, every job fascinated me.

In the evening we dined with Lady Marie. She never looked at, nor acknowledged her daughter. Red bore with it stoically; more so than I did at times. Conversation never flowed easily, especially since anything I had to say usually involved Red in some way.

After dinner, Red would retire to her room and I would sit with Marie and the Reeds around the fire in the parlor. One day I started talking to Marie about Red. Not by name, or with any design in mind, just to ruminate about the strange woman I was beginning to know. To my surprise, Marie asked me how my friend was doing every evening after that. I never tried to make Marie understand exactly who we were discussing, knowing that she wouldn't be able to bear it. But it pleased me to think that she could discuss her daughter that way. *And maybe someday she'll be able to break through whatever wall is holding her back.*

I was jolted back to reality as the wagon next to me rumbled forward. *I'm getting lost in my thoughts.* I turned to scan the field once more. Red was no where in sight. John Reed was driving the wagon along the cartpath toward the main barn. John Jr was at the other end of the field, walking toward the tree line to a path that led to the hamlet. *Maybe she already headed home?*

"Home," I muttered to myself, trying out the word as I pulled a handkerchief out and wiped the sweat from my brow. Somehow in the last month or so, Barnsdale had begun to feel a little like home.

"What about home?" Red's voice sounded from behind me. She emerged from the trees cradling her upside down hat. Blackberries peeked over the brim, threatening to tumble out at every step. She grinned at my raised eyebrows.

"I remembered there used to be a blackberry patch right around here so I went to see if it was still there." She popped a ripe berry into her mouth before offering one to me. I took it and savored the sweet sun ripened juiciness that burst over my tongue. Red's smile grew as I snatched a handful of blackberries from her hat. "Mrs. Reed might make blackberry cobbler if we ask nicely," she said conspiratorially.

"Then let's ask nicely," I urged around a mouthful of fruit. "Should we pick more?"

"No, I got most of the ripe ones. The others will be ripe in a day or two. But what were you saying about home? Missing it?"

I shrugged, falling into step next to her and accepting proffered blackberries every now and again. "Yes and no. I miss my family, and the old familiar places. But as strange as it is, this place feels like home too. Not the same as Croiseux, but the people here are good, and the land could be good, if it was tended properly."

"Don't let John Reed catch you saying that," Red chided with a laugh.

"He's the one that said it to me!" I protested. "He thinks your brother should send more staff down. If you ask me they probably don't need much more help to make a success of things... but anyway. It caught me off guard when I was looking over the hay harvest: all these cares and concerns and good people, it just feels like home."

Red chewed on her blackberries thoughtfully, jerking her hat away when I reached for more. "If this place feels like home, I think I've been doing a poor job as your jailor," she said, raising her eyebrows at me.

I laughed. "You've been working me to the bone on your farm and learning all the Pelerine fighting techniques I know. I think you've been getting your money's worth out of me. If our countries ever go to war, not only will I have set you up with increased food supplies, but you'll know all our fighting strategies. You should get a medal!"

Red let out a snort of laughter, and I grinned even wider. It was nice to see her like this, open and free. These moments were still rare, though she let me behind her masks more often, especially after a long day of working together. Strange though the circumstances were that brought me here, a part of me was glad. Red was worth knowing. I doubted I would ever meet another person like her in my entire life.

"Well, when you're back to your real home, you can think back with pride over the resistance you put up. After all, you're getting to spend an entire summer with the famous Red Rider, and although I'll deny it if you ever tell, you're starting to beat me in sparring matches half the time. Not many can say that!"

My smile dimmed a little at her mention of my real home. Croiseux and it's concerns seemed far way at the moment. A tendril of guilt snaked through my heart. I should be overseeing the hay harvest there, making sure things ran smoothly, not working myself to the bone for Barnsdale Lodge.

And what about my men? I still didn't know who had made it through the battle, and whether the ones who needed work had been given positions at Croiseux like I planned. My father would take care of anyone who needed it, but many of the men would have too much pride to ask.

"I feel free here because all my burdens are at Croiseux," I said suddenly, plummeting our teasing mood into seriousness. "This place is interesting, and new. I can work on problems and suggest solutions all while knowing that I won't have to deal with the fallout if my suggestions don't work. It's easy to help grow and heal a place when you know you don' have to live with the consequences."

Red reached out and snagged my hand, giving it a little squeeze. I smiled at her friendly touch. She didn't seem to like touching people very much, so I knew it to be a mark of our deepening friendship. She held on for another beat as we walked, then dropped it and flicked the side of my head.

"What was that for?!" I demanded, rubbing my temple.

She crooked a smile at me and raised an eyebrow. "Maybe you feel at home here because you actually *like* living with heathen mages like us. Maybe *you're* a mage and you never knew it!"

I rolled my eyes and she laughed, stepping ahead of me

through the gate to the courtyard.

Her accusation about not minding mages anymore stuck in my mind. *I guess I really don't mind it anymore. How could that be?* I slipped my hand into my pocked where I kept my lucky charm. Rubbing the frayed blue silk, I considered this revelation. *Friendship with Red is making it too easy to accept their ways. I need to remember I don't belong here.* A little portion of my heart rebelled at the thought and I passed into the kitchen behind Red with a string of tension across my shoulders that wasn't there before.

* * *

Buttery goodness filled my mouth as I finished the last of the shortbread scone Mrs. Reed had given me at lunch. Rain was keeping us inside for the day, so we ate our lunch in the kitchen for a change. Usually we ate wherever we happened to be working when the sun reached it's zenith. Today we were enveloped in the warm draughts of Mrs. Reed's kitchen, steaming mugs of tea and a few scones fresh from the oven to launch us into the afternoon.

The housekeeper stood dithering at the end of the kitchen table, hesitating to speak whatever request that seemed to weigh on her mind. "Lady Red, may I make a request of you and Captain Marchand?" Red looked up from the letter she was reading, and nodded.

"I do hate to ask it of you because I know you don't… well, and it's not proper to be asking the upstairs folk. Though Lady knows we're all mixed around at the Lodge. Upstairs folk living above the kitchen, downstairs folk living in the family rooms, heaven knows what my mother would say."

Red tapped the table with the corner of her letter impatiently and shot me a covert look before responding. "Mrs. Reed, I'm well aware of your thoughts on the running of the Lodge. If you're going to ask us to rearrange the room assignments again, please don't bother."

"No, no milady, nothing like that. It's only, I need a cask of wine and ale moved up from the cellar. I've been puttin' it off since you've all been busy with some of John Jr's projects. It's no matter for me to be going down to get the wine for dinner, but now the ale's gone too, and my bones won't take me going up and down those stairs ten times a day for everyone. Mr. John Reed usually does it with our John Jr., but you know he threw his back out last week, and our son is stuck at home today what with all this rain. I know it's an imposition…"

I crunched the last bite of my scone slowly, observing the two ladies in front of me with confusion. Mrs. Reed always showed deference to those of higher rank, although she treated Red and myself with a little motherly kindness as well since we were in her kitchen so often. But the nervous chattering was out of character for her. Red had frozen in the act of putting her folded letter in her pocket. As the caretaker continued rambling, Red moved again, stiffly, holding up her hands to halt the flow of words.

"That's enough. Eddie and I will get the casks. You should have asked us when the wine ran out."

"Oh, but milady - "

Red interrupted again as she stood up from the table. "The running of the house is more important than any… consideration… you may want to give me. You keep them in the treasury storage room, correct?"

"No, Lady Red. I'm so sorry, but we moved them down to the apothecary storage area. John Jr. Said that the treasury storage was much better for cheesemaking, since they had started with the new cows, so we moved the ale and wine to the lower level."

Red nodded once, her face a shade paler than usual, then stalked out of the kitchen with jerky movements.

"Well go with her, Captain!" Mrs. Reed admonished me, flapping her hands at me and casting a distressed look after Red.

I brushed my hands off on my trousers as I jogged after Red, catching up to her as she stood before the main entrance to the old tower. I hadn't yet been inside the old monstrosity, which seemed to be in disuse and disrepair. When I had asked Mr. Reed about it, he had only grunted and said there wasn't money enough to get rid of the ghosts yet. When I had probed further into that enigmatic statement, he had changed the topic.

Before I could speak, Red pulled open the iron wicket gate in the ancient tower door. It continued to creak open wider as she stepped through to the gloomy interior. She muttered a spell under her breath, igniting a few torches on the corridor walls. I followed, eying the raised rusty portcullis dangling above the old gateway. Red's breathing echoed strangely in the ancient entrance hall and I drew closer, peering around in curiosity. Shadows flickered and danced across each dusty surface, the burnt orange flames illuminating our way forward while revealing little of the rest of the tower.

"It's cold in here," I commented to Red's back as we made our way to a stone spiral staircase in the middle of the entrance hall. She ignored me, so I tried a different tack. "Why isn't it used anymore?"

Red's back remained tense and I frowned at it. She gave no indication that she had even heard me. I followed her through the archway of the spiral staircase, brushing at a few stray cobwebs as she murmured another illumination spell. More rust-flamed torches sprang to life, providing only enough light to prevent us from tripping as we went down the stairs.

Our footfalls scratched on the stone steps, filling the heavy silence. Dirt and dust made each step slightly treacherous as our shoes slid on the gritty surface. The tower smelled dank and musty. *Has anyone even come in to clean in the last year?* At the bottom of the first landing we stopped. Heavy iron latticework blocked our way and a heavy padlock dangled underneath the latch. Red stared at it.

"So, do you know the magic words?" I quipped, gesturing toward the lock. Red turned her head my way slightly, her eyes still focused on the lock. "The magic words?" Her tone was wooden and dull. I frowned.

"You know, like from fairytales? Just say the magic words and the door opens... nevermind. I'm assuming you have a key then."

"I forgot the key," she replied. Eyes still on the lock, hands at her side.

"Okay. So, do you want me to run up and get it? Would Mrs. Reed have it?"

"Yes. Yes, she would have it." I made a face at her odd behavior, then turned to trudge up the stairs again.

In the kitchen, Mrs. Reed looked at me with eyes raised as I came back through the door.

"We forgot the key apparently. She said you'd have it."

"Oh Lady Above. Never say you left her down there on her own!" Mrs. Reed pulled out a ring of keys hooked on a belt at her waist. She took the entire ring off it's buckle and handed it to me. "Here Captain, it's these two big ones," she said, indicating two dark iron keys next to each other. You'll need the second one for the bottom landing. We don't keep the wine room locked usually. Now get back down there!" She put her hands to her cheeks as I backed away, worry creasing her brow.

Rain pounded heavier than ever as I walked back across the cloistered breezeway connecting the kitchen to the main Lodge. The humid warmth of heavy summer air billowed across my skin as an errant breeze picked up, leaving a chill in it's wake. The chill only intensified as I passed through to the shadowy tower.

Burning torches led my way down again, the darkness at their edges full of menace. A shudder passed through my body as I descended the stairs, and I rolled my eyes at the horrors crowding the edges of my mind. Something about this place seemed to call to my darkest memories. Pictures of Beasts I had killed at the war flashed through my mind, the numb despair at brothers in arms that had been lost through the years pulling at my heart. I shook my head, concentrating on the stairs between me and Red.

I froze with one foot suspended toward the next stair as I came into view of the landing. Red had turned at my approach. Every line of her body was tense, but it was her expression that arrested my progress. She looked half feral, like a kicked dog, her lips curled into a snarl and her eyes wild. She hadn't transformed, like she did that day in the woods, but looked just as wild. Her eyes pinned me down, then blinked once, twice, and finally relaxed.

She turned back toward the ironwork gate, shrugging her shoulders to dissipate the tension there, and pointed. "Open it. It should be the large key with the diamond design."

I stepped down the remaining stars slowly, my eyes glued to her as she stepped out of my way. She wouldn't look at me, staring at the gate instead and keeping carefully out of my way. I turned toward the door, finding the key she had mentioned, and inserted it into the lock.

The gate opened with a noisy protest and she ghosted through behind me as I stopped to tug the key from the lock. We descended another flight of winding stairs. The darkness grew thicker with each step. Although the walls and floor were dry, the air felt slimy and cloying. I pulled the other iron key forward, opened the next gate and we stepped forward into a murky stone passage.

Red's whisper was barely audible as she murmured the illumination spell this time, her words swallowed up by darkness and gray stone. The passage held only two torches, one at each end, and they spluttered halfheartedly, as if reluctant to lend aid to any visitors. Red took a deep breath and exhaled quietly, a little puff of white streaming out of her mouth as she did. I realized my hands were cold and rubbed them together a few times for warmth.

"So, where are the wine and ale stored? Let's just get this job done and move on to a warmer task."

She started a little, flashing a glance in my direction as my words fell flat in the still, dead air. Instead of replying, she started forward, hands balled at her sides as she stalked to the very end of the corridor. The wall to our right held a series of closely set doors, all of them open to yawning darkness within. I shuddered again, and hurried behind Red.

What's with this place? And me? There's can't be anything scarier than a rat down here.

Red stopped at the last door on the lefthand side of the hallway, her gaze never straying to either side. Her hand shook slightly as she opened the latch, but she stepped through briskly, turning on the lights and looking around. I followed on her heels and together we located the wine and ale casks.

"Let's do the wine first. I hope Mrs. Reed drew enough for dinner over the next few nights already. Your mother will spit it out all over the roast tonight if we we serve unsettled wine," I joked.

Red flinched again at the sound of my voice. Irritation warred with concern at her jumpiness. "What's going on, Red? This place is creepy, I'll give you that, but it's just a cellar. Unless there's something down here?" A sense of dread crept up on me as I imagined something terrible enough to make Red nervous lurking in one of the open cells on the other side of the hall.

Her only response was to get into position on one side of the wine cask. I sighed and did the same, muttering instructions as we lifted the cask and started down the hallway. As we reached the stairs, I maneuvered so that I was the one going up backwards. Red was strong enough to take the weight of the cask, and was so distracted that I didn't want her slipping on the dark, gritty steps.

We were almost at the next landing when I missed a step, my foot sliding out from under me. I grunted, shifting to try and maintain my balance and keep the cask from hitting the ground. Red hadn't noticed my misstep in time and continued to move forward, bumping the cask into my chest, and shoving me backward into the stairwell. The cask ricocheted off of me and back toward Red.

"No - sorry!" I exclaimed as the barrel slipped out of my hands, dropping toward the steps between my legs. Red stooped to try and catch it, crouching down slightly and leaning forward to take the weight, but to no avail. The cask crashed loudly against the stone, splitting open one side and sending a gush of dark red wine flooding down the steps and all over Red's arms and legs.

I groaned, pushing the ruined barrel to the side and kicking a piece of the lid out of the way. "Are you all right?"

Red's head was bent as she braced herself against the steps, seemingly staring at her wine soaked forearms, the red drink staining her tunic.

"I'm so sorry. I should have been more careful. My foot slipped on the stair," I explained, checking to make sure the remains of the cask had settled securely before maneuvering the few steps that separated us.

I took out two handkerchiefs that I had on me, the last two I had from Pelerin, and reached forward to sop up some of the mess on her arms.

Her movements were a blur. I dropped my handkerchiefs as her arms snapped up to my throat. Feral, maddened eyes stared out from behind a curtain of black hair that had slipped from her bun. Her work roughened hands scratched at my throat and face, searching for my neck even as I grappled to keep them away, just as we had done in our sparring matches. Her breaths came in ragged gasps, hot blasts of air over my face, eyes tinged red with madness.

"Red," I gasped, desperately trying to keep her from strangling me even as I struggled to keep us both from overbalancing on the slippery stairs. "Red! It's me. It's just me!"

Her eyes latched on to mine and she froze, staring like a lost soul.

"Red, what is going on? What just happened?!"

Angry hate drained out of her gaze to be replaced with a tired horror, the tinge of red encircling her irises fading into their usual storm cloud gray.

Her eyes dropped to her hands and her breathing sped up as she stared at the red stains. I tightened my grip, pushing her arms down out of sight before sliding my hands up to her shoulders. My grip wasn't harsh, just enough pressure to anchor her in front of me, forcing her to look at me instead of her arms.

"Red, it's okay. We're okay. Whatever is going on in your head, is not happening for real right now. It's just me here with you. I'm not a threat." Her eyes cleared a little more with every word I spoke, but her muscles were still hard under my hands. She gripped my biceps like she was dangling off a cliff and I was the only anchor to stable ground.

I breathed in through my nose and out through my mouth, trying to guide her as she sought to relax her own heaving chest. After several minutes her fingers loosened slightly on my arms. She was still as stiff as a board, so I kept one hand wrapped around one of her arms and gently pulled her up the gloomy staircase. She walked with jerky motions but was compliant, her jaw set so hard she might be cracking teeth.

I kept a steady pace as we left the tower, not stopping until we made it to the dismal rain filtered light of the veranda. She looked even worse in the gloomy light, skin taught, posture defensive, eyes only slightly this side of sanity. The cord she used to tie her hair up had fallen out completely, the inky black locks corkscrewed around her face in a shaggy mane.

"What happened back there? Can you talk about it?" I asked, gently but firmly. She shook her head. I watched her for a second, my mind racing.

"You need a minute to pull yourself together. That's fine. But once you feel calm, we need to talk."

She jerked a nod. "Let me be alone. I need to be alone."

I hesitated, then squeezed her arm one more time and continued down the veranda to the kitchen. I would need Mrs. Reed's help cleaning up the mess and we would have to figure out what to do about the other casks. I glanced back at Red just before I stepped through the door. She was where I left her, staring at her red stained hands.

CHAPTER THIRTEEN

Red

As soon as I heard the door to the kitchen close I pushed off into a sprint. *Where can I go that's safe? Where?*
I stumbled down the few steps off the veranda and skidded to a stop. My eyes scanned the courtyard, nerves jangling harshly as I considered my options. *Not the storehouse.* My eyes darted toward the grassy spot we used for sparring. *No shelter there from the rain. Besides, that's a place for fighting. You're weak right now. Hide.*

The fields? Being far away from that cursed tower sounded good right now, but there would still be no shelter, and I would be exposed. To what, I didn't know, but the need to find even a moderately defensible position was overwhelming.

My eyes snagged on the wooden palisade surrounding my mother's flower garden. The heads of giant sunflowers peeked over the top, bowed beneath the rain. I took a few faltering steps toward it, stumbling into a run by the time I reached the gate. I took a quick glance around to make sure I hadn't been seen. The courtyard was empty. *Safe.* Passing through, I latched it carefully behind me, stumbling over uneven stones on the narrow pathway. The leaves of the sunflowers trailed sympathetic touches along my arms as I pushed my way through; leaving cold, wet smears across my skin.

Winding my way through the sunflowers, I followed the narrow stone pathway to the back corner of the garden. Just beyond a large tangle of hydrangea bushes sat a well, mostly obscured by the flowering shrubs and sheltered by a tall maple. It was as good a spot as any, hidden from view where the wooden palisade met the thick stone outer wall. Trembling, I collapsed with head in hands, leaning my back against the well.

It was covered by a small roof, which provided some protection against the rain. Frequent gusts blew curtains of water across me, and I held my hands out, watching as the sky's tears washed rivulets of red off my hands. I closed my eyes, enjoying the feel of cool water on my face, flicking them open anytime a flash of memory cut across my vision: of all the other times my hands had been soaked red in the tower, and the reasons why.

Slowly, the intrusive memories faded, coming less frequently and less vividly as the wine washed off my shirt and hands. Tendrils of hair were being steadily plastered against the sides of my face as the rain soaked into them, trickling down my neck. I tipped my head back, placing the palms of my hands down flat against the stone slab beneath me. It was warm and rough. Inhaling, I caught the scent of rich earth, wet stone, zinging rain, and the green scent of life that plants give off. I breathed it in greedily at first, then slower, the image of Eddie standing in front of me in the tower, firmly staring into my eyes, anchoring me to the present with deep breaths. I furrowed my brow. I didn't want to see him right now. I didn't want to see anyone.

I flicked open my eyes only to find the same man standing in front of me in reality. I startled slightly, my hands coming up reflexively, but without much conviction. I was too tired, and my heart knew I was safe, even if my mind was still unconvinced. Elne, the coward, was still nowhere to be found, leaving me to fend off ghosts for myself. The lack of her presence in the tower was an ache I was used to.

Eddie crouched in front of me, rain hitting his face and sliding to drip off his nose and chin. "May I?" He motioned to a spot next to me on the ground.

I nodded and he leaned forward on one hand, spinning slightly to sit by my side, his back to the well, his legs stretched out into the curtain of rain.

"Mrs. Reed told me about the the cellar. She said..." he swallowed hard. I could see his adam's apple bob from the corner of my sight, but I kept my eyes trained on the dirt in front of me.

"She said you had been tortured down there when you were a girl. Why - why didn't you say something?"

I licked my lips, my mouth too dry to respond. When I didn't answer him he continued, his tone still calm but holding a slight bewilderment to it.

"We're friends, aren't we Red? I know we haven't been friends for long, but we've been forthright with each other. You had a rough upbringing, more than most in a country that seems full of tough people. I'm not saying you should have talked to me about all that by now, but you could have at least given me a warning before we went into the tower today. Then I could have helped you, or at least monitored whether you could handle it or not. I could have hauled you upstairs before you snapped! Why would you hide that from me?!"

The accusation of weakness stung, and my temper go the best of me. I brought my knees up to my chest, crossing my arms around them and hunching over. "Why *wouldn't* I hide that from you? I'd hide it all from myself if I could. If you knew what it was like..." I gave a harsh laugh. "You couldn't even fathom it. Your stories of growing up in Pelerin, the golden boy, beloved by all. You're not capable of understanding where I come from."

He shifted toward me, close enough that I could feel the warmth rolling off his shoulder where it almost touched mine. It sent a tendril of unwelcome comfort across my skin and I shuddered.

"You shouldn't judge my understanding before you give it a try. I doubt I could fully know your pain. As you said, I had a charmed childhood. But maybe I could understand it if you let me in. You're carrying so much." His voice broke off in anguish and he stopped for a minute, turning toward me. "I don't think there's a way for me to carry any of it for you. But you don't have to do it alone. I'll carry my own burdens next to you, if you'll let me."

The heat off of his body continued to roll across my skin, and I shrugged the shoulder closest to him, unconsciously trying to shake it off. I didn't want his care. I knew him well enough by now to know that he would ground me completely if I let him. As tempting as that sounded, the glow of calm reassurance and steady friendship, there was a wild part of me that resisted the idea. It lashed out before I could close my mouth.

"Your own burdens? And what are those, exactly? Working during your house arrest in Sherwood, and sighing all over the estate over Princess Belle?" He stiffened beside me, turning a frown in my direction. The hint of disapproval stroked the flame of irritation in me, giving my flailing emotions something to focus on. "What? I've heard you at it every day since we've been here. If I'm hiding from my past, then you're stuck in yours."

A thread of offended anger rumbled through his voice as he spoke, "That's different and you know it. I would certainly never compare what I felt losing Belle to what you've been through, so don't bother. And when it comes to my feelings about my house arrest... well, those don't matter right now. It's not fair to try and rank our suffering. It's not a competition. And I didn't say I was suffering anyway." I rolled my eyes and hugged my knees tighter. His steady gaze stayed on me and I chafed under it, fidgeting and wishing I was anywhere else. Finally he reached out, putting a hand on my shoulder and, when I didn't pull away, sliding it around my back and pulling up next to me.

"Won't you talk to me?"

I shook my head.

He sighed. "Then let's at least get you warmed up. It might be summer but you're soaked through, and your skin feels like ice. It's nearly dinnertime anyway."

I looked up at sky and was startled to find that the gray had darkened considerably, the rain having eased up to a light mist.

I met his eyes finally, just for a second, and nodded. He stood up, held out a hand and pulled me up too. I snatched my hand back and folded my arms tight over my chest. As we started toward the lodge, hunched tight against the tremors wracking my body. He followed behind, keeping a warm hand on my shoulder, the touch both welcome and irritating. The windows of the kitchen glowed yellow and we passed through the gathering fog of the courtyard toward their light.

❊ ❊ ❊

Eddie was lounging in the loft area when I came out from my hot bath, having changed into a clean set of clothes. He led the way down the stairs and into the cozy, almost too warm, kitchen. The heat of my bath on top of the warm kitchen soothed my still fluttering nerves. Mrs. Reed was finishing the washing up, having already dined with my mother in our stead. She fussed around, setting a bowl of soup and fresh bread on the table in front of me, bringing over a cup of hot tea and a shawl to put around my shoulders. I accepted her ministrations stiffly, eating and drinking mechanically under Eddie's watchful eye, irritated at Mrs. Reed's mothering and Eddie's relentless concern. *I haven't gotten to where I am now by letting people in. It feels foreign, and dangerous.*

Once I had finished, and refused repeated offers of sweets, Mrs. Reed followed the two of us upstairs with a hot pan, murmuring to Eddie as we all trouped up together.

"Warmth is good for shock you know, even if she's a little too warm. She'll need the hot pan. You bring it down when it goes cold. But I really think she shouldn't be alone tonight. I hate to suggest it because I should be upstairs in case Lady Marie needs me, she often does at night, but I can't in good conscience let Lady Red go without…" she stuttered to a stop as she caught sight of our sleeping pallets. We made our respective beds every day, but they were still slightly rumpled and had a collection of books and handkerchiefs and other items next to them that would make it obvious they were in use.

Mrs. Reed turned accusing eyes on Eddie.

"It's not what you think!" he protested, then gave her a stern look. "You know me well enough by now not to doubt my honor. And Lady Red is certainly above reproach. But don't ask, and don't mention it to anyone else." He used his most commanding tone, and while she pursed her lips in disapproval, she nodded her head in agreement. The ridiculousness of the situation pulled a laugh from me. I turned my head away when Eddie glanced over.

Mrs. Reed deposited the hot pan, retreating back downstairs and bustling around the kitchen with the washing up while Eddie and I prepared for bed. She left, turning the lights off as she went, just as I folded myself under my blankets. Instead of getting into his, Eddie walked around the other side of his pallet, bent down, braced his hands against the side and pushed. The wooden support beams scraped across the plain wooden floor as he pushed it across the foot of space between our beds until it was flush with mine.

A flicker of amusement went through me. "I thought you told Mrs. Reed we were both above reproach."

He cast me a repressive look. "Don't start." The corner of his mouth quirked up. "Besides, didn't you recommend I sneak up on you in your sleep to be released from our binding spell? Now I'll be able to wake up and smite you at any moment if the fancy takes me."

I snorted. "What, by rolling over and crushing me?"

"If needs must," he responded, peeling back his covers and sliding under. I snuggled deeper into mine, laying on my back and staring at the ceiling.

"Tell me about it," he urged after a minute, his tone gentle but with a hint command in it.

To my surprise, I found myself doing just that. "My father took up arms with the loyalists when Prince John usurped Marian's crown. He died in battle when I was eleven, fighting John's forces." I paused. "Did you know John was my uncle?"

Eddie voiced quiet surprise.

"Yes, he was my mother's younger half brother. They shared a mother, Eleanor, who was such a strong woman, and still alive then. One day, maybe a year after my father had died, we received word that she was coming to visit us." I swallowed, that last day of freedom flashing through my mind as I quickly pushed it away. I felt Elne's confused curiosity surface, tinged with shame.

You should feel shame, I told her. *You left me alone there. Again.* Elne whined and retreated again. I rolled my eyes at the ceiling.

"We thought Grandmother was coming to announce clemency for myself and my mother, Robin having already been declared an outlaw. Instead, John came, dragging Marian as well. He had decided we were dangerous, connected as we are to Asileboix. To silence us, he had me entered into the military early, no doubt hoping I would be killed in my first battle."

Eddie stirred next to me, turning on his side to face me. "How could that be? What commander would take you at that age?"

I pressed my lips together. "I didn't go into a unit right away. John had brought an old crony of his to prepare me. Those preparations mostly consisted of torturing me until I passed out, trying to force my companion to the surface. I had only made contact with her a few months before. Elne was just a pup, so she hid, far away from the pain and hurt."

I paused, drawing in a long breath and releasing it. "It was only natural. I don't blame her. Although I did for a time. I was only a child myself after all."

Eddie's hand searched through the covers, finding mine and giving a steadying squeeze. "Tell me what happened next, he commanded, keeping a gentle grip on my cold hand.

I obeyed. "The torture went on for months. John stayed, using Barnsdale as his headquarters to secure the south. He forced my mother to listen to what happened to me. That's when she... she stopped acknowledging me. I think it was easier to just pretend she didn't have a daughter than to sit for a whole year and listen while her daughter was pushed beyond endurance." Eddies hand tightened on mine as he drew in a breath.

"Finally, Elne came back, and we transformed fully, just as John suspected I might be capable of. A full transformation like we're capable of is rare and is usually conscripted into the military. The next day, he let healers attend to me. A few days after that I was packed off to a forest guard unit, with just the clothes on my back. It was a hard winter. I learned to fight, and hold my own. I wasn't allowed to be a squire, as is usual for youths entering the service. John specifically instructed that I was to be absorbed into a unit and sent into battle immediately. I think he couldn't decide whether he wanted to push the potential I had displayed by shifting early, or whether he just wanted me to die. Either way, I survived. Then I thrived. I rose through the ranks quickly, becoming one of the best soldiers in our unit.

By that time the resistance had started to coalesce: Robin's Merry Men. John was scared that Robin might reach out to me, or that people would rally to me because I was his sister, so he had me transferred to a border unit. I know he wanted me to die then, because my unit commander told me. She was a strange person. Spent too much time in the wasteland, I think. She followed John's instructions, sending me out on the most dangerous missions, putting me in situations that were guaranteed to kill me. But we survived, Elne and me. I don't know how, really. My commander became proud of my skill. She started sending positive reports to John and he became convinced of my loyalty, so he recalled me to his personal guard. I spent time guarding him and his household, doing some of his dirty work. Then one day, Robin got to me."

I paused, tears threatening to well up as I thought of that day. The day my prison of a life had a door open beyond survival.

"And then?" Eddie urged, after I had been silent for a time. I drew in a long, shaky breath.

"Then, I saw a way to be free. I threw my lot in with Robin and

Marian, hunting John down so he could face justice."

"And did you ...?"

"Yes." I grinned, a wild satisfaction welling up within me. "I captured him alive and gave him over to Robin and Marian for trial. He was sentenced to death. I volunteered as his executioner."

Eddie was silent for a moment and I wondered if he was judging my obvious bloodthirst. Sometimes I wondered if it was wrong to delight so much in that execution, but I couldn't, and I couldn't see a reason to lie. Finally he spoke, his tone somber.

"So he met with justice. More than he deserved from the sound of it."

I turned toward him, mildly surprised. "That's what Marian and I said. I had originally suggested assassination that day Robin and Marian got a hold of me, but Robin wouldn't hear of it. Marian agreed, but Robin was firm. Said the country needed to see justice done properly. And we needed to see who was on which side up to the end. I guess he was right, seeing how things worked out."

Eddie gave me a sad smile. "So The Red Rider. That name came from your part in the coup?"

I smirked, some of the heaviness of the day leaving me as the opportunity to tease him presented itself. "Partly. But I won't be telling you that story tonight."

He rolled his eyes. "Why am I not surprised?" He sobered, giving me a serious look. "Thank you for telling me all of that. For trusting me. I'm sorry all of that happened to you."

I shrugged. "It's over. Or at least it's supposed to be. Sometimes, like today, it all seems so real again." I hesitated, the words choking me but needing to be spoken. "Thank you for listening. And caring."

He squeezed my hand, then tugged his free, putting it up to my face and pressing his thumb to the center of my forehead. "Go to sleep. I'm right here, and I'll wake you if you have any nightmares. Tomorrow will be better."

Gleams of gold flashed through his pupils as he spoke, and his thumb felt warm on my forehead.

"I was right!" I mumbled sleepily, as I felt my body slide toward oblivion. *He's a mage.* I lost my train of thought as delicious rest took over.

CHAPTER FOURTEEN

Eddie

Weeks turned into months and time passed quickly at Barnsdale Lodge. My friendship with Red deepened with each passing day, built on the trust we had established that day in the tower. At times, our differences in personality aggravated us, which usually resulted in a longer and more aggressive than usual sparring bout. We were evenly matched now, each test fight a long, hard, claw toward victory for whoever won. They were one of my favorite times of the day.

My other favorite time, not counting the quiet moments of teamwork during chores, our muscles burning as our skin darkened in the sun, was just before bed. We still slept in the pallets next to each other in the loft. As the evenings got longer, we found ourselves going to bed earlier, laying in the dim light and talking - laughing, more often then not, over stories we told or funny things that happened that day.

Our friendship soothed over any aching place in my soul when I thought of Croiseux and my former homeland. I missed LeFeu more than ever, but Red had become just as familiar as LeFeu had always been, although in a different way.

In rare moments of solitude, I wondered at our friendship. Less than a year ago, I would have scorned someone like Red, thinking her unfeminine and dangerous. My idea of what a woman should be had been centered around Belle.

I haven't thought about Belle in ages. Letting her go was relatively easy on my heart compared with accepting the idea I would never be allowed in polite society in Pelerine... or possibly never see Pelerin again. Although I had devoted myself to Belle, she had never inspired much depth of emotion. *I spend more emotion trying to keep up with Red in a day than I ever did on Belle,* I thought with a chuckle.

The memory of Red accusing me of being stuck in the past flashed across my eyes. *Jealousy,* my thoughts whispered. I shoved them down. She hadn't been jealous, just angry and defensive. She wasn't flirtatious, like she was when we first met. I preferred this deep knowing of her to the surface level interactions of our first meetings.

But if I was honest, in the deepest dark, when all, including Red, were asleep and I was left with my truest thoughts; there was a part of me that missed the flirting. When she had been willing to dish it out to me, I had been disgusted, thinking that no proper woman would be so obvious.

Now I caught myself quietly flirting with her at times, almost unconsciously, a forlorn hope that she would respond in kind driving me. I never pushed the boundaries though, not wishing to ruin the closeness we had as friends. But I found a new restlessness rising up in me. When I first came to Barnsdale, I had itched to get away. Now I itched for a change, not in circumstances or location, but in my standing with Red. Just a bit of hope that we could grow even closer. *Maybe a relationship with Red is one of the fates the gypsy prince took from me. If so, I'll need to find that Prince and have a reckoning.*

When change finally did come, it was unsettling. We were sitting at the kitchen table after a meal, each absorbed in different tasks. Mrs. Reed brought in a letter from Robin before bustling back out to another part of the Lodge.

"Well this is something," Red said, setting the letter down and looking across the kitchen table at me. I raised my eyebrows at her.

"We've been recalled to Nottingham," she said bluntly.

"When?"

"Next month. For Yuletide."

"And what of..." I gestured to myself.

She shook her head. "He only writes that they're still in negotiations. But he thinks they'll have an answer by Winter Solstice." She hesitated, chewing on her lip. "We're invited to Asileboix for the holiday, and we'll learn your fate then."

I caught her eyes, and we shared a charged look. Our slow, quiet, interlude at Barnsdale was almost over, and I felt the coming separation seeping into the present. I wanted to cover the ache I felt with a laugh.

"Well," I said, standing up and dusting off my hands. "Seems like a waste of time now to kill you in your sleep. I suppose I'll just have to skip it. It'll be more efficient to just go along with orders."

She grinned. "That comment just shows your distinct lack of backbone and creativity. Shocking really, considering you're one of us."

"I'm *not* a mage," I told her, rolling my eyes. She had been trying to get me to practice magic for the last few months, claiming that I had natural talent for command.

"Saying that doesn't make it true, you know," she shot back, pushing off from her own chair and coming around to grab my chin. "Those pretty blue eyes aren't capable of deceit. And I saw magic there."

I jerked my chin out of her grip, catching her hand as it fell without thinking. Our joined hands hovered between us for a moment, while we stared at them. Our connection thrummed, reminding me of when she first laid the binding spell. My eyes flicked up and met hers, grey and intense. We both jerked away at the same time, turning to head back to our chores. After a few minutes of hard work, we relaxed back into our usual friendly banter. But I couldn't shake the buzz of our connection, nor the growing desire to explore where it would lead.

* * *

The glow of candlelight reflected off of Lady Marie's red cape. She often wore it when the nights got cold, though it was old and patched. I watched as her hands traced the embroidery along the edges of the cloth, stopping to pick at snarled pieces here and there.

It was our last night at Barnsdale. Red and I would leave in the morning, retracing the path that led us here. She had parted ways with us at dinner, kissing her mother's forehead as she headed towards our loft, her mother still unresponsive to her presence.

Will she ever see Red again? I often wondered what it would take for Lady Marie to confront the pain and horror of her failure to protect Red all those years ago. But it wasn't my knot to unpick. It was nice enough just to be able to talk to her about Red, in my roundabout way, hoping she understood somehow.

I cleared my throat, drawing Lady Marie's eyes in the direction of my feet. She rarely looked straight at a person, instead picking a point near them to focus on during conversation.

"I mentioned that I would be leaving tomorrow, and taking my friend with me," I told her.

She nodded. "Yes, Eddie. I wish you both safe travels," she hesitated a moment, eyes darting from one of my feet to the other, "and you must take care of each other. Your friend needs you. It's always good to take care of a friend."

"I'll take care of her, for as long as I have the opportunity. Don't worry. I'll do a better job than I did on our journey here, you can be sure." I chuckled, and Marie's perpetually worried face broke into a hesitant smile.

"We weren't great friends when we first came down here. Now…" I trailed off, mind wandering along the edges of mine and Red's relationship.

"You might be more than friends, is that it?" Lady Marie asked, gentle amusement threading her voice. My eyes snapped to hers, and she met my gaze briefly, a teasing sparkle glinting there before her eyes wandered away again.

I glanced around, checking to make sure the Reeds were still in conversation on the other side of the room, before leaning forward in my chair. "What makes you say that?" I couldn't disguise the eagerness in my voice and felt my face flush.

Lady Marie gave a quiet, rusty laugh. "The way you talk about her of course. It's changed. Your tone, your understanding of her: you admire her, that's plain to anyone." I leaned back, stunned.

She murmured to herself for a few minutes before directing her gaze back toward my feet and addressing me. "From what you've said, she needs someone to rely on. But she won't take to the idea easily. You need to decide if she's worth the effort to you before you start."

I began to protest but she held her hand up. She had never interrupted me before during our discussions. That she did so now meant she had something important to say.

"If you begin to pursue her, and then quit the field because it becomes difficult, you will do more damage to an already damaged person. You must be prepared to fight for her, even against herself sometimes, before you start. If you cannot do that, there's no shame in it. Just don't start something you can't finish." She cast a stern glance my way, holding my eyes for an elusive moment before dropping them to the carpet near my feet again with a small smile. "At least, it seems that way from what you've told me of her, dear Eddie."

"Yes, milady. I promise I'll be sure before I... before anything changes."

She nodded, a smile hovering around her mouth. "I've come to think of you as a son these last few months, Eddie. If you should return here with a bride, I should like to think of her like a daughter." Her smile wavered, her voice plaintive. "I've always wanted a daughter you know."

I gave her a gentle smile in return. "I know, Lady Marie, and thank you. As I've told you before, my fireside chats with you have made me feel at home. My mother's name is Marie, so it's not quite a stretch to view you as a second mother." A sudden whim took me, and I pulled out my old good luck charm, the faded blue ribbon and it's trinkets winking at me in the palm of my hand. I held it out to Marie, who took it with shaking hands.

"What's this?"

I shrugged. "My good luck charm. I've had it most of my life, and it saw me and my best friend through many a battle in Pelerin. Since I've been in Sherwood though, I feel as if I've outgrown it. I was wondering if you might like to have it. Silly, I know, but I'd like to think of it protecting you while we're gone.

Lady Marie's smile creased her face as she lay her head back against her wingback chair wearily. "Thank you my dear boy, I shall be happy to carry it with me. Let it put your mind at ease."

I stood, bowing over her proffered hand. "May the Lady keep you and guide you," I said, using the formal Sherwoodian farewell I had learned over my time here.

"And you, Captain Marchand. Until we meet again."

I bowed one more time, then bid farewell to the Reeds and headed toward the loft, possibilities flashing like lightening in my mind.

* * *

Our journey back to Nottingham was uneventful. The air was frosty, the days short. We spent as much daylight as we could walking, and set up camp quickly at night, huddled either around a campfire, or next to each other in the tent. When we weren't talking, our hiking gave me a good chance to search my own heart and mind regarding Red. She captivated me.

When we first met, her recklessness and the differences in our cultures had repulsed me. Now, gravity seemed to pull me closer to her every day. She was inevitable. Of all the fates the gypsy Prince burned to keep me alive, the only one I wanted was one that included her. *Could that be the pull between us? The tug on my heart?*

I wanted to fascinate her too; to win her heart and mind, to win the right to keep her safe. Not locked away, but to be allowed to watch her back on whatever insane adventure she went on next. To hold her hand while she healed. To push her forward when she needed a friend.

Her own feelings toward me seemed murky. Our trust in each other had become like bedrock. The spark of attraction that had always skittered between us was still there. But she had backed away from the domineering pursuit from our early days, and I didn't see that she had any desire to start it again. *Does she only view me as a friend? Could she be open to more?* I knew she thought me controlling and a little tight laced, forever teasing me about the handkerchiefs I kept on hand. If I wanted to win her heart, I would need to curb my own tendency to issue commands. These thoughts swirled as I followed her through the woods to whatever fate awaited me.

We entered the city of Nottingham late in the morning, just a few days before we were scheduled to leave for Asileboix. After stabling our horses, we stowed our belongings in our guest chambers, and were escorted to a meeting with Robin and Marian.

We entered Robin's study to find him seated at his desk, Marian ensconced in a nearby windowseat, her infant son asleep on her shoulder. Red went over to them directly, offering congratulations and peering at the sleeping lad as he drooled on his mother's fine dress. After a few minutes of greetings between the family members, Red motioned me forward and we took our seats across the desk from Robin.

"Thank you for coming to see me," Robin said, sitting back in his chair. "Red, your reports have been lacking of late, I have to admit, but since I wanted you to rest, I suppose I can't complain."

Red grinned and slouched in her chair, flicking a look over to Marian. "Here's my report: all is well. Eddie is a lamb. I'm rested. Can I get back to work?"

I swallowed a laugh, turning it into a slight cough and drawing Robin's eyes my way.

"And how did you find your house arrest, Captain Marchand?"

I straightened in my chair. "Perfectly adequate, Lord Robin. I trust I wasn't a burden to Captain Hood." It was Red's turn to snort. Robin raised an eyebrow at her.

"Nothing, brother dearest. It's just that prim and proper Eddie is back. I haven't seen him in some time so I forgot how ridiculous he could be."

I shot a glance at Red, pressing my lips together slightly. Her smile just widened. My eyes threatened to roll toward the ceiling but I resisted the urge. She was trying to get rise out of me in front of her brother for a laugh and to get under my skin. I didn't want to make it easy on her.

Robin went through a few instructions as to our travel arrangements for Asileboix, then dismissed us after handing Red a letter for Prince Andrus. Red hovered over her still sleeping nephew, Marian inviting her in quiet tones to a family dinner later in the evening. I cleared my throat as I stood up, drawing Lord Robin's attention once more.

"Sir, might I have a word with you in private?" I asked. Red shot me a curious stare, but swept out the door when Robin nodded.

Once the door was shut he motioned for me to proceed, and I swallowed heavily, my throat dry as the question of my fate loomed before me. "Thank you for seeing me. I am requesting permission to join the Sherwoodian military upon news of my sentencing from Pelerin, unless I am taken back for execution of course," I said, opting for bluntness rather than explaining the background for my request.

Robin shot a glance at Marian, then looked back at me. "You want to join our military forces?"

"Yes, sir. Specifically, I would like permission to join Captain Hood's unit."

Robin rubbed his temples and Marian rose from her seat to drift toward him. "Why?" he asked after a strained silence.

I took a moment to collect my thoughts, even though I had

prepared for this question when the idea first dawned on me. "I have come to feel at home since I've been in Sherwood. I've healed a little, both in body and spirit. I believe I've helped Captain Hood heal a little as well. I'd like to continue." I paused, but when Robin didn't respond, I couldn't help voicing some of my deeper feelings. "She's worth following. I didn't see it at first, but since I've come to know her, I've realized I'd follow her anywhere." I snapped my mouth closed before I revealed too much.

Marian's skirts swished at the corner of my vision as she edged toward Robin, bobbing gently to keep her son asleep. Robin looked up at me, his brow furrowed. "If I didn't know any better, I would think that all of this... your capture, your maneuvering to be placed under Red's charge for house arrest, the request to remain by her side... well it would be a perfect plan for a spy to execute if he wanted to destabilize Marian's throne with the only other viable candidate."

Anger flared up my spine at the affront to my honor. I pushed my temper aside, keeping my voice even as I responded. "I take that accusation personally, Lord Robin. I am not here to destabilize anyone's throne. Indeed when I first arrived, my only thought was to return home, to bide my time and find a way to hide the gypsy tattoos on my face so I could live freely in Pelerin again. If you want an accounting of how I changed from that to wanting to make this place my home, I don't know if I can give it because I don't know how it happened. But I can tell you this: I'm not a spy, and I only want to keep Red safe, wherever she goes. If you doubt me, I'll submit to any truth spell you like." I struggled to keep my tone calm, not wanting to endanger my request by making them think I was volatile.

"An excellent suggestion, don't you agree, my dear?" Marian's voice floated across the desk like a spring breeze, soft and lovely. I had forgotten her presence and looked at her in surprise. She smiled down at her husband, a secret conversation passing between their eyes. Finally, her smile widened and she turned toward me, extending a hand across the desk, the glow of magic pulsing there. Slowly, I reached out, until our palms met, and felt a surge of warmth pass across our hands, tracing through my veins up to my head and heart, making me feel a little dizzy.

"Are you a spy from Pelerin?" Robin's voice rang out, cutting across my vertigo. I felt a tingling in my blood as the question reverberated through the spell.

"No," I replied simply.

"Do you intend harm to Sherwood or any of it's citizens, including Marian and our children?"

"No. I would only hurt another citizen in self defense."

Robin pressed his lips together. "Do you truly wish to live in Sherwood the rest of your days?"

The rush of magic in my veins tingled, distilling my thoughts until the truth was left. "Perhaps. I'm not sure about all my days." Robin didn't seem reassured so I rushed to add, "but it's where I want to be for now, and for as far into the future as I can see. It just depends…"

"Upon what?"

"Red. If she wants me to stay." The answer bubbled out of my lips before I could prevent it's escape. I looked at Robin and Marian warily.

Robin's look of surprise plunged into something darker and he leaned forward on his desk. "Why would it depend on Red? If she doesn't want you in her unit we can assign you elsewhere. Your experience could be valuable if you can adjust to our ways."

My skin itched as I tried to distill a truthful answer without revealing more than I wanted. "If she doesn't want me here, I don't think I would want to stay. I would travel elsewhere I think."

Robin's eyes darkened even more and he pushed out of his seat, his voice smooth and deadly, "And what exactly is the nature of…"

Marian's hand broke away from mine, and the tingling buzz of the spell broke off. She laid a calming hand on Robin's forearm, drawing his attention.

"How reassuring to hear that Captain Marchand's intentions

are pure. Especially since we wouldn't normally submit an applicant for the military to such a spell. It sounds to me like the only thing left to do is wait for Red's decision, doesn't it Robin?"

Robin gave her a stormy glare, then turned his face toward me. "I will ask Red if she would be willing to take you on. And of course it all depends on the sentencing in Pelerin."

"Would you prefer to ask Red yourself?" Marian's soft voice inquired.

I nodded. "If that would be possible. I know my request is highly irregular."

Robin ground his teeth together, casting an exasperated look at his wife. "Fine."

Marian stifled a smile and looked back at me. "You had better go now, Captain Marchand, unless you have other business with us."

I bowed and beat a hasty retreat, eager to leave Robin's presence. The pair of them saw far too much for my liking.

Red caught me as I walked across the Great Hall toward our guest chambers.

"What was that about?"

"Just a few questions... for after my sentencing."

She looked at me skeptically then shrugged, leaning closer so she could whisper. "I'm feeling claustrophobic. Let's spar."

I laughed. "Now? Where?"

She nodded, still leaning close enough I could feel her breath on my ear. "There's a sparring gym near the kitchens. I can get us in to a private room. Follow me."

I laughed, falling into step next to her as we walked toward the rear entrance of the castle. "Scared someone will realize a wimpy Pelerine like me can put you on the ground in less than a minute?"

She shot a quelling look at me. "That was *one* time, and you haven't been able to do it since."

"I don't want to be predictable," I replied, using her criticism from our early sparring matches. She tipped her head back in laughter, and I drank in her joy contentedly.

CHAPTER FIFTEEN

Red

Eddie fell in behind me as we strode out of the stables at Asielboix Castle. After several days traveling in the cold from Sherwood Castle to Asileboix, I was happy to be off my horse and in a place well known for hospitality. Glancing over my shoulder, I reached out and snagged his sleeve, dragging him next to me.

"Come on, I told Belle you would use the spare room in my suite. Let's go clean up before dinner."

I showed him into the disused apartment suite, permanently reserved for me and my mother. The week or so Eddie and I would spend here would be the longest it had been occupied since I was a child. After putting away the few articles of clothing I had packed, and changing into a clean pair of breeches and tunic, I waited for Eddie in the sitting room.

Will my nightmares start again here? I wondered. Since Eddie and I had begun sleeping next to each other, they had all but disappeared. During the two nights we spent at Nottingham Castle, in separate rooms, they hadn't returned. While we traveled to Asileboix, our party had slept huddled together in a handful of tents. Each time, Eddie and I had managed to put our bedrolls next to each other, and as usual, the nightmares didn't surface. Our stay here would be longer, and I was curious to see if they returned after a few nights sleeping alone.

If I knew it just took a warm body next to mine at night to keep them at bay, maybe I would have gotten married already, I thought sarcastically. Marian had been hounding me about a political marriage for years, and Robin had hinted and wanting to see me settled as well. There had been offers, apparently, although not to my face. It appeared that I was too intimidating for any man to propose such folly directly. Instead they lobbied Robin or Marian for my hand.

None had interested me. None had known me very well. They had each wanted to marry The Red Rider, not the person underneath. *I suppose Eddie has a point though. I haven't let many people get to know the person underneath,* I mused.

Eddie's footsteps drew my attention, and I looked up in time to watch him close the door to his bedchamber before turning and walking toward me. He had changed from his riding clothes, wearing Pelerine style dress coat over his shirt and breeches. Overall, he looked much more like the stuffy Pelerine Captain I had met over six months ago now, instead of the hard working friend I had come to know. The only betrayal of the wilder, Sherwoodian Eddie was the twin tattoos snaking down from behind his ear and disappearing into his stiff collar. My eyes traced down his collarbone and over to his shoulder, where I knew his medallion tattoo sat. It felt wrong that the beautiful piece of art was covered by so many layers. It made me want to rip up his coat so he couldn't wear it again.

"Red?" Eddie asked, and I tore my eyes from his broad shoulders back to his face. He looked amused and I fought a flush, hoping he didn't think I had been ogling him. *Even if I had been doing just that.*

Silly of me really. He would be going home to Pelerin for better or worse in a few days. *It had better not be for worse or I'll start an international incident by kidnapping him. He would protest the whole time that it's his duty to go back and die, but I'm not going to give him a choice.*

"Did I do something?" Eddie asked, cutting into my thoughts

again. This time I did feel heat creeping up my neck.

"You're looking at me so angrily, like I knocked the haystack over again," he joked, referencing an incident from the summer.

I rolled my eyes, brushing off his question. "I'm still not recovered from that. You deserve many more angry looks than I've given you so far." I started for the exit, "Come on, I'm starved. We're having a family dinner with Andrus and Belle tonight. Mathilde and Clement might be there too."

He followed me out the door and we set out toward the Royal Tower side by side, our hands almost grazing as we swung them at our sides. I resisted the urge to flex my palm and release the charge building between us.

"I'm surprised I'm invited," Eddie said, his tone serious.

"You weren't," I replied cheerfully, "but I told Belle in my letter that you'd be dining with us, and I haven't had a refusal so I assume all is well."

Eddie shot me a repressive look. "Red! This is going to be awkward enough even if they *were* expecting me. If I show up unannounced they'll probably banish me straight away. Why *do* you enjoy putting me in situations like this?"

"You put yourself in this situation," I protested. "You're the one who attacked Andrus like an idiot. It will be for the best, you'll see. You'll both have to talk about it and then put it behind you, so you can eat your dinner. Like ripping a bandage off."

Eddie shook his head, his eyes trained ahead of us so I couldn't see his expression. I snagged his hand and pulled him to a stop just as we started up the stairs to the Royal Tower. He was a step above me, so I had to look up into his eyes for once.

"If it turns out to be a problem, we can just order a tray to our suite and I'll catch up with them later," I said, a hint of remorse tinging my confidence that things between three of the most important people in my world would work out smoothly.

Most important? I asked myself in surprise. Elne whuffled a snort in reaction to my thought. I realized with quiet wonder that Eddie's friendship *had* become very important to me. His capacity to accept and encourage me, while simultaneously pushing me to do better had been an anchor in the last months. *Why am I realizing this now, when he's about to leave?* I sighed internally, to Elne's continued annoyance. She had mostly been ignoring me the last few days, but she missed no opportunity to make her irritation toward Eddie known.

Eddie looked down to our joined hands and squeezed gently. "It will be fine. Belle is always magnanimous, and by all accounts Prince Andrus is too. You're right, it will be nice to have a chance to make amends. Besides, even if they're cold toward me, *I* at least have a basic grasp of manners, so I trust I'll conduct myself appropriately, unlike someone else I know." He grinned as I pulled my hand from his and started back up the stairs.

"You told me I need to stop wearing masks, my friend. Manners are just another mask the new Red is refusing to wear."

"A likely story," came his reply as he caught up to walk beside me. A moment later I heard a sigh and glanced over to catch an apprehensive look on his face. It suddenly hit me that this was the first time he was seeing Belle since the Battle of Asileboix, when he thought she had died. He hadn't mentioned her at all the last few months, but I knew he had spent most of his life in love with her. That didn't change easily. This meeting would be difficult for him, especially because he would be apologizing to the man who ripped Belle away from him.

I shrugged my shoulders discretely. *He's a bit of an idiot with this unrequited love for Belle thing, I'll give you that,* I told Elne. She snuffled in disdain. *But he's my friend, and I care for him. I'll try to make it easier for him if I can.* Elne turned her disdain toward me and I smiled inwardly.

We reached the top of the stairs and reached out to knock on the door to the first level of the Royal Tower. Andrus' voice rumbled for us to enter. As I glanced over at Eddie, I caught his uncomfortable expression. I reached out and tugged on his ear, grinning as he looked at me in consternation, then strode inside.

Andrus stood a few feet inside the door, looking expectantly toward us. I put my fist over my heart and strode up to him, catching his outstretched forearm in a tight grip of welcome.

Slapping his back, I peered around until my eyes caught sight of Princess Belle. Warm friendliness shot through my heart, ghosted by a sliver of jealousy that made me want to roll my eyes. *Yes she looks like she's a fae queen stepped out of a fairytale of old, but she's your friend and the love of Andrus' life. If she's the love of Eddie's life too, well I guess I can see why.*

Elne snorted in my head, and her desire to get outside the castle walls and run drifted across my mind. *We just got here,* I scolded. But her secondhand emotion remained, prickling tension across my shoulders. I took a few steps toward Belle and bowed slightly. She floated across the room with a wide smile and I stooped to exchange a kiss on each cheek.

"You really did bring him?" she demanded in a scolding whisper. The smile on her face belied her tone and I grinned, unrepentant.

"I know you all have had a bit of a spat, but Eddie's sorry now and I thought it best to get it all in the open and move on."

Belle pressed her lips together and raised her eyebrows. "A bit of a spat?! He *attacked* my husband! Not to mention wouldn't listen to a word I said while the Beasts were invading."

I cocked my head to the side and raised an eyebrow back. "Something tells me you may be more irritated by him not listening to you than his attack on Andrus."

Belle forgot her dignity so far as to put her hands on her hips. "First of all, Andrus' wellbeing is always my top concern, so I resent the implication you're making. Second of all, Andrus could obviously take him in a fight, so of *course* I was more irritated that he wasn't listening to me." I burst out laughing and she couldn't help joining in, stopping only to look over my shoulder, her expression inquisitive.

I turned to find Andrus and Eddie conversing quietly as they walked slowly toward us. Eddie's face was very serious, and a little pale. I realized he must have apologized to Andrus while I had been joking with Belle, and was now coming to do the same with the princess. I took a few steps back, allowing the three of them some space.

The smile fell off of Belle's face, and the haughty mask I had seen at times during the council after the Battle of Asileboix took it's place. She could be more intimidating than some of the fiercest warriors I knew. Not that she was threatening in a physical way. I knew for a fact she was terrible at combat and had only rudimentary self defense skills. But she could be as icy a winter's day, her words as sharp as the edge of a sword. She looked every inch the Asilean princess this evening, dressed in a simple, but luxurious, plum gown, with matching amethysts at her throat and in her upswept hair. My own breeches and tunic, while comfortable, seemed lacking in a way that hadn't a moment ago. She gave Eddie a cool look as the two men came to a stop in front of her, declining to offer her hand and looking at Andrus instead.

"Well?" She asked, her tone even.

He gave his wife a little smile. "Eddie has something to say, dear. He's already apologized to me, and I've forgiven him."

A look of mild exasperation passed across Belle's face. "You would. You're entirely too tenderhearted some times." Andrus rumbled an amused chuckle, and Belle turned back to Eddie, somehow looking down her nose at him even though he was several inches taller.

"Princess Rosebelle," Eddie began, after a formal bow, "I would like to extend my sincere apology for my actions last spring. At the time, I felt that I was acting appropriately on the information I had, and to a certain extend that's true." Belle's frosty demeanor turned positively frigid and my eyes flicked to Eddie's face to see how he was holding up. He still looked pale. There was an earnest light in his eyes, and my heart skipped a beat in sympathy as he continued. "I can also acknowledge that there was a large part of me that was operating out of prejudice and arrogance. I didn't believe you. I thought you needed saving, and that I should be the one to save you. I'm sorry for not listening, and for not trusting that you knew what you were doing. Will you forgive me?" My eyes flicked between Eddie and Belle. Their Pelerine birth was on full display in their interaction. Both stood stiff, Belle with disdain, Eddie with open remorse and shame. Andrus and I hovered on the perimeter, waiting to hear what Belle would say.

What would it be like to open yourself up to another, so vulnerably, knowing you may be, or probably will be, rejected or scorned? That's a type of bravery I've never considered worthwhile. I had always kept my heart to myself, but for the first time, it felt cowardly instead of smart.

"*If* you have truly seen the error of your ways, and have truly apologized and gained my husband's forgiveness, then I suppose I can forgive you as well," Belle said finally, extending her hand toward him. Eddie took it gratefully and bowed over it, and Belle gave him a small smile.

She looked up as Andrus stepped to her side and slipped an arm around her waist, and her smile lit up fully, drawing a similar response from the normally taciturn Andrus. It was almost painful to see their connection, and I stepped over to Eddie's side almost reflexively. I couldn't bear to look at his face and see his reaction to the two in front of us, but I could stand by him while he composed himself.

Andrus turned to look at us again, more relaxed and happy than I had seen him in a long time. "Well, I'm glad that's all in the past now. Especially because we have an announcement about our future. We're expecting the next Prince or Princess of Asileboix this spring."

My eyes snapped to Belle and her look of shy excitement confirmed everything. Stepping forward, I slapped Andrus on the shoulder once again and squeezed Belle's hand. "Congratulations, both of you. I don't know whether to congratulate the rest of us or not. Any child of the two of you is going to be a beastly terror!"

Andrus roared in laughter while Belle raised her eyebrows and shot a look at Eddie. I turned to see his expression, hoping he had had time to compose himself. He shook his head and shrugged his shoulders at Belle as if to apologize for me, then offered his own congratulations. *He's doing well at hiding his emotions,* I told

Elne. She remained firmly disinterested.

"Come on, let's eat," Andrus said, capturing Belle's hand in his own and drawing her away to the small dining table in the corner of the room.

Eddie's whisper tickled against my ear just as I made to follow, making me jump. "Mocking the sovereign's unborn child Red? Perhaps I *should* help you with a basic grasp of manners," he said, offering me a sly grin before starting forward. I gaped after him, torn between laughter and bemusement. *He really is hiding his emotions well.*

Dinner was a comfortable affair after a few minutes of awkwardness when we sat down. Mathilde and Clement had been called away for a few last minute wedding details and couldn't join us, but Eddie's charming conversational ability, and dare I say, *grasp on manners*, set us all at ease quickly. Belle was every inch a lady, as usual, and although Andrus could never quite get away from an impression of a quiescent bear, he and Eddie warmed up to each other rather faster than I would have thought possible, bonding over discussion of Pelerine fighting tactics that Andrus had observed in the Battle of Asileboix.

Both warriors, I suppose, I told Elne. Her disagreement pricked at my thoughts, almost making me chuckle. *Yes, Eddie is a warrior, even if you don't like him. He fights like one. And he couldn't have risen to Captain during wartime without being a real warrior.*

Once the meal was completed, we quickly parted ways. Belle was yawning before dessert, tired from her pregnancy, and Andrus seemed anxious over her. I passed the letter from Robin into Andrus' hands as we said goodnight.

Eddie and I should have been tired from a long day of riding, but I felt a buzz of tension that made me want to move. As we reached to door to our chambers, I touched his arm to get his attention.

"Is there any chance you're up for a sparring match or two?" He stopped with his hand on the doorknob, turning a grin toward me.

"After the nervous breakdown you almost put me through with that dinner, yes I'd love to go take my payback through a fight."

I laughed and pushed him through the door as he opened it. "Big words, Pelerine. Get changed and we'll find a practice room."

* * *

"Here," I called over my shoulder as I stepped into a dimly lit practice room that face the back courtyard of the castle. Moonlight shone through several long windows, illuminating the room in a gray pallor. With swift steps I crossed to the windows, pulling their drapes closed before muttering the spell to turn on the lights.

Eddie gave me a quizzical look as he shut the door behind us. "Don't want anyone to see you sully yourself by practicing with the me?" he asked. I snorted, beginning my usual series of stretches without responding.

"What was I thinking?" he asked conversationally, as he began his own warm up. "You never mind who you're fighting. Quite egalitarian of you actually. You just don't want to be seen being defeated by a 'fancypants Pelerine army captain' as I believe you've called me once before."

My scowl met his grin across the chilly room as I pulled one arm across my chest to stretch my triceps and shoulder. "If the boot fits, there's no reason to mince words."

His grin only widened. "You no doubt noticed my boots at dinner. My friend LeFeu ordered me my exact size in dress boots, much fancier than officers in Sherwood and Asileboix wear. They *did* fit exceedingly well now that you mention it." He was wearing a different pair of boots now, less showy than the ones he had worn to dinner, but still more elegant than anything I would wear on a regular basis. He looked altogether too refined.

I was used to a rougher version of him, wearing work clothes on the farm as we sweated together. The image of him standing with Belle before dinner earlier flashed through my mind. *That's the type of company he belongs with. The type he misses. It will be a relief to get back to the sophistication of Pelerin for him. No doubt he'll amuse his companions with tales of the rough and tumble female army captain who acted as his jailer during his time in Sherwood.*

The thought annoyed me more than usual. *Who cares what a bunch of foreigners think?* But I knew it was the idea of Eddie laughing at my unpolished ways that made me self conscious, and I didn't like knowing his opinion mattered so much.

Irritation buzzed around my head as I moved on to stretching my neck. I stared at the man in front of me, smiling to himself as he mirrored my posture.

"You're using humor to deflect," I accused him finally.

He shrugged. "Deflect what? I'm just using humor to get a smile out of you."

I sat on the floor to begin a series of leg stretches and pointed to my face. "Doesn't look like it's working. And for all you tell me not to put up walls, to find ways to connect, you do it just as much. You project this image of a content, self assured ... *aristocrat* who's in command everywhere he goes."

I pushed to my feet as he did the same, and we stood facing each other. He was no longer smiling and a faint blush crept across his cheeks. I couldn't help some of the bitterness I was feeling from tumbling out of my mouth, my habit of openness with him overcoming my desire to start detaching in preparation for his departure.

"You're facing the results of your trial tomorrow, maybe even a death sentence, and you're acting like everything is fine, like you're at a house party and you're just here to enjoy yourself. Talk about a hypocrite!"

Eddie pulled his knife out, tossing it's sheath to the floor and began circling me, his jaw set tight and anger building behind his eyes. It was simultaneously soothing and irritating to see his usual calm slip away at my accusations, and I pulled out my own knife and began circling as well, murmuring the shield spell we used during practice bouts.

"I *am* at a house party, as if you forgot. Your aunt is getting married in a few days. I'll be attending the Winter Solstice Ball. There will be feasting, and I daresay I'll be reunited with a few friends while I'm here. Whatever my sentence is, I see no reason to worry about it until it's handed down." He ground his words out through clenched teeth, tension and anger cording the muscles of his forearms. Part of me wanted to back down, create a safe space for him to avoid the future. Most of me wanted to push him over the edge into the well of emotion I knew he was avoiding.

"Liar. You're scared and you don't want to face it."

A growl escaped his chest and he closed the distance between us in a few steps, his motions efficient and unembellished as they always were. I drew in a breath and blocked each one easily, letting him push by me as I spun out of reach. Usually we would regroup and go back to the center of the room after each contact at the beginning of a fight, until we caught the feel and mood of each other. Instead, Eddie re-attacked immediately, almost catching me on my left shoulder as I spun to face him more fully. Giving ground slightly, I couldn't help picking at our binding spell with my mind, not surprised that a sense of anger came across it, matching the mildly unhinged darkness on his face.

I had sensed him sliding toward chaotic intensity over the last few months as he processed the changes to his life and understanding of the world. How I knew that, when he was so consistently cheerful and self effacing I wasn't sure. I assumed it was either from our constant proximity to one another, or because of the strangeness of our binding spell. I had refrained from pushing him over the edge, as I had been dealing with my own issues, but tonight I couldn't help it. I was about to lose him, and my despairing anger over it was too much to bear. Whether to a death sentence or a return to his homeland, he would be beyond my reach in a few days. And he clearly wasn't as bothered as I was. So I wanted to bother him the only way I knew how. Making him bleed first.

Our shots blended into each other, fast and furious, neither of us landing a scratch on the other. I couldn't tell where his attacks began and mine ended as our aggression poured out on each other.

After we broke apart for the third time, catching our breath and still circling each other, sweat dripping down my nose, I couldn't help goading him further.

"You'll have to think up some lies for when you get back. Wouldn't want your buddies knowing you were bested by a woman during our fights."

Hot fury swept across his face at my comment, making my heart stutter for a moment as he surged forward. *I may have pushed him too far,* I told Elne. As I braced for his attack, my own anger surged up again. *After all this time supposedly becoming friends based on mutual respect, and all it takes is a comment about a woman beating him to push him over the edge.* I felt the cold detachment that used to be my every waking moment during my service to John settle over me, as despair touched my heart, and we met in a flurry of movements too fast to follow. My brain couldn't comprehend our motions. I reacted on instinct alone, the desire to prove mastery over him at the forefront of everything. After several minutes, the only sound our mingled breaths and bone knocking on bone as we blocked and parried, broken by the ring of steel as our knives met infrequently, I sensed an opening. Taking it before I could think it through, I swept my knife up towards his ribs. At the last second, he knocked my wrist away, my blade cutting only through the fabric of his shirt before he managed to knock it out of my hands.

He used my distraction to bring his own knife around, and I caught his wrist with both hands, barely stopping him from slicing at my neck. My eyes bulged in offended rage.

"You went for my *neck?!*" I demanded, shocked that he had broken our sparring rule of below neck only. His only response was to snarl, and I had to prevent Elne from surging forward with the last shred of my willpower. With a quick series of motions, I broke his grip on his own knife, feeling his fingernails scrape down my wrist as I tossed it aside before bringing my fist up to punch him in the jaw. He put a hand up to his face in surprise, but responded to my taunting look with a series of jabs and punches. We locked into a flurry of handfighting before I sensed another opening that I couldn't resist: I head butted him in the nose. He stumbled back, hands covering his nose and eyes wide in shock again. As he took his hands away I crowed in triumph, raising my fists in the air. A gush of blood was sliding down his lips and chin, making inroads into the white shirt I had already slashed to ribbons.

"I win! I got first blood!" I told him as he pinched the bridge of his nose and tipped his head back.

"That doesn't count. You did it with your head," he said, his voice thick with blood. "Besides, look at your wrist. I think you'll find I got first blood actually."

Nonplussed, I lowered my hands and examined both wrists. Sure enough, a long scratch ran down my left wrist, drops of blood welling here and there and dripping to the floor. I looked over at him in shock.

He started laughing before the blood dripping down his nasal cavity became too much and he started to choke, still laughing as he watched me jog over.

I pressed both hands to the side of his face, tipping his head back down so I could see his nose, and muttered a healing spell to clot the blood vessels and realign the cartilage and bone. It was a spell I was very familiar with, but had never had to use on Eddie. We had always stuck to our training rules before. I felt a pang of remorse as the healing spell completed and my eyes focused on his again. For a moment, we just looked at each other, my hands framing his bloody face, the only sound our mingled breath and my own blood dripping in a slow pattern to the floor.

He broke contact first, pulling a handerchief out from his waistcoat pocket to start mopping up his face. I took a few steps away and kept my eyes off him, calming my heart rate and healing my own wound.

I didn't look up as he approached. He reached around me and gently pulling my injured arm toward him, tugging so that I faced him fully. My eyes watched his hand press another clean handkerchief over the spot where my injury had been, wiping away the smears of blood until only pale skinned remained, covered by white cloth and his sun browned hands. I swallowed reflexively.

"I'm sorry I went for your throat," he said quietly, not letting go of my arm. "That was dishonorable of me. I was out of control, and I just wanted to beat you. I heard you say the spell, so I knew I couldn't hurt you really. But it was wrong."

I twisted my arm around so I could grip his forearm, grabbing his chin with my other arm and tugging his face up so I could look him in the eye. "I'm the one who should be sorry. I pushed you over the edge on purpose, even though I know you're on the brink of your sentencing. I just wanted you to feel what I'm feeling, before you leave. That was selfish. I hope..." I hesitated, trying and failing to gage the emotions in his eyes. "I hope you can forgive me, and remember our friendship when you go instead of all my wildness."

He drew in a shuddering breath and closed his eyes, shutting out the sight of me. *He's leaving. He's already withdrawing. Tomorrow he'll get his news, and the decision will be made. Every day this week he'll draw further away until he leaves.* I wanted to cry, but instead I let my eyes drift over his face. They landed on a smear of blood he had missed to the right of his mouth. I rubbed at it with my thumb absently, tracing around the corner of his lips until it was gone. His mouth dropped open slightly as I did, and when I glanced back at his eyes they were watching me, heavy with an emotion I couldn't identify.

"I asked Lord Robin for permission to join your unit," he said, his voice low and halting. "He granted it, but said the final decision was yours. Will you let me join you?"

My eyes searched his for the truth, a lump growing in my throat as my brain denied the possibility that I had heard him right. Elne's displeasure leaped around the edges of my mind but I pushed her firmly away until I couldn't feel her presence anymore. I wanted privacy to wade through whatever murky waters Eddie and I had just entered.

"Why would you ask that?" I whispered, my voice hoarse. "You might be allowed to go home soon. You don't owe me anything. You're *going* to be free," I insisted, blatantly ignoring the fact that he might be sentenced to death.

"Why would you ask me to forget your wildness?" He retorted softly, his brow furrowed. I blinked, confused at the direction of his question. He licked his lips, his tongue passing within millimeters of my thumb and drawing my eyes. I let go of his face, but his hand came up to snatch mine in the air, enclosing it in his slightly larger one. We sat frozen for a moment, cross legged and staring at each other, our hands clutched together as our thoughts filled the space between us, unspoken. Eddie's breathing became a little ragged, his eyes still filled with that slightly unhinged look, tampered with something else I didn't recognize. He licked his lips again and I swallowed as I forced my eyes not to watch.

"I want you -" he broke off at the sound of the door opening, whistling mingling with a rumbling clatter proceeding a uniformed servant into the room. I ripped my hands from his, pushing off the ground and turning to scan the ground for my knife and it's sheath, in effort to calm my pounding heart and avoid detection of the heat that had ripped across my face.

I felt, rather than heard, Eddie push up from the floor more slowly behind me, turning to face the worker and assure him that he wasn't interrupting, and we were finished anyway, and to apologize for interrupting his work. By the time I had cleaned my knife and secured it to my leg again, he was engaged in a discussion on magical cleaning methods with the worker, shaking hands with him as I stalked by and jogging to catch up with me in the hallway. We didn't speak as we walked, and I sped up slightly so I could pull ahead of him, instead of feeling him at my side. He matched my pace and we were practically jogging by the time we reached our rooms, awkwardly navigating the doorway and spilling inside one after the other.

I rounded on him as soon as he shut the door.

"What were you going to - "

He spoke at the same time, "What will you decide to - "

We stopped, staring at each other, both breathing hard as if we were in the middle of a practice bout.

"I'm going to pretend I didn't hear your request to join my unit until tomorrow," I told him, trying to bring my thoughts into order.

He started to speak but I held up my hand, cutting him off. "If, after the council meeting and your sentence, you still want to join my unit, you can make your request again."

Eddie choked off a few more words, his expression tinged with anger. After a moment, he nodded. I hesitated, the churning emotion in my chest a sure indicator that the nightmares would be dogging me tonight. Instead of asking for him to sleep with me, I turned and took refuge in my room, ruthlessly pushing down the echo of his words in my mind as I cleaned up and made ready for sleep.

I want you.

"That's not what he meant and you know it," I muttered angrily, pulling my covers over me with an impatient tug. The bed and room seemed empty and cold despite the cheerful fire crackling nearby. "Even if he did mean it that way, you wouldn't be a good fit. You'd just end up hurting each other. Whatever you're feeling is probably a result of that cursed binding spell anyway." Despite a scratchy weariness behind my eyes, sleep eluded me for some time.

CHAPTER SIXTEEN

Eddie

I felt wound up and unraveled, berating myself repeatedly for almost revealing my heart to her in the practice room, and cursing myself even more for not pouring everything out when I had an opening.

"If only that cleaner hadn't come in when he did," I muttered as I cleaned off the remaining evidence of my bloody nose. After changing, I stared at my bed for a few minutes, a comfortable looking proposition, especially after months of sleeping on either a hard pallet or camping on the ground. I turned away finally, puttering around my room, rearranging the way I had stored my clothing and examining the few decorations on the walls, before finally surrendering to the bed.

Red's soft cries reached me sometime in the middle of the night, waking me from my own fitful dozing. I hesitated only a moment, before throwing aside my covers and striding into her room, pulling the tangled covers off her restless form.

"Red." I called, as I straightened the blankets and pulled them over her again. "Red, it's me." She didn't wake up, but I saw tears slipping down her cheeks in the glow of her banked fire. I walked around to the other side of the bed and slipped under the covers, pulling myself toward her slowly.

Reaching out, I pulled one of her hands in mine, squeezing

gently and repeating her name in a low voice until she woke from whatever had been tormenting her. She didn't startle awake, like she had the other few times I had woken her up from a nightmare. Instead, she came awake gradually, turning to look at me, tears still streaming from her eyes along with a pathetic vulnerability. My heart wrenched, and I knew she didn't want to ask for help.

"I'm not here," I told her soothingly, gripping her hand more tightly. "I'm not here, I'm back in my own bed. Don't say anything. Just sleep."

She nodded slowly, closing her eyes as I settled in next to her, our hands still clasped between us. She stared at the ceiling for awhile, the tears welling up from her eyes slowing gradually. I kept my breathing measured, and after awhile she began to match it, drifting back into an untroubled sleep.

I couldn't bring myself to let her hand go as I drifted toward sleep as well. *Just this once,* I told myself. *She might push you away soon, you might not get another chance.* I lifted her hand up, pressing a kiss on her calloused and scarred knuckles, before settling our joined hands down again and letting myself go.

I walked out the doors of the cabinet room, Henri and Hazel LeFeu at my side, a shaky, fluttering feeling in my chest. Red was still inside, deep in conversation with her cousin, Prince Andrus. I had just received formal word of my banishment from Pelerin, and after an official pardon from Prince Andrus, she had released me from our binding spell that had yoked me to her for the last six months. I had gotten so used to it's presence, and the feeling of connection between us, that I hadn't expected to feel it's lack so palpably.

My old friend Hazel was chattering next to me, directing most of her comments to, her husband, LeFeu. He offered encouragement in the form of noncommittal grunts every now and again. She had linked arms with both of us and was practically dragging us forward. I wrenched my thoughts away from the cabinet room, and the lack of connection to Red as I recognized the corridor my two Pelerine friends were leading me down.

"...and I know they're waiting to hear as well, so I'm glad it all worked out. I wish I could come, darling, but Belle needs my help with some last minute alterations for the ball tomorrow. Her stomach finally started to show this week so she has a fitting with Clothilda, and is probably going to need some emotional support."

I cast a bewildered look at Hazel. "Why would she need emotional support for a dress fitting? And why are we at the stables?"

Hazel made a mildly disgusted noise. "Don't bother trying to wrap you head around what emotional support looks like, Eddie, it will just make you dizzy." I snorted as she turned to confer with a groom, gesturing to me and LeFeu as LeFeu stepped up to a nearby horse and patted it's nose. I couldn't help my mind drifting back to the emotional support I had offered last night, the feel of Red's work roughened hand in mind, the quiet warmth of our steady breathing in the dark.

"Eddie," Hazel called, snapping her fingers in front of my face. "I know you've just had a shock, but can't you listen to a word I'm saying?" She put her hands on her hips and gave me a fondly exasperated look.

I rubbed at the missing spot in my chest and gave her a crooked smile. "Sorry Hazel, I'm sure I'll get used to the feeling soon enough. I just didn't realize what it had meant."

Her brow furrowed, she scrunched her nose, darting her eyes between my hand rubbing small circles on my chest and the sad smile on my face. "I meant your sentencing and banishment. What feeling are you talking about?"

Realization dawned on me and I snatched my hand away. "What? Nothing. What are we doing in the stables?"

She gave me a suspicious look but turned to gesture to the horse next to LeFeu. "As I *already* said, some of the men from your unit attended your hearing in Pelerin and insisted on coming with us afterward. They're waiting for you at the Piper's

Inn.

Warmth blossomed in my chest and I looked toward Henri who gave me a confirming nod. "That's wonderful!" I said, walking over with renewed vigor to the mount a groom was leading toward me.

Hazel stood on tiptoe, pulling LeFeu's head down far enough to give him a kiss on his cheek. "Have fun you two, but don't be out too late." We said our goodbyes and mounted up, LeFeu taking the lead out of the castle gates.

* * *

Hot air and the scent of hops blasted our faces as we pushed through the door of the pub, a roar from the back corner indicating where our party was located. We pushed our way through the crowd, LeFeu peeling off to get drinks and food from the barman while I greeted our old unit. Most of those who remained from our former unit had come, excuses readily given for the ones that couldn't make it.

"Creator's Breath, it's not justice!" Lieutenant Hevre said in a dark voice, after we had finished our food and drinks and sat huddled in our dark corner, away from the other groups. "The trial was a farce, and anyone with eyes could see it. They wanted to pin their decision to invade on someone, and chose you just because you reported the facts of what was going on at the border. If you ask me, the Pelerine lawyer appointed to represent you was in someone's -" I held my hand up and Hevre cut off, everyone's eyes swinging to me.

"I've already heard it all from LeFeu, my good man. It's too late for that now. I'm content with the ruling, so long as it doesn't affect my family in any way."

LeFeu rumbled a rare laugh. "Not one bit. They've had more trade than they can handle these last few months. Prince Andrus made his favoritism for them known, so anyone who wants anything to do with Asileboix goes through the Marchands.

You'll hear all about it when your parents arrive tomorrow."

The men rumbled in agreement, breaking into scattered conversation about their own protests of the trial. I listened with half an ear, my fondness for them warming my heart, even as my head couldn't help noticing the differences between who they were expecting me to be, and who I was now. They spoke in the same way, focused on Pelerine news and politics, pride for our country and a desire for injustices there to be righted. I approved of their sentiments, but I shared them much less than I used to. My interest lay in Sherwood, with Barnsdale Lodge and it's inhabitants, with righting the wrongs that had been done to Lady Marie and others like her. The old call to offer my life up in defense of something greater than me was still there, but instead of Pelerin, it was transferring to Sherwood, and even more so to Red. Nothing seemed so important to me anymore than protecting her at any cost.

I could see that the difference in me wasn't wholly unnoticed by the men, either. Their respect for me was obvious, and their devotion in coming here to see me and voice support for me was a balm to the empty place where my homeland used to reside. But their eyes flicked to my visible tattoos quite often, and some couldn't bring themselves to look me directly, so uncomfortable were they with the magic that marked me.

I cleared my throat, drawing everyone's attention back to me once again. "Thank you all, for showing up for me tonight, and showing support. You've raised valid concerns about our beloved Pelerin, but unfortunately, as of today, I have no way to aid you in solving those issues." I gestured toward my tattoos. "Even if the verdict had been in my favor, I wouldn't be able to show my face in society again. No one would want to follow someone marked my magic, like I am." I hesitated, then plowed ahead, hoping my words wouldn't diminish me in their eyes, but wanting to be as honest as I could. "In truth, my understanding of magic has changed during my time in Sherwood. I was snatched from death's door twice by mages, once by the one who gave me these marks, and the other by the one who had been appointed my jailer, risking her life to save me from a folly of my own making." The men were quiet, the roar of conversation in the main part of the room providing a contrast to the still attentiveness before me. "They asked nothing in return, demanded no debt for their work. I've had other experiences too, of course, but those were the ones that impressed me the most." I drew a breath, looking at each man in turn. "I've applied and been accepted into the Sherwoodian army," I said bluntly. The other stirred gently, looking from one to the other. "My path is here. Yours is not. If you take my advice, you will go home to Pelerin and each seek a way to serve your country best. But know this, the old story of magic being evil is more complicated than that. I hope you won't hold my decision against me."

A chorus of murmurs rang out in protest, Private Oger's voice rising above the rest. "I've already decided to move here if I can," he said, defiantly. He glanced over at LeFeu. "Sergeant LeFeu said he's put in a good word to see if we can transfer. My aunt too. Apparently they have a laundry here she could work at that uses magic instead of some of the harsher chemicals. She said it would be nice not to have her hands peeling every day of her life." Some of the men nodded and patted him on the back, while others cast him anxious looks. I steered the conversation to safer waters, saying goodbye not long afterward and riding back to the castle with LeFeu in companionable silence. We chatted for a few minutes at the stables before parting ways, LeFeu back to Hazel, and me to my former captor.

❈ ❈ ❈

She was lounging on a sofa in front of the fire when I walked into our rooms, tossing a knife up into the air and catching it again.

"What is the point of that?" I demanded, exasperated. "If you miss it will land point down in your stomach!"

She laughed, sitting up and slipping the knife back into it's sheath. "I had a shield up of course. But never mind that. Andrus is waiting for us in his study. I told him about my suspicions and he's willing to test you."

"Your suspicions?" I asked, drawing a blank.

"That you're a mage," she reminded me patiently, crossing the room to the door just behind me. She looked back over her shoulder. "It won't take long, just a prick on your finger to test your aptitude."

I put my arm out to stop the door from opening, and she looked at me over her shoulder.

"I'll go," I conceded, "if you tell me whether you'll allow me to join your unit."

She gave me a wry look. "That's precisely why we're doing this. If you're going to be in my unit, I have to know your mage level."

"And if I don't have any magic?"

"Then you won't be given any magical tasks, obviously," she replied.

I beamed. "So you're saying I'm in."

She nodded, laughing a little at my happiness. "I already told you I don't have any open positions, so it may take awhile to find where you fit."

"Let me be your bodyguard," I urged, pushing the door closed again as she went to open it. She raised her eyebrows.

"You're coming in as a former captain in the Pelerine army and you want to be assigned as my bodyguard? Never mind the fact that I have no need of a bodyguard, aren't you going to be bored to tears? I'm sure after awhile we could find a role that plays to your strengths."

I shook my head. "My strengths will work just fine guarding you. And you do need someone to watch your back." She opened her mouth to protest but I continued on without giving her an opening. "Think of it this way, I'll be there to guard your back so you can focus on killing more beasties. You know our fighting styles work well together."

She snapped her mouth shut and tried to hide her grin. "Fine, bodyguard it is. But don't get in my way. And don't try to stop me from doing my job. I know you can't help being bossy."

I shook my head, straightening up so she could wrench open the door, and following her out into the hall. "No bossing, boss. Just keeping you in fighting shape so you can tear up more of the enemy."

She skidded to a stop in front of me and I stumbled trying to prevent a collision. Turning back, she put her hand to her chest and gave me a fake smile. "Why, Eddie Marchand, I do believe that's the kindest thing anyone has ever done for me."

I barked out a laugh, falling in beside her as we made our way to the Royal Tower.

* * *

As it turned out, I *did* have magic. I stared at the test tube Andrus was holding up in astonishment, not really listening as he and Red discussed the results. Apparently I was a decently powerful mage. They were going into the intricacies of power expansion, and where I should start working to improve since I never really used my magic.

Andrus set the test tube down and they both turned to look at me, Red folding her arms across her chest and giving me a satisfied smirk. I stared at her in shock.

"It's his tone of command. He's *very* bossy. But it just seems like a natural personality trait because he's so sure of himself. No wonder no ever noticed. And no wonder he was such a good officer."

My mind scrabbled at their conversation, searching for purchase on individual words. "A good officer? You think I'm a good officer?"

Red scoffed. "Didn't you just get back from meeting with a group of soldiers who came all the way here from Pelerin just to show support for you against their own government's ruling? *That's* a good officer."

Her words trickled through my shock, leaving a warm glow as

they burrowed into my heart. "Yes, they did want to cheer me up. They were a bit surprised when I told them I was joining the Sherwoodian army."

Andrus chuckled. "From what I've heard of your tactical abilities, I'm sure they're mourning your loss. But now at least you know you have magic at your disposal. You can train with it, if you want, so you can use it in battle."

"And if I don't want to train with it?"

"Then there's no need. You'll probably continue to draw on your command capabilities without even thinking about it, but that's your natural tendency - it's like breathing. You won't be able to stop it even if you try."

We sat for awhile, discussing possibilities and potential, until the clock chimed the hour. Andrus showed us out and Red and I walked in silence back to our chambers.

"Told you," she said, as we made our way inside. "Bossy."

I pulled a decorative pillow off a nearby chair and chucked it at her, missing by a mile and making her laugh.

CHAPTER SEVENTEEN

Red

I let Mathilde envelope me in a warm hug, taking care not to damage her intricate hairstyle in the process. She was the only one I allowed to hug me, because she was the only one who dared to do it. My thoughts strayed to the times I had woken up to a certain person's arm flung over me, or vice versa, but I pushed that aside and focused on my aunt.

"You look beautiful, Aunt Mathilde," I said truthfully. Though middle aged and having seen more than her fair share of tragedy and hard times, she was glowing in her wedding finery.

She gave a little twirl and laughed, her long gold and cream colored dress trimmed with snow white fur swirling out around her. "I suppose I should demur the compliment, but I can't help agreeing. I feel like a princess!" She sent me a mischievous look. "Which is a good thing, because today is my last day *as* a princess. It's time for change."

I smiled at her, glancing over at Belle, who looked resplendent in a wine colored gown with gold underskirts and trimming. She was dabbing at tears in her eyes as she looked at Mathilde.

"I think your departure is causing despair in some quarters," I stage whispered, nodding my head toward Belle.

"Oh my dear!" Mathilde said, sweeping over to her daughter-in-law and guiding her down to sit on a nearby sofa. "There's no need to cry. I'll still be living here, after all, and when the baby comes I'll be happy to help with whatever you need. We've discussed all this!"

"I know, I know, I'm just being emotional. I'm so happy for you and Clement! But these days I'm a watering pot. I'm blaming the baby." Mathilde laughed and rubbed her back, regaling both of us with stories of her own pregnancies until Belle had dried her eyes.

"I only wish Marie were here," Mathilde said, looking at me with sad understanding as she stood from her seat. "If only we could have had it at Barnsdale Lodge. It's been far too long since I've seen her. But Rosebelle was right, combining our ceremony with the Winter Solstice Ball gives everyone a chance to celebrate with us, and mark the end of a ruling era. Perhaps we can come visit your mother in the spring?"

I nodded. "That would be kind of you, and I think good for her." Mathilde reached out and patted my hand, then started shepherding the two of us toward the door. "You go ahead out, my dears, I'd like a moment alone before I head down the aisle."

I trooped out after Belle, pulling the hem of my own crimson dress up slightly as we walked down a flight of stairs before heading toward the ballroom. I wasn't dressed nearly as extravagantly as Rosebelle, but I couldn't claim to be comfortable in the dress and it's voluminous, bell shaped sleeves. The velvet fabric was soft, but it was tailored along the bodice and waist, flaring out only slightly at my thighs. Not a silhouette that would hide many weapons. My hair was also combed and unbound, spilling down my back in heavy waves. I left it that way sometimes when we were riding, but in a stuffy ballroom, I would have preferred my usual severe bun or braids.

I left Rosebelle with Andrus near the royal balcony, and made my way down to the lobby outside the main entrance of the ballroom. It was buzzing with guests, just beginning to file in through the open doors, and all dressed in shades of red and green as requested on the party invitation. I let my eyes wander over the festive scene until they caught on Eddie, not far from where I was standing, dressed in forest green.

His family was grouped around him, chatting amongst themselves, along with Hazel and LeFeu. My heart twinged to see him surrounded by so many people he loved, but that he wouldn't be allowed to live with again unless they uprooted their whole lives and moved to a strange country. His eyes glittered like dark sapphires in the candlelight as he noticed me, and I felt a rippling awareness pass between us, almost like the feeling of connection I had taken for granted through the binding spell. He started toward me, and my feet mirrored his, something drawing us both forward until we met under the main chandelier, just a step away from each other.

"You look -"

"Odd? I know. It's the dress. Can't get away from the color red, of course, and these sleeves are big enough to fit a small child inside. Not exactly practical if a fight breaks out." Words bubbled out of me, betraying the nerves I felt at his presence and the tug in my chest.

Amusement flared in Eddie's eyes. "Do they get many fights at Winter Solstice balls in Asileboix?"

I laughed, grateful for our familiar banter. "Not that I'm aware of, no. I just don't enjoy feeling like I'm not dressed for the occasion, if one does break out."

"I see," he said, grinning before offering his arm. "Come over here, I want you to meet my family."

I nodded, eyes flicking toward the group he had just left, a thrill of nerves flaring in the pit of my stomach before I quashed them down mercilessly. *Who cares if they think me rough and uncouth in comparison to Belle, whom they've known so long. They won't be wrong.* I took his arm gingerly.

As we started forward together he tilted his head closer to mine. "For the record, I was going to say you look beautiful before. Not odd."

A different thrill went through me, which I cut off as

ruthlessly as my nerves, just before we stopped in front of his family. Introductions were made, too quickly for me to catch everyone's names, and we moved in through the door as a party, my arm still tethered to Eddie's.

Andrus and Rosebelle made a grand entrance down the staircase, and I made my way to sit with them as the wedding ceremony began, leaving Eddie and his family behind. Mathilde and Clement looked radiant as they exchanged their vows, and I felt of an ache in my chest. For the first time, I wished I had a relationship like that to rely on, someone that would see me for me, and still want me. To have my back, and let me fight for him too. To build something together.

After the ceremony, the ball began in earnest, with Clement and Aunt Mathilde leading the dancing. Soon the entire floor was covered in couples, including Andrus and Rosebelle from time to time. I traced my way around the perimeter. People made room for me wherever I went, few of them daring to speak to me. *Why don't people want to speak to me? They all go out of their way to bow and make room, but not reach out.*

A soft tread behind me sent me whirling, my hands on the pair of daggers tucked up my voluminous sleeves.

A surprised Eddie held his hands up and I relaxed. He quirked a smile. "Why are you prowling around the edge of the dance floor, instead of dancing?"

I shrugged my shoulders, trying to dissipate the sudden tension scittering across them. "I'm not prowling. I'm pacing. There's a difference." His eyebrows went up but he didn't challenge me. " And I'm not a very good dancer. Besides, no one is daring enough to ask me."

His hand went out. I stared at it, confused.

"Will you dance with me?" He asked finally, amusement coloring his voice.

My eyes flicked to his. "Why? I just said I'm a terrible dancer."

He laughed, leaning forward to take my hand. "I happen to be an excellent dancer, so I'll make it easy on you." His eyes sought mine, a question in them, and I nodded slowly.

His face creased into a smile and he tucked my hand under his arm, pulling me into a slow waltz.

He was easy to follow, keeping our steps simple and unembellished, signaling direction changes with clear, gentle pressure. To my surprise, I didn't stumble. I even began to relax and enjoy myself toward the end of the dance, the whirling colors and chattering happiness providing a festive atmosphere. We didn't talk much, for which I was glad. I needed to concentrate on what we were doing, and the feel of Eddie's firm hand on my back, pressing me almost against him was distracting.

When the waltz ended, he led me back to his family, who chattered around me, talking to me every now and again but mostly leaving me alone and directing their remarks to Eddie, who remained at my side. Finally, during a lull in the dancing when everyone was getting food from the buffet, I managed to slip away, up to the quiet of my room.

What a confusing night, I told Elne, who flitted at the very edges of my mind like a ghost. Eddie had been strangest of all, giving me compliments and keeping me by his side. I had liked it, to my dismay, and not just because I enjoyed his presence as a friend. I snapped a lid on that thought before it could go further and made ready for bed. I couldn't help a sliver of anticipation at the thought that he would most likely end up next to me again soon enough, but it was dampened by the thought of him pining for Belle. *Is he dancing with her now? Or just watching from afar?* I pushed those thoughts away. *Don't waste your time Red. You have other things to focus on.*

* * *

The next morning we made ready to leave early that morning, Eddie stealing out before me to bid farewell to his family. I had tossed and turned all night, not with nightmares, although since Eddie hadn't come in to my bed I wouldn't have been surprised if they had shown up, but with restless thoughts of him. Jealousy, for one, of his continued infatuation with Belle. The haunting conviction that the only reason he was joining my unit was as a distraction from her, especially since I'm the last woman in the world that could take her place. Fear that having him always near me was becoming distracting and would be a problem when our next mission was assigned. By the time I was heading down to the stables I decided I needed to corner him before we left, and force him to make sure he was joining my unit for the right reasons.

I found him at the entrance hall, waiving off his parent's carriage. I waited in the shadows until he turned around, his gaze catching mine almost immediately. I beckoned to him and he followed silently, his expression uncharacteristically serious and unreadable. That alone flared my irritation. *If we're supposed to be such great friends, why is he obviously hiding something from me?*

We turned down a corridor toward the stables, ducking into a tack room I knew housed ceremonial items. We wouldn't be disturbed unless there was a sudden need for the best of Asilean livery.

"What are we doing in here?" Eddie asked as I shut the door. His voice was dark. I crossed to the back of the room, and he followed. I turned as I reached the back wall, keeping it's steady presence behind me.

"I need to ask you something," I replied, finally. His eyes snapped to mine, his gaze compelling. My mouth went dry, and I swallowed heavily, putting my hands on my hips. "I want to make sure you're serious about joining my unit. You've been acting strange since I agreed to take you on, and I'm concerned that you're joining for the wrong reasons."

Eddie's face lit with surprise, then darkened to something like anger. I continued on, wanting to finish this conversation as soon as possible so we could leave.

"I'm assuming you regret asking, so I want to give you the chance to back out before I announce it to the rest of my unit.

We'll be forming up again on our return to Sherwood, so this is your last chance."

Eddie balled his fists at his side, grinding out his response through a clenched jaw. "I am *not* regretting asking. If I'm acting strange, that's not the reason. Furthest from it actually."

Relief streaked through me at the knowledge that he wanted to stay. But my troubled thoughts forced me to press him further. "Then tell me what's going on. You're clearly keeping something from me, something is bothering you. If we're such good friends, you should tell me so I can share your burden."

"Of course we're friends!" Eddie threw up his hands in exasperation, pulling at his hair slightly and turning away. "Why are you upset? Why are you asking me this?"

I scoffed. "I'm not upset. But I know you well enough to know something is bothering that normally calm mask you like to wear. Admit it!"

"Fine. There is something troubling me. But I don't know what to do about it, or even if I *should* do something about it, so there's no point in talking about it."

I stepped closer, putting a hand on his shoulder in sympathy. "I thought so." His expression was wary. "Selfishly, I want you to stay with me. But maybe you should travel more before you settle down, go see the sights in Spindle, visit the ocean. New adventures will cast Belle out of your heart for good, you'll see. I can't bear to think of you pining over her your whole life, never letting someone else in to love you. You *deserve* love, and there's someone out there that deserves your love in return. Maybe once you've done some healing you can return to my unit and I'll help you find her."

Eddie's breathing had become more ragged as I spoke, my hand feeling the rise and fall of his lungs as his eyes took on a raw light. "Belle is gone from my heart, what little of her actually ever held it. But I'll take you up on your offer of helping me win the one to give my devotion to. I already know who it will be. *Must* be."

A surge of jealousy swept over me and I knew I hadn't hid

it well from the way his eyes sharpened on mine. *Hopefully he ignores that, or thinks it's something else.* I snatched my hand back, trying to hide my continuing disappointment, cursing myself for even having disappointment when I knew a relationship with him could be problematic.

Edging along the wall toward an alcove used for storing funeral livery, I felt every footstep Eddie took behind me, each one reverberating up my spine and shaking loose the hold I had on my heart. Finally, I reached the end of the alcove, shadows hiding my face well enough now that I hoped he couldn't see my emotions too much. I turned back toward him, startled to find him only a few inches behind me.

I forced my eyes to his, my heart pumping in my chest so hard I couldn't focus long enough to read his expression. "I hope you'll tell me who it is, especially if it's someone in my unit."

"Oh, it's someone in your unit all right," he replied, voice harsh again.

Anger shook my vulnerable heart around in my chest. *Who?!* Aeflaed seemed the most likely to take his fancy, but I couldn't remember if he had even met her during our ride to Nottingham all those months ago. I couldn't picture him falling for Edda or Edith, but the only other woman in our group was Eileen, and she was married.

"Who?" I demanded, my voice hoarse. "I'll have to put up with your pining all day and all night, assuming you'll still sleep next to me, so I think I'm entitled to know. I can't have you distracting my soldiers."

A growl escaped Eddies throat, making my skin stand on end and sharpening my attention on him. "I don't want to distract your soldiers. And I don't plan on doing any pining. But if I can turn her heart toward me, I'll do whatever it takes, however long it takes." He pushed forward, crowding me further into the alcove. "I want to invade her mind and heart, inch by inch, until our souls are so mingled we don't know where one stops and the other begins. I want to light her skin on fire, until everything she feels reminds her of me, of what I'm feeling for her."

He stepped forward with each sentence he spoke, and I stepped back in response, my eyes wide at his words and the strength of his feelings. My own heart pounded in my ears, aching in exquisite agony as it reached for him, called for him to say it was *me* he wanted, and no one else.

When my back hit the wall behind me, my breath caught, words tumbling out of my lips before I could stop them from drawing a line in the sand. "Who is it?" I asked, my voice plaintive. I couldn't even care how vulnerable I sounded, wanting only to hear the words from his mouth.

He reached out, first one arm, then another, planting them on either side of my body against the wall, and leaned toward me until our faces were only a few inches apart. "You know who, Red. It's been you since the day you jumped in the river after me, you reckless, brave, beautiful woman."

Heat swept across my skin, warming me from the inside out. I closed my eyes at his words, swallowing the thick lump in my throat before I opened them again, not daring to look him in the eye and let him see how pathetically vulnerable I was at his admission.

My hand reached out of it's own accord and I stroked down the column of his throat with my fingertips, the rasp of stubble tickling my skin pleasantly. He shuddered at my touch. "You want to light my skin on fire?" I asked. "That doesn't sound very pleasant."

His voice was low and rough as he answered. "It's not. But it's the sort of torment you've been giving me, so you'd deserve it."

My eyes flicked up to his lips, not daring to travel further and see what was in his eyes. My gaze became unfocused as he slipped his hand around my waist, slowly, giving me more than enough time to pull away if I wanted. I couldn't. I was frozen in this endless moment, feet stuck still while I waited on the threshold between our friendship and the unknown of how our feelings fit together. He put just a bit of pressure on my lower back, pulling me forward a step, then another, until I was flush against him, my eyes never leaving his lips. His other hand slipped up my arm, trailing along my shoulder until it snaked up my neck to cradle the side of my face, his thumb tracing along my lips lightly.

"We shouldn't cross this line," I said breathlessly against the skin of his thumb. He stopped his tracing, gripping my chin instead, tilting my head slightly to the side as he put his lips by my ear.

"I don't see any lines here, Red, just you."

My eyes fluttered closed as the sensation of his breath across my ear overwhelmed me, and then fluttered open again, unseeing.

"Kissing. Your lips. I shouldn't kiss you," I managed to stutter out, as I felt rather than heard him inhale the scent of my hair. He dipped his head down, dragging his stubble roughened cheek up my throat, mirroring my touch from earlier.

"You say I have the gift of command. Will you listen if I tell you to kiss me? I hope you do, because I'm going to kiss you, and I want you kiss me back."

My mouth dropped open at his words and I hissed in a little breath before his lips met mine, smooth and dry and urgent. I couldn't help pressing myself into him, responding eagerly, imparting all the trembling in my heart into every press of our lips. My hands came up of their own volition, tracing the muscles on his upper arms and shoulders before curling behind his neck and tangling in his hair, pressing him to me and making him groan.

We both pulled apart slightly at the noise, laughing breathlessly before our lips sought each other again.

Suddenly, the door to the tack room creaked open, and voices reached us as footsteps stomped inside. We froze, out of sight in the alcove we occupied. If anyone came to the back of the room, they would be able to see us easily.

"Here it is. They're taking the brougham, so they don't need much. And she specifically instructed the stable master not to put full ceremonial tack on, just enough to be festive."

Another voice murmured something that made the first

speaker laugh, and then they fell silent, the only sound the scrape of boxes and then heavy footsteps leading back into the hallway and the door creaking shut. We kept still for a few more minutes, relaxing only when it became clear that they wouldn't be back.

My anxiety at being discovered pierced through the fog of desire in my brain, and I disentangled myself from Eddie's arms. "We need to forget this happened," I told him roughly, stepping past him and heading toward the exit. "Just leave it all in here, and when we walk back out, we'll be in the same place we were before we came in here." My voice wobbled as I spoke my next words, not daring to look at him as we approached to door back to the corridor. "I don't want to lose your friendship. You have no idea what it means to me. I can't risk that."

His hand snaked around me, pressing against the door, preventing me from opening it. I looked back at him over my shoulder. His face was fierce, eyes full and earnest.

"I don't want to keep this just in here. There's no way I can forget your lips on mine when we walk out of here. I'm not saying we need to move forward right now. I'll let you set the pace. But I don't want pretend this didn't happen."

I swallowed heavily, distracted by the heat of his body on my back. My voice sounded small as I replied. "If you think I could really walk out that door and forget this ever happened, you're insane. But that's exactly why this isn't a good idea." I leaned back against his chest, and he tipped his head down to rest against mine. "I'll be dreaming of this at night," I whispered, too raw to tell anything but the truth. "When we're all talking around the campfire in the evening I'll remember the heat of you on my skin. When I'm eating dinner I'll be thinking about the feel of you on my lips. When we're joking and talking with the others I'll be wishing I could find a place to hide and kiss you again. When we're laying down to sleep, I'll be thinking… just thinking…" A blush spread across my skin, despite the anguish I felt.

I heard Eddie's breathing catch and he spun me around,

pushing my back against the door as I slipped my hands on either side of his face and guided him down to me again. Our kisses were more like a battle of wills this time, desperate and emotional, but Eddie slipped his palm over my heart, soaking up my frantic heartbeats until I gentled, able to give him my care and concern and, yes, *love*, instead of frustration and anger. I was the one who groaned this time when he pulled away, following him and winning a few more soft kisses before falling back against the door.

"We need to go," I whispered and he put his forehead to mine.

"I know."

"I don't know when we can talk about this again," I said, brow furrowed.

"I know. And I promise I won't distract you. But don't make any decisions without me."

I quirked one side of my mouth up, nodding slightly. "When we get to Nottingham, we can talk in our rooms."

He nodded, easing down to press one more slow and gentle kiss to my lips before backing off. We stood still for a few minutes, catching our breath and trying to put ourselves back together, before I turned and carefully pulled open the door.

No one else was in the short hallway to the stable, so we started forward, falling into step next to each other, our strides becoming more purposeful the further away from the tack room we got. When we passed into the actual stable itself, Andrus was there, motioning to me as he finished speaking to a groom.

I gave Eddie a nod, sensing his understanding and knowing that he would be nearby without needing to fully look at him. I went over to Andrus, crossing my arms as I waited for him to finish his conversation and hoping my face didn't betray what was still on my mind.

He sent the groom off with a handshake and turned to me. "Red, as always I wish you could stay longer. Sometimes I think back to our days swimming in the moat and wonder why we thought we had forever to run wild."

I grinned, remembering a particularly long day teaching

ourselves to catch fish with our hands, before Prince John changed everything. "Yes well, our countries call, and duty is our first love," I reminded him, echoing a popular phrase amongst older people in both our countries.

He smiled fondly. "Robin wrote to inform me of a mission he is going to give your team when you get back. He says you're doing better, and I have to agree. Something about you is different, although I can't put my finger on it. It's not that you're at peace, because you've always been at peace with your lot in life, as much as one can be. And you've always been reliable, trustworthy... but I don't know. You seem more, grounded, I guess. If that even makes sense."

I shot him a sarcastic smile, but inside a sense of understanding dawned on me. Maybe Eddie had been helping me more than I knew, forcing me to confront my past, and encouraging me to drop the masks I wear. Maybe those things would not just help me feel at ease with myself, but help the people that love me feel more at ease about me as well.

My smile turned more sincere and I shrugged. "I think that does make sense actually. My time at Barnsdale these past months has been... healing, in some ways." I shrugged, surprising him by pulling him into a hug when he went to shake my hand. "Take care, cousin. May we meet again soon."

Turning, I strode over to Eddie, taking the reins of my horse from his hand and flashing him a quick look. We mounted and our small party fanned out, heading back to Sherwood.

CHAPTER EIGHTEEN

Eddie

A knock sounded at my door as I toweled my face off at my water basin.

"Come in!" I called, and watched in the mirror as Red slipped into my room, closing the door behind her softly.

"You should always ask who it is first," she scolded, her smile betraying any real attempt at censure. I turned in time to catch her in my arms, accepting her kiss as my heart flipped over.

"But we're inside the castle. The only one coming into my room would be a servant, or you," I murmured when we broke apart.

She pursed her lips. "I should hope there would be no one else coming in here. Still, Nottingham Castle isn't exactly the safest place on earth. Marian could tell you from experience. But never mind. I'm probably being paranoid."

"If being paranoid brings you to my room with kisses, I'm not protesting," I replied, tightening my hold on her and pressing a chain of kisses down her neck." She hummed in approval but pushed out of my arms after a minute.

"That's what I came in here to talk about. We're about to embark on a mission, and we can't be doing…*this*… the entire time. We need to be focused."

I nodded, taking a seat and forcing my brain to focus on the needed conversation in front of us. She stood a few feet away, arms crossed and slight frown pulling at the corners of her mouth.

"We're both professionals, Red. As much as I can't deny that you make my heart trip in a way no one else has ever done, I also know myself well enough to say that this won't get in the way of the job. I don't think you'll have a problem either."

Red scoffed, turning away slightly. "That just shows what you know about how I feel."

I looked at her with interest, but tamped down on the desire to pursue that line of thinking with more kisses. Instead, I gave her a soft smile. "That's the most encouraging thing I think you've said to me so far, and I can't pretend to be sad about it."

She laughed softly, coming over to sit down in the chair next to me. "It's not uncommon in the Sherwood for military couples to serve alongside one another. It's usually encouraged as long as their jobs are complementary. But I've just never navigated anything like this myself. And..." she hesitated, then looked into my eyes with a frank expression. "I'm worried that these feelings are a result of our forced connection: the binding spell. And our time together all those months, and, well you know, sleeping next to each other."

I frowned, considering her words. "Well, this is all new to me too. As much as I fancied myself in love with Belle all those years, it was never like this." I reached out tentatively and she laced her fingers with mine. "I can't deny that I'm feeling the loss of that binding spell. I almost wish you would put it back. I hadn't realized how much it had let me... I don't know, sense your presence, your closeness?"

She drew in a breath and released it in a slow, steady stream. "I feel the same. What if these emotions will fade, the longer it's gone?"

My heart roared to life with a desire to protect her, from what I didn't know - our own feelings? The potential for heartbreak? Myself? Red gave me a quizzical look as she felt my hand tighten on hers. I relaxed after a minute, turning more fully toward her.

"I suppose your concerns are logical, although in my heart I know what I feel for you isn't going to fade. But we haven't had time to test that, and you're right to be cautious. So before we start making plans for our future, let's give ourselves time. Let's get through this mission, and settle into how I fit as your bodyguard. No kissing, no endearments, nothing. Then we'll talk afterward about where to go, and if our feelings are still the same."

Red's eyes strayed to my lips when I proposed a ban on kissing, and a stubborn look came to her face. "I wasn't saying *no* kissing, just that we can't keep meeting for trysts like couples in the books Marian used to read."

A slow smile pulled at the corners of my mouth. "Is that what we're doing right now? Meeting for a tryst? Because if that's our objective, I might have a few ideas on where to take this conversation."

Red huffed out a breath, color rising in her cheeks. "This is what I mean. You can't say things like that when we're on a mission."

I watched her closely, soaking up each betrayal of feelings that crossed her face. I couldn't help trying to stake a claim on her affection, even though I had just agreed to back off. "To be clear. I'm going to pursue you openly whenever I'm able."

She cocked her head to the side, considering. "Will it interfere with our mission?"

"No, never."

"Then fine. But to be clear, I'm not sure whatever is between us right now is real. It might just be a by product of our attraction and that binding spell."

"But you'll allow me to try and convince you?" I moved closer and her eyes flicked from mine to my lips breathlessly, the beating of my own heart matching her erratic breaths.

"If that's what you want to waste your free time doing, then I won't stop you." She bit her lip, unconsciously leaning toward me.

"Then fine. Let the hunt begin," I said, grinning wolfishly

before seizing her lips with mine, teasing her with short kisses before they could deepen into something more passionate, and laughing gently when she growled in frustration. I gave in, meeting her more slowly until our breathing quieted, finally breaking apart and resting our foreheads against one another.

"I *am* making plans for us, Red. Don't push me away just because you don't like plans."

* * *

Red's unit was already assembled in the great hall, grouped around a roaring fire at one end of the room. I fell back a few steps as we made our way over to them, letting Red take their salutes and greet each one after months of absence. They eyed me curiously over her shoulder, but I stayed quiet, offering only a nod and letting them get caught up. They would learn about my presence soon enough.

Robin strode in the room a few minutes later, a sleeping baby in his arms. He walked up to Red and gave her a peck on the cheek, which she returned, and after a whispered exchange, handed over his infant son for her hold while he gave us orders. The sight of her with a baby in her arms did something strange to my stomach, and I couldn't help stealing glances as she drifted toward me, bouncing the little man deeper into sleep.

"Alpha team - it's good to have you back. I shared a little bit of your mission with your Captain yesterday, but I received more intelligence a few minutes before I walked in here that's changed the main objective."

Red looked up, still bouncing the baby gently and raising an eyebrow. Robin grimaced and moved to take his son back, settling him into his arms before continuing.

"You may be aware that tension has been building between Sherwood and Spindle ever since we lost contact with their Border Team One. Losing a team would be bad enough, but one with their princess..." he sighed. "There was nothing we could do obviously, and I'm sure Rapunzel would be reminding everyone that they were responsible for themselves alone. Understandably, her family doesn't feel the same. At any rate, we haven't had enough information to renew the search: until now. A ripple of alertness went through the group, like a pack of dogs catching a scent. Robin looked around grimly.

"One of her teammates was rescued near the border. He's in bad shape, but before the doctor put him into a medical coma, he was able to confirm that at least one of their unit was captured by the beasts, and taken somewhere instead of being eaten or killed outright. He claims that he was held in a cage until he managed to escape last month."

My jaw dropped in astonishment at the implications. *Beasts detaining a person instead of outright killing or eating them? How is that possible?*

"This changes everything," Red said darkly. The others nodded, grim expressions settling on their faces.

"Yes. Several of you reported that the Beasts you fought alongside Border Team One seemed alert and coordinated, almost like a human unit. This information substantiates your claims. Our escapee didn't know why he was held for so long. Apparently he was left in his cage and had no interaction beyond receiving food and water sporadically."

Eoforde spoke up, cracking his hairy knuckles audibly. "What's our new objective, then? Scope out his prison and see if we have any leads to the rest of his unit?"

"Partly. Your first objective is to find where he was held and recover any additional surviving personnel. But I'm considering gathering intelligence about how these "enlightened" Beasts are organizing, and what their objective is to be just as important. If they're becoming a tactical force, Sherwood will need more allies. But we'll need evidence to convince the other countries to take this seriously."

Red nodded, crossing her arms and looking at each of us in turn with a wicked smile on her face. "Sounds like we have a fun trip planned. It's a good thing we're all rested, because we're going to need it. And we have a new team member." She jerked her head toward me. "You all remember Captain Marchand. He'll be joining us as my bodyguard." I watched as her team members shot each other discreet looks of surprise before they nodded to me. "He's serving directly under me, and is only attached to the team, not technically part of it. But I may order him to work directly with you depending on the situation, so expect to treat him as a brother." She glanced at me before looking to Robin once more.

"I had expected to integrate him during a normal border mission, but since we're going behind enemy lines maybe he should sit this one out."

Refusal swept through my body, but I was careful not to let it show, cognizant that any signaling I did could undermine Red's authority.

Robin looked at me thoughtfully. "Have you had any prior experience in the Wasteland, Captain Marchand? It can do strange things to people while they're there, and we couldn't afford a greenhorn going on this mission."

I threw a quick salute, keeping my tone even as I responded. "I've done many border runs into the Wasteland during my service in Pelerin. Much of our war was fought at and around the border, so I'm familiar with the way it can play tricks on you. I've never spent more than a day or two inside at a time, but the majority of my service was spent in and around it."

Robin nodded, looking back at Red. "My advice is to take him. Your unit is yours to command of course, but his fresh perspective may be valuable. And from what you've told me, his fighting skills will be useful."

Red nodded glancing at me long enough that I could interpret her command for me to stay put before turning back to her unit.

"Okay, that's settled. We'll form up after early mess tomorrow, and leave with the dawn. We don't know how long this will take so snag a few extra food and water charms from the supplies office. Dismissed."

Her soldiers saluted, then filed by one by one, stopping to

either shake my hand or murmur a welcome before they left.

Red rounded on me as soon as the door closed on the last person. "Staying in the wasteland for week or more is different than a day or two. You're going to be a liability if it pulls something out of you, especially since you have latent magic that you're not trained in!"

Robin looked at his sister in surprise, before transferring his gaze to me when I responded with a skeptical look.

"I've already said I'm not going to challenge your orders, so I don't know why you're assuming the worst."

She scoffed, putting her hands on her hips. "Are you going to try and tell me you didn't immediately think to yourself, 'there's no way I'm letting her leave me behind' when I questioned your fitness for this mission?"

I fought back a grin. "I can't help thinking that, and I can't help that you know I was thinking it. I certainly would never voice such a thing in front of your team. You said you'd let me watch your back. Are you backing out of that?"

She rolled her eyes. "That's not what this is about. Questioning your fitness for your own safety and that of my unit is different than not letting you have my back. It's the *opposite* of recklessness actually, which should be making you happy."

"It does, Captain Hood, you have no idea. But you're forgetting I have extensive experience with the Wasteland, so I think I can handle whatever it throws at me, if not perfectly, at least so as not to be a liability. I'll have to bow to your expertise in the area of untrained magic, but if I felt myself being compromised, you know I'd self report before you even noticed, and you could send me back home."

She chewed on her lip, eyes narrowed as she considered my words. We turned toward Robin at the same moment, and I had to choke down a laugh at the shocked look on his face.

"What?" Red asked, confused by his expression. "I'm sure I mentioned in my report that he tested positive for mage craft. No minor amount of it either. My hypothesis is that he's been using it unknowingly since he came of age... well I won't go into my theory. Anyway, do you have information on how an untrained mage might react to prolonged exposure to the Wasteland?"

Robin schooled his expression and shook his head slowly. "I don't know that we've come across that situation here, or in Asileboix, but I'll check with Marian to get her take on it. She would know best probably."

Red nodded. "That's good enough for me. If she gives us the go ahead, you can go." She shot me a warning look, then turned to smile as her brother shifted the baby from one arm to the other.

He caught her look and returned a rueful smile of his own. "I wanted to give Marian a break and tote the little guy along to my meetings today, but I forgot how heavy they are even though they're tiny at this stage. His older brothers won't stay still long enough to snuggle so I'm trying to soak it all in."

"Just get one of those slings the nannies use, you'll be more comfortable," Red said, ruffling her older brother's hair.

"I know, it's just, I always feel like a bit of an idiot when I use one. I don't exactly look like a commander of the realm when I'm wearing a baby."

"No parent does, whether he's running a country, or just trying to keep the house clean. You're all just a tangled mess until they're out of the house and dating people you don't approve of." Red chuckled as he shook his head at her.

"Besides," she added, "you always talk about how Dad carried me everywhere when I was a baby. You look so much like him, I like to think I can picture it."

The siblings shared a sad smile and Robin tapped his son's nose. "Auntie Red has convinced me, little man. Let's go see Nanny about a baby sling." A cooing gurgle reached him in response, and he drifted out of the room, describing the schedule of meetings they were going to have to get through together, leaving me and Red alone in front of the fire.

The silence between us was thick and charged, dust swirling in the shafts of sunlight and the crackling from the fire giving voice to the crackling of my nerves at her presence. She reached out a hand to me and I took it greedily.

"We'll see what Marian says," she said finally, rubbing her thumb along my wrist. I squeezed her hand and she pressed a quick kiss to my lips before tugging me toward the door. "Let's go get our packs together. We have a lot to discuss."

* * *

"You can't put your bedroll next to hers! No one sleeps next to the Captain."

I looked over at Eoforde in surprise, pausing as I bent over my ground pad from our campsite. We had left Nottingham Castle early in the morning, making excellent time, and were expecting to cross the border tomorrow afternoon. I had a few nerves about the mission ahead of us. They were easily shoved aside by my gratitude that I could keep an eye on Red, and assure her safety with my life if need be.

"I do," I said, simply, then turned back to my task, unrolling my sleeping bag and making sure Red's was centered on her ground pad. The tent we would share was small, and huddled next to the other's around our fire. *I hope she has extra heat charms for tonight. Maybe I should learn how to make some when we get back. If I have the ability, I may as well use it.*

"No, you don't understand," Edith said, drawing my attention and giving me a kind smile as Red trooped back into view, several rabbits hanging from her game pouch. "The Captain always insists on sleeping alone." She hesitated, glancing at Red out of the corner of her eye. When Red ignored us in favor of handing over the fresh game to Broc over near the stream, Edith added in a lower tone, "she's a restless sleeper. I've heard she slashed her last tent mate's face from ear to chin when she was a foot soldier. She's always said that only a warrior able to beat her in a three out of three bout could be trusted to sleep by her side and not be murdered in their sleep. It's a bit of a running joke, but she's also dead serious about it."

I pursed my lips to hide my smile, thinking back to the first time I had bested Red in a three out of three, two months ago now at Barnsdale. My eyes slid to her back, watching as her hands slowed from the food preparation, her face turning just enough that I got a glimpse of a grin on her profile before she refocused on her task.

I turned my attention back to Edith and the others. "And no one's managed to beat her in a three out of three?" They shook their heads, Eoforde looking stern, Etta glancing at her sister ruefully, and Hreremus staring into the cookfire.

Eoforde shifted in his seat, his face his usual hue of beet red with glowering brows. "No, young man. And as much as we enjoyed your fighting style in those bouts when we first met you, no Pelerine could hope to match our Red Rider. Not meaning any offense, Marchand, but you're new here and don't know how these things go. Best put your bedroll in with Hreremus and and Aeflaed. Usually one of them is on watch so there will be room for you most nights."

"Ex-Pelerine. They chucked me out, remember?"

Eoforde barked out a laugh. "I remember, Marchand. And now we're stuck with you, heaven knows why. I would say that our bark is worse than our bite but then I'd be lying."

It was my turn to laugh as Edith threw a twig at Eorforde's head, earning a glower.

"Be nice," she hissed around her sister's storm of laughter.

Edda sobered up and turned to me as Edith started repacking her bag. "You earned a bit of our respect when we first took you in, prisoner though you were. And we're willing to accept you since the Captain has given her approval. But we're not going to baby you. If the Captain finds you in her tent, and she doesn't like it, none of us are going to defend you when she takes her frustration out on you in blows. She sleeps *alone*."

I gave her a grateful smile. "She *is* sleeping alone. I'll be sleeping alone too, just next to her."

Eoforde opened his mouth, a sarcastic retort obviously on his lips, but Red's guffaw of laughter interrupted. She had finished helping Broc and was walking toward our tent, quiver and bow held loosely in her hands.

"I guess I can't argue with that logic, can I?" She asked the group at large, shaking her head at me and chuckling as she ducked into the tent and began strapping her weapons back onto her pack. I hid a smile and went to help Broc carry our dinner ingredients over to the already boiling cauldron.

CHAPTER NINETEEN

Red

We made good time slipping across into the Wasteland, following a stream bed that had gone dry sometime in the last year. The escapee had mentioned using the white caps of the Northern Wilds mountain range to guide his way home, so we had a general idea of his escape route. It would be pure chance if we could stumble upon his exact point of capture, but with Edda's ability to sense Beasts from a great distance, we expected to be able to avoid detection while making a methodical sweep over the next month.

The sweep started out smoothly and we encountered few Beasts. It was hard going, the terrain ugly and mountainous, game and edible plants hard to find the further we went into the Wasteland. Most water sources were oily and foul, although we had built maps over the years of clean freshwater springs so we weren't in any danger of dehydration.

As the scouting team, Eileen, Hreremus, and Aeflaede felt most of the strain, working around the clock and often in tandem with the rest of us to find a trace of the escapee's trail. Finally, the only course left for us was onto a northern plateau that no Sherwoodian had ever explored.

Eileen stood atop the cliff we were scaling, monitoring two

ropes she had secured for the rest of us to use. Hreremus was up there somewhere too, already scouting ahead. Aeflaed was probably an hour behind us, scouting our rear. *Creator you've given me what I've been asking for, a mission to rescue Rapunzel, but I could do with a bit more rescuing and less touring the countryside.*

A sharp intake of breath snapped my eyes to Edda, waiting at the bottom of one of the ropes for her turn to ascend.

"Captain," her eyes were unfocused as she spoke, concentrating somewhere inward, "there are Beasts nearby. An entire pack. Maybe fifteen?"

Wystan stepped away from the other rope, and I felt Eddie turn behind me, his concentration focused on the scraggly treeline behind us.

"Where? Top of the cliff or down here?" I demanded urgently, keeping my voice low as I glanced up in time to see Eileen help Broc scramble over the edge of the cliff.

"Hard to tell," she replied, gaze still unfocused. "They're closing from the East, but I haven't caught their scent yet. Mise can sense their presence."

Edda's mouse companion seemed odd to many for a warrior, but it's sense of Beast's presence was parallel to none. That, combined with Edda's skill with a blade made for a formidable addition to my unit.

I tapped my moonstone brooch, getting Eileen's attention, not daring to risk a voice spell. Casting magic in the Wasteland while Beasts were nearby would alert them to our presence easily. Spelled objects used magic that had already been cast, so they weren't as easily detectable.

Eileen looked down, making an exaggerated questioning motion. I used a series of hand signals to convey the news and ask her to scan the area for hostiles from her perch. Her hawk companion, Trewe, would help her spot anything moving above or below the cliff. I hissed to get the rest of the team's attention.

"Edda senses a Beast pack nearby, closing from the East. Eileen is attempting to obtain a visual. We'll wait for her signal. If they're above, Edda and Barden, you'll go up next since you're the best climbers out of the rest of us. If they're below, we'll have the others pull up the rope and we'll face them down here as best we can."

Each soldier nodded, loosening weapons and taking a minute to stretch or secure packs that might get in the way during a fight. Eddie's eyes were dark and serious as he moved to put himself between me and the incoming pack. His shadow, which had been flickering oddly for the last week at least, seemed a writhing mass of darkness as he moved, making my eyes blink. We had been teasing him about the Wasteland's gentle treatment as soon as it had appeared. *Will the stress of this fight bring out something even worse?* I shook my head. *Too late to worry about that now.*

"Wystan, contact Aeflaede and Hreremus and tell them to fall in as quick as possible. We may need everyone's help given our position." Wystan moved to comply when I felt a pulse on my moonstone brooch. Snapping my head up, I saw Eileen crouching at the edge of the cliff. Using exaggerated hand signals, my eyesight not being as sharp as her companion enhanced sight, she confirmed a visual on the pack.

"They're down with us," I relayed. I replied to Eileen with a few instructions, and she and Broc began pulling up the ropes while I turned back to the rest of my pack.

"Okay, we'll have a little aerial support from Eileen and the others, but I don't think Aeflaede is close enough to be able to help." I glanced around at the terrain.

"Not much coverage here, so if they aren't aware of us yet, they will be once we're in sight. *Don't* use magic unless there's no other recourse. There could be other packs close enough to sense it and we don't want to draw their attention." The others nodded, and Wystan glanced toward the slight cover the scrubby trees provided. I knew him well enough to guess what he was thinking.

"Wystan, take Barden and Eoforde. Fan out to create a funnel toward us. Once they're within sight, begin forcing them toward the cliff." Without taking a breath, I turned to the others. "Eddie and Edda, you're with me at the bottom of the funnel. Edda, I want you against the wall. Eddie, on my right. Let's try not to let anyone through to Edda, yeah?" I sent him a challenging grin, but his only answer was to tighten his jaw, his shadow flickering around him like wind whipping a flag. Elne surfaced in my mind, tense and prowling, sending waves of reassurance and battle hunger as we anticipated the fight.

Wystan threw a salute, then jogged toward the treeline, moving quickly and quietly, Eoforde behind him. Barden grinned at me, then clapped Eddie on the shoulder. Eddie jumped, barely biting back a snarl.

"Don't be so serious, Marchand," Barden admonished, "it's the first fun we've had since we got here. And don't let the Wasteland distract you." He nodded toward Eddie's shadow, then jogged after the others. Eddie's eyes followed him with a sullen look before he took his position, a few yards from me. I made a pass over my weapons, anticipation thrumming through my veins, dilating my pupils and making every breath echo oddly.

A few heartbeats later, an arrow arced off the cliff, followed in quick succession by several others. *Eileen.* She must have taken the forward position along the cliff top. Several huge boulders followed, slightly closer down the cliff line. It had to be Broc, since the others wouldn't be able to lift that size without magic. I glanced at Eddie and Edda, both standing at the ready, their eyes trained ahead of us, Edda's gaze going slightly unfocused every now and again as she and Mise tracked the Beast's progress.

The sound of scrabbling feet on rocky terrain heralded the arrival of two Beasts that had gotten through the other's efforts. Elne's rage swirled through me and I joined her spirit, feeling my jaw elongating, and fur rippling off the back of my hand as the battle rage took us. Before I could jump forward, Eddie sprang out of his position, preceded by his shadow. The shock of what trailed him into the fight momentarily stilled my motions.

Eddie's shadow had grown darker, almost an entity unto itself. Still amorphous, it whipped around Eddie in a frenzy as he tore out the throats of both Beasts in powerful, efficient motions. One moment, I had been preparing for a good fight, the next, Eddie stood between both dead Beasts, blood running down his forearms, clutching nothing but his fighting knives.

I closed my jaw, torn between chuckling at the quick change in events and growling in irritation that my blood was up and I had no one to spend it on. Elne growled freely and resentfully at Eddie, although I could tell she was curious about his shadow too.

Eddie turned his eyes on me, a quick assessing glance before facing forward again, just as the next wave of Beasts reached us. This time, he wasn't quick enough and I was able to dispatch one myself, a fact which obviously annoyed Eddie based off of his body language. We had no time to discuss it, as another wave of Beasts came through, Barden coming into sight with them. We fought them off, mostly with knife and shortsword work, as Eoforde came into view as well.

"We're almost done," Barden shouted, jogging toward us slightly as Eoforde killed a Beast a few yards beyond him. "Lucky we had Eileen and the others up above, they finished half of them off before the Beasts even knew we were there."

I grinned at him as Eoforde and Wystan appeared behind him, Wystan signaling that we had killed them all. "I was looking forward to more of a fight truth be told."

Edda's voice ground out next to me, sounding strained. "We may get it. There's another pack headed our way," she dropped her sword, face drawn as her eyes looked inward.

"Where?" I demanded, pressing a warning into my moonstones to Eileen and looking back toward our recent battleground.

A roar went up, and Eddie fairly leaped by me, growling savagely. I spun around, shocked to see a group of Beasts bearing down on us, and equally shocked to see that Eddie's shadow had morphed into an enormous, silently howling black wolf, moving along with him as Eddie danced from Beast to Beast, using knife, sword, and when that failed, his bare fists to put them down. Eoforde sprang into motion just behind him, and Elne urged me forward, the others fanning out to engage as best as possible. Ten minutes of intense fighting followed, gasping breaths between engagements, fighting tooth and claw, Eddie at my side, Eoforde fighting any who skirted by us.

Finally, a flash of white blonde hair caught my eye: Aeflaede. *She's trying to catch them in a pincer movement.* Wystan must have seen her before I did, because a moment later he appeared by her side. Their quick work meant the skirmish was over with a few last blows.

After making sure the new Beasts were all dead, we all turned to Eddie as one.

"How did you do that?!" Barden demanded, looking in awe at Eddie's shadow, which was now prowling back and forth behind him, stopping to sniff at each team member and any dead Beasts it came across.

I chuckled, shaking my head and lifting my eyebrows at Eddie. "I have to say that was a neat trick, did you have any control over it?"

Eddie's eyes were locked on mine, his chest still heaving deeply as he recovered from our work. My eyebrows drew together as I realized he was still recovering.

"It's fine. We've won, Eddie. They're all dead." I turned to the woman next to me for confirmation. "Right Edda?"

She nodded looking tired, "As far as we can tell, yes. Although I don't know why I didn't sense this group until they were directly on top of us."

"You're safe?" Eddie's voice rasped out, quietly, and I turned to find that he had made his way next to me while I talked to Edda. His hand snaked out to my shoulder, hesitant to touch me, but obviously wanting to reassure himself.

"Yes," I whispered, taking his hand in a swift, fierce grip before releasing it. The tension seeped from his shoulders and I turned to the others, most of whom had turned away to examine the bodies around us. Eoforde was giving Eddie a narrow look, but I focused back on Edda.

"Have you ever experienced that before? Not being able to sense them very far out? I've never known it to happen to you since you've been under my command."

She shrugged. "When I was younger I wasn't as good at sensing as I am now, but even then I could sense Beasts much further off than the others. I grew up on a border town you know."

I nodded, concentrating on cleaning off my knives and drying them before turning to look around us. "Well, don't let it get you hung up. Could be because they approached during a fight and you were distracted. Or maybe it's something about what type of Beasts they are. Either way, you were still able to give us a warning."

"Captain," Aeflaede's calm, ethereal voice drifted to my ears from behind Eddie. He turned, stepping next to my side to reveal the beautiful intelligencer, trailed by Wystan.

"Well done, Aeflaede. You arrived back just in time."

She nodded deeply, saluting with her fist over her chest. "My sweep took less time than I thought, so I was already heading back when I received your message. I caught site of the second group not long before you became aware of them. But that's not what I wanted to show you."

I raised my eyebrows at her. "What then?"

She held out a scrap of coarse brown fabric. Stamped onto it was the outline of a wolf's paw print, filled in with distinctive swirling designs, bound in twisting chains under a crowned heart. My hand drifted to my right cheek, touching the wolf prints etched there by gypsy magic when I was barely a teenager: the exact match of the wolf print in the insignia before me.

"What is this?" I whispered hoarsely, tearing my gaze from the cloth to Aeflaede.

"I tore it from around the neck of one of the beasts here." She flicked her eyes to a body nearby. "They all have have it."

Eddie took a step closer to me, looking between my face and the cloth. "Maybe it's a coincidence," he said, his gravelly voice low in my ear. Aeflaede and Wystan saluted, then turned away, murmuring to each other.

I shook my head. "I've never seen that wolf print outside my own tattoo." I swallowed, pushing the memory of the day I got it away. "I almost died that day, but John let a gypsy healer in to save me, just when I had embraced death." I coughed a dry laugh. "I felt the life draining out of me, so I told John I was going to die and laughed in his face at the thought of what Andrus would do to him." I paused as Eddie growled. "I should have kept my mouth shut. John obviously didn't like that idea, so he grabbed a nearby gypsy healer and let her heal my wounds. You've seen the tattoos during training." He nodded, lifting his hand up to trail the backs of his fingers along my cheek and under my chin for just a ghost of a second. I swallowed hard. "They track all across my body, most of them covered by my clothes, but all in the same pattern: an outline of a wolf print, filled with a swirling design." I gestured to my right cheek. "Like these."

"It's just a coincidence, whatever that insignia means," Eddie said softly.

I shook my head. "I've never seen that design before, and…" I crooked a smile at him, wanting to move past this somber moment. "The Queen said she had used many of my fates to pull me back from death, and that this symbol is the one of my true destiny. It means something that I'm seeing it now."

"The Queen?" he asked, suspicion clouding his forehead.

"Yes, the Romany Queen," I replied, suppressing a shiver as her face floated before mine. "She happened to be passing by at the time. No one else probably could have saved me, it was that bad."

"And she didn't intervene with Prince John?! You were a child!"

I shrugged. "I doubt she had the power to force him. But that's over now." I turned back toward Aeflaede. "Take the entire piece of fabric off the Beast you tore this one from. Someone obviously marked them. I'd rather they think this one lost it's collar entirely than wonder who tore this piece. Hopefully they'll guess they were fighting another pack."

I started back toward the cliff face, raising my voice to reach my entire squad. "Night will fall soon. Let's get up to Eileen and the others and put some distance between us and his battle." I paused mid-step to turn back. "Except you, of course, Aeflaede. You stay here and watch. If someone comes to find them, get as much information as you can. Depending on what you find you may want to head back to headquarters instead of joining up with us." She nodded as the rest of us turned back toward the ropes Eileen was lowering our direction again. The Wasteland was giving up more secrets than we had bargained for.

* * *

"I need to talk to you," Eddie murmured as he passed me by the campfire. He bent to tighten his bootlaces, his head level with mine as I bent over my map.

"Can it wait until tonight?" I replied quietly, my eyes darting around to make sure no one was watching our exchange. The touch of heat on my cheeks had nothing to do with the nearby campfire, and everything to do with the whispered exchanges I looked forward to at the end of every day, right before we fell asleep next to each other. By rights, my sleep in the Wasteland should be troubled and light, as it had been during every other trip here. I could see the effects of everyone else's restlessness on their faces each morning. Mine and Eddie's faces alone were as rested and full as they usually were. *Now that I think about it, he has been a little withdrawn the last few days.* I had put it down to the usual anxiety that settled on everyone after a few days in the Wasteland.

"No. It's not about… anything like that. And we might want to talk to some of the other team members."

Our eyes met briefly and my brow furrowed at the implication of something wrong. "Okay, let me finish what I'm doing, and I'll meet you at the well to help with the water. We can talk there." He gave me a brief nod and straightened up, picking up the flasks he carried and heading toward the hidden spring used by border units during sweeps like ours.

Forcing my brain to cooperate, I scribbled the last of my notes onto my map, tracing over our next area of exploration before folding it up and putting my things away.

Eileen nodded as I passed her by, then turned back to chopping the limp vegetables she had managed to gather for dinner. I forced my steps to be even and confident as I approached the spring, hidden down in a little dell behind a patch of dense brambles.

Eddie was filling the last of the flasks as I came into view. He set it down next to the others before turning to me, grabbing the edges of his cloak and wrapping it tight to keep out the wind. I did the same, looking at him expectantly. "Well? What's this about?"

"I need to report something to my Captain, although I want to stress that I don't think it's going to present a problem in the discharge of my duties."

I braced myself for whatever Eddie thought important enough to report to me so formally, and away from the others. "Fine. Spit it out," I ordered, pushing my emotions down and forcing my brain to focus only on facts.

"Something strange is going on in my head," Eddie said, hesitantly.

I pressed my lips into a thin line. "Define strange."

"You know what's going on with my shadow..." he said, breaking off as I nodded. We all had unnerving experiences with magic in the Wasteland periodically, although my team had been out on missions so often it was almost as if the Wasteland had come to accept us. My eyes would probably be glowing red by the end of our trip, the main reaction I had to the Wasteland, and Aeflade's skin would begin to sparkle if she didn't have her camouflage charm on her, but the others rarely had noticeable physical reactions anymore.

"Well, it's not just with my shadow anymore," he said, his tone crisp and emotionless, a soldier giving a report. "I can only describe it as some sort of presence, hovering around the edges of my mind, and for some reason I know it's a wolf." I gaped at him in shock.

"A black wolf actually, like the night sky, or my shadow," he said thoughtfully. His eyes flicked to mine and his thoughtfulness disappeared under the guise of a soldier in report. "Like I said, it's not affecting my ability to discharge my duty, but I am getting a sense of it's… emotions, or feelings, every now and again, so I thought I would mention it."

I chewed on my lip, irritation mounting as I turned over his information in my head. *Wasn't there a more convenient time to allow his magic to wake up in his all his years?* I asked the Creator. *I know I said this trip into the Wasteland has been uneventful, but this wasn't what I had in mind.*

I turned my attention back to Eddie, who was standing stiffly in front of me. "So it turns out you're a shifter. This sort of thing is precisely why I didn't want to bring you out here," I said, turning and pacing away a few steps to collect my thoughts. He was silent, letting me process until I paced back toward him.

"The Wasteland is never kind, and I should have expected it to do something like this. We've had too easy of a time up until now. The problem with a shifter's first change is that it can quickly get out of control. And you've never had any training, or even spent enough time around shifters to know what it will be like." I put my hands on my hips, ignoring the blast of wintry air that swept over my armor as my cape fell open. "This can become a liability, very quickly. You should probably go home as soon as we figure out a way back around that rockfall."

Eddie looked at me steadily, waiting to make sure I had finished before offering his opinion. "If you order me home, I suppose that's that, but I'm telling you that as of right now, I feel fit for duty… just, a little strange. I would tell you immediately if that changes."

I huffed out a disappointed breath, the only sign of my mounting irritation and concern I allowed past my lips, although I was sure Eddie knew my mind. "Come on, let's go drop off these water skins and go talk to Eileen. She helps with the new recruits when we're stationed at Nottingham, so she might know what to expect."

Gathering up everyone's water bottles, we trudged back to camp, seeking out Eileen where she was skinning the few pieces of game we had managed to hunt for supper. Broc sat with her, preparing the rest of our food, and they both looked up at our approach.

After a quick explanation of the situation, and some more detail from Eddie, I asked for their advice. Broc looked thoughtful as Eileen launched into an explanation of some of the usual expectations for a late shifter.

"As you know, usually the later you shift, the less dramatic it will be, the thought being that the older you are, the more control you have over your response, and the better your communication skills will be with your companion. Although I've *never* heard of someone's first shift occurring past age 18." She looked Eddie over with professional curiosity, and I chewed on the inside of my cheek.

Broc's voice interjected cheerfully over the chopping noise of his knife. "He looks alright to me, Cap'n. Just a bit spooked. My advice is we watch him closely, but let him be. Send him back with one of them scouts if he gets a bit peaky. They could run information home and bring back supplies while your bodyguard over there recovers." He flashed a smile at Eddie who sent him a repressive look.

Eileen shrugged when I looked at her again. "It's as good a recommendation as any. Worst case scenario, we send him west into the Northern Wilds Mountains. As soon as he passes out of the Wasteland, he'd probably be able to get himself under control, assuming he doesn't die of frostbite. He could skirt the border south until he reaches Sherwood again. Or if he's lucky, runs into one of the Wilding Camps. Eddie, you'll report in if your symptoms get worse, correct?" Eddie nodded and Eileen dug around in one of her pockets. "Here. A suppressant charm. They're issued to new recruits in case of emergencies." I shot her a funny look and she laughed. "I keep one or two on me just in case. Sometimes I modify them when I'm out in the field to suppress traps. They don't always work but it's a force of habit."

"Fine," I said, dusting off my hands and looking at Eddie. "You're to check in every morning with Eileen. She'll give you guidance on any additional manifestation of your companion. Let me know if anything changes. If it gets out of hand, I *will* send you back to Sherwood." Eddie through up a salute, then looked toward Eileen as she spoke as well.

"You should start thinking about a name for your companion. That's the first thing we teach our children to do, anyway. Often times a particular trait or characteristic that you want to encourage in yourself, or a skill you want to have. Or if you get a sense of your companion's personality, you can use that as inspiration for a name."

"Okay," Eddie said slowly, looking around at each of us. "What are your companion's names? I can't believe I never thought to ask."

Broc burst out laughing, and Eileen suppressed a smile before replying. "Telling someone your companion's name is an intimate thing, so it's not exactly appropriate for you to ask us that."

Eddie grinned repentantly, holding up his hands. "My apologies, I had no idea."

Broc chuckled again, turning back to chopping vegetables. "While I don't want you to take this as an invitation toward intimacy, Captain Marchand, since you're supposed to be one of us now I'll tell you mine if you like." When Eddie protested he just laughed again. "We all know each other's companions, having worked together for so long. I can see you'll be with us for a long time too, so I don't mind being the first to welcome you." His eyes slid to me for a shadow of a moment, and I caught my breath, wondering if he had guessed at the feelings between me and Eddie. I shoved that aside as Broc looked away, reaching up to tug on the white shock of hair on his forelock, stark against the rest of his black mane.

"Beric, his name is. A badger, as you might guess. My mother named me Broc at my birth, having an inkling from my hair as to which way my companion would go. Runs in the family you see."

"Grain farm?" Eddie guessed at the meaning tentatively.

Broc gave him a wide, gap toothed smile. "Aye, indeed. Someone knows the old tongue. I thought those in Pelerin didn't pay it no mind anymore."

Eddie shrugged. "Not outside the church very much, no, but my father is a trader, and some of his clients in Spindle prefer the old tongue, so he made sure his children could speak it passably.

Broc nodded in understanding. "Well, I won't get into the why and how of choosing my own name as the details would be long in the telling, but suffice to say, I was raised on a grain farm, and my wife and children live on that same grain farm, and my heart is there whenever I have to fight for my country. My companion feels the same. You understand?"

Eddie nodded slowly. "Yes, I believe I do." Broc chuckled and stood up, pulling together the ingredients for our food and trooping over to the fire with one last nod at Eddie. "Ye'll do fine lad, just keep your wits about you and let the Captain know if you have trouble. No shame in that."

Eileen cast him an encouraging smile, then gathered up the chopping board and knives they had used to prepare the food and lugged them down to the spring to clean with a quick spell.

I turned my head to where Eddie sat beside me. He met my eyes and I gave him a soft smile. "Mine is named Elne. She's a wolf too."

"Courage," he replied. "You have it in spades. Thank you for telling me."

"I didn't have it when I named her. I thought I did. But I was quickly disabused of that notion," I replied bitterly, standing up quickly and stalking away. The Wasteland pulled at the dark thoughts my naming always produced, distorting and amplifying them the way it did any potential weakness. I pushed myself into campsite chores to distract myself, with only moderate success.

CHAPTER TWENTY

Eddie

When we slipped into our bedrolls that night, Red's irritation was palpable, her motions jerky and responses short. The wolf in my head scented her distress, and a tendril of his desire to fix it drifted across my mind. I agreed with him.

"I have no need for a shadow to protect me, Eddie," she hissed waspishly. "You don't have to sleep next to me. I've had nightmares my whole life, and done just fine without you here. If anything, I should be protecting *you*, especially since you're actually starting to shift."

I turned on my side toward her, surprised at her protestations, and a little hurt. "Everyone needs someone at their back. There's nothing to be ashamed of, and although it's strange, the wolf in my mind is not out of control."

"Not the Red Rider," she protested harshly. "I can protect myself. I'm no Princess Rosebelle, a new object to fix your devotion upon because I'm fragile and need protecting. You want me to become her, and I can see why. Her need for a champion appeals to the protector in you, but I won't be like that. I won't change who I am for you." I could feel the seems ripping between me and the wolf, feel him urging me to fight for my pack.

"I don't want that," I hissed back, angry and wanting to reassure her at the same time. "I *know* you don't need me to save you, but have you ever thought that *I* might need someone to protect? And that I want that someone to be you? I don't want you to change. I just want you to choose *me* for who I am, and let me love you the way I know how."

Her mouth dropped open in a small 'oh', a look of surprise sitting on her face before closing up like granite. I reached out toward her tentatively, and she let me take her hand as I ordered my thoughts. "I don't want to weaken you by protecting you. I want to make you stronger, make *us* stronger. The whole pack." A wild urge to pull her close and kiss her passed through my brain, and my hand tightened on hers. She met my eyes with a softening gaze and a surge of triumph passed through me. I couldn't separate my own feelings from that of the wolf prowling at the edges of my mind.

An almost inaudible hiss sounded from the direction of the campfire as Broc dumped earth over it to smother the flames. I stroked her hand under the blanket, not wanting to give up the connection between us.

"I know we need to focus on this mission. But don't let the Wasteland play tricks on you either. I've told you Belle has never possessed my heart like you do. You *know* I love you for who you are, not for who anyone else thinks you are." I felt the tension in her hand drop away slowly and I let out a quiet breath.

"We're not supposed to be talking about our relationship on the job," she reminded me in a gently teasing whisper.

I smiled, squeezing her hand and breaking the connection between us. "You are my job, so I'm starting to think that talking about anything between us counts."

She huffed a laugh and rolled her eyes, tucking her hand under her face and turning toward me more fully. "Sorry," she whispered after a minute, so quiet I almost couldn't hear. "What I said about Rosebelle... I don't know why I feel jealous about her sometimes. Just that she's so different from me, and a voice whispers in my head that if you loved her you could never love me, just use me as a... a palate cleanser of sorts."

I suppressed a smile, knowing that she couldn't see into my heart to know how ridiculous that was, and wanting to make sure she felt safe opening up to me.

"And I do fear that you're going to try and control me - that you won't be able to help yourself. Command, remember?" Her lips curved up in a sad smile, and I instantly became serious.

"That may be my natural tendency, but the minute I use it to make you do something you don't want to do is the minute I become a coward and a fool. Your own tendency toward rushing headlong into danger makes my shoulder blades itch. If you can let me watch your back, it would make it easier on me."

She smiled, closing her eyes and giving me a nod before rolling to her back. I smiled too and rolled over. *Creator, Lady of the Woods, whoever, if you could give me whatever fate is left that has her in it, I'll be grateful forever.* The sound of her deepening breaths called me to sleep quickly.

*　*　*

Frith? I tossed at the wolflike presence in my mind. It's only response was to settle more comfortably against my own thoughts, like a solid wall at my back. *Well, I like it. I think I'll call you Frith.* I nodded to myself, glancing at Red a few steps ahead of me.

We were a week into our exploration of the plateau. The pace was slower but the plateau itself was much narrower than the plains below, moreso the closer we got to the ring of mountains in the distance. Thankfully, there was more of the sickly trees that seemed ubiquitous to the Wasteland, and less of the oily, marshy fenland we had slogged through for weeks before hitting the cliff face.

Although the wolf presence in my mind had grown steadily stronger, and was disturbing on an objective level, he was generally a steady presence, and didn't interfere with my ability to live life, or even engage in the few fights we had entered into as we worked our way north. The only time his emotions left the steady even keel I had come to expect from him, were in response to my own surge of aggression when Red seemed to be in danger. Each time, we fought blindly until she was safe again, and afterward, once we were assured of her safety, his presence faded almost completely while we recuperated. We were slowly settling into a balance.

"Had a message from Aeflaede," Wystan muttered from the other side of Red.

She cocked her ear toward him, her eyes still on the broad roadway that had appeared in the distance. "What did she say?"

"Confirmed mission complete. Requested we stay put and wait for her intel. Thinks she's two days out."

Red sat still, staring at the road while she considered our options. I could feel the wolf in my head wanting me to urge her to stay put and mentally shrugged at it. *Not our decision. She's in charge.*

"Okay, let's set up temporary camp here. We'll be waiting until tomorrow for Eileen and Hreremus to get back with more intel on that road up ahead anyway. We can wait another day before moving forward. Confirm with Aeflaede and have her keep you updated on progress."

We set up shelters in a thick stand of twisted trees. There was just enough space in the middle of them to construct a few tents. We would be screened from the nearby road as well as the surrounding plateau. There was a stinking bog nearby that would hide our scent too. It didn't make for a comfortable wait, but it was the best we were going to get.

Hreremus and Eileen made it back not long before Aeflaed, the first two having taken longer in their scouting mission, and Aeflaed having gone faster than her initial estimate. Their information turned out to be related.

"The road continues in both directions for quite awhile. We weren't able to confirm where it leads," Eileen reported, huddled between Hreremus and Aeflaed as they all reported to Red. I sat at Red's back, eyes trained away from the little group, scanning for any hostiles. The entire area felt wrong to me. More wrong than usual for the Wasteland.

"Saw several Beast packs moving along it during our surveillance. Hard to believe that the Beasts built the road. Maybe it's a holdover from before whatever created the Wasteland happened," Eileen added, Hreremus murmuring agreement at her side.

Aeflaede sounded grave as she gave her report. "A Beast stumbled upon the remains of our battle several days ago. It checked over all the bodies, and I believe it noticed that the one collar was missing because it crouched by that body for awhile and then looked around the site exhaustively. Finally it gave up, scaling the cliff and heading north. At first I thought it had caught your trail, but after awhile, I determined that it was simply heading in the same direction." A tremble passed through her voice, the first emotion beyond calm serenity I had noticed from the intelligencer. I flicked a look over my shoulder to see tension radiating from her eyes, still fixed on Red as if about to deliver a blow. "It was the Beast Captain."

Red flinched at my back, and I turned my head outward again seeking reassurance that our position was still secure while Red processed whatever that news meant.

"Are you entirely sure?" She asked, her voice hoarse and low.

"Yes," came the simple reply. Eileen and Hreremus shifted in their seats. Nothing else moved outside our camp. I knew the others were spread out in strategic positions, waiting for the Captain to make a decision.

"Do you think it noticed our presence?" Red asked finally, her voice grave but steady. I relaxed slightly, the knowledge that she was under control soothing to me and Frith.

As Aeflaed hesitated, I couldn't resist throwing another glance over my shoulder. She looked paler than usual, although that could be the charm I knew she wore to suppress her usual highly visible reaction to the Wasteland.

"I think he knew it was you," she said finally, causing Red to sit up straighter.

"How?"

"He picked something up by the base of the cliff. I was able to get close enough while he slept the next day to see it. It was one of Eddie's handkerchiefs, and I know you used one to clean up after the fight that day."

It was my turn to stiffen, as I silently berated myself for not keeping track of the item after I had given it to Red. She used so many of mine, I practically considered them hers by now, but usually I took them back and cleaned them when she was done. That day I had been distracted by the change in my shadow, and the emergence of my wolf, that it had slipped my mind to double check.

Red sighed, leaning back against me slightly. "I noticed it missing the next night when we camped. I had hoped it would be blown away or that I had dropped it somewhere that wouldn't come back to bite me. What did the creature do with it?"

"He hooked it onto one of those bandoliers he wore across his chest. After the first night of rest, he didn't stop at all, and I lost track of him about a day ago. He was heading East, away from your location, so I decided to stop in and get orders from you before pursuing him."

Red let out a frustrated huff. "You did well. As much as I hate to admit it, our orders are to find where the escapee had been held, and try to locate Rapunzel. We can't spend resources on that Beast Captain. Now that he has information on our presence here, we had better get our job done quick. I don't want to face him on his home turf." She sat still for a minute, thinking. "Aeflaede, I want you to act as scout for Wystan, Barden, Edith and Edda. You'll go East along the road we found, to see what you can discover. If you've found nothing after a week of travel, plot everything you've found, and head home. We've been out too long already, and if we don't find anything now, there's nothing left to find. I'll take the others along the western leg of this road, and do the same. When you reach the bottom of the cliff as you head back, send us a pulse on the moonstones. If we're within reach, I'll reply and we'll meet up there. If not, continue back to Sherwood without us."

"Yes, Captain," Aeflaede saluted, then slunk away from our group.

The others got up as well, Eileen stretching and shooting a look at Red. "It would be nice to have Reynold right about now," she said with a smile.

"I know. He would even up the numbers at least. But I had to leave someone behind with the rest of the company. He's gotten used to that job in the last few years." Eileen chuckled, and she and Hreremus melted away too.

"Don't start," Red ordered, turning to look at me fully. I pressed my lips together.

"It's not your fault that I dropped it. It's mine," she said, her face stern. "It doesn't matter now. We just get the job done, and head home."

I drew in a deep breath and released it, giving her a nod. She pushed to her feet and went toward our tent, drawing the flap closed as I settled in to continue my watch. *We'll be moving out soon,* I told Frith. *We'll need to keep a closer eye on her if someone knows who she is, and that she's here.* His agreement flooded my thoughts, and we grimly continued our guard duty.

CHAPTER TWENTY-ONE

Red

We certainly missed Reynold's good cheer over the next few days. After splitting with the other half of our unit, we crept slowly forward, keeping to the scrubby tree line, with the road just visible in the distance, so as not to be seen. The going was slow, but thankfully we didn't run into any Beasts. However, the Wasteland itself seemed determined to deal with us since the Beasts hadn't yet.

Only a day into our new direction, Broc fell into a firepit. These pits were common in some areas of the Wasteland, distinctively named because they were large holes filled with fire. Worse, they were frequently covered by a thin layer of earth, held together by Wasteland magic and evil, resulting in any unsuspecting traveler falling to their death as the surface gave way. Luckily Eoforde had been close enough and quick enough to catch Broc's hand, but not before Broc's legs were badly singed.

"Have to go on without my cooking now, Cap," Broc said. I pressed my lips into a thin line, considering what we needed to do. "Let's heal you up enough to get you mobile again. Hreremus, you'll head back to Sherwood with Broc now. You can act as an advance scout since we'll be heading home within the week anyway. Take your time and just remain out of sight. Contact us on the moonstones if you run into anything."

The two men nodded, and we each contributed a little healing magic until Broc's legs didn't run the risk of infection. We all rested, and the next day, parted ways. After another two days of cautious progress, made slower by the knowledge that firepits could be under our next step, and conscious that perhaps that was why the road had been made, although by who, we still didn't know, we were arrested by something unexpected.

"You'll want to see this," Eileen called when we caught up to her at what passed for mid afternoon in the hellish morass of the Wasteland. She had been acting as our sole scout now that Hreremus was gone.

"By the Lady," Eoforde swore as he came to stand next to her. I walked up to peek over the shoulders, Eddie trailing a yard or so behind, more focused on our surroundings than seeing whatever Eileen wanted to show us.

A quarter of a mile from our position, and the obvious destination for the road we had been following, sat a large house. It was built next to the gaping mouth of a cave system that backed onto the first mountain we had seen up close so far. The rest of the range swept away, high and menacing as far as we could see to the east, and marching west until it met with the snow covered Northern Wilds range.

"He was telling the truth," Eoforde murmured, referencing the escapee's information, and Eileen bobbed her head.

"Let's rest here tonight," I said finally, recovering from the shock of a house in the middle of Beast territory. "Tomorrow we'll have to find a way in."

✱ ✱ ✱

We slept in shifts. None of us felt comfortable with the nearby mystery, undoubtedly the location of the escapee's detention and torture. The next morning, we split up. Eddie and I took the left flank, Eileen and Eoforde took the right. Our plan was to scope out entrances, activity, and any outposts in the area. The next day we would try to find a way in.

"Here," Eddie said, handing me a piece of dried meat, and shoving another in his own mouth.

"Doesn't exactly beat Broc's cooking, but it'll do," I told him with a grin. He crooked the corner of his mouth in response, then went back to scanning our perimeter. Out of the corner of my eye, I saw him stiffen.

"There's movement in the yard below," he relayed quietly, shoving the last of his food into his mouth and crawling forward to get a better look. I followed suit, just in time to see Eoforde dash away, with several Beasts in pursuit.

"We need to help them!" I cried, pushing off the ground.

Eddie put a hand out, arresting my motion. "We need to run - look!" He pointed to our right and once I turned my head, I saw a group of Beasts running toward the woods near us, clearly starting a sweep. There were too many for us to take down quietly. If we got into a fight, others would notice and come to our enemy's aid.

"Come on," I said with gritted teeth, and we started forward as carefully and quickly as possible. The motion of the Beasts ended up driving us ever closer to the house.

Finally, we found ourselves hidden in a thicket close to where the back of the house met the mountain face behind it, straining to listen.

Footsteps crunched on the rocky ground, and I shot a glance at Eddie, a stab of fear for the both of us worming it's way into my heart. *They're coming toward us still!* My eyes looked around wildly, and I spotted what looked like a service door on the wall of the building. Jerking my head toward it, I motioned to Eddie to watch my back, then sprinted over on quick feet, praying to the Lady that it would be unlocked. Fumbling, I couldn't get it to open, pulling with all my might. Suddenly, Eddie appeared right behind me, reaching around to push, and we both went stumbling into the darkness beyond.

"They were almost on our position. Let's find a place to hide," he hissed in my ear as we untangled our limbs and got to our feet.

Eddie quickly shut the outside door while I tapped my moonstone brooch, putting forth a dim gray light. It was enough to make the edges of the hallway we stood in visible, but not enough to draw unwanted attention. Double doors stood closed at the end of a short corridor, with additional doors leading off on each side. The one to the left led straight into the rock face of the mountain. The idea of being surrounded by impenetrable rock didn't appeal to me, so I started for the door on the right. Eddie followed at my back, facing away to cover any intrusion from the outside.

Quietly, I lifted the latch and opened it a crack, covering the light from my moonstone as I did. The interior was dark, so I opened the door wider and looked around.

"Some sort of storage area," I whispered back to Eddie, "come on."

We passed silently into the room and secured the door behind us, scanning the boxes clustered at random around the room. A scuffling sounded in the hall, followed by a door slamming. The noise sent us scrambling. Eddie dove behind a tower of boxes to the right of the door, I settled down behind one at the back.

We waited, each breath seeming too loud, and my muscles screaming at their forced stillness. Eventually all was quiet again. I crept towards Eddie's position, settling down and leaning in close so we could talk quietly.

"We need to find out what's going on in here since we've gained entry. Let's try to make contact with Eoforde and Eileen too."

Eddie's face was just visible in the dim gray light from my brooch. His jaw was set, and I could tell he didn't like the idea of moving around the facility.

"Eddie, it's no time for cold feet. We have to figure out what's going on here. We haven't come all this way to turn around and leave just as we get to the most important discovery in the

Wasteland in centuries. I'll make sure you get out alive."

His lips curled up in a snarl, his eyes seeming to glow in the dim light. "I'm not worried about me, Red."

I huffed out a laugh. "This is my job, Eddie. It's what I'm good at. So if that's a problem, you shouldn't have volunteered to be my bodyguard."

This time he did snarl. "It's not just me, Frith agrees. You need protection, to stay safe with the rest of the pack. I need to get you out of here."

A surge of interest washed over me from Elne, and it gave me pause. "Eddie, did you say Frith?"

He looked a little bashful. "Yes, that's what I named him. My... companion."

I grinned. "Peace and stability, right? A good name for a companion to you."

He rolled his eyes. "Yes, but I'm not likely to get either if you won't fall in line."

I stuffed down another laugh. "You can't say I didn't warn you. But I think I know what's going on. If you're communicating enough with your companion to name him, then you're pretty far progressed in your shift. The only other thing that may happen is a physical manifestation. It's probably a good time to use that suppression charm Eileen gave you, otherwise your wolf's desire to protect your pack is only going to get stronger. It's not really a good time for all that, is it?"

He looked like he wanted to argue for a minute, then sighed and pulled the charm out of one of his pockets. "Fine. How do I use it?" I showed him how and he turned it on, laying his head back as the spell washed over him.

"The magic shouldn't attract any Beasts since it's low level and has technically already been cast. There won't be a surge of power unless something messes with the spell work."

"Okay," he said, eyes still closed. "Not sure if it's working yet, but let's talk next steps. How exactly are we going to sneak around this house, or whatever it is? And how do we get in touch with the others?"

"I already sent out a pulse to Eileen and Eoforde. They'll contact me when they get to safety. If they're in range, that is. Otherwise we'll have to rendezvous at the cliff or the border, like we planned."

He nodded. "Right." After hesitating for a minute, he spoke again, reluctance shading his words. "This might sound funny, but this place reminds me a little of Croiseux... my parent's house. Not in shape exactly, but the style we have in Pelerin. If it's the same, there should be servants corridors in some of the thicker walls. That would allow us to move from place to place without being seen... as long as these Beasts don't have servants waiting on them hand and foot."

I snorted. "I doubt it. But do you think you can find them?"

He grinned. "I spent my youth running around the ones at Croiseux. If I'm right, there's probably one in this room. It's just like the larder near the kitchens in Croiseux.

Moving quietly, we walked around to the back wall, close to where I had first hid. He searched around the filthy wood paneling until he found something. Pressing firmly, I heard a snick, and then watched as the paneling slid into a recess in the wall, revealing a wide opening onto a light-less passage.

"The kitchen is probably directly across from here. Makes it easy for deliveries to be placed in the pantry, and then accessed by the kitchens without having to lug them all around the halls."

"Well, lead on. Let's see where these go."

We traveled in silence after that, eventually tracing the passageway around half of the first floor, and finding a rickety staircase leading up to an additional cramped passageway on the second floor. The rooms up there clearly hadn't seen use in a long time, so we decided to use the upstairs for sleeping in relative security, and the downstairs for gathering intelligence. Just as we had finished our explorations of the passages, I received a pulse back from Eileen.

"They're injured, but safe," I relayed to Eddie. "I told her to head back to Sherwood as we planned and let them know what we found. You and I should be able to follow in a few days."

* * *

The first day was quiet. Nothing much happened inside, especially since we didn't know the patterns of the Beasts or whoever was using this place, so we didn't know where to go to get intel. The next several days were spent tracking the few Beasts that did pass through the house, their growls and screeches audible through the walls. Most seemed to enter and either stop in at one of the front rooms, or pass straight through the house and into the mountain. It was dull work. We both had a fair supply of dried food in our packs, but it was beginning to run low, as was our water. There was a freshwater spring not far from the entrance we used to get into the house, but we didn't like risking being caught, so we rationed our trips out.

"You may as well tell me," Eddie said, about a week into our uninteresting surveillance. "We're going to die here, either from boredom, or from discovery by the Beasts."

I shot him a look. "Tell you what?"

"Your name. The real story of why you're known as 'The Red Rider', and not one of those campfire stories please."

I sighed, feeling sluggish from mild dehydration and the cramped walls. *He's probably right,* I told Elne. *We're either going to die, not learning a thing about this place, or once we've uncovered it's secrets, die from a Beast attack trying to get back.* I shrugged.

"I guess you've earned a bit of my trust over the last year, Marchand. And since you're right, and we'll probably be dying here soon, why not?"

"Really?" He asked, sitting up straight and scooting a little closer to where where I sat against the wall in the upstairs passage.

I rolled my eyes, then gave him a twisted smile. "The truth is, my brother Robin gave me the nickname Red when I was little. The color has been following me since before I could remember. It was always my favorite. My mother said I would reach out to it before I could walk or talk, always wanting any red thing that came near me." A sad smile curled my lips as a memory flashed across my mind. "We used to grow sunflowers at Barnsdale. There must have been a market for them for some reason, I'm not sure. I loved running through the fields of them. But my favorites were these dark red sunflowers my mother grew in her own little garden. Whenever they bloomed she would cut half of them and put them in my room, or let me play with them."

"And that's why Robin called you Red?" Eddie asked.

"No. Or maybe partly. But mostly it was my red cape. My mother made me a bright red winter cape one year for Christmas. It had beautiful embroidery and was of course, my favorite color, but was also practical since I was half wild and it would make me more visible in my rambles in the woods around our home. I loved the thing, wearing it almost year round, except on the hottest days. My mother took to adding strips of red fabric to the bottom instead of making me a new one, that's how attached I was. And so Robin started calling me Red to annoy me."

"Well. That's not at *all* how I thought this story was going to go, I admit."

I laughed. "Yes, it's not an impressive origin story, that's true. Nor is the one for The Red Rider." He raised his eyebrows and settled back, watching me intently as I continued.

"I was wearing the cape when John came. I ran out to meet the carriage, thinking it was just going to be my grandmother. Instead it was John, and, well you know what happened after that." I shook the images of that day away before they could drag me down. Elne whined and growled in my head, not liking my recitation of the events.

"Anyway, after a time of... deciding what to do with me, I suppose, John decided to send me to join the forest guard early. He made the decision in the dead of winter, and on a whim, packing me up with a few hours notice, and just the clothes on my back. My mother had added a length of fabric to the end of my cape not long before, and it was the only winter ready one I had, so it's the one I wore to the unit. Unfortunately, since they didn't have advance knowledge of me joining, and had orders to put me to work immediately, I ended up wearing the red cape on our patrol duties."

"That doesn't seem safe for patrolling," Eddie commented, his eyes tracing my face.

I shook my head. "I can tell you the others in my squad didn't like my visibility. They blamed me every time something went wrong, and perhaps they were right. I was a rookie, and visible to any Beast or enemy within fifty yards."

"But you survived."

"Yes. I survived. I even thrived despite my lack of training and youth. Elne helped. By the time my standard issue uniform, including a woodland cloak, arrived, my red cape had become something of a mascot to my unit. My commander ordered me to continue to wear it, so I did. Evenutally, I rose through the ranks, even after being put on border patrol, and when I was older, John pulled me into the Royal Guard, second in command after Guy de Gisbourne. When Robin and Marian convinced me to join their cause, I didn't hesitate. I rode across the country, convincing my old units, and as many others as I could to join us, as well as stirring up the people with Robin and Marian. My red cape was easy to follow, and I had become famous already anyway. So after the revolution, that's what I was known by, The Red Rider, who raced across Sherwood to bring John to justice."

Eddie sat quietly for a long time, studying the floor. I was too lost in my own thoughts to wonder what his were. Finally, he cleared his throat.

"So, if Red isn't your real name, what is?"

I snorted. "Even if it wasn't the name I had at birth, Red has become my name in every way that matters." He just looked at me steadily and I sighed. "Tournesol. My mother named me Tournesol when I was born. It means-"

"Sunflower," he interrupted, one side of his mouth turned up in a smile. "In the Pelerine old tongue."

"Yes. My mother is Asilean, you remember. Your countries

share more history than Sherwood and Pelerin. It's one reason why I didn't like using it, as I grew up. Too Pelerine. Reminding me of the court Prince John was always trying to imitate. And being named for a flower... wasn't exactly something I wanted to flaunt when I joined the military. So I became Red instead."

"I like Tournesol. I wish you would let me call you that."

"No," I said, slicing my hand through the air in finality. "Tournesol died in that tower when Prince John came. I'm not her anymore. And I wouldn't want to be."

Eddie pressed his lips together. "Well you don't have to be Red your whole life you know. She saved your life when all you could do was survive each day, and she saved Sherwood, but she doesn't seem like the type that could settle down and live a full life."

I gave him a sad smile. "I'm not sure *I'm* the type to be able to do that."

"I don't know. We settled into something that... worked... at Barnsdale. Didn't you think so?" He leaned over, pushing his shoulder next to mine. I leaned into the contact, glad of his presence beside me.

"Yeah, actually. I did."

He slipped an arm around my shoulders, and I let him hold me for a minute before pulling away and grabbing some of the dwindling food in my pack to eat.

"Well if your names have represented a part of your life, why not take a new one to represent a new part of your life. A more peaceful one."

I gave him a look, then gestured around the cramped space we sat in.

"Well, the dawn of a more peaceful one then." His eyes lit up. "Sol. From your name. It means sun. How about Sunny?"

I choked on my beef jerky. "No way."

He grinned. "I bet that's what you said when Robin started calling you Red all those years ago, and now you're defending that nickname!"

I froze, my anger on my face dissolving into amusement. "Just because you're right about that doesn't mean I want everyone calling me Sunny!"

He moved toward me, capturing my face in between his hands. I could feel the grit on his palms from the dust in each passage we patrolled, smearing against my unwashed face.

"Just me then. When we're alone. Let me call you that, as a promise that there are clear skies ahead, and better days." He pressed a kiss to my lips, not an earthshattering one, just a soft, slow promise of warmth, and trust, and loyalty. I pressed my lips back, basking in the moment, daring to let my armored heart crack just a little, at the thought that something steady and good could grow from this moment.

"Okay." I whispered, when we broke apart a minute later, rolling my eyes. "But we need to complete this mission to see where that promise could lead." His grin lit up the dark.

CHAPTER TWENTY-TWO

Eddie

Just as we began debating heading back to Sherwood, a break came. We were sitting at opposite ends of the servant's corridor down stairs, listening near the front rooms which seemed to be used periodically. We had decided to stay one more day, the absolute limit based off of our food stores, then head out in the morning if we discovered nothing else. There had been almost no movement in the cavernous house for the last few hours, when suddenly I noted Red shift closer to the wall, pressing her ear flat. She was scarcely visible in the gloom both our moonstone brooches threw into the passageway, but over the last month in the Wasteland I had grown attuned to her every movement, especially since gaining sharpened senses from my wolf companion. She motioned me forward and I crept silently down the corridor. As I settled down next to her, I could hear what had caught her attention.

A deep growling voice sounded from the other side of the wall, speaking in a barely discernible form of Old Tongue.

"...have received a report from my underlings that humans have been here, and I can indeed smell their scent at the House."

A pause ensued, while a whispering murmur brushed at our

ears, too soft for us to make out.

"That unit pursued, but they failed to capture them my Queen. I have already dealt with the weaklings."

I shot a look at Red and she nodded. *Aeflaede and the others must have escaped.* The voice spoke up again after another pause.

"I do not know. I wanted to report in first. I will check on the prisoner immediately."

My eyes shot back to Red, the alarm I felt matching what I saw in her eyes.

'Rapunzel?' she mouthed, and I shrugged. *If the princess has been nearby all this time, I'm going to go nuts,* I told Frith. His presence had been muted by the suppression charm, but I could still feel him and talk to him. For some reason I found that comforting.

Red and I exchanged a series of hand signals, then moved out, using the servants passages to get as close to the mountain entrance as possible. We watched as a hulking Beast, walking on two legs, passed through the doors.

Red stiffened at my side, whispering almost inaudibly, "That's the Captain. The one that took down Rapunzel's unit and killed half of my company on my last detail."

I put my hand on my shoulder to steady her. "Let's focus on the mission. If that was him talking, there's more here than meets the eye. We need to get intel back to Sherwood." She nodded, and we settled down to the difficult task of waiting. Based on the previous patterns we had observed, we guessed that the Beast… Captain… would come back out in a few hours, which is when we would slip through the mountain door to check on the prisoner ourselves.

An hour later, we were in luck. He stormed back through the doors, stopping in at the front room again, before leaving the house entirely. Red tapped my shoulder, and we swept through the door.

* * *

A rough hewn corridor lay on the other side, damp and fetid, making both of us gag at our first step through. It branched off a few paces ahead and Red stopped, sniffing the air even as she gagged again. She motioned me down the righthand side and after a few minutes I could smell what she did. The Beast Captain's scent, and fresh. We followed it, meeting no one else, to a chamber about one hundred yards from the door. Quietly, we confirmed there were no guards and stepped inside.

A gaunt form hung front chains secured to bedrock, it's dark hair and clothes filthy, it's head hanging forward to obscure it's face.

"Rapunzel?" Red asked, and the prisoner's head snapped up, haunted eyes boring into hers.

"Ritter," she breathed, and moved toward him. I turned, taking up a post near the door while she figured out a way to release the prisoner. After several long minutes of rattling chains that I feared would give us away, she appeared next to me, half supporting him as they limped across the filthy space.

"Eddie, this is Ritter Weidmann. He was in the Princess' unit."

I nodded, noting his thin frame and sunken eyes. "Can you walk? We'll need to run, fast."

"Yes," he gasped, pain etched into his face. "Not very fast, but now that I'm free, and Red removed the charm they had on me, I think I can give us an advantage."

Red smiled at the confused look on my face. "Ritter's natural magic forces confusion on his enemies, giving him time to hide or escape."

"Well, not to be a pessimist, but seeing where we found him, maybe we should rely on stealth and speed instead."

Ritter shook his head, flexing his hands, so recently bound in manacles. "When they first attacked, they must have known of my powers, because the first Beast that reached me slipped a charm over my head, incapacitating my magic. I killed it, but was quickly taken by another. Now that I'm free, I can help."

"Enough talk, let's go," Red interrupted. "Eddie's right. We need to get out of here fast. I'd rather be in the Wasteland when they notice you're gone than in here. It will give your magic more room to work."

We walked as quickly as possible, Ritter hissing and limping with each step. I took up the rear guard, every nerve raw as I expected Beasts to stumble across our flight. Our footsteps scraped and echoed on the stone floor, marking every step toward freedom with a warning to any sharp eared Beasts nearby. We had just reached the main passageway again when footsteps sounded down the other tunnel, accompanied by scraping and growling. Red broke into a trot, practically dragging Ritter along, and I took up a defensive position while she maneuvered the door. We passed through, pulling it shut behind us just as someone came into view.

We pulled Ritter into the servant's passage, closing the secret panel just as the other door began to open. Growling and snapping filled the air as we all held our breaths. Ritter put his hand to his head, and suddenly the noise on the other side of the wall changed, filling with yelps and hissing. The Beasts seemed to scuffle around for a few minutes, then turned and went back through the mountain doors.

"Okay, that should occupy them for at least a few minutes. Can we get out of here?" Ritter whispered hoarsely.

"I'll take him," I said to Red, and she nodded, transferring Ritter's weight from her shoulder to mine, and pulling out her sword.

She led us out the side entrance we had used the first day. Luck was with us, and we met no resistance, although the sight of the sinking sun was a blow. Night would be upon us soon, and with it, Beasts.

"If we can get a few hundred yards away, I could probably work a healing spell without any Beasts here noticing," Red said in a hoarse whisper, panting as we looked toward the tree line.

I grunted, and nodded for her to lead on, before turning to Ritter and shrugging his army more securely over my shoulder. We shambled forward, sticking to a stand of trees not far from the house. Just before we reached the edge of the trees, a patrol of Beasts swept by so closely I saw leaves on the bushes in front of me tremble. The shock of our near discover froze every single one of us for a moment, our breath caught in our chests. Red was the first to recover, peering around covertly and motioning that the coast was clear. Ritter and I followed her out as quietly as possible. Soon enough I was dropping Ritter down onto a patch of dead leaves, several hundred paces into the forested scrub land just past the road. Red immediately started an examination.

She had begun her healing, when a keening howl went up somewhere behind us.

"Well, I guess they realized I'm missing," Ritter said, coughing as Red resumed her healing spell.

After a few more minutes she pulled away. "That's all I dare attempt now. You should be able to walk. But it'll be faster if Eddie carries you. We need to get away or hide, now."

We looked at each other grimly and I offered Ritter my hand, pulling him up and noticing that he didn't flinch with every moment anymore. I pulled him over my shoulder in a fireman's carry and turned to Red.

"Lead on."

* * *

The next two weeks were a long nightmare. How we escaped detection the first night I didn't know, but every night after that seemed to be one near miss after another. By the time we reached the cliffs again, we were exhausted in body and mind. Instead of camping there for the night like we planned, we doggedly ran on, stopping just before nightfall at a cave marked on Red's map.

Before we sealed ourselves in for the night, Red and I went outside to conceal our trail.

"Boost me up," she said, indicating a tree branch just out of reach. Going over, I cupped my hands and she stepped into my grip, catching a hold of the tree limb and pulling herself up. I stood below, watching her climb almost to the top. She shaded her eyes and looked north for several long minutes, then shimmied down, sending a scattering of tree bark and dried needles down on top of me.

"They've reached the cliffs."

"They?" I asked, dreading her answer.

"Beasts." She let out a long, steady breath. "An army of them. It looks like they'll try to scale the cliffs tonight. We'll need to pick up the pace tomorrow. If they're headed for Sherwood, we have a full scale attack on our hands."

We exchanged grim looks and went back in to Ritter, not daring to think how close our enemies were.

* * *

"There," Red gasped, pointing toward a distant dark splotch on the horizon. "That's the Northern Outpost. Once we reach it, we'll have a wall between us and the hoarde."

"And hopefully an army at our backs," I replied, taking a swig of water from my canteen before checking on Ritter. He looked better than we had found him, but not by much. Running for two weeks straight didn't seem to aid in the healing process.

"Yes, that too," Red said, taking a drink from her own canteen. A growing sense of protectiveness swept across me as I watched her, the desire to find her food and shelter and safety getting harder and harder to ignore. Frith's emotions were becoming stronger and more aligned with my own drives despite the dampening charm.

"Getting worse?" Red asked, looking at me with understanding in her eyes.

"Yes. I thought this charm should suppress this sort of thing? It's getting hard not to just pick you up and run all the way to the sea - as far from the Wasteland as we can get."

Her mouth crooked into a smile. "That sounds like a nice vacation actually. I've never seen the ocean."

"Nor have I. But we have business to take care of here first, I know."

"Exactly. So tell Frith if he wants to see us safe, we have to see Sherwood safe first."

Ritter trudged toward us, a stoic look on his face. "I'm ready. Can we make it there by nightfall?"

"If we're quick, and nothing else happens, yes."

"Let's be quick then."

※ ※ ※

We stumbled through the gate, all three of us falling into friendly arms that helped us to our feet again as we gasped for breath. Torchlight flickered in my eyes as we were given food and drink, and I followed blindly as Red led the way toward an audience chamber off the main courtyard of the outpost. We stepped into a small, unadorned room, the only nod to comfort a roaring fire and a few chairs. Red strode over toward a man standing by the fire, whom I recognized as Robin after a few minutes. I stood dumbly as they greeted each other, exhaustion pulling at my eyes and every limb.

"Brother. I'm glad you're here." She clasped his arms and they gave each other grim smiles.

"I got your message. Marian stayed in Nottingham with the children. What news?"

"There's no time. We came with an army at our backs, though our news will be worth the fight. I have no doubt they'll attack at sundown."

"Our scouts saw signs of a hoard, but you think it larger than the usual pack?"

"Very much so. We saw them amassing behind us, a company or more. We need to prepare ourselves."

"Fine. I have the rest of your company here, including the rest of your team that made it back."

Red and I exchanged a quick hope filled glance. "Who?" She asked.

"All save Eileen and Eoforde. The others are stationed at the wall right now." Red swallowed a curse and met my eyes for a second before focusing back on Lord Robin.

"Hopefully Eileen and Eoforde found a place to hide. They were injured and started back about a week before we did. I want the rest of my unit with me."

"All right. Otherwise we have the usual patrol here, my honor guard, and at least one company of Foresters on standby.

Red smiled grimly. "That should be more than enough to take the hoard, unless they picked up more Beasts along the way."

"Good. I want you to go to the healers, and then present yourself to Little John. He'll be directing things, but I want you front and center with your cape on. You know the drill."

Red drew in a deep breath as Robin's words dawned on me.

"The Red Rider." The first words I had spoken since we entered the room. They drew Robin and Red's eyes on me, the first held a question, the second, an invitation.

"Yes. And will my shadow be fighting with me?" Red asked, quirking an eyebrow.

I saluted with a fist to my chest, and Red's smile deepened. "Let's go," she said, helping Ritter up and slipping an arm under his shoulder. I took his other side and together we found our way to the infirmary.

* * *

A set of healers descended on us as we entered the cramped, sterile healer's chambers. One led Red behind a screen, another took Ritter away, and a third directed me behind the screen across from Red.

My healer turned to his tray of supplies after a quick examination. "No injuries, thankfully, just fatigue, malnutrition, and dehydration. Easy enough fix. But you'll need to take off that suppression charm you're wearing. Will that be a problem?"

"Not as far as I know. It was just a precaution in the Wasteland."

"Good. Take it off, and we'll begin. This will only take a few minutes."

I took off my charm as I lay down on the bed, and Frith bounded into contact with my mind. I closed my eyes at the onslaught of his emotions, and after a minute, opened my own up to him. Our concern over the coming battle mingled with determination to see it through, and see Red safe.

"I said you're all set soldier," the healer's voice cut through the turmoil of my exchange with Frith, and I realized he was giving me an odd look.

"Oh. Yes. Actually I feel in top shape, thanks."

"Glad to hear it. Is there anything else I can help you with?"

I shook my head and got to my feet, catching sigh of Red as I came around the curtain.

"Let's go," she said, striding toward the exit. I trailed in her wake, almost overwhelmed by Frith's presence and my newfound clean bill of health. *Overwhelmed, but ready.*

❋ ❋ ❋

Little John belied his name, being one of the largest men I had ever seen. Preoccupied with trying not to stare, I missed most of his short conversation with Red, and we were headed toward the armory before I could do more than salute the General and follow Red once again.

A servant ran up as we were strapping on our bracers, carrying a red cloak. Red thanked him and slipped it over her shoulders, pulling the moonstone broach off of her travel stained brown and gray one, and using it to fix the crimson cape over her armor.

"It's good for moral," she said, as if trying to explain.

I stepped up to help as her fingers slipped on the catch. "I'm sure it is." I replied, securing the pin and stepping back again. I knew she struggled to live under the cape of the Red Rider, even it was good for moral.

We stared at each other for a moment, but just as she opened her mouth again several more soldiers streamed in to retrieve weapons. She turned and grabbed something on the bench beside her.

"Here, the servant brought this for you." She pulled a black cape out of the parcel, and handed it over.

I grinned as I swapped it out for my own torn and dirty travel cape. "The color seems appropriate for The Red Rider's Shadow."

She tipped her head back and laughed, drawing the attention of the soldiers to us. "Well let's see if my shadow can keep up in the coming fight. I'll wager you won't."

"Then you'd be wrong, as usual, milady," I teased, with a formal bow, drawing another laugh. She shook her head and led the way out of the room, ignoring the mildly shocked expressions on the faces of the soldiers.

The next hour was a blur. We met up with the rest of Red's unit, shaking hands and comparing brief notes, studiously ignoring Eileen and Eoforde's absence. We formed up with the rest of the main body of troops, listening to a brief, and to my ears, undecipherable rallying cry from the General. Red stood by his side, looking like life's blood about to be spilled in her crimson cape and array of weapons, expression wild and tinged with bloodlust. I stood behind her, grim and ready.

She led the vanguard out of the gates into the Wasteland, and I stayed a few steps behind, heart pounding in my chest as it always did before a battle, my nerves coming more alive with every step we took. Once we got into position, we heard a warning blast from the wall. *Enemy sighted. Engagement imminent.*

Red turned to scream at our fellow soldiers, eliciting an answering cry. She turned to me then, her eyes wild and full of life, and I couldn't help the surge of desire that rushed through me, desire for her, for our cause, for goodness and victory and peace and life with the woman in front of me. I saw the same desire reflected in her eyes and I pulled her to me roughly. She reached for me too, our lips meeting in an insistent exchange of emotion, impressing each other with reassurance, promise, and strength. We broke apart too soon, our breath ragged.

"The Beasts are threatening our pack. Let's teach them why that's not a good idea," I told her.

Red tipped her head back in loud, wild laughter, then spun and pulled her sword, rushing forward as the first Beast swept into view. I sprinted at her heels, Frith's snarling focus mingling with my own until I couldn't tell the difference between us.

The next hour was a flurry of steel and claw, blood and bone, mud and darkness, as Red and I worked in tandem, needing no verbal communication to face each wave of opponents. Almost a year of daily sparring made sensing each other's intentions effortless, and I couldn't help answering Red's exhilarated grin with one of my own as we viciously put down our opponents. At some point, my brain noticed black fur had sprouted up my arms, and my face felt different, but it hardly mattered. I kept my focus on the task ahead of me, fighting at Red's side, and removing Beast after Beast from this earthly plane.

As I looked around for my next opponent, two vaguely feline forms dropped on top of me from a nearby tree. Red was several steps ahead, fighting something that resembled a bear, too far away to hear my grunt of pain.

Teeth tore across my back, catching the seam between the side and back portions of my fortified leather jerkin. I spun, clubbing one of the Beasts with the pommel of my sword before the other leapt on me, knocking me to the ground. It was at my throat in a flash, teeth sinking in, drawing a hot gush of blood before I could get my hands to it's neck. Dropping my sword I grabbed it bodily, pushing it away with all the force my rage could muster and managing to get to my feet. The first Beast took the opportunity of my distraction to sink teeth and claw into my hamstring, pulling me down on one knee as I pulled knives out of my bracers. Flipping one around so it faced behind, I stabbed backward in a swift motion, catching it in the eye by sheer luck. The shock loosened it's grip and I used my momentum to twist, bringing my other knife around and catching it in the joint behind the ear. It twitched as I pulled out my knives, snarling even as it's eyes rolled back and the body dropped to the ground.

A groan escaped as I put weight on the leg that had been mauled. My eyes flashed back and forth, seeking only Red. Finally I caught sight of her crimson cape whipping around as she turned her head and caught my eye.

Concern broke through the battlelust there, and she took a step toward me just as a looming figure of a wolf sprinted out of the dark mist behind her. The Beast Captain.

"No!" I screamed as it caught her by her cape, jerking her backward as shock swept her face. Despair and rage lit up every part of mine and Frith's being. *Protect the pack.*

CHAPTER TWENTY-THREE

Red

My mind raced as my body flew through the air, rushing backward toward the Beast Captain. I tightened my grip on my shortsword, bracing for an attack on my neck and back. I could only trust that my armor and shield spell would protect me from any mortal wounds until help came.

When the inevitable blow came, it was like a boulder slammed into my right kidney. Pain radiated through my torso, ejecting every scrap of air from my lungs. Decades of training meant my reflexes didn't need even a minute to recover. Drawing in an agonizing breath, I used the momentum of the hit to lean all my weight on my left foot and whirl around, driving my sword upward with all my strength. It grunted in response, tightening it's grip on the nect of my cape, cutting off my air.

The edge of my sword skittered along the front of the Beast's torso, my momentum tightening the cape around my neck even more. Frantically, I reached up, working to find my moonstone brooch under the twisted layers of fabric, parrying weakly as the Beast Captain swung at me with his free hand. The contact sent a jarring shock through my arm, just as my fingers found my brooch. Hastily, I used the last of my breath to splutter a command and opened the brooch, pulling with short tugs until my cape loosened and I was able to rip it away.

A growl reverberated through my ears, foul, hot breath rolling across my face, making me gag as a heavy blow hit the side of my head. My vision doubled for a moment. Staggering backward, I managed to bring up my sword in a blocking motion as the blurry figure in front of me stepped forward. His howl of pain told me the edge of my blade had done it's work, and a surge of triumph stabbed through my pain.

My vision cleared just in time for me to notice the kick he aimed at my gut. I doubled over, borrowing Elne's quicker reflexes, and managed to escape his hit only to have my sword knocked from my hand in a powerful swipe. A quick flurry of blows were exchanged between us, exhilarating even as I began to realize I wouldn't be able to end this fight anytime soon. Like last time I had fought him, his intelligence seemed almost human, paired with the savagery of a rabid animal. A stab of icy fear cut through my heart, which I met with grim determination. *We have to end him, or he'll deal a blow to Sherwood we can't afford,* I told Elne. *I need Eddie.*

As if he heard my thoughts, Eddie appeared at my side, blocking a blow from the Beast Captain before it could reach my thigh. The Beast roared his frustrated aggression, and I used the opening to plunge a knife into his unprotected neck. His hide was so thick it only went in about an inch, sticking out at an odd angle as I danced backward out of reach. The Beast pulled the blade out, throwing it and narrowly missing Eddie. Stickly blackish-red blood dribbled from the wound, and I shared a glance with Eddie. *This monster won't die easy.*

Eddie tightened his grip on his sword, pulling a knife from one of his bracers and I recognized his intention from our hours of training together. Pulling another knife from my left boot, I dodged sideways, timing my run so I leaped just after Eddie's thrown knife lodged in the Beast's side. Aiming a blow toward our opponent's jaw, I swung up with my other hand, catching it in the armpit with my knife as Eddie used my distraction to push his sword into it's gut.

Joy ripped through me at our successful teamwork, even as the Beast pushed me away. Eddie ripped his sword out, but not before the Beast lunged forward. Eddie wasn't fast enough to escape it's enormous teeth, which tore a chunk out of the side of his neck right before my eyes.

Bright red liquid gushed from his wound, sliding down his neck and staining everything in it's path, including the edges of my vision. I don't know if I even breathed, so focused was every part of my being on ending the one who was ending my pack mate. It was short work. A few blows, and the timely application of my last knife forced the Beast to the ground, it's eyes rolling back with one last snarl. As it died, a ripple seemed to roll through the air, and the relentless barrage of Beasts seemed to snap in an instant. The others either flew back into the Wasteland, or broke in disjointed packs.

I didn't stop to observe their behavior, sprinting back to Eddie and pressing my hands to his neck to stem the blood.

"No no," I shouted at him. "We're about to win this thing. Don't you *dare* die on me!"

His hands fluttered, one grabbing onto my wrist and squeezing, as light as a butterfly. "Worth it," he wheezed, his words coming in wet gasps. "You're worth it."

"No I'm not, Marchand. I'm a wolf girl with anger issues, not someone worth dying for." I poured magic into his wound trying to find the edges of every blood vessel and heal anything broken. There was too much, and it was too delicate for my skill level.

"Healer!" I yelled frantically, looking around even as I poured more magic into the man at my side. I glanced back down at his pale face, his eyes tracking my every move with tired slowness.

"You will *not* die on me Eddie Marchand, and that's an order," I demanded harshly, willing him to live. He crooked a sad smile at me and closed his eyes, his body relaxing under my hands.

✻ ✻ ✻

Curses streamed out of my mouth almost faster than my magic, certainly faster than the blood still gushing from his wound. A medic dropped down on the other side of him, a hiss of air whistling through her teeth as her magic probed into Eddie's wound. I held my tenuous grasp on the worst of the torn flesh and blood vessels as still as I could while I felt the medic begin repairing the damage.

She looked up at me after several minutes of frantic work, brow furrowed and eyes strained. "There's a Romany healer back in town. Got here just as the battle began. I heard it's the Prince. If that's true, he may be able to heal this. Otherwise, all I can buy is more time for this soldier to die."

"Do what you must so that I can transport him," I growled, my concentration slipping, resulting in a surge of blood gushing from Eddie's neck. I snarled, clamping back down on the veins and making the blood shrink to a trickle. The medic nodded and resumed her work. I continued my own slow assistance, rebuilding smaller veins and preventing larger ones from bleeding out. I was exhausted by the time the medic sat back.

"That's all I can do. It will probably keep him alive while you get him back to the Romany, just keep him steady and go slow. If it's not the Prince..." she trailed off, giving me a grim look before saluting and running off in a tired shamble to the next emergency.

There was no time to prepare a stretcher, so I layered a stretcher spell under Eddie carefully, making sure every inch of his body would be supported evenly, before I whispered the words to raise him in the air. I lifted him to hip height, grabbing his hand to ease the flow of magic between us, and looking around to chart the best way back to the wall.

With mild surprise, I noticed that the battle was well and truly over. Medics dotted the field, rushing between bodies as soldiers milled around. Some supporting others as they limped toward the wall, others sustaining stretchers like the one I had just created for Eddie, and still others moving to pursue the Beasts into the night. Hreremus jogged over, just as I began moving.

"There's a Romany healer in the fort, apparently. We need to get him there or he'll die," I gasped, stumbling over a rock and almost breaking concentration on my spell. Hreremus nodded grimly and began examining Eddie, sending magic into him to fix some of the smaller injuries here and there as we walked, while weaving his own magic into the stretcher spell for extra support. Blood dripped from Eddie's dangling hands to the earth as we progressed. My desire to stop walking and find each wound and close it itched unbearably, but we pressed on. People around us stopped and stared. At first I thought it was because of my presence, but after awhile, I realized they were staring behind us. I turned my head and sucked in a breath. There, a few paces behind our group, stalked a huge dark wolf: Eddie's shadow. I looked back to his sleeping form and smiled. He still had my back, even when he wasn't conscious of it.

We reached the walls without incident. Painstakingly, we maneuvered Eddie into the infirmary, Hreremus taking the lead while I followed behind and kept the stretcher aloft. To my relief, the gypsy healer was right inside the door and came to Eddie's side with a quick step.

"Your Majesty," I sighed in relief.

He offered a wry grin, motioning toward a bed. "Don't call me that, Red. Put him here and let me see what I can do."

I floated Eddie over to the bed and gently released the spell, sitting down as the gypsy prince began his examination. After a moment, I could feel his strange tingling brand of magic reaching out in tendrils along Eddie's wounds, binding them closed with magic, ink snaking across Eddie's skin. After what seemed forever, the healer moved his hands to Eddie's head, healing some moderate cuts on his face.

My heart skipped a beat at the tattoo that formed there. Wolf prints, identical to mine snaked up the side of his face. The sight made my chest feel warm and raw at the same time. *We're walking the same path. He's choosing my path each day. Could I choose his too? Is this what love is? Choosing each other's path?*

"He'll live," the prince said, coming to my side and putting a hand on my arm. "Though I had to take many fates to ensure it." He hesitated a moment before adding in an undertone. "You saw the markings?"

I nodded. "How could I miss them?" I drew a deep breath, drinking in one more look at Eddie, before turning fully toward my old friend Petro, the Romany Prince. "You know how many of my own fates your mother had to use to save me from John."

He nodded, giving me a curious look. "And you've had more gypsy healing since that day. To be expected in your line of work."

I offered him a weak grin and shrugged. "It's true. But I have a question, although you may not be able to confirm my suspicions."

"The only way you'll know is to ask."

"True enough. The the thing is, when we first met, he was a prison. I place a binding spell on him, just the usual one we use for prisoner transport." Petro nodded.

"Well, when I placed the spell there was a... a jolt, is the best way I can describe it. I've never felt the like before. And the longer we had the spell on, the more I could, I don't know, *feel* his presence. Not just that pain you feel when the other bound person is too far away, or the compulsion to walk toward each other when one is escaping... I mean I could feel his presence, and even find him by focusing on the spell if I wanted. He could with me as well." I trailed off, at a loss for how to proceed.

Petro folded his arms, considering what I had said. "That sounds interesting, very interesting in fact. Have you asked any specialized magicians? Marian is probably the most knowledgeable in your country, and she's your sister in law."

I shook my head. "No, it's not something Eddie and I..." I broke off, letting out an exasperated breath. "We've developed feelings for each other. But I've been hesitant to explore where they lead because we thought it had something to do with that spell. It reminds me of the Romany marriage spell a little, which I know you can't speak about. Is there any way they could be related? I don't want a palm reading, but I know you can see peoples fates when you heal. Is there anything at all you can tell me?"

I watched Petro's frown deepen, and my heart began to sink. I knew it was rude to ask for readings, and he was the prince no less, but I couldn't help wanting to know whether our feelings had been created by magic, not nature.

Finally, he spoke. "I won't reveal much of what I saw. It's never a good practice, because your fate can change given a big enough disturbance elsewhere. Here's what I do know. Your binding spell could not have accidentally become a marriage spell. They have similar origins, so I can see why you might make a connection, but they aren't the same. It sounds like you got a taste of what the old marriage spell is like, so if you do get married, I'd be happy to perform the real version for you." He grinned and I gave him a broken smile, nerves at Eddie's still form beside me clashing with the small seed of hope in my heart.

Petro continued more seriously. "Here's what I think happened, based off of what you told me, and what I've seen of Eddie's remaining fates. Both of you have sacrificed many possible destinies to continue living, so they have narrowed considerably; although as you know, we are never denied free will. You've obviously been led to this moment, where you're walking together with your remaining fates. As fates become fewer, they can seem clearer, more potent than destiny seems to an average person, walking around with infinite fates within their hands. When you linked with Eddie in the spell, I believe each of your magic recognized the other as a part of your fates, and naturally reached out."

I froze, my muscles and joints achy as his words settled in my brain. "So, you're saying that are feelings aren't true. It's all been created by magic."

Petro laughed and I gave him a stern look. "Red!" he exclaimed softly, squeezing my shoulder. "I haven't said anything of the sort. And this is why we don't talk about our magic with outsiders much. It's confusing. What I meant to say is, your destiny is narrow. It includes Eddie, that I have seen. Whether you love him as a husband, or friend, or hate him as an enemy is up to you. We live in a world of magic. It will be part of any relationship you have, so don't go blaming it for not pursuing the one you want. That's your choice." He gave my shoulder one more squeeze, then got to his feet wearily, moving down the infirmary ward to another patient.

His words chased their way around my head, and hope blossomed in my heart.

* * *

"I need you to be our liaison. You're good in the field, obviously, but the people love you, and not just in Sherwood. You know that. If they see you heading up this mission, they'll get on board, particularly Spindle."

I gritted my teeth as Robin's words needled me. Eddie was a silent presence at my back, but I already knew he agreed with Robin from our conversations after he woke up yesterday. I looked back at my brother and sister-in-law.

"If you order me to go, I'll go. You know I'm loyal to you. But negotiations and diplomacy isn't my skill set."

Marian smiled and glanced behind me to Eddie, before pinning me with her gaze. "You do well enough. Your presence is more persuasive than most people's words. And of course, you wouldn't be without your Wolf. Maybe he can share the load of the talking?"

I glanced back at Eddie with a raised eyebrow. He smirked and shrugged his shoulders, then bowed toward Robin and Marian.

"I go where Red goes. If she requires assistance, I will happily supply it."

A bubble of warmth radiated through my chest at his words. *He goes where I go*, I told Elne. *He won't leave. And we won't be leaving him either.*

"Fine. Between the two of us, with the diplomat's assistance, I'm sure we can strong arm everyone into a council of war. But what will we be presenting? How much will we tell them?"

Robin sighed and leaned back in his chair. "Everything, and more." He flicked his hand toward the door and it opened. Ritter strode through a moment later, still looking half starved, but much more energetic.

"Ritter, Captain Red and her Wolf have agreed to spearhead mustering the Council, but they don't know all. Tell them what you told me."

Ritter bowed and turned his attention to us, his mouth set in a firm line as he stood to attention.

"We had little time to discuss the place where I had been held during our journey back. From what you said, it seems you spent some time there, and know it's being used by the Beasts."

I nodded, excitement beating in my chest at whatever he was about to reveal. He drew in a breath and continued.

"The mountain behind the house is a coal mine, which is still operational. The house itself is in disuse, although it serves as a base of operations for the area."

"So they are organizing then? If they're collaborating well enough to mine coal, they're progressing beyond just wild hunger."

Ritter nodded grimly. "Oh yes. There is someone controlling them, who holds power over their actions and is somehow calling forth their intellect. My captor often spoke of his Queen's orders when he was torturing me for information. I also overheard garbled conversations between him and subordinates as they argued about mining quotas, and when they would be rotated back out to the "front". They were becoming more and more excited and agitated about an attack planned on the "Southern Lands". And just before you rescued me, the Beast Captain revealed that he was finally going to be allowed the annihilation of my homeland. He had been given permission to lay waste from here to the ocean. He offered me a place in their army in exchange for information on Rapunzel's whereabouts.

They mean to use her to strike at the rulers of Spindle somehow. They don't want to start their full offensive until they have her."

I shot a look back at Robin. "Then you should send us back out. It's imperative that we find her!"

He shook his head. "We need you to get this Council pulled together. If they're truly organizing, and have a leader that is ready to launch against all of us, our countries need to put aside our differences and fight together, before it's too late."

I opened my mouth to argue but he put his hands up, forestalling me.

"You didn't even get a reliable lead to her whereabouts during you month in the Wasteland, did you?"

I shook my head and he gave me a gentle smile. "We won't stop searching for her, of course. Since the Romany Prince is here, I've asked him if there's anything he can do to find her, any magic that they have that would help. He wouldn't promise anything, but he said he would do what he could. He's known her since they were children, actually, so he may know even more than we do about where she would hide." Robin shook his head. "If she hasn't been found or made it back by now, I'm not holding out much hope. But we won't stop until we have answers."

We discussed logistics for another hour, then were dismissed. Marian pulled me aside as we walked out the door.

"Go visit Barnsdale. It was good for your mother to have you home for so long. She has started writing to us regularly, and asks after the children. We'll summon you once we have the official envoy together."

I gave Marian a look of surprise before she swept away toward the nursery. Eddie's hand came to my back, putting gentle pressure there as we started toward our rooms. His voice sounded in my ear. "It's not a bad idea. Better than sitting around here in meetings that slow time down to a crawl."

I smiled. "You know, you do have a point."

CHAPTER TWENTY-FOUR

Eddie

As soon as I was given the all clear by the infirmary, Red and I left for Barnsdale. We went on horseback this time, as the stables needed a few horses sent to an outpost near the Friary anyway. Our journey on the main roads was much less eventful than our first trip from Nottingham to Barnsdale. The air was still sharp with Winter's bite, but the ghost of Spring hovered; a whispered promise that life would be made new soon, and it sped our journey.

After stabling the horses at the outpost, we continued on foot toward the Friary, making it just as the sun was beginning to sink into red and gold splendor. Friar Tuck was visible, drifting in and out of the abbey's beehives as we approached the ancient building. We lifted our hands in hello when he finally caught sight of us and jogged to meet us.

"Hello young travelers! Truly the Lady is smiling on us if we're blessed with your presence tonight."

Red laughed and I couldn't help smiling at his effusive welcome.

"We're glad to be back," she said, shooting a roguish grin my way. "Although Eddie's on the mend from a life threatening wound again, so I'm not sure we've made much progress since the last time."

I rolled my eyes and shook the Friar's hand as we all turned toward the Abbey together.

His eyes traced both of our faces with a faint smile, lingering on Red's the longest. "Well, I'm sorry to hear about another brush with death, but it's as plain as pie that you've made progress together, since last I saw you. It suits you." I glanced at Red, who wouldn't meet my eyes, and I hid a smile. *Not much gets past this old one,* I told Frith.

As we entered the living quarters of the abbey, the scent of spiced ale and roasting meat hit our noses, eliciting grateful grumbles from our stomachs. The Friar laughed. "Don't fear, there's more than enough for all of us. Wren has been cooking up a storm."

Just as they had last time, the Friar and Friaress enveloped us into the circle of their enormous and cheerful family, plying us with hearty food, a warm fire, and listening ears. Red told them an abbreviated tale of our journey in the Wasteland, leaving out the bits that Robin ordered to stay secret. I regaled them with the story of our trip to Asileboix, of the Beast Prince's forgiveness of the foolish knight, and the Beautiful Maiden at the ball who bewitched his heart. Red busied herself with one of the youngest children when I reached that part, the tips of her ears pink. We stayed an extra day, helping with chores and enjoying our time. There was something about the magic of the Abbey that felt as though it was a sanctuary that would stand forever, humble and free, even though it were surrounded by howling beasts.

Soon we had to press on, and we left with our rucksacks refilled and a spring in our step.

* * *

Barnsdale popped up in the distance suddenly as we rounded a bend in the road. Both of us slowed gradually and then stopped, taking in the view of the ancient Lodge. It's farm and fields were sleepy in the midday sunshine, green grass coming alive again, dotted with tiny daffodils and hyacinths, daring to fly their colors in the face of fading winter.

"It's beautiful," Red said in surprise. I glanced over. She looked as if she had never seen Barnsdale before. *Maybe she hasn't. Maybe she's seeing it as it is now for the first time.*

"It's good to be home," I said, admiring the view again. We stood quietly for another minute, the only sound a rustling among the trees and burbling water from a stream not far away. I felt Red turn toward me, and looked back at her with a smile.

"Would you like to make it your home?" she asked. My smile turned fragile as my heart picked up. *Am I reading into this too much?*

"What are you asking?" My heart beat in my throat, making my words thick. Red's neck and face were flushed, and she looked uncomfortable, but determined. "I guess I'm asking if you want to live there. Here. At Barnsdale. When we're not on assignment, obviously. I mean, we could live at Nottingham, we have rooms there too. Or even Asileboix, if you really wanted. Our apartments there are almost never used. But that's a bit far away for a home, and not even technically in Sherwood. It's just that you seemed to really like it here last summer, so…"

I caught her hand, tugging her around to face me fully.

"I would have a condition," I said, my voice low. She took a breath, squaring her shoulders and looking up into my eyes. "Yes?"

"That we live here together."

She released her breath and crooked a relieved smile. "Well, obviously. I wouldn't just dump you here with my family and run off."

"As husband and wife," I continued, and her grip tightened on mine.

"You know my feelings for you, and it's not just because of that binding spell. I'll die for you. I'll live for you. I'll help you build any world you want here, but I want to do it as one pack. Do you?"

She drew in a sharp breath and closed her eyes for a fraction of a second, then opened them, a slow smile dawning on her face. "Yes. One pack. Always."

My own smile grew in response to hers, and she drew me toward her, pressing a gentle kiss to my lips before deepening it into something wilder, more urgent and primal. I met her there in the joy of the moment, before gentling our kisses until we broke apart, leaning our foreheads against one another.

A throat cleared behind us, and we turned, startled. Mr. John Reed stood there with a frown, his son as his side trying to hide a smile. "I do hope we'll be able to announce wedding bells to my wife when I get home, Captain Marchand. She wouldn't take kindly to any liberties with our Red, you know."

Red laughed and tugged me toward Barnsdale. "Come on, Eddie. We had better go redeem your honor, or they'll run you out of town before nightfall."

* * *

"Eddie!" Marie lifted wrinkled, but graceful hands to me as I entered her parlor, and I paced over to her with a smile. "Welcome home, my boy." She placed a kiss on my cheek, and I settled into the chair across from her.

"Thank you, Marie, it's unbelievably good to be home."

"And will you stay long?" she asked, a hint of worry in her voice.

"Not as long as I would like," I told her gently. "Lord Robin has business for me and my... friend. The one I told you about. We'll need to travel a fair amount to complete it."

"Ah yes, I remember. Don't worry about me." She fished in a pocket and pulled out my old good luck charm, holding it out for me to examine. There were a few more trinkets added to it since last time: some red thread, a tiny sparkling gem, and what looked like a tiny embroidered flower. The dainty objects seemed out of place among the bits I had added during the war, but the more I looked at it, the more I realized they belonged. Each was a token of Marie's past suffering: red thread, perhaps the same she used when she made her daughter's first beloved cloak, the gem might symbolize Marie's own past as a princess, even though she lives so differently now, and when I looked closer at the tiny flower, I realized it was a sunflower. *Her daughter, whom she can't even speak about.*

I handed it back to Marie. "You've made it your own," I said, and she smiled.

"I've added some of my cares, as you can see. I thought the magic you put into the charm might help.

"The magic?" I furrowed my brow, looking back at the tokens in her hand suspiciously.

"Yes. Didn't you know you put magic in it, Eddie?"

I shook my head. "No, not at all. I didn't even know I had magic until just a few months ago. Could I have done it accidentally?"

She stroked the ribbon with her thumb, her face thoughtful. "It's certainly possible. Perhaps even probable since this is a token you used for luck in desperate times. And perhaps that's why the flavor of the magic is so sweet and sharp at the same time. It picked up on your wishes and desperation as you leaked magic into it." She glanced up at me, her eyes suddenly sharp with with. "I suppose I should offer it back to you, but I'm afraid I've become rather fond of it."

I laughed, as much in surprise at how much less scatterbrained she seemed to be as her little joke. "No no Marie, it's yours. As I said, I've outgrown what it means to me, so if it's helpful to you, then I'm happy you have it." She smiled and we sat in companionable silence for a few minutes. I was contemplating the history of my good luck charm, and all the twists and turns my life had taken since I had first found the original blue ribbon now binding all the trinkets together, when Marie's voice creaked out into the quiet parlor again.

"And how is she? Your friend, I mean. You've been taking care of her, I hope?"

My heart warmed at the mention of Red and Frith whuffed contentedly. "Yes, I haven't left her side. And we've discovered we work best as a team." I cleared my suddenly dry throat before continuing. "Actually, I've convinced her that we should always be a team. She's agreed to marry me."

Marie's eyes lit up, and a smile creased her careworn face. "Is that so? Oh I do love a wedding. I missed my sister in law's you know. She got married again this last winter. I couldn't attend as it was so far away. I don't like to leave Barnsdale."

Compassion filled my heart, an uncomfortable feeling. *She doesn't like leaving Barnsdale because she was threatened on Red's life by John if she ever did. She still doesn't feel able to chance it.*

"Well, with your permission, we would like to have our wedding here at Barnsdale Lodge. We already discussed making this place our home, if we're able."

"I would be honored my dear boy." Her face crinkled in happiness and then faded into anxiety. "Only, it can't be a large affair you know."

I laughed. "I know. A small ceremony and celebration would suit me and my bride exactly."

Marie looked at me doubtfully. "Well, if you think she'd like it, then of course. Only, just be sure she *would* like it. A bride should feel happy on her wedding day. And Barnsdale isn't for everyone you know."

I reached out and squeezed her hand reassuringly. "Lady Marie, I was wondering if you would like to meet my betrothed? Then you could see for yourself that she's comfortable. I know she would like to get to know you."

Marie's eyes fluttered, and she glanced rapidly between me and the fire. I let go of her hand and she wrung them together Part of me wanted to rescind the offer since she was so agitated, but a whisper in my mind told me to wait a moment. "Well, my dear boy, I would be delighted, of course I would. If only she wants to meet me of course."

I smiled, tears threatening my eyes and nodded. "She wants to meet you more than anything Marie."

Her hand went up to her mouth, her eyes wide. "I've always wanted a daughter you know. Have I told you? I've *always* wanted a daughter."

"Then perhaps she will be your daughter. If you'll let her."

❖ ❖ ❖

"She wants to meet you." I whispered to Red, as we prepared for bed later that night.

Red stilled, slowly turning to look me in the eyes. "Is that a good idea?" She licked her lips. "If she still won't look at me I don't know what I…"

I pulled her into my arms, holding her tightly. "If you don't want to chance it, I understand. But maybe this is how you can start, well, not back to where you were, but towards a real relationship with her. Just a small step at a time."

Red's breathing became more even after a few minutes, and her head tipped upwards. I looked into her eyes, seeing hope, and caution, and a little fear there.

"I'm here," I whispered. "Whatever you decide, I'll be here. Always." She closed her eyes and I pressed a kiss to each one, willing peace into each brush of my lips.

"Okay," she said finally, opening her eyes to reveal the resolve I knew she had to her core. "Even if it doesn't go that well, let's take that first step. After all, it may lead somewhere beautiful."

"It already has," I whispered, and pressed another kiss to her sudden smile. She pinched my arm and I yelped, jumping back.

"Don't be taking liberties before the wedding, Eddie. Do I need to get Mr. Reed up here to warn you off again?"

I gaped at her for a moment as she doubled over in laughter. Rolling my eyes I grabbed my pillow and hit her over the head before settling into my bed, chuckling despite myself.

CHAPTER TWENTY-FIVE

Red

Eddie's hand was steady as he led me through the garden gate, little puffs of earth escaping joyfully toward the sky when I stumbled off the gravel path. He turned and pulled me forward, pressing a kiss to my forehead and folding me into a hug. I bent my face to hide from the sun while I gathered my nerves, then pushed away and nodded, squaring my shoulders. He let me go, retaining my hand and we started forward together, the hem of my plain green gown catching on leaves from the rows of tiny, newly sprouted sunflowers we walked between.

My mother came into view at the back of the garden, her form ramrod straight and wrapped in a colorful shawl as she sat at her little garden table, a pot of tea in front of her. She turned her head at our approach, not quite looking at us, and I saw the tremble of her lip as she swallowed heavily.

My feet floated the last few steps, nerves closing my throat.

Eddie squeezed my hand soothingly before turning toward my mother. "Marie, I've brought someone to meet you."

Mother's eyes flashed up toward his, creeping sideways to take in my form but not quite meeting my face. She pushed a smile onto her lips as tears welled up and started trickling down her face.

"Oh really dear? And who is this young lady?" Her voice wobbled, and her first reference to me since before John's betrayal threatened to break me. Tears tracked down my face. Elne whined in sympathy, offering a warm presence in my mind for support.

"She's the friend I told you about, the one I love. It turns out she loves me too, as you suspected." Eddie cleared his throat. His voice was thick but he struggled to keep his tone light. "She's agreed to marry me, and I wanted you to know her."

Mama's eyes flashed up to mine and I let out a sob as she saw me for the first time in a decade.

I trembled as her eyes darted between Eddie and me, only daring to look at me for a second at a time before seeking refuge elsewhere, only to return to me again like a hummingbird hovering.

Eddie stepped forward, tugging me gently with him. "May I present the soon to be Tournesol Marchand?"

My mother's eyes were brimming with so many tears she obviously couldn't see, but she held her hand out to me and I took it, pressing a kiss to it and crying all the more as she squeezed mine.

"It's nice to meet you, my dear. I... I've always wanted a daughter, you know, and I think you'll do nicely."

I choked out a laugh, treasuring every moment that her eyes met mine. A smile played at her lips through her tears, and I dared to pull her slight figure into as gentle an embrace as I could manage, raw hope blossoming where darkness used to be.

EPILOGUE

A beam of light flashed through the dirty, ancient window of the attic, landing on a pair of low heeled shoes an older woman was pulling from the bottom of a battered trunk. Wherever the sunbeam touched, a fractured rainbow danced out, scattering colors on the dull, faded wallpaper.

"Wait, but Mama, aren't those the-"

"Hush, Aria. Don't say even speak it out loud."

"But Mama! If that's what I think it is, it's too dangerous! You said you had a gift for her to borrow!"

The mother opened a bag at her side, placing the beautiful dancing shoes inside with great care, before turning to her daughter.

"It's a longstanding family custom my dear. It's how I met your father, and hers' too. They never fail. And even though she doesn't share our blood, she's family."

The daughter pressed her hands to her chest nervously. "Mama, of course she is. But I don't think Ella would want them if she knew what they-"

"Aria!" Her mother hissed, pursing her lips. "That's not the point. No one will know, the magic isn't detectable by the methods those anti-magicians will be using. And as long as *you* don't tell her, she'll never know either. It will just confirm whether his love is true, or not. She'll be thanking us if it's the latter, and I'll feel better about letting her fall into the life he leads if it's the former. It's harmless."

Her daughter worried her lip with her teeth, looking unconvinced. "I don't know Mama. I just don't think it's a good idea. Have they ever been used on someone without fairy blood?"

The mother gave her daughter a gentle look. "I've never witnessed it personally, but yes, of course they have. In the days when these shoes were first made, fairy and human lived together peacefully." She picked up the bag and pulled her daughter into a hug. "Don't worry Aria dear, your true love will come soon, and then you'll have a chance to wear the shoes, never fret."

Aria smiled as they let go and helped her mother settle the strap of the bag over her shoulder. "You know that's not why I'm worried, Mama. Shame on you."

The mother laughed. "I know darling. Still, you saw how tiny they were. Is there any doubt that they know their next mission? They probably won't change size to fit anyone else until Ella wears them. If you want your turn, I suggest you let her have hers."

Aria laughed, stepping ahead to open the attic door. "Good point. But we better not let Alessia find out either. She'll have both our hides."

AFTERWORD

Thank you for reading The Red Rider! I hope you enjoyed immersing yourself in a new world as much as I do. The next book in the Istoire Awakens Series is available for pre-order now. Search my author page on Amazon to buy a copy of Glass Slipper today.

If you want to read more of my work, sign up for my newsletter and receive Forget-Me-Not, a free novelette set in Istoire. You'll meet a few characters that will appear in future books.

My newsletter is released quarterly and contains updates on current and upcoming projects, freebies, and other exculsive content. Thank you for your support!

Discover more at:

www.rebeccafittery.com

www.facebook.com/Rebecca-Fittery-Author

www.instagram.com/rebecca_fittery_author

www.pinterest.com/rebeccafittery

ABOUT THE AUTHOR

Rebecca Fittery

Rebecca Fittery is a fantasy romance author who writes clean, immersive fairytale romance. Her characters grow through relationship while adventure unfolds. Everyone who deserves a happy ending gets one, and even those who don't deserve one have a chance. Whether they take it or not is up to them!

She lives in rural Pennsylvania with her husband, their two children, and a friendly dragon disguised as an orange tiger cat.

Made in the USA
Middletown, DE
16 June 2024

55905306R00175